RIDIN' FOR A FALL

RIDIN' FOR A FALL

Cornbread Mafia Book Three

NINIE HAMMON

STERLING & STONE

Prologue

February 26, 1978
Indianapolis, Indiana

THE MAN who strode into the conference room in the Indianapolis field office of the Federal Bureau of Investigation that blustery winter day in 1978 bore a striking resemblance to Sidney Poitier. Special Agent Elijah Bradigan had been plagued by that likeness since high school and not once in all those years had it been a good thing. Well, okay, once. Juliette had admitted after they got married that she'd only agreed to go out with him on that first date because he looked like the movie star.

"Welcome home," said Bill Thomas. The two of them had trained at Quantico together back in the day.

"You can take the boy out of Indiana but ..." Eli said, as he walked to the big table and deposited a file box on it. He nodded toward the window, where the snow outside fell in flakes the size of nickels, the kind that would deposit at least a foot before it was done. "South Texas does *not* have winter, in case you were wondering, but the barbecue's better."

Agent Thomas introduced him to the other four agents seated around the table.

"Better than R's Barbecue?" asked the tall, blond agent on the end — Peterson — feigning offense.

There'd been an R's Barbecue across the Ohio River in Louisville, Kentucky when Eli was growing up. He remembered the slogan: "If it's bad barbecue, it ain't R's."

"Yup, better than R's. Mexican food's waaay better." Eli reached into the box and retrieved three files and laid them on the table beside it. "Buuut … in four years, I never had a bite of any dessert as good as derby pie."

Then he took a breath, and Juliette would have said he "put his game face on." She claimed she could see it happen — something about how he furrowed his forehead, and formed a "pleat of concentration" between his eyebrows. In poker, that would be called a "tell" — which was probably why Eli lost his shirt every time he played.

"I didn't transfer to this field office and move back home just to work on this case," he indicated the files, "but it's a big part of the reason." He pulled from his pocket a sealed sandwich bag filled with what appeared to be dry grass clippings. "*This* is Righteous Weed. Sometimes it's called Baby Bear's Bed … because it's 'just right.' It showed up on the streets out of nowhere a couple of years ago and has taken over as the premier domestic marijuana on the market. We've been actively tracking it for about eighteen months and we have reason to believe the source is a drug enterprise operating in Kentucky. We're going after it …"

He took another breath.

"… using the Kingpin Statute."

The other agents exchanged looks, and leaned in.

The Kingpin Statute — actually the Continuing Criminal Enterprise Statute — was a federal law that targets large-scale drug traffickers responsible for long-term and elaborate conspiracies. The statute made it a federal crime to commit or conspire to commit a continuing series of felony violations of the Comprehensive Drug Abuse Prevention and Control Act of 1970 "when such acts are taken in concert with five or more other persons." For conviction under this statute, the offender had to be "an organizer, manager, or supervisor of the continuing operation and must have obtained substantial income or resources from the drug violations."

The sentence for a first CCE conviction was a mandatory *minimum* twenty years in prison — with a maximum of life.

"These are our suspects." Bradigan stepped to the large cork board at the front of the room, took a blown-up driver's license picture from each of the files, and affixed them to the board with stick pins.

"This is Riley Hannacker," he said, indicating the first picture, then tapped the second. "Willie Ray Taggart." He nodded toward the third. "And Jessica Monaghan. They are the corn-pone version of South American drug lords. They're proud of it, too — call their organization the Cornbread *Mafia*."

He paused.

"We're going to take them down."

Chapter One

Monday, October 9, 1978
Callison County, Kentucky

"CHOPPER JUST TOOK OFF, headed your way," Joe Joe said.

"DEA?" Riley Hannacker asked.

"Nope, not crickets. State-ies. Gray-babies."

Joe Joe had a wealth of colorful names for the Kentucky State Police helicopters, manned by gray-uniformed troopers, that buzzed over Callison County every summer looking for fields of marijuana. He called the green Drug Enforcement Agency choppers crickets, flying pickles ... sometimes bug guts.

"Took out down Versailles Road" — pronouncing the word in Kentucky fashion, Ver-*sails* — "and hung a left over the Bluegrass Parkway south, best Larry could tell."

As soon as he hung up, Joe Joe would call Larry and his other spotters to get a bead on what part of the county the Kentucky State Police helicopter was scouting, searching

5

the windswept foliage below it for a particular shade of "marijuana" green. That was harder than it might sound — even now, with the trees a riot of bright fall colors. Riley had rented a chopper a few times to see what the law saw when they flew over his fields. Of course, Willie Ray Taggart was all the time flying Kiwi so low over them that one of these days he was gonna get a wheel tangled up in some woman's clothesline and drag her wet laundry across the sky like a tail on a kite. He *said* he was scoping out the aerial view of the pot fields, but Riley knew Willie Ray just wanted an excuse to do acrobatics, a reason to experience the world out there on the edge. That was Willie Ray.

Gratefully, today's chopper would have to get real lucky to spot any of Riley's weed in the field. Most of what little the Cornbread Mafia grew in Callison County these days was already cut and drying. There were maybe a half dozen or so small fields, and spots where it'd been planted between the rows in a cornfield — which took longer to mature because the plants didn't get as much sunshine that way. All the Callison County fields were test crops where Willie Ray kept track of which hybrids exhibited the traits he was breeding for — a mama plant's size, maybe, along with a papa plant's resistance to mold — that kind of thing. Willie Ray couldn't find out what he needed to know just growing a single plant all by its lonesome, needed to see a whole crop develop under normal growing conditions.

With an advance warning from Joe Joe, it was possible to spread out camouflage nets over small fields and they'd worked real well earlier in the spring. But that was just luck. Unless there were already workers on site, there wasn't time — even with a warning — to get the nets in place.

All Riley could do with the alarm Joe Joe'd sounded

today was cross his fingers and hope. It'd be a real shame to lose any of those fields, a setback for Willie Ray's hybrid breeding program that had already produced the world's premier strain of marijuana — Righteous Weed.

"Keep me posted."

"All over it, boss." Riley could hear in his voice the grin on his face.

Riley was proud of Joe Joe. His nephew could have drifted along like so many of the other Callison County boys did right out of high school, content to work just enough to get by — in tobacco if they were skittish and marijuana if they weren't. Not Joe Joe. He'd graduated this spring with a BA in Business Administration, courtesy of Riley's offer to fund a full ride at the University of Kentucky in Lexington — in exchange for Joe Joe getting a job at Bluegrass Field so he could continue the career he'd started when he was nine years old, fishing in the creek down from Nate Hannacker's moonshine still.

Papa.

His grandfather's image bloomed bright in Riley's mind and a dagger of grief stabbed into his heart. Papa had been gone for five years now and Riley still missed him so much it took his breath away. Someday, he would find out who'd murdered Papa. And when he found that person, he'd put a bullet in the center of their forehead just like they'd done to Papa.

After Riley hung up, he stepped out onto the second-floor balcony that opened off his office and looked down at the little blond boy swimming laps in the pool below. He squinted up into the sun and shook his head — temperatures had hovered near ninety degrees well into October. But Riley was glad Drew could use the pool today, with school out for some kind of teachers' in-service day. Swimming was one of the *few things* the boy enjoyed. He

7

watched his perfect form, courtesy of hours of swimming lessons. Drew could be on the school swim team when he got older … except Riley couldn't imagine Drew ever joining a team of any kind, and his heart ached.

Drew had been emotionally hammered by his grandfather's death every bit as hard as Riley had been. But he was just a little boy, didn't know how to deal with the pain and couldn't seem to get past it. His grief had morphed into something more, something worse, something bigger and uglier and more emotionally dangerous. Riley didn't know how to help him.

But he *did* know it would take more than some stupid bouncy castle to make Drew Hannacker smile. Sherry Lynn had delayed the boy's ninth birthday party to schedule it. The party was excessive, over the top, of course — featuring a bouncy castle *and* a clown *and* a puppet show *and* pony rides. But that was Sherry Lynn's specialty — over the top. Excess was her mission in life. He honestly wondered sometimes if she woke up every morning thinking, "What is the most extravagant, lavish, overindulgent thing I can do today?" And then set about doing it.

Lord only knows what the woman would have brought to the party if Riley hadn't reined her in — which he seldom did anymore — what was the point? But when he'd heard her on the phone setting up hot-air balloon rides, he'd put his foot down. And there'd been hell to pay. Her explosion of temper had likely shown up on some seismograph somewhere as a shifting of the tectonic plates in the earth's crust.

Which was probably what she wanted. Riley was pretty sure that most everything Sherry Lynn did was an effort to get a rise out of him. That had to be the reason she was staging the party of the century for Drew. She knew how the boy felt about crowds.

"It will be a crowd of *children*, so he'll be fine," she'd snapped when Riley'd brought up the salient point that their son was always tense, never relaxed around a lot of people, climbed into a shell of uncomfortable-almost-frightened silence every Sunday at church. It was like she had erased from her consciousness what'd happened two years ago at the Callison County Burley Festival. But that was to be expected, Riley supposed. After all, it'd been "unpleasant," and Sherry Lynn Hannacker did not *do* unpleasant. No sir-ee, she did not. As soon as she'd lost the mountain of weight she'd gained after Drew was born, she'd become again the vivacious girl she'd once been — the perpetual high school cheerleader, smiling/happy/bouncy/giggling/fun-fun-fun. She was the reason they'd attended the Burley Festival in the first place, because *everybody will be there.* Translate that — Sherry Lynn wanted to see and be seen, wanted men to ogle her and women to be jealous of her and she wasn't about to pass up an opportunity for both.

Chapter Two

Sherry Lynn had taken Drew to the Burley Festival Parade and all the other kids' events that morning, got Riley to load up the boy's Big Wheel into the back of the pickup truck, though it was clear to Riley that seven-year-old Drew wasn't nearly as excited about Children's Morning at the Burley Festival as Sherry Lynn was. The boy had gotten a ribbon for coming in third in the Big Wheel race and you'd have thought he'd just brought home the first-place trophy from the Indianapolis 500.

It's five o'clock now, and they've returned to tour the booths, have supper and watch the other contests that will be conducted onstage this evening.

Brewster certainly knows how to throw a party and they pull out all the stops once a year for the Burley Festival. Over the course of its three-day run, the festival will bring twenty, maybe thirty thousand people to a town with a population of about six thousand. Downtown streets are blocked off to provide three traffic-free blocks of Main Street and the same space on Kendall Avenue, on one side of Main, and Chambers Street on the other — by the train depot where a National Historic Landmark sign designates the spot where rogue Confederate General John Hunt Morgan's youngest brother, Tom, was killed in a battle during Morgan's daring raid through Union lines across Kentucky into Ohio in 1863.

Set up along the side streets, stretched out for as far as you can see on both sides of the streets, are booths where you can buy a handmade quilt, a pound of fudge, an original oil painting, lawn art, crocheted doilies, Appalachian Apple dolls, hand-knitted scarves/shawls/hats, statues carved in coal, every conceivable kind and type of hand-made jewelry, hand-thrown pottery ...

Sherry Lynn demands to stop at every booth.

The Band Boosters booth is selling cookies, the Baptist/Methodist/Presbyterian/Pentecostal churches each have a booth passing out pamphlets and selling homemade cakes, pies, banana and pumpkin bread and cream cheese danish. The mouth-watering aroma of grilled meat wafts up and down the streets from booths selling barbecued beef, pork and chicken, along with hamburgers, hot dogs and brats and slabs of barbecued ribs — cotton candy and funnel cakes, too, of course. Picnic tables are set up on the street in front of the food booths and they plan to eat supper there when Sherry Lynn tires of purchasing all manner of things she has no use for and nowhere to put. The beer booths along Main Street don't open until late afternoon, so Willie Ray won't likely show up until then.

Riley can't help scanning the crowd for Jessie's face. She'd said she was going to the festival but in a crowd this size he doesn't expect to run into her. The festival brings in Callison County folks from the countryside along with people from adjoining counties, a hodgepodge of people who wouldn't gather together anywhere else. He hadn't seen Big-un McClusky, of course — he didn't go anywhere! Oh, he'd seen other McCluskys at the event, buying or selling goods, and of course caught sight of Kentucky State Police Detective Booth Graham, who turned up like a bad penny everywhere. Riley could even lay claim to a Mama Bert sighting, and she seldom ventured outside the tavern for anything but church. She was standing in line to buy a funnel cake and their eyes met. She'd nodded, he'd nodded and that was all. But a

Jessie sighting — that *would put a spring in Riley's step for the rest of the day.*

A huge stage has been set up in the intersection, under the traffic light of Main Street and Proctor Knott Avenue. It's where the blue-grass band, country-western and rock bands would provide music for the dancing in the streets all around the stage from eight o'clock to midnight. Cloggers are performing at the intersection of Main Street and Brandenberg Road, a block north, and square-dancers at the intersection of Main and Partridge Street a block south.

Contests attract a constant crowd around the main stage. A jalapeño-eating contest, hog-calling and husband-calling contest and hay-bale tossing. The crowd moves judiciously back away from the stage during a tobacco-spitting contest. As Mayor-for-Life Malcolm Murdock announces the contest winners from the main stage, Riley spots Winona McClusky standing behind him, a woman Willie Ray once described as "so ugly she'd make a train take a dirt road." Drew seems to be enjoying himself and that's what matters to Riley. The boy'd changed overnight three years before when his grandfather was killed. The bubbly, laughing, happy child became withdrawn, fearful and quiet. Riley finally demanded that they take him to counseling a year ago, but it didn't appear to be helping. He'd heard of a really good child psychiatrist in Louisville and if Drew didn't start making progress soon, Riley'd try that.

"Want another cotton candy?" *he asks the boy as Sherry Lynn oohs and aahs over some pottery that* "will be just the right color for the sunroom we're adding to the house next year." *News to Riley — apparently they will be adding a sunroom to the house next year. Drew looks up at him with eyes the same color as Sherry Lynn's — a bright blue that almost looks purple.* "Mommy said I could only have one." *Riley almost says he can have a second one anyway, but doesn't. He has learned it is prudent to save opposition for hills you're willing to die on.* "How about a funnel cake instead?" *he asks and the boy offers him an achingly adorable gap-toothed grin.*

"Riley!" *Sherry Lynn calls.* "I need you to carry the big pieces of pottery back to the truck. Will you help me, please?" The wattage of her smile could light up Westminster Abbey. He digs into the pocket of his jeans and comes out with a handful of coins. He hands Drew two fifty-cent pieces and three quarters. "You can get your own funnel cake while I help Mommy. You're a big boy."

The boy clutches the coins tight in his small fist and runs off toward the booth, which is across the street from the pottery booth where Sherry Lynn crinkles her brow at the sight.

"Where's he going all by himself?"

"He probably won't get kidnapped between here and the funnel cake booth." She doesn't like it but turns back to the pots. Riley picks up the box with the bigger pieces and heads down Main Street to Court Square, where he'll cut through to Kendall Avenue, where they parked. He sets the box in the bed of the truck and returns to Main Street where he finds Sherry Lynn in a total meltdown.

"Drew's gone!" she cries, her voice somehow managing to convey genuine fright and I-told-you-so glee at the same time. She has already enlisted the aid of half a dozen bystanders to look for him. "I turned around and he was just … gone!"

Riley feels fear clutch at his throat, even though he knows the boy is in no real danger here. He's just gotten lost in the crowd, that's all. Half an hour later, Riley is close to frantic — particularly when he notices a fifty-cent piece in the street shoved up under the skirt that covers the front of the funnel cake booth. Did Drew drop it? The police are searching the crowd. The stage manager has announced, "Drew Hannacker, please come to the main stage," and Sherry Lynn is waiting there, teetering precariously on the edge of hysteria, no longer gloating that Riley is at fault.

"Riley," Spud Walters calls out. Spud has a farm where he raises alpaca sheep and llamas out by Double Springs Distillery. "I think I found your boy." Riley follows him to the hand-woven rug booth on the other side of the pottery booth. "I b'lieve they's a little boy hidin' behind them boxes."

Riley moves through the forest of thick wool rugs dangling from *overhead rails and out the flap at the back of the booth where the boxes used to haul the rugs to the booth are stacked.*

"Drew!" he calls out. "Drew, are you back here? Answer me." A pile of smaller boxes tips over, spilling them out on the ground as the little boy crawls out from behind a bigger box leaned against the wall of a nearby building. He rushes at Riley, hurls himself at his father, grabbing him around the legs, not even crying, just trembling violently.

"Spud, would you mind going down to the main stage and telling Sherry Lynn we found him?"

Spud leaves and Riley peels Drew off his legs so he can get down on one knee and talk to him.

"What are you hiding from, Buddy?" he asks gently. "What's got you so scared?"

Drew won't say, just shakes his head violently back and forth, almost like he's trying to fling an image out of his mind, then clutches Riley's neck so tight Riley can barely breathe. Drew doesn't have a funnel cake or the money he had in his hand to purchase it. Did he just drop the coins in the street? No amount of coaxing can pry a response from the boy. Something scared him terribly, but Riley has no idea what it was.

AFTER THAT EXPERIENCE, Drew didn't want to leave the farm, didn't want to go into town, to Bardstown to a movie, out to get a pizza. It took six months to get him to be willing to go back to church and even now, two years later, he refused to venture more than a few feet from his father during the service and always requested to go immediately home. Surprisingly, he wasn't reticent to go back to school, and Riley supposed it was because he felt safe there in that environment, with those people. Why he didn't feel safe around crowds of strangers, Riley had no idea.

Drew caught sight of Riley standing on the balcony and called out, "Hi, Daddy."

"You been working on that cannon ball I showed you?"

Drew swam to the edge of the pool and got out, his golden-brown tan coupled with his white blond hair always striking. He backed up from the edge of the pool and then burst into a sprint, hurling himself out over the water while he wrapped his arms around his bent knees. He landed with a satisfying splat sound and water sprayed everywhere.

He came up sputtering.

"Good job! You splashed water up almost as high as the diving board."

Drew offered the scraps of a smile and nodded. What Riley wouldn't give for the exuberant cries he heard from other children who came to play in the pool.

"Lookit me, Mommy!"

"Watch this, Daddy."

"See what I can do!"

Drew Hannacker wasn't exuberant about anything.

Maybe he would enjoy the birthday party. Shoot, maybe the bouncy castle would make him smile after all. But in his heart, Riley knew it wouldn't. Something was seriously wrong with Drew. Riley had tried everything he knew to find out what it was, had taken the boy to three different counselors, and the best he could get out of them was that Drew had "internalized some kind of trauma." Of course, Riley knew what the trauma was. Drew had seen his Pop Pop lying dead in the barn that autumn night five years ago with a bullet hole in the center of his forehead. The wound that trauma stabbed into the boy's soul had never healed. And Riley was beginning to wonder if it ever would.

His office phone rang and Riley stepped in off the balcony to answer it. It was Bucky Reagan, who'd been working in a small field off Hester Pike.

"I'm afraid we got ourselves a hermie," Bucky said. "I been trying to call Willie Ray for three days but couldn't track him down. You might ought to come give it a look-see."

A hermie … goody.

Chapter Three

RILEY'S ARMS WERE SCRATCHED, his pants legs slathered with thistle stickers from plowing through the weed barrier between the thick woods and the small field of marijuana on Grist Mill Lane. Turned out, Riley had been right all along — back in high school when Riley accused Willie Ray of being interested in horticulture because it was plant sex.

"We got to keep the male plants away from the female plants," Willie Ray'd said that hot July day as the three remaining members of the Cornbread Mafia sat together in their clubhouse in Jessie's tobacco barn.

The other two had thought he was joking.

"YOU MEAN boy plants on one side of the field and girl plants on the other side?" Jessie asks, and shoots Riley a look. He takes the handoff.

"Right, and then we'll do what them Shakers did," Riley says, recalling a junior high field trip to the Shaker Village outside Lexington where several hundred members of the off-shoot Quaker sect

had made their homes. "You remember — in them big buildings, they put the men on one side and the women on the other side, then they'd spread flour on the floor of the hallway in between so's there wouldn't be any hanky-panky."

"You know, so they couldn't shake, rattle and roll." Jessie's full-on laughing now.

Willie Ray adopts a patient smile.

"You guys done yet? You ain't bad. Maybe you ought to take your act on the road — the Amazing Jessie and her trained chimp."

"I resent that remark," Riley says pompously.

"Wait a minute — you can't be … serious." Jessie is incredulous.

"As a heart attack."

Then he proceeds to tell Riley and Jessie about the birds and the bees and cannabis plants.

"Cannabis can be male or female. The hemp growing out behind the barn comes back year after year because the male plants fertilized the female plants and they made little baby seeds to drop on the ground when they die."

Riley loves to see Willie Ray engage like this — earnest and concentrating, intelligence lighting his eyes. Riley thinks if things had been different perhaps Willie Ray would have become a teacher. Maybe a horticulture scientist like Dr. Archibald Waznuski, the University of Kentucky professor who is their silent partner, the purveyor of all knowledge when it comes to marijuana.

"Just like with people, them fertilized seeds has got the genetics of both parents — the male and female cannabis plants. Only female cannabis plants produce the buds and when they're pollinated the seeds grow inside the buds. But if they're NOT pollinated — no seeds, which leads to a harsh smoke anyway but getting the seeds out of the final product isn't the most important thing. Seedless cannabis — sinsemilla   it's like topping the plants. You top them so they don't concentrate all their energy into growing seven feet tall — so they grow out instead of up. Same's true of seedless marijuana — if it's not diverting energy and resources to producing seeds, it just produces bigger, better flower buds. And because buds have the highest concentration of THC in the whole plant — if you make them bigger and better you get more bang for your buck. Sinsemilla is a seedless cannabis flower from unfertilized female plants and it's the most potent form of cannabis there is."

He sits back and grins.

"What you get with that high concentration of THC is seriously, seriously righteous weed."

"And you know that how?"

"I thought you'd never ask." Willie Ray grins and produces a baggie out of his pocket and cigarette papers. As he rolls a small joint — none of them has time today to sit here getting stoned — he says he thinks they ought to grow both Sativa and Indica strains of cannabis this year — mostly Indica because it has a shorter flowering cycle and they've learned it grows better in Kentucky, which isn't as warm as South America and has a shorter season. But the effects produced by the two different types of cannabis plants fascinate him, and he wants to try to make a hybrid that has the best characteristics of both.

"That's like making a hybrid of day and night and the light's just dim — none of the good characteristics of either," Jessie puts in. "Smoke a joint of Indica and you want to take a nap. Smoke a joint of Sativa and you feel energetic, mind-high. So how can you feel both productive and creative, and relaxed and lethargic at the same time?"

As Willie Ray lights the joint, inhales deeply and hands it to Jessie, Riley says, "I want to go back to the boy plants and girl plants mating. Or not mating. What …? Are we talking condoms here? Chastity belts?"

Riley takes the joint from Jessie and Willie Ray exhales as he speaks.

"Nope, not good enough. You gotta get them rangy boy plants plum out of the field."

"And you can tell the difference between boy plants and girl plants — how?"

"I'll show ya. It ain't hard."

Riley is certain it is way harder than Willie Ray makes it sound. Willie Ray sees all kinds of differences in plants — cannabis, sure, but flowers and trees, too — little details the others would never notice. Obviously, Jessie's thinking the same thing. She passes the joint back to Willie Ray.

"That's gonna be your job. You're in charge of making sure there's no bump and tickle out there in the field when our backs are turned. You're the Plant Sex Police."

THAT JOB HAD FALLEN to Riley today, though.

Bucky spotted him, put down his pruning shears and walked down a row of chest-high plants to where Riley stood.

"I think we're already too late," he said.

He led Riley down the row of plants to the end, where Bucky pulled the leafy stems out of the way and pointed.

"If this here's what I think it is, the damage's already been done."

Telling the difference between male and female cannabis plants was in some sense more art than science. Male plants grew pollen sacks on the joints of the stalks; female plants had the same bulbs, but on the bulbs would be long hairs called pistils. Unfortunately, some marijuana plants appeared to be female but were in reality hermaphrodites — both sexes. And a single hermie plant could pollinate not only its own female parts but other plants all around it.

Riley examined the plant and sighed.

"Yup, looks like a hermie to me, too. Get it out of

here." That plant had just devalued five, maybe ten thousand dollars' worth of marijuana growing near it.

Bucky grabbed hold of the stalk and carefully pulled the plant up out of the dirt — careful so as not to scatter any pollen the male parts of the plant had already produced. They'd know soon enough which nearby plants had been pollinated, since the pistils on a pollinated female plant turned an orange-brown color.

As Riley made his way back through the weeds and bushes to where he'd parked his truck, he allowed himself to transition from annoyed to pissed off at Willie Ray for being so hard to reach, a butterfly, flitting from flower to flower in a meadow. Willie Ray could spot a hermie before anybody else had any idea — certainly could have seen it three days ago, and maybe Bucky could have gotten the plant out of the field before the damage was done. Riley wouldn't likely get a chance to tell Willie Ray about the hermie before Willie Ray flew out in the morning. He'd call in, of course, after he left — but he always called Jessie when he was on the road because she had a schedule, would be home caring for Davie on certain days and during certain hours, while Riley stayed away from home as much as possible.

Willie Ray would be gone ten days at least, longer if he ran into any trouble. Riley didn't regret the decision to blow the doors off this year with marijuana fields all over the country. Most of the time he didn't. Papa had taught him not to undertake a task unless he intended to do it right, and the decision to expand made good business sense. But growing weed on some farm where you didn't know your neighbors, where *you* were from Away From Here, still spooked him. There were all kinds of things that could go wrong.

Chapter Four

WILLIE RAY TAGGART pulled his pickup truck off Big Rock Lane and wound down a dirt road to the back of a piece of land that had too much brush and weeds on it to be much good for anything. But it suited his purpose fine. He got out of the truck, took a deep breath and his eyes watered. And he was glad of that. It was, after all, part of the place's charm.

He was right proud of his greenhouse. Wouldn't nobody in the world ever figure out that was what it was. And wouldn't nobody stumble over it, accidental-like, neither. Not where he'd put it. The spot where he produced seed to grow the best marijuana in the world was safe from prying eyes, so to speak.

Oh, it had drawbacks. Jessie would not come anywhere near it and Riley only showed up when he absolutely had to, and left quick as he could.

Willie Ray supposed it was a little like motion sickness. Some people got sick to their stomachs if they's in a car going over hills and around corners. Weren't many of those kinds of folks in Callison County, of course. A kind

22

of natural selection, the ones who got sick driving in hills and curves didn't live long enough to reproduce themselves and the trait was just about bred out of the species.

Willie Ray didn't have a speck of motion sickness anywhere in his body, could eat Thanksgiving dinner and go out and do barrel rolls in his plane all afternoon — actually did that last year. Didn't nothing like that make him sick.

Bad smells was the same way. Oh, he couldn't say he liked to smell things like sour milk, bad meat or dead animals. But it didn't make him sick, neither. That's why he was able to camouflage his greenhouse as a pig barn, and the pigs all around kept nosey people away.

It didn't really smell that bad, and after you's in the greenhouse for a few minutes you didn't even notice it anymore. Riley argued that point, but Willie Ray believed he'd never give it enough time to get used to it.

Willie Ray'd got a lawyer to buy a little piece of property in the name of some phony corporation, built his greenhouse on the back part of it that you couldn't get to any way but a dirt road. Then he'd bought half a dozen sows, made a pigpen out front of it. You couldn't tell there was any way to get to the building on the back side of the pig pen except to go through the pigpen, sink up to your shins in the stinky mud and slog through it. In truth, there was a back door hidden in the bushes.

He'd gone to so much trouble because the hybrid marijuana he'd created with Wazzi's help had made the Cornbread Mafia millionaires many times over. It was the best weed around, hands down. The proof was in the pudding, as Grandma used to say — they charged a premium price for it and customers was fallin' all over themselves to buy it. It was way better than the "righteous weed" Ace had given them all those years ago in 'Nam. Now Ace traveled the world to bring back seeds — exotic strains of marijuana grown in Thailand, South Africa and on big ranches in Brazil. They'd given their weed that name, though, called the marijuana the Cornbread Mafia produced "Righteous Weed." Jessie'd hand drawn a logo with a big R and a W stuck on the bottom of it that was real pretty, though Willie Ray 'spected they wouldn't never have no need for stationery.

The seeds to grow that weed — Willie Ray produced them in the greenhouse behind a pigsty.

He'd figured out he had to have a greenhouse after the first year, when he tried to do the whole thing outdoors — a total disaster. Male marijuana plants were prolific pollen spreaders. It was staggering how far the wind carried that pollen, and a single male plant "impregnating" the female plants would ruin the whole bud harvest, 'cause a polli-nated bud was pretty much worthless for anything except seed — you couldn't even use the leaf 'cause it was bitter.

So Willie Ray'd built his greenhouse to isolate the specific female and male plants he wanted to make seed from. Next spring, he'd plant small fields in Callison County, using their seed, a dry run before they committed to growing it by the acre in other states. He'd had to put the greenhouse twenty miles away from the nearest of their current test fields so he wouldn't have to go to the trouble of putting filters on the air vents to keep out pollen from some random male — male pollen really was that sneaky. Once his chosen male plant did its pollenating, he'd destroy it, clean out the whole greenhouse. Kept everything clean and neat, with no risk a particular strain of plant he was seeking would accidentally get impregnated by some little pollen soldier left behind by previous males.

After that, the rest was simple. He put a clear plastic cape around the base of the female plant, extending out six or eight feet. Then he waited. Fertilized female plants were seed-producing machines! Once the seeds were fully developed, the seed'd start to drop off the plant and down onto the cape. You could hear plop, plop, plop as the seeds hit the plastic. Sounded like popcorn. Then he'd just sweep up the seeds and clean out any puny-looking ones. You could get a quart jar of seeds from a single fertilized plant — a gallon jug from four of them.

They'd decided to move their growing operations out of state a couple of years ago 'cause Callison County had gotten too famous — needed its own air traffic controller to keep all the law's helicopters from running into each other. Willie Ray didn't know exactly how the land transactions worked in other states — he had a foreman at each site who took care of leasing a farm and equipment.

The seed for those different sites had been produced here, from strains of marijuana Ace found all over the world, some places Willie Ray had to look up on the map to know where they were. About every country in Central America and a bunch in South America, but places more exotic, too, like Burma, New Zealand — even Tibet. Willie Ray didn't know there was anything in Tibet except mountains. Ace found cannabis that'd grow where it was hot, or dry, or wet, or cold, and every place in between. They'd develop a hybrid they liked, working with their "silent partner" Dr. Archibald Waznuski, a *former* professor at the University of Kentucky School of Agriculture whose "hobby" was raising cannabis. (Wazzi'd retired from teaching, bought hisself a horse farm up by Lexington.) They'd grow a small amount of the hybrid in isolated test fields in Callison County — you needed more'n one plant to determine the quality. Those were the little fields snuggled up in hollows or individual plants planted between the rows in cornfields.

They'd started small, rented a little farm in Arkansas down the road from where Bucky Reagan's grandmother lived when he was a kid. The next year they'd rented land in two more states. Not just random farms. Every site was recommended by somebody they trusted, and they'd spent a couple of weeks in each place, scouting around, making sure. This spring was their most ambitious venture ever. The money it would generate literally boggled Willie Ray's mind. It was absolutely *staggering.* Their crews'd planted Righteous Weed crops on farms in *seven* states — outside Martinsburg, Minnesota; Abbyville, Arkansas; Middletown, Nebraska; Foster Mills, Wisconsin; Thurston, Iowa; Empire Township, Missouri and Clayton, Kansas. Willie Ray was leaving in the morning to do an "inspection tour" of all the sites — each in a slightly different stage of production, depending on the growing conditions of the location.

He'd developed Righteous Weed seed specific to where it'd be growing, slightly different strains. He needed weed that was particularly mold resistant for crops in the more southern states. But the fields farther north didn't need that characteristic. Those plants needed to mature rapidly because the growing season in Minnesota, Wisconsin and northern Iowa was a lot shorter. Particularly in upstate Minnesota, where local farmers claimed they'd seen winter storms swoop down out of Canada before Halloween.

Soon's the pigs heard the sound of Willie Ray coming, they'd started raising Cain. That was another drawback. Had to feed the pigs. His specimens ate better than most such beasts because he brought them real food, corn, instead of feeding them slop like most farmers did, using them as garbage disposals. Of course raising pigs on straight corn made the meat high in fat and low in muscle. He coulda added some lysine and other vitamins and minerals — and a little protein — to get a lower fat percentage. But he didn't bother because he wasn't raising these pigs to eat, he was raising them to stink, and they did a right fine job of that. He filled up a big water tank about once a month to turn the dirt in the pen into mud and to provide drinking water in the trough.

After checking on the water, he unloaded feed out of the truck — his work truck, an old Chevy held together with duct tape and Bondo. He'd bought the clunker because he wasn't about to get mud on his other truck, a Night Train — 1955 Ford F-100 custom pickup. That beauty was fitted with a 427 cubic-inch V8 engine, four-wheel disc brakes, 20-inch chrome wheels, and amazing coil-over shocks, factory-fitted air conditioning unit and stereo system. He'd paid fifty thousand dollars for it and it was worth every penny! He'd bought a couple of motorcycles that same year, but riding 'em hadn't been as much fun as he'd always thought it'd be. He woulda spent some of his millions to build a house but it was too dadgum much trouble picking everything out. Why, there was twenty different kinds of toilets in the hardware store catalogue and without trying 'em out, how was he supposed to decide which one he'd rather sit on? He finally settled for moving into the old Hannacker place in Hickory Stump Hollow off Gallagher Station Road — in the house them South American drug dealers shot full of holes. He'd let Jessie fix it up for him and she'd made it real nice! It was good to be there, felt like home — though he probably didn't spend half a dozen nights a month under that roof.

After he gave the feed to the grunting, snorting hogs, he went around behind the building at the back of the pen to the door there hidden by the tall brush.

Careful not to close the door fast — he didn't want the whoosh of air to blow off the seeds his female plants were busily depositing on the plastic spread out around them — he moved slowly between the rows of plants. There were twenty of them, ten on a side. Easing down on one knee, he scooped up a small handful of seeds into his palm, turning each one over with his thumb. Willie Ray didn't think there was many things in God's green earth that was prettier than marijuana seeds. A little smaller than dried pinto beans, each one was different, like picking up pretty shells on a beach. Pinto beans was blotchy, like somebody'd splattered brown paint on a kinda pinkish-tan seed. Marijuana seeds was golden — not gold as a chickpea, more golden-brown, and the markings on them was patterns, like a terrapin shell or cracked dirt where a puddle had dried up. And most Righteous Weed seeds was tiger-striped! Wazzi didn't know why that was. They'd started out with all kinda different sizes, shapes and colors of seeds — little bitty black ones from Thailand, dark brown ones from New Zealand, grayish-brown ones from Florida that had tiger stripes and golden ones from California. Cross-breeding had produced a patterned/striped seed that grew weed that smoked so smooth it was like you was breathing the mist hanging over a creek on a spring morning.

Wazzi'd said them seeds would germinate five years from now, ten maybe — indefinitely, if they'd store them in a dark, cool, dry place.

And Willie Ray had done just that. Yes, sir-ee, he surely had. When he got these seeds sealed tight in jars, he'd take them to the tree house to store with all the other seed jars, carefully labeled. He kept meticulous records.

The storage facility was safe and secure, of course.

It'd be hard to find anywhere safer to put somethin' you didn't want nobody to find than in a place that didn't exist.

Chapter Five

SHERRY LYNN HANNACKER flipped down the visor and checked her lipstick, then sat for a moment studying her face. Was she starting to look … old? That was crazy, her thirtieth birthday was still months away. Twenty-nine was *not* old. Still, there were lines around her eyes and mouth that she was certain hadn't been on the face of the head cheerleader at Callison County High School.

She smiled, relaxed, smiled again. Yeah, there were lines.

Maybe she should get plastic surgery. Not some kind of facelift or anything like that but she'd heard of something called a chemical peel that all the women's magazines said removed fine lines and blemishes. She'd look into that.

Flipping the visor back up, she looked at her watch. She was early, wasn't supposed to meet Glen Youngman until after he left the store at five o'clock, but she'd finished her shopping. She had the big banner with "Happy Birthday Drew" on it that she'd had specially made, along with the balloons that'd be filled with helium, each of them emblazoned with a post office box address and a plea to "let me know where you found this" and a couple of sentences explaining that a nine-year-old boy had set the balloons free and would love to know how far they went. Drew would like that. He'd get out a map and plot where they all landed, she knew he would. He'd find out the wind direction and speed. He'd be so excited when he started getting responses in the post office box.

No, he wouldn't. Drew didn't get excited about anything. He was a ghost, the faint apparition that had come to inhabit her son's body the night—

Nope, not going there. No sir-ee, *not*. Drew was fine, just fine. He'd have a wonderful time at his birthday party. He would. And wait until he saw what she'd gotten him. She hadn't said a word about it to Riley, not because he wouldn't have approved but because she wanted the gift to be hers — Drew's best possible birthday gift *from his mother.* Riley let the child do anything he wanted and she had to be the disciplinarian, the one to make sure he didn't grow up into some wild creature who had no self-discipline, no judgement and no manners, if he lived to grow up at all, and when she considered all the things her stupid husband allowed the boy to do, she feared he'd never see his twenty-first birthday. She was the one who said no to absurd things. She was the one who wouldn't let him take ridiculous chances. She was always the bad guy and Riley got to be the good guy and she hated that. *Hated* it. Well, wait until Drew saw his birthday present — an electric train. And not just one — three of them so he could combine the pieces into one gigantic train. Sherry Lynn'd purchased the Lionel 6-1867 Limited Production Milwaukee set — the newest set on the markct, the Workin' on the Railroad Logging Empire set *and* the Chattanooga Choo Choo set that came with a seventeen-piece Bridge & Trestle unit. She'd also bought *twenty feet* of track extensions. Drew could run track all over the house. He would love—

A Lincoln Town Car pulled around the side of the motel main building and into the back lot where Sherry Lynn waited in the far corner, and her heart skipped a beat.

Glen Youngman was older than she was, and she could remember being in elementary school, watching the high school boys play football and swooning over the dark-haired quarterback who moved on the field like a cat.

He owned the furniture store in Brewster now, and was opening a second location in Bardstown. And though he'd gained considerable weight since high school, he still had a mane of unruly black hair and still moved with the grace of a big cat.

She shivered. She'd run into him at a school board meeting, of all places. She had gone to complain to the board about the merry-go-rounds at the three elementary schools, had come prepared with facts and figures that proved they were far too dangerous to allow small children to play on. Drew had come home with a badly bruised leg and a skinned knee after he fell off one the children were pushing too fast, and that'd sent Sherry Lynn on the warpath.

Glen was at the meeting to get the specifications for the bids the board would be taking on new furniture for all the teacher's lounges in the elementary, middle and high school buildings.

He had sat down beside her, smelled of her favorite aftershave, English Leather, smiled at her and asked why she'd come. She saw that he was interested in what she had to say. Didn't roll his eyes at her the way Riley did when he'd offered a half-hearted attempt to change her mind about going to the board.

"Kids have been playing on merry-go-rounds for generations," he'd said. "I played on one, so did you. We both survived. Why would you want to take away something the kids enjoy?"

She'd given him a piece of her mind about the importance of safety versus having a good time, but Glen didn't think she was overreacting at all. They'd talked. The board had tabled both their requests until the next meeting … so they'd both had to return a week later. They'd gone out to get a cup of coffee with some other parents after the meeting. He'd sat beside her, casually bumped her knee with his.

That'd been six months ago and they'd been getting together at least once a week ever since. Today, their rendezvous was in a Lexington motel near Keenland Racetrack. She'd bought a sexy see-through negligee at Fayette Mall after she ordered the balloons for Drew's party. She could have worn the lacy white one she'd bought when she was seeing Bud Peters. He'd told her she looked as hot as any teenager in it, but she'd wanted something new and different for Glen.

She watched him pull the big car into a spot in front of the row of outward-facing motel rooms, enjoyed watching him get out of the car — still moved like a big cat. He unlocked the motel room door and went inside. She'd wait a couple of minutes so he wouldn't know she'd come early. In fact, maybe she'd wait longer — fifteen minutes maybe. Perhaps she should be late, make him wonder what'd happened to her. Make him wonder if maybe she'd found somebody else … gotten tired of him. She hadn't, of course. At least, not yet.

With a wicked smile, Sherry Lynn leaned her head back on the headrest and watched the shadows of the trees on the hood of her new Mercedes. Not fifteen minutes. She'd make him wait half an hour.

Chapter Six

ELI BRADIGAN COULD HEAR the beginning of the welcoming chorus as soon as he opened his car door. Their new place in Indianapolis had a picture window and he hadn't realized the ramifications of that when they were looking at the house. In truth, he'd been so desperate to relocate his family from Texas, the size and placement of the house's windows had been of supreme unimportance.

At least one of the three dogs had been stationed at that window when he'd arrived home the past couple of evenings — watching for him. Did the dogs get together and decide who? *Moe, it's your turn on guard duty.*

The designated guard dog would sound the alarm, which would reverberate all over the house so that by the time Eli opened the front door, the welcoming committee would be assembled and waiting. The dogs had been trained to *down-stay.* But the likelihood that all three of them — Larry, a mostly dachshund, Moe, a mostly beagle and Curly, a droopy-eared basset hound — would actually obey while Eli got all the way into the house, was slim.

Today, he did manage to make it down to one knee

before Gabrielle came barreling at him full steam, lights and sirens.

"Daaaaadeeee," the little girl squealed, as if Eli had been gone for a month instead of just since breakfast. The sight of that child always did tangling-up things in Eli's heart so his chest was tight.

Gabrielle was strikingly beautiful. Her mixed heritage had put an eclectic collection of genes into a Mason jar and shook them up and produced a genuinely rare loveliness. Eli's mother had been Jamaican, his father an Irishman. Juliette was Creole. She only knew that much because she had literally been left in a basket on the steps of St. Louis Cathedral in New Orleans as an infant.

So where, in that mix of genetics, had Gabrielle gotten the red hair — dark red, the color of rubies? Eli's father had been Irish, which presupposed some redheads in the lineage, but his father'd never mentioned any. Juliette's hair was glossy black hanging in long curls down her back.

Gabrielle made no effort to slow her wheelchair — just angled it at the last second to keep from bowling her father over. Leaning out of the seat to throw her arms around his neck, the seven-year-old launched into a stream-of-consciousness babble that barely left space between the words. "... a yellow butterfly on the roses by the back porch and a white one and a blue one and Mommy said she'd get me a butterfly net but I'm afraid a net would hurt them. Will it hurt them, Daddy?" She didn't wait for an answer. "And there are hummingbirds in the backyard, too, but I haven't seen any so we have to put up a bird-feeder with sugar water ..."

Eli turned his attention to the animals as she babbled, patting heads, scratching behind ears, rubbing bellies. Juliette appeared in the doorway to the kitchen, six-month-old Daniel balanced on one hip and something with lots of dangling wires in her other hand. It looked like the autopsy of a robot. She held it out to Eli. "Here."

"Awwww, and I didn't get you anything."

She tried unsuccessfully to choke off a smile. "This was under the kitchen sink. I suspect it might be a garbage disposal. Am I supposed to — what? Hook the thing up?"

"My bad. The real estate guy called and said he'd have somebody come by and install a new garbage disposal tomorrow morning. He did *not* say he had left the carcass of the dead one in the cabinet."

Eli stood and took the chubby baby that Gabrielle called Dan-Dan out of his mother's arms and the child favored him with an adorable toothless smile before sending a warm stream of baby barf down the front of his suit coat. Eli looked helplessly down at the coat, and then up at Juliette. She shrugged.

"I'm considering launching my own line of perfume. Eau de Upchuck. Think it'll sell?"

It was a chaotic couple of hours before the kids were asleep and the dogs banished to the backyard. Eli would be leaving for Callison County in the morning, but only needed to add a few items to his perpetual "go bag" that sat in the back of his closet. He'd learned about the prudence of having such a bag already packed and ready to grab when an instructor at the FBI Academy, in the Quantico Marine base in Virginia, had picked him to accompany the agent to Chicago and assist with the forensic work in a serial-killer case. They'd found a third body, but it'd been in Lake Michigan for a week and forensics would be "challenging." Translate that: the body was ripe and likely falling apart. "Wheels up in fifteen," the agent had said, which gave Eli roughly five minutes to pack for an indeterminate amount of time, a couple of days to a couple of weeks. He had managed to grab a change of pants, goulashes and a winter coat — and his shaving kit, so he hadn't looked like he was coming off a three-day drunk on the job. The other agents didn't know he washed his shirt, underwear and socks out in the sink every night, used the hotel-furnished blow dryer to dry them and the accompanying curling iron to smooth the wrinkles out.

Juliette came to sit with Eli in the spare-room-someday-soon-to-be-an-office as he went over his files, made her way through the obstacle course of unpacked boxes, and perched on the edge of a chair piled with sand toys and beach towels. She held two paper cups of wine and she handed him one. He took a sip, wrinkled his nose at the paper cup and Juliette shrugged.

"It was either set up the baby bed, the bouncy chair and the playpen or unpack the wineglasses. I picked Door Number One." She winked at him. "And I didn't have time to roll a joint."

That had been a running joke with them ever since Eli'd landed on his first marijuana detail at the bureau. Now, the "harmlessness" of weed was always a subject he dealt with quick whenever he started an operation.

"HOW ABOUT WE get rid of the elephant in the room first thing," he says, as snow like he hasn't seen in five years begins to accumulate outside on the window sill. "Marijuana. Grass. Mj. Mary Jane, dope, weed, pot … whatever you call it. What's the harm in it? Hard not to think about our comrades-in-arms out busting drug dealers who sell heroin to kids on the street and smuggle truckloads of cocaine across the border … and we're stuck here chasing farmers."

He pauses, looking from one agent to the next.

"I'm not asking for a show of hands here, just putting it out there that … I may or may not have smoked a couple of joints when I was in college."

The agents chuckle.

"I might or might not have done some research myself," says Agent Thomas. "Satisfying my scholarly curiosity about the effects of THC, of course."

"That's his story and he's sticking to it," says Agent Nakamura.

The men are grinning, relaxed. This isn't the first time Eli has had to step into the shoes of a well-liked boss, and if he'd learned anything from his first experience it was he had to be real. Puff up like a frog on a lily pad and you're done.

"So I get it. It feels like expending a lot of resources on rounding up people producing an innocuous substance that's not hurting anybody." He shakes his head. "I won't even go down the rabbit trail of the 'gateway drug' concept. Anecdotally, I could personally document chapter and verse the progression of half a dozen kids I know through weed to uppers, downers, cocaine, heroin — they're all dead now from overdoses. But, to be fair, a lot of people smoke it who don't move on to hard drugs. I think that case has yet to be made."

He pauses.

"For the past five years, I've been working out of the field office in El Paso, Texas. And I've watched the sale of marijuana fund one massive drug operation after another — the largest run by a Colombian man named Pablo Escobar. You might have heard the name. Three years ago, he started developing his cocaine business, and this year, he and Jorge Ochoa, Juan Vásquez and José Rodríguez formed an organization called the Medellín Cartel."

Eli nods to the second picture he'd pinned up on the cork board.

"Like Willie Ray Taggart, Escobar is a pilot, used to fly a plane smuggling drugs into the U.S. … before he bought fifteen *bigger planes, including a Learjet, and six helicopters. Now, that original plane hangs above the gate of his Colombian ranch called Hacienda Napoles.*

"The Medellín Cartel is only one of the sources of illegal drugs — everything from cannabis to heroin — that are smuggled from sites in South America into the U.S. — somewhere between forty and sixty

tons every month. Using the proceeds from marijuana sales, these guys branch out. Some of them are heavily involved in sex trafficking, young girls from Central America, but they've gotten more brazen, started kidnapping girls from Eastern Europe — blondes, mostly, to satisfy their customers. We know they're producing and marketing snuff movies, though we've never been able to prove it. We can prove they make millions on pornography and kiddie porn."

Eli has resisted the urge to pace as he speaks, a bad habit that's hard to break. But he surrenders now, gets to his feet, and crosses back and forth in front of the cork board.

"There are other, smaller cartels — Los Indios, Cinco Pesos, Muerte Negra — and one is called Los Asesinos. That translates to 'killers, assassins, butchers.' They have close ties to the Genovesi crime family in New York.

"We busted one of their mules hauling a hundred pounds of pure cocaine in the side panels of his pickup truck, crossing the Rio Grande south of El Paso, and he cut a deal. He was too far down the food chain to give us anybody big, but he did provide information about marijuana-growing operations in the U.S. that are selling weed by the ton all over the world. Three were in California, one in Florida. We're tracking down all the leads. He claimed Righteous Weed" — Eli holds up the baggie — "comes from right next door in Kentucky." Stopping in front of the cork board, Eli gestures toward the pictures.

"Los Asesinos had a run-in with the Cornbread Mafia five years ago and got their asses kicked. This guy said Riley Hannacker and his army use their competitors as pig food, described human bones and 'leftovers' lying around — apparently hogs don't like shoes and belt buckles."

Eli takes a breath.

"Let me be clear. I'm not talking about feeding dead bodies to pigs … I'm talking about men being eaten alive."

One of the agents cringes. The others' faces are impassive.

"Look, everybody agrees Prohibition was a bad idea — in large part because selling booze illegally for huge profits funded the birth of *organized crime in this country. And the sale of illegal marijuana has funded criminal enterprises all over the world."*

He stops in the center of the room, and his voice turns hard.

"The bottom line is that possession, manufacturing and selling marijuana is against the law. We get paid to arrest people who break the law — that's reason enough. If you harbor any warm, fuzzy feelings about Ma and Pa Kettle growing a little weed out behind the barn to ease Ma's arthritis, now's the time to ditch them. These people are criminals. This is organized crime *— on a multi-million-dollar scale. It's our job to put them out of business."*

JULIETTE TOOK another sip of paper-cup wine, then turned and looked at the door. A second later, Eli heard the baby cry. She was all the time doing that — *how?* He'd prefer to believe that she had more acute hearing than his, but the truth was sometimes she just *knew.* Were all mothers like that?

Dropping the file onto the desktop, he got to his feet. "My turn." He held up a finger. "Unless it's a—"

She joined her voice to his in a sing-song chant, "— poopy diaper and you don't *do* poopy diapers."

Chapter Seven

SUNSET PAINTED the western sky shades of orange, pink and lavender, and granted the fading light a golden hue that sparkled on the autumn foliage, making the red and golden leaves almost incandescent. But the colors were muted by the tinted glass, so he rolled his window down, enjoyed the damp, earthy smell of tilled fields and black dirt as the lengthening shadows deepened from purple to black.

He told the driver to pull over to the side of the road as soon as they crossed the bridge. The two Harley Davidsons that followed pulled off the road, too. Then he got out of the sleek silver limousine and walked back to the bridge, leaned on the railing, looking down into the muddy water of the Rolling Fork River.

In truth, Jackson McClusky would really rather be riding one of the Harleys than sitting in the limo. Those were sweet machines for a fact and he intended to spend some quality time cruising the highways and byways of Callison County aboard one of them. That would come later, though, when there was time for recreation. Now it was time for business.

The sandbar was gone. Musta been a big storm that raised the water level of the river, sent it rumbling down the riverbed, washed it clean away. A lot of things can get washed away in five years. He'd played on that sandbar when he was a kid, and there was crawdads in the creek that fed into the river about a mile up. He'd caught a couple once and put them down his sister's shirt collar, woulda got his hide tanned for it good if he hadn't planned ahead, planted a dead crawdad in his brother Wade's pocket so he'd get the blame.

That was the key to success — good planning. And he'd been planning and organizing what he was going to do in the days ahead for almost a month now. And if you counted the time he'd spent fantasizing and imagining it, he'd been planning it for five years.

Jackson looked down at the black brace that ran from an inch below his elbow to the top of his left hand — the brace that held his wrist motionless so the bones couldn't move and grate against each other, the wrist bones that'd been broke, set wrong, broke again, and then put back together by a Tijuana surgeon who'd been too drunk at the time to line up the bones right. Jackson coulda had another surgery, but he was done with that. Suffering through years of constant pain in silence had strengthened his character. The mangled wrist was a moment-to-moment reminder of what he'd been through — that goaded him, prodded him, kept his mind focused and alert. The brace was a badge of honor now, and the "special feature" he'd recently added would serve him well. Jackson McClusky would never again be without a weapon.

A pickup truck appeared on the road approaching the bridge, coming fast, a bat outta hell, and Jackson turned back toward the limo and hurried to it. He only managed to get the door open before the truck sped by, though. He saw a face, saw that the face saw him, but it was only for an instant and then the truck was gone.

Bruce Puckett. Looked like Bruce, anyway. He'd put on weight, cut his beard off — if it was Bruce at all. If Jackson had recognized the man in the truck, maybe the man had recognized him, too. He stood where he was as the pickup sped away.

Then he shook his head. No, he couldn't afford to take a chance. His plan — his *real* one, not the elaborate charade that'd saved his life — was the basic battle plan he'd learned all those years ago by watching the daily brawls in the yard at the Kentucky State Penitentiary in Eddyville. Always strike first with a devastating blow. The man who came out on top in those fights wasn't necessarily the bigger or more powerful man. The winner was the man who planned his attack and *surprised* his opponent.

It'd worked in Vietnam, too, when he and the others had been on the receiving end. An involuntary shiver ran down his spine. He never thought about that time, about the attack at Tweety Bird that had left so many soldiers dead. He'd solved all his problems with a single, spontaneous act that day ... and set himself up to be the victim of catastrophic revenge when the war was over.

Well, this time, Jackson McClusky would be the one doling out the revenge. He would strike before his victims even knew he was here.

He turned to Alejandro, who was still straddling his Harley. Paco had already put his up on the kickstand.

Gesturing toward the pickup truck that had already rounded a curve and was out of sight, he said, "Run that guy off the road. Make sure he's dead."

The biker didn't blink, just turned on the ignition key,

jumped up and onto the kick starter and the engine rumbled to life. He left a spray of gravel and dirt hanging in the air as he sped away.

Then Jackson got into the backseat of the limo and instructed the driver to pull back out onto the road and continue into Brewster. He told the man to drive slowly down Main Street, so he could watch the folks on the street ogle the sleek silver limo, watch them squint trying to get a look at who was inside. This was pure theatre and Jackson knew it, just self-indulgent grandstanding. But he'd earned some grandstanding, thank you very much, and he intended to squeeze all the gusto out of his return as he could. Tomorrow, he would settle down to business. And after he'd done what he came here to do, wouldn't be a man, woman or child in the whole county who didn't know Jackson McClusky was *back*.

Chapter Eight

THERE WERE no windows in the back room of the Club Cherry so Willie Ray didn't see the sleek silver limo cruising slowly down Main Street. He had gone home and got cleaned up so he wouldn't smell like a pigsty before he came in to Brewster to deal poker.

And to perpetuate the legend.

Willie Ray had decided at the very beginning that the best possible way to keep his secret was to tell everybody all about it. And so he did.

"Yep, I got me a propane tanker buried out in a field. It's where I keep the ... proceeds from my ... various commercial endeavors." He let out a loud burp at the end of the sentence and the men gathered around the poker table laughed.

Willie Ray had once been an interminable gambler. That all ended when he went to Vietnam and his brother Andy was killed. But the thing was, it hadn't been a conscious decision on Willie Ray's part. He didn't wake up one day and think, you know what, I b'lieve I'll stop gambling. It wasn't even so much that he'd decided not to

45

gamble. He didn't decide. He just … *couldn't*. Every time he did, he invited the presence of his brother, who almost a decade after Vietnam, still showed up every now and then in Willie Ray's life. Although he had grown accustomed to it after all these years, visitations from Andy were still a horror no one would ever willingly repeat.

He couldn't gamble, but he *could* deal and there was none better than Willie Ray Taggart. Besides, he was good company and the other gamblers who hung out in the back room of Club Cherry liked to have him around.

"So you got yourself a whole propane tanker full of money, do ya?" asked Smitty Alesworth. He was a small man with delicate features who lived in Taylor County.

"Well, money and … other valuable stuff. But it ain't *full* of money … yet."

"So what do you do when … you know, when you need to go buy a roll of toilet paper to wipe our butt with … how do you get to the money?"

Willie Ray laughed easily.

"Now if I's to tell you that, it'd be like giving you the key to my safe deposit box in the bank. Just know I can get in and out any time I want. I's there just this afternoon as a matter of fact, making a deposit."

The propane tanker wasn't *full*, of course. It was a propane tanker, for crying out loud. But Willie Ray did believe it might be full of money someday. That wasn't his goal in life — to have a buried propane tanker stuffed with thousand-dollar bills. Fact was, he didn't really care about the money anymore. It was just a way to keep score. But he had to put the money somewhere and he sure couldn't go into the Farmer's National Bank on Main Street in Brewster and open up a savings account. He gave away as much of it as he could, they all did — anonymously, of course. Pete Cunningham's mortgage when the bank was about to foreclose and take his farm, a big double-wide trailer for the Purcells after their house burned, college educations for Willie Ray didn't know how many cousins. But giving money away was dangerous. People knew where it was coming from, though they pretended they didn't. And the more people who knew you was growing weed ...

Riley and Jessie had numbered accounts somewhere in the Cayman Islands. Ace had set the whole thing up for them, but Willie Ray said that was too high-tech for a good ole boy from Callison County. He'd keep his money in *bills*, thank you very much. Of course, eventually there had been so many bills he had to figure out somewhere to store it.

"Ain't you afraid somebody's gonna steal your money, just stuffing it in a propane tanker like that?" asked Roy Burchel, who winked and grinned at Smitty. Roy worked on the production line at General Electric Appliance Park in Louisville and Smitty was a mechanic and neither one of them could pour sand out of a boot if the instructions was on the heel. They was just egging him on, making fun of him. But that was the point. He *wanted* people to make fun of him. The only way to keep folks from trying to find his buried propane tanker full of money was to convince people it didn't exist. He couldn't stop the rumors, so he fed them, piled logs on the flames and roasted marshmallows in the fire. After a couple of years of his tall tales, Willie Ray Taggart's buried propane tanker full of money had passed into legend — kinda like Bigfoot and the Abominable Snowman.

There were only three other people who knew the propane tanker was real — Riley, Jessie and a man named Cornelius P. Butterworth, better known as Ace. Only Riley and Jessie knew where it was located. Riley had operated the backhoe to dig the huge crater in the field off

McCubbin Lane, a couple acres of Monaghan farmland that was so rocky it wouldn't grow nothing.

He'd dumped his idea on the other members of the Cornbread Mafia five years ago, and Riley'd had two words for his plan: "You're crazy."

THEY'RE SITTING in their clubhouse — Jessie's old tobacco barn. She has brought a pot of pinto beans, three dishes of cornbread still hot from the oven and a big chunk of butter to slather all over it. They're here to discuss hiring more hands to work in the pot fields come harvest, but Willie Ray derails the conversation with a non sequitur.

"I've decided what I'm gonna do with my money!" Willie Ray's mouth is stuffed with cornbread, but his words are clear enough.

"Finally," Riley says.

Jessie chimes in with "It's really not that hard, the numbered accounts. Ace showed us how, just said we had to memorize the numbers — not to write them down anywhere—"

"I ain't putting my money in a bank account on some island I ain't never been to."

"What difference does it make if you've ever been there? The numbered accounts offshore make it so the government—"

He waves Riley off.

"Last time we talked about this you gave me the off-shore-account rap. It wasn't for me then and it still ain't."

"Then what are you talking about, if not a numbered account?"

"I'm thinking about putting it in The Treehouse."

"A treehouse?" Jessie asks.

Willie Ray rolls his eyes. "Not 'a' treehouse — The Treehouse. It's a cave we stumbled on as kids when we were on our way to the woods to build a treehouse."

"You can't be serious. Put your money in a cave?"

"No, not 'xactly in the cave. I'm thinking about putting it in a propane tanker and putting the tanker in the cave."

Riley chokes.

"Are we in the same conversation?" Jessie asks.

"The inside of a tanker is clean and as secure as the inside of any bank vault. Cut you a door in the side, fix it with hinges, like we learned in shop class. You could put all kinda valuable stuff in there.

He lights up.

"Seed! That's where we could store it. Wazzi says it's got to be a dark, dry place and the inside of a tanker's dry. The cave's dry, too. Limestone caves don't drip water 'cause all the water's already come and gone a couple million years ago."

Riley decides to humor him. Riley don't seem to know Willie Ray figured out what he was doing a long time ago and is just playing along.

"Fine. Your tanker idea makes sense. Just got one question."

He pauses and Willie Ray knows Riley thinks he's got him now.

"Just explain to me how you plan to jam that tanker through the three-foot opening of that cave."

"Ain't gonna take it in through the front door. I'm gonna dig a hole in that meadow, bust through the top of the cave, lower the tanker down, then fill in the hole with dirt around it — just leave a little space in front so's you can get into the cave and open the tanker door."

The other two look at him like he'd grown a third eye.

"You're serious about this, aren't you?" Jessie asks.

"As a—"

Riley and Jessie chime in "... a heart attack."

IT REALLY WASN'T the tanker they's upset about. It was the principle the plan was based on. *You just don't go dig a hole in the ground and bury money!* You put it in a bank, or buy stuff, stocks and bonds and the like — houses and boats and real estate, maybe. But just bury it in the ground?

He finally wore them down, though. They didn't agree with him, but they did agree to help him do what he wanted to do. It took the better part of the summer of 1975 to set the whole thing up.

In truth, Willie Ray'd wanted to do *something* with that cave since he was ten years old. He had gone with Riley and his grandfather to the farm of one of Riley's cousins who lived so far back in the knobs even they called it "the boondocks."

The two boys'd decided the woods around the place would be a great place for a treehouse because they had never been logged and the trees were gigantic. Then Riley scared up a rabbit and they chased it across a meadow on top of a good-sized rise with woods along the slopes leading up to it. They come to a big pile of boulders, like big as tanks, piled up against the side of the hill. The rabbit darted in among the boulders and they went after her, clambering around on the huge rocks. And right smack dab in the middle of them rocks was a kind of empty place and that was the first they realized that the rocks had piled up at the front of a cave entrance.

Caves were common all over Kentucky. Shoot, the largest cave system in the whole world was Mammoth Cave National Park — with four hundred miles of explored caverns and who knew how many more miles that hadn't nobody ever seen yet.

Wasn't much in life more exciting to two ten-year-old boys than finding a cave! The entrance was a big crack in the rock and the cave lay beyond. Not no Mammoth Cave, though. It was just a big hole in the ground, didn't go nowhere. Still it was a cave and it was their own private cave. They didn't tell anybody about it. It was their secret.

When Willie Ray'd first got to considering where he was going to put all the money he was making selling weed, he thought about that cave. He got Jessie to buy it so he wouldn't own the property — and her lawyers done it in the name of some kinda corporation. But he couldn't bring himself to leave a trash bag stuffed with hundred-dollar bills laying on the cave floor.

Then he thought about the tanker, and it all come clear to him. He done what he needed to the tanker — cut a doorway, welded a door frame to the hole and set a door in it with a big old hasp and padlock. Later, Riley made him swap out the door for one that'd come out of a real bank vault, had a complicated combination lock and pins that went into the door frame and everything.

Soon's they'd got it finished, the three of them went down into the tanker, carrying flashlights and a bottle of wine, christened it The Treehouse. It likely had a couple million dollars in cash in it by now … but what was in the jars that sat on the shelves was worth waaaay more than that — *seed*.

Chapter Nine

THE NEXT MORNING, Juliette stood in the doorway of the bathroom watching Eli shave. He hated it when she did that, mostly because the only time she did was when he was going out on an assignment. She was good at keeping her worry to herself, but the bathroom-door-standing was a definite tell.

"What's this Callison County like?" she asked.

"Beautiful. Gigantic hills the locals call "knobs," green pastures, secluded hollows."

"And those locals are ...?"

"Not toothless and barefoot and married to their cousins, if that's what you mean. What they've built ... an *empire* ... Not a thing dumb hillbillies could put together." He winced when he nicked his chin with the razor, grabbed a piece of toilet paper and dabbed at the wound. "I'm told they don't warm up to strangers, but I already knew that part."

Eli had grown up with a great aunt and uncle in a little town called Sellersburg in southern Indiana after his parents were killed in a drive-by shooting in Chicago. His uncle had been a fisherman and they spent most of every summer weekend at lakes in Kentucky, on the other side of the Ohio River — Lake Cumberland, Barren River Lake, Cave Run Lake.

"And, of course, I'm not their favorite color."

Racism was a fact of life. Eli'd had to work twice as hard to get half as much out of every class/job/situation for as far back as he could remember, had to out-perform every white kid in grade school, and still didn't make the team; had watched white agents leap-frog over him for promotions in the bureau. But he'd bulldozed his way through. Things were way better than they used to be, but true equality … no, not happenin'. There were worse places to grow up for a black kid than Indiana, though. A whole lot worse.

"Mmmm … *Blazing Saddles*," Juliette said and they nodded in shared understanding.

They had seen the movie when it came out two years ago and liked it so much they went back twice.

Juliette had known what she was signing on for when she married Eli. They'd met when he was finishing his master's degree in criminology and criminal justice at Northeastern University in Boston. She'd known he was one of those rare sorts who had always known "what he wanted to be when he grew up." He'd decided in second grade he wanted to be an FBI agent and never gave serious consideration to doing anything else with his life.

Perhaps Eli was imagining it, but it appeared to him that Juliette got wound tighter now when he was working on a case than she did in the beginning. He suspected it might have something to do with the children. They'd waited to have kids. Juliette had been a trauma nurse in a big-city hospital emergency room — wrecks, fires, shootings — she'd known how ugly it could be out there, but she loved her work. And when she'd accidentally gotten pregnant ... well, the world went into a whole new orbit around the sun. They'd found out Gabrielle had spina bifida from an ultrasound when Juliette was only four months along, and from that moment forward worry and anxiety and fear became as much a part of everyday life as breathing.

Juliette's obstetrician left a lot to be desired in the bedside manner department.

"You need to abort this fetus," he'd said, saw how horrified they were and raised his hand for silence before either of them could speak. "This kind of life-altering decision can't be a knee-jerk, some kind of emotional 'oh, I could never do *that*.' Yes you can. And you should, but that decision rests with you. Just make sure it's a *decision* and not an emotional reaction." He looked at Juliette. "I don't have to tell *you* what you're going to have to live with for the rest of your lives unless you end this here and now."

Eli wished he could say that they did decide, that they weighed the alternatives and made a rational choice. They didn't.

He wished he could say they never doubted. They did.

He wished he could say that the wonder of their precious little girl was worth everything they went through — and she was, but not in the beginning. In the beginning ... the surgeries, the complications, the hospitalizations. He questioned their decision every day, sometimes every hour, as he looked at the tiny baby's swollen head and useless legs ... and wondered — will she be a *person* on the other side of this?

Maybe it was all that — the struggle that had bonded them together — maybe that's why Juliette found it harder now to let him go.

Eli dressed — and didn't even have to come up with a

good excuse this time because Gabrielle called her mother from the kitchen.

Juliette turned to go see what the child wanted and he rose quickly, put on his shoulder holster that held the SIG SAUER .45 Auto and slid his jacket on over it. It was one thing to know your husband is armed, and another to watch him strap his gun on. Juliette probably knew the little game he played, but that was okay, too.

After a sticky kiss from a jelly-faced Gabrielle, they performed their question-and-ridiculous-promise tradition:

"Daddy, will you bring me home a ... a walrus?"

"Won't fit in the trunk."

"How about a parrot?"

"If you want a bird, the best I can do is a pterodactyl."

"What's a terry-back-tal?"

"Ask your mommy."

Then he stood at the front door with his bag and the dogs jumping all over him.

He gave Juliette a peck of a kiss.

"Be safe," she said. She *never* told him goodbye.

When he got into the car, he unhooked from home. Had to. Carrying your family around in your head on the job could get you killed. And from everything he'd learned about them, the Cornbread Mafia were *dangerous* people. Anybody who'd feed a live person to pigs ... they were *monsters*.

Chapter Ten

THE MONSTER ATTACKED Drew Hannacker as he sat at the breakfast table, eating his cereal.

Daddy was as quick as a frog catching a fly, came up behind him and marched his fingers up Drew's ribcage to that special spot under Drew's arm that only the Tickle Monster could find.

Drew burst into a gale of giggles.

"Riley, stop that. Let the boy eat his cereal. He'll miss the school bus."

Daddy ignored her, grabbed Drew's University of Kentucky baseball cap and sailed it out of the breakfast nook into the vast expanse of the formal dining room beyond it.

"What happened to your hat, boy?"

"Leave him alone and let him—"

"Why … is that it yonder? Lying on the floor by the chair?"

His father flicked him a look and Drew leapt to his feet, bounding around the right side of the table into the dining room. Riley barreled around the other side of the table.

"The house is not the place to play rowdy games—" Mommy said as Daddy sidestepped past her and raced toward the hat. Drew dived, sliding on his belly across the shiny hardwood floor, grabbed the hat as his father loomed overhead, trying to snatch it away. He curled into a ball clutching the hat to his belly, knowing the coming attack would be swift and delightful.

"The Tickle Monster is comin' to get you," Daddy said in a deep voice, and then gave a ridiculously scary laugh. "Bwa-ha-ha-ha-ha."

"Ri-ley!" Mom said it like it was two words — Ri and Lee, in her mad voice.

The monster struck and Drew burst into giggles, wiggling around on the floor, trying-but-not-really-trying to get away as his father stood over him, tickling his stomach, his sides and up under his arms.

"Stop that roughhousing right now — you'll break something!" his mother said, marching into the room. "Riley, the boy can't breathe."

He could too, but Daddy stopped anyway, reached down his hand to pull Drew to his feet.

"Need to be more careful with that hat, son, or—"

The phone rang and Daddy went into the library to answer it.

His mother was still talking to Daddy when he walked away, so she just kept on, like he could hear what she was saying.

Maybe she knew Daddy didn't listen to her.

Drew went back to the table, sat down, picked up his spoon and chased Cheerios around in the puddle of milk in his bowl. He watched his mother scurrying around to finish what she was putting in the crockpot for dinner, and she reminded him of a squirrel. She was small, dark and her movements were quick, even a little herky-jerky like the movements of a squirrel.

Sometimes he thought of her as a fox, with a black jelly-bean nose and its whiskers twitching.

His father was always a bear. Not one of those big, ugly scary ones, the grizzly bears he'd seen pictures of. They had claws that were six inches long — or Kodiak bears, more monster than animal.

A black bear. Yeah. There wasn't anything more powerful than a black bear. Well, the grizzly bears and Kodiak bears were but they didn't count because they were just killers. A black bear was strong and determined, and protective. A mama black bear would rip your arms off if you got between her and a cub.

Drew had almost found out for himself last year when he and his father had gone deer hunting. Hadn't shot anything, but on their way back to the truck they crossed a stream and his father had grabbed his shoulder and squeezed as hard as he could. Didn't say anything, just gestured with his chin. About fifty feet away were two black bear cubs, drinking from the stream. Drew watched his father look all around, trying to find the mother.

Then he'd just dragged Drew back the way they'd come, through some bushes where they could watch and sure enough the mama bear had been downstream of them, so if they'd kept going, they'd have been between her and the cubs and Daddy said later that she might have charged.

"You coulda killed her with a deer rifle, couldn't you? A .30-06 will kill a bear, won't it?"

His father had said that it would indeed kill a bear, but he absolutely did not want to shoot it. The bear had as much right to be in the woods as he and Drew did, he said,

58

and it would be wrong, just *wrong*, to shoot a mother for protecting her young.

That's when Drew'd decided his father was a black bear.

The image of a lion flashed in front of his eyes. Like it looked when it growled, like the MGM lion that growled before the start of a movie. His father wasn't a lion.

Pop Pop had been a lion.

The ache of longing was still there. Drew missed his grandfather, but moving out of the old house and into this one had changed everything. He couldn't picture Pop Pop at the head of the table at Christmas dinner, or sitting in a rocker on the front porch, or helping Daddy and Uncle Willie Ray put together his swing set. He couldn't insert the image of his grandfather into his new environment because his grandfather had never been there. The house hadn't been finished when he died. He'd never been in it. Drew and his mother had moved in with his Grandma Aggie and Grampa Fred Bennett after … and Drew never went back. Not one time. His mother had packed up his things and moved them to the new house. His father had gathered up the toys that'd been in his secret playroom in the storage room in the barn and brought them to the new house. Not the GI Joe doll, though. The first one, the one Mommy got so mad at Pop Pop for buying. Daddy said he had looked in the playroom and all over the house and couldn't find it.

Drew knew where it was. It was in the tall weeds outside the outside door of the tack room, the door he'd used to go into the barn, and then to run out of it and back into the house. He'd had the doll in his hands when he peeked through the crack, then turned toward the door with it and ran. Somewhere in the dark weeds it had slipped out of his fingers and he never set foot there again to look for it.

He didn't tell Daddy where to look because Daddy would wonder why Drew had been coming into the tack room through that outside door. Might wonder *when* he'd done that. Drew didn't want the doll bad enough to chance being asked about how it got there. Leave it there. In the weeds. Let it stay there.

"… listening to me?" his mother said and he realized she'd been talking to him.

"Yes ma'am, I'm listening." He hadn't been and hoped she didn't ask what she'd said.

"So what kind do you want? You get to pick what kind of creatures you want in the bouncy castle. They have cartoon characters, like Donald Duck and Porky Pig, or farm animals — pigs and goats and cows — or jungle animals—"

"Jungle animals," he said firmly. He didn't really care at all one way or the other, but knew if he admitted that, she'd want to know why he didn't care and she'd poke and prod and …

"Jungle animals it is, then," she said. "Are you excited?"

"Sure, I'm excited."

She looked keenly at him.

"Well, you might want to let your face know because it didn't get the memo."

He didn't know what to say, so didn't say anything at all.

"Finish that cereal or you'll be late. I have too much to do today to take you to school if you miss the bus."

Then Drew thought to make sure, again.

"There's just going to be kids coming, right? Not any grownups — your friends or daddy's."

"No adults. How many times do I have to tell you that?"

As many times as it takes to convince me it's true, he thought, but had better sense than to say it. Daddy *knew* the Thing. That's how Drew thought of the killer in his mind. Just a Thing. Not a person. People had souls. Father Donavan had said so lotsa times. And no person with a soul coulda done what the Thing did. He'd seen Daddy speak to the Thing. Maybe it was even one of Daddy's friends. Drew lived in abject terror that one day he would look up from the television or a comic book and Daddy would be standing in his very own living room with the Thing, had brought the monster home to dinner.

The Thing knew that Drew had seen, knew he'd watched his grandfather's murder. Drew was sure it did. The Thing knew where he lived, too. And one of these days, the Thing was going to come for him.

Daddy came out of the library into the kitchen. "I'll see you at supper," he told Drew. "See if you can manage to keep up with that hat until then."

"Was that Uncle Willie Ray on the phone?"

Drew adored his Uncle Willie Ray.

"Nope. He's flying to Minnesota today."

Flying! Drew had fantasies of sneaking into Uncle Willie Ray's airplane and riding with him wherever it was he went — someplace a long way from Callison County where Drew would be safe from the Thing.

Chapter Eleven

As Winona McClusky sipped her second cup of morning coffee in the breakfast nook in the little house on Booker Street in Brewster, she considered how far she had come in such a short time, all the arrangements she'd made, plans she had set in motion. Now, when she stood up in life's canoe and looked out ahead, she could see sparkling water and a brighter tomorrow. She reminded herself to be profoundly grateful for that because it hadn't always been the case. The future had looked pretty grim until … when? Well, it wasn't like there was some big event, some moment that Winona could point to and say, that's when it happened. It was more the turning up of a dimmer switch in a dark room. It got brighter and brighter until she was finally able to see the world clearly. The world as it really was.

She did, however, remember the exact moment when she decided to do something about what she saw. It was before dawn on the Monday morning after Steve Cauthen rode Affirmed to a one-and-a-half-length victory in Saturday's 104th Run for the Roses. The McClusky family's derby party had been epic, she'd gotten drunk, took all day Sunday to recover, and now had to get to work early to prepare for a rare court appearance at nine o'clock. It was pouring rain when she pulled into her parking slot near the courthouse, reached for her umbrella and realized she'd left it … somewhere. Instead of sitting in her car until the rain let off, she decided to make a run for it — go from her car to the roof overhang in front of the pool hall down the street and from there to the courthouse.

By the time she collided with the front wall of the closed pool hall, she was soaked to the skin, standing like a drowned rat beside the dirty window. What was affixed to the outside of the window caught her eye then. It was her own picture — what passed for a glamour shot for a woman with zero glamor to bring to the party. Red, white and blue colors on the poster, big word "VOTE" at the top above her picture. Beneath were the words "Elect Winona McClusky, Callison County Attorney."

The poster had been defaced, of course, a mustache drawn under her nose, elephant ears on the sides of her head and big devil horns protruding from her skull — but that's not what bothered her about the poster.

Winona had become the Commonwealth's Attorney of Callison County in 1975, had taken the position for a variety of reasons, chief among them that she was absolutely bored out of her gourd working in the offices of Tanner, McClusky and Fowler, attorneys at law. She hadn't joined the firm because she knew she'd enjoy the line of work. She knew she'd hate it, though she was surprised at how quickly she had come to detest it and how profound was her loathing. She'd left an interesting and sometimes exciting criminal law practice in Louisville to return to her hometown of Brewster and join the law firm her father had helped to found and where he had been employed until he vanished in a puff of smoke on the same day her brother Shep had been killed in a "traffic accident" nine years ago.

She'd come home to find out what happened to her father. And she had unraveled the mystery, at least she believed she had. Winona had no smoking gun to confirm her suspicions but she was completely satisfied that she had found out. She was certain that Nate Hannacker had run her brother off the road and through a guardrail and that her father had figured out what Nate had done and went after him. Then Nate had killed her father.

She never found any "admissible" evidence, any evidence at all unless you counted the medallion the little Hannacker boy'd found, or the blood stain in the loft of the Hannacker barn that marked the spot where her father had died. Or so she believed.

Though Kentucky was not a death penalty state — and though it was likely Hannacker could have mounted a pretty convincing case for self-defense, the death penalty had been exacted for his crimes. Nate Hannacker was dead, buried under a stone in the St. Augustine cemetery, and her quest to find out the truth was over.

Every time she thought about that, she smiled.

So … now what? Or that's what she'd thought five years ago when she looked around and realized she'd landed a dead-end job in a dead-end town and a future stretching out there in front of her conducting title searches or making out wills or … oh, how could she stand the excitement — getting to defend somebody charged with driving under the influence of intoxicants.

The route out of that miasma of tedium fell out of the sky and hit her in the head. Political office. The position of county prosecutor — called Commonwealth's Attorney — was an elected position and the man who'd held it since shortly after the earth cooled off had dropped over dead in the middle of a Chamber of Commerce luncheon in 1976 and Democratic Governor Julian Carroll had appointed Winona to serve out the remainder of his term.

Now, if she wanted to keep the job, she'd have to run for election, so she'd filed the necessary paperwork, horrified at the prospect of having to campaign, give speeches, show up at county events, fish fries and festivals, pressing the flesh, smiling and greeting people and drumming up votes.

But there was more than one way to skin a cat in politics. Like most other endeavors in life, getting elected to public office had little to do with *what* you knew and everything to do with *who* you knew. Her uncle, the sheriff, had promised to grease the skids, call in favors and perhaps twist an arm or two. And he would have to do just that because Winona certainly couldn't run on her record of success! She had yet to make a significant conviction, had watched helplessly as farmers in Callison County who hadn't grown an ear of corn in five years built multimillion-dollar houses, went on European vacations and drove jaguars and BMWs.

Shoot, she couldn't even get an *indictment* on marijuana charges because the jury pool was tainted. Oh, the voter registration rolls from which potential jury members were selected was legitimate — nobody was cooking the books. The issue was that in Callison County, Kentucky it was impossible to seat a jury of twelve county residents without one of them being a weed grower. Maybe they weren't growing it themselves, but their uncle/brother/father/boyfriend/husband or Great Dane was!

Or they were selling their appliances/farm equipment/shoes/groceries/dental services and jockey shorts to people who could afford to buy what they were selling because their pockets were full of weed money.

Or they were what she called *hardcore*, that small but powerful group of county residents who wouldn't spit on a law enforcement officer if he was on fire. The ones who'd grown up in the moonshine tradition and still played by the rules of that game.

Winona wasn't sure exactly what her uncle's tactics were and didn't really care, knew only that she was assured a win in the November election, would continue to claim residence in the big drafty office in the courthouse she'd moved into after moving out of the tidy little offices of Tanner, McClusky and Fowler. That was a good thing. At least it had been until the demon-horned, big-eared creature on the poster five months ago had stared into Winona's eyes and asked her a simple question, "Do you really want to sign on to another four years of this?"

Well, it was better than working on land transfers and shoplifting cases.

So, are those your *only* alternatives, the image asked: wither away in a small-town law office or chase criminals you'll never catch?

No, she'd decided, as she shivered and dripped on the sidewalk that morning, those were *not* her only options. She wouldn't let them be! She would start thinking outside the box ... outside the box the first box came in. She'd find a way to take the lemons in her life and make lemonade.

As soon as she set her thoughts free, a world of delicious possibilities opened up before her like the petals of a rosebud. *Yeah!* And she wouldn't settle for mere lemonade, either. She'd find a way to drink it in the shade of a palm tree somewhere far, far away.

Later today, she would take yet another step toward her new life. She'd already taken many steps, both large and small, but this one was particularly pivotal. Today, Winona McClusky would inform the Callison County Clerk — with deep regret, of course — that she must withdraw from the county attorney's race and forgo her shoo-in victory.

Chapter Twelve

As soon as Willie Ray pulled Kiwi out of the hangar he'd built for her — at the end of the runway he'd also built for her — he methodically went down the list of preflight inspections. This morning's weather check revealed clear skies all the way from Kentucky to Canada. A storm system was due to roll in late this afternoon, but he'd be long gone by then.

A clear day, blue skies — a few puffy white clouds, maybe — autumn colors blanketing the earth beneath.

It was a perfect day to fly. But then, for Willie Ray Taggart, every day was a perfect day to fly. The only time Willie Ray ever felt free, completely free, was when he was soaring among the clouds. He'd learned to fly four years ago as just one more activity to give him a buzz of excitement — the kind of buzz that only came from doing something at least mildly dangerous.

He'd actually intended to go skydiving that day — what Riley called "jumping out of a perfectly good airplane," but he'd gotten the scheduling wrong and didn't figure it out until he had already driven to Louisville to

Bowman Field. He'd figured if he couldn't jump out of an airplane, might be cool to learn how to fly one. So he'd gone looking for somebody at the airport to teach him.

THE FLIGHT INSTRUCTOR at Bowman Field was a man named Harold Tobin — Toby — a Navy pilot who'd earned his wings flying an F6F Hellcat and a P-47 Thunderbolt during WWII. He was used to people like Willie Ray Taggart, folks who'd never spent any time in a small plane, suddenly getting a wild hair that they wanted to learn how to fly.

It was a warm July morning, that'd likely top out at more than a hundred degrees by mid-afternoon, when Willie ray showed up wanting to take a test ride with an instructor. Fine by Toby. It was clear that the young man with flaming red hair and more freckles than not — and a scar that sliced across his cheek from his eye to his chin — seemed to have plenty of cash. He had trouble getting his wallet out of his pants pocket because the money stuffed into it made it hard to fold over.

"What'll it be?" Toby asked. "A test ride costs fifty dollars."

The young man quickly peeled three twenties out of the wad of bills and held them out to Toby, told him to keep the change.

Instead of taking the money, Toby launched into his don't-barf-in-my-cockpit speech. Oh, he knew it wouldn't do any good. If somebody got airsick and had to puke, no amount of cajoling on the ground half an hour before was going to stop them. But he gave the speech as just a part of the service because while it had never deterred any vomiting in the air, it had convinced more than a few people not to even try.

"You know what motion sickness is?"

"I do. And I ain't got it."

"You get car sick, sick on a carnival ride or anything like that?"

"I threw up after Riley and me rode the Beast at Kings Island — an amusement park outside Cincinnati. But that don't count 'cause I'd spent the whole morning stuffing myself with hot dogs, funnel cakes, cotton candy and ice cream and I was ready to chuck my cookies before they strapped me into the seat."

"It's hot today. That means a couple of things are going to happen. For starters, when it's hot, the ride's bumpier because there's more turbulence. And there are no air conditioners on a Cessna Skyhawk. So it will be a hot, bumpy ride. If you think you might get sick—"

"I ain't gonna get sick. And if I do, I'll stick my head out the window to throw up, won't dump it on the seat or floorboard."

Toby rolled his eyes.

"Son, you can't get your head out a window on a Cessna Skyhawk, and if you could, your puke would blow back in your face at a hundred and thirty miles an hour."

"Oh. Well then, I just won't puke."

And the kid was true to his word. He didn't vomit. What he did was fall in love.

Toby had seen that before, too, though not nearly as often as he'd seen people turn green and throw up on his floorboard. Something in the freckled farm boy just *clicked* the instant the plane lifted off the end of the runway and leapt into the sky. His face registered surprise, then shock — those were typical. But then all expression left his face and he looked around like a little kid on his first day in heaven. Up at the sky, down at the ground sinking rapidly away from them, taking it all in with unrestrained wonder and delight.

Toby gave the boy his spiel, but he wasn't listening. Told him about the various parts of the airplane's interior, what the dials on the instrument panel meant, how the controls lifted the plane's nose up or pointed it toward the ground. He gave a massively simplified form of "how can something as big and heavy as an airplane get off the ground and stay there?"

The boy never said a word, just looked around him in wonder. Though he didn't do it, Toby was sure that he could have performed all manner of acrobatics, barrel rolls and fake stalls and the kid would have shown no fear. And no excitement, either, and that was what was unique. He wasn't a typical thrill seeker, somebody who was just into the experience to scare himself. Oh, he was that, alright, but he had fallen in love with flying — the act of soaring above the earth — and that sense of awe and wonder never left his face, from takeoff to landing.

"How much does it cost to learn how to fly?"

Toby took a deep breath — it was a long spiel.

"There are different kinds of pilots' licenses. With each one you're certified to do some things but not others. There's a VFR — Visual Flight Rules — license, which basically allows you to fly if you can see but you can't fly just by relying on the instruments. IFR, Instrument Flight Rules, kick in if the ceiling is less than a thousand feet and visibility is less than three miles. And there are commercial grades beyond that. For each one of them you have to take ground school classes and clock a certain number of hours in the air. Ground school is a flat fee, but then you have to rent an airplane, too — have to carry renter's insurance with a minimum physical liability coverage of forty thousand dollars. Hourly plane rental rates are wet rates —

including fuel and oil — but the rate goes up or down depending on what aircraft you rent."

"How about if I just buy an airplane? Then I wouldn't have to rent one."

In almost a quarter of a century as a flight instructor, nobody'd ever asked Harold Tobin that question.

WILLIE RAY BOUGHT A CESSNA 170, used it to get his VFR license, then traded it in for a Cessna Skywagon. He almost traded that one for a Piper Apache, but a test flight of the twin-engine plane felt too much like driving a car. In a smaller plane, you could really get the sense that you were flying. Not the airplane, *you*. Flying.

He did trade up for a Cessna 182, the Skylane, because he liked the tricycle landing gear, struggled to find a name for *her* — assuming if ships was always female, so was airplanes. Finally decided to call her Kiwi — because a kiwi was a bird that couldn't fly, and that made some kind of profound sense to Willie Ray he could never have explained.

He quickly discovered that Andy never came to see him when he was flying. Didn't really surprise Willie Ray. Andy didn't like to fly, had singlehandedly kept the troop transport in the air from California to Vietnam by pulling upward on the armrests of his seat.

The plane was useful to the Cornbread Mafia; what he saw from the air told them how successful their efforts to disguise their crops had been. When they'd started growing weed out of state, it had become a necessity for Willie Ray to make his rounds. Particularly now, at harvest time.

The telltale sign of harvest-ready weed was when the hairs of the plant, or pistils, had fully darkened and curled in. If the buds was looking thick and dense, but they was still some straight white pistils, it wasn't time yet. Of course, Willie Ray had hired experienced crews to work the crop, but he liked to keep a personal eye on such things as when to harvest it.

Harvest was the most labor-intensive part of the process — it flat out took a long time, a *really* long time, to hand trim the buds off *every single marijuana plant* in the field, and you'd best have lots of help!

Willie Ray used the dry-trim method — chopping the plants down and hanging them up to dry for several days before trimming. He could wet-trim if he had to — chop the plants down and take off the buds immediately. That was for emergencies, though, when you had to get the crop in fast, and he hadn't never had an emergency. Not yet, anyway.

As the ground fell away from the Skylane and Willie Ray felt that glorious sensation of freedom deep in his belly, he briefly considered turning south and buzzing Riley's house before he headed north.

Drew loved it when Willie Ray flew low over his house, wagging the wings in a greeting. The boy always jumped up and down, waving both hands high over his head.

But Sherry Lynn hated it, said Willie Ray was going to crash the plane into the house and kill them all.

Willie Ray felt a brief pang of sympathy for Riley then. A random Proverb leapt into his mind from a long-ago confirmation class: "It is better to live on the corner of the roof than to share a house with a quarrelsome wife."

Sounded like whoever wrote Proverbs had made the acquaintance of Sherry Lynn Hannacker.

Chapter Thirteen

THE BIG TRUCK in front of Jessica Monaghan was too wide to pass on this narrow lane, so she puttered along behind it, grateful for the delay. It looked like a UPS truck, but it wasn't brown and the word KISS was painted across the back — though not in the frilly script you'd expect to see on that word. She recognized the truck, watched it turn off at the big brick house set back from the road behind concealing oleander bushes where old Dr. Dawson had lived until he died. He was the doctor who'd held her upside down by her ankles and slapped her pink baby's butt almost thirty years ago.

She had loved that old man. Everyone did. The last of a dying breed, she supposed — a doctor who still made house calls. He had come to her house often in the early days when she had just gotten Davie settled at home and was still terrified of all the medical equipment she and his mother had to operate. She missed Ruth Monaghan — even the post-stroke woman who spent the final three years of her life on her way to a royal wedding, with her diamonds and pearls and furs hanging just around the

74

corner in the closet. Before her stroke, she had been a force to be reckoned with, so abrasive and … oh, call it what it was … *rude* that she had run off her two daughters and would cheerfully have run Jessie off, too, if Jessie had let her.

When the truck started down the driveway of the Dawson place, she could read the words on its side — Kentucky-Indiana Security Specialists. She watched it drive toward the beautiful home — understated charm, classy and tasteful — between the sentinel trees. Stately oak trees … *not* big concrete lions. She cringed at the comparison. The lions were one of hundreds of tip-offs that Sherry Lynn Hannacker had no taste. No, she had taste. Bad taste. Sherry Lynn could be counted on to pass up every opportunity for elegance and classic style in favor of grandiose, garish and tacky.

Riley had told Sherry Lynn she could have anything she wanted and what she wanted was anything he didn't like. The tennis courts, badminton courts, and sand volley-ball court that was used so seldom it had become a litter box for all the feral cats for ten miles around. And the pool. Correction — pool*s*. Plural. Three of them — an Olympic-sized pool for adults, one for children, though there were no small children in the house, and the third a hot tub large enough to accommodate a dozen adults.

Most people didn't know, however, that the concrete lions out front concealed cameras that were part of the house's elaborate surveillance system.

Jessie knew all about the surveillance equipment — which had been installed by the KISS company — and all about the house. Sherry Lynn had drowned Jessie in unwanted minutiae as the construction progressed, since Jessie was the perpetual teenager's reluctant "bestie."

"I told Riley I was not going to spend another night in

that house — would not let my son spend another night there!" Sherry Lynn had said, describing how she had packed up and moved back into her parents' house until construction was complete on her ... castle. Jessie'd tried to comfort her, to reassure her, but she would have none of it. And in truth, if it'd been Jessie instead of Sherry Lynn who had walked into the barn and found Nate Hannacker with a bullet hole in his forehead, she might have been pretty spooked herself.

"I know it was those South Americans," Sherry Lynn ranted. "Riley says that's not possible but I know what I know. Those men came down here and shot bullets into that house and not a week later Nate gets murdered — who else could have done it? The Tooth Fairy?"

What began as justifiable fear had morphed into full-bore paranoia for Sherry Lynn, and she'd insisted on every conceivable surveillance tool and the most sophisticated alarm system money could buy. She had the workers tear out a bathroom and install what she called a "safe room," somewhere she and Drew could run and hide if those monsters came back with guns blazing.

It was excessive, of course. Everything Sherry Lynn Hannacker did was excessive.

Glancing in the rearview mirror as she passed the driveway entrance, Jessie thought to wonder who was moving into the Dawson place, and why they needed a surveillance system. It certainly wouldn't be the only house in the county with one. Nate Hannacker had insisted Jessie have KISS put in "some kinda burglar alarm" and she'd done it because he asked, not because she'd been afflicted by the surveillance-camera paranoia that tended to go hand-in-glove with growing weed.

Even with the slow-moving truck out of the way, Jessie didn't drive fast. She was in no hurry. Harriet Porter was at home with Davie, looked after him with the kind of care you couldn't pay for. She'd been the first nurse Jessie'd hired years ago when she'd finally had the money to do it and Harriet had cared for both Davie and his mother until his mother's death. Since Harriet was a widow — her only son had been killed in Vietnam — Jessie'd added an apartment for Harriet onto the house when she'd renovated it, with its own outside entrance, its own driveway, its own private phone line. Harriet could live as independently as she cared to be. And Jessie suspected that one day, their roles might be reversed, with her looking after Harriet — because Harriet was *family*.

When a truck pulling a hay wagon turned into the road ahead of her, Jessie was almost grateful for another delay. She was *not* anxious to get where she was going, and this morning's weather forecast had said there was a possibility of "afternoon thunderstorms." If the freaky weather that had produced such incredible fall foliage this year — temperatures down into the forties at night for two weeks in August, and then this *hot* Indian Summer — plowed a storm through here, it would rip all those gorgeous leaves off the trees. Today was a perfect autumn day, the colorful foliage set against a blue sky dotted with cotton-ball clouds tethered like hot-air balloons to the treetops. There was a medley of color splashed on the sides of the knobs and running down into the hollows — claret-wine red, the gold of a riverboat gambler's front tooth, smiley-face yellow, the deep russet of a chestnut foal's coat or an auburn-haired toddler, half a dozen different shades of green and an amber shade that was almost caramel brown.

Jessie took it all in because that beauty could be gone tomorrow. *Gone tomorrow.* Something like a shiver ran down her back at that thought.

Pulling off Gallagher Station Road, Jessie drove her

truck around the house and through the open bay doors of the barn, and came to a stop on the back wall beside an old tractor and an equally ancient tobacco setter. When she got out, she glanced at the tobacco setter and remembered how much trouble it'd been to haul that thing up the side of the knob to that first pot field — where they proceeded to grow weed that was nothing more than that — weed. They'd worked so hard in that field, struggling to produce a crop of a plant only two of the four of them had ever seen, and that none of them had ever seen growing in the wild. They'd lost their shirts, almost lost all hope. If they'd given up then ... she shuddered to think where she would be now if they hadn't kept on keeping on.

Three years later, the law'd busted that field and they'd worked all night, cutting what they could of the weed crop and hauling it away as friends and neighbors filled the backs of their pickup trucks with the rest of it. How could she have cared for Davie — and then his mother! — without weed money to pay for nursing care, expert therapists and the right kind of equipment?

Davie would have ended up in a Veterans Administration hospital.

Davie's face flashed in her mind and she banished it instantly. It was the face of the vacant-eyed man who never actually looked at anything. The man who smiled ... at nothing. The man who made noises, all kinda noises, but if any of them had any intellectual significance, she'd never found it. He wasn't talking. It was like the doctors had said — it was a biological response, not a cognitive one.

Jessie almost never saw the face of the old Davie, the man she'd married, the man who'd ridden with her on a magic carpet and promised he'd return from Vietnam "without a mark on him." If she saw that Davie, the ache of longing was still strong enough to take her breath away.

Nine years had passed, but she loved that man still, would surely love him until she died.

And the other Davie? The one with vacant eyes who drooled sometimes in his sleep? She loved him, too, the way you love a puppy or a kitten — something helpless and dependent, something that would die if you didn't care for it. Not a puppy or a kitten, though. They gave back. They loved you back in whatever manner they could. Davie didn't. Couldn't. Davie Monaghan had left the building and he had never returned. Never would.

Stepping out of the barn into the sunshine, she pushed the barn door closed behind her and headed toward the backyard of the house. She stopped in midstride when she saw the flower in the vase that was supposed to look like cut glass but was really made out of plastic. A single long-stemmed yellow rose waited for her on the table by the door.

All her will and resolve drained out of her, leaving her empty and vulnerable. Tears sprang into her eyes so suddenly they almost squirted down her cheeks. She shook her head and whispered, "Oh, Riley."

Chapter Fourteen

A LIGHT WIND stirred outside in the fading afternoon light, making the sycamore tree's limbs sway, scattering shadows to dance across Jessie as she made another pot of coffee. Riley studied her face, did that often. In every kind of illumination — bright sunshine, deep shade, inside and outside. He had fantasized a thousand thousand times what her face would look like illuminated in the strip of moonlight that always shone in through the partially open drapes in his old bedroom. The soft light of a full moon would reveal the perfect harmony of the planes of her cheeks, her wide forehead, rounded chin — lips like the red bow on a box of Valentine candy.

Beauty was all about symmetry, or so said his resident beauty expert Sherry Lynn. She liked nothing more than sitting in front of a mirror admiring herself — and she *was* beautiful — had been when he married her and after a few lost years was beautiful again. She'd told him once that the human eye unconsciously seeks symmetry. Looking at the human face, if both sides were the same, it presented a more pleasing aesthetic than a face that's asymmetrical.

Didn't have to be off much. It would require a concentrated, focused examination to see the difference. One eyebrow higher than the other. One side of the mouth turned up farther than the other in a smile. Nostrils not the same size. Little things, taken as a whole, their uniformity would make a subconscious impression that would determine the assessment of beauty.

Sherry Lynn was proud to point out that her face was perfectly symmetrical ... well, it was when she carefully plucked her right eyebrow, which was slightly closer to her nose than her left. She was always careful not to curl her upper lip under when she smiled so you couldn't see her gums.

Riley'd never stared at Sherry Lynn's face long enough to know if it was as symmetrical as she seemed to think it was. But he had studied Jessie's face, had stared at it with longing for years. He couldn't have said whether all the pieces parts were the right shape, size and position, all he knew was that she was the most beautiful woman he had ever seen.

There was a distant rumble of thunder and Jessie tensed.

"A storm," was all she said, but he could see anxiety tighten the muscles in her shoulders and her jaw. She still hadn't gotten over the terror of the harrowing day three weeks ago when the two of them had braved a tornado together. It had been an awful experience, but it was one of Riley's most treasured memories. The storm had blown them into each other's arms — literally.

"WHAS JUST ISSUED A TORNADO WATCH," *Sherry Lynn tells him, the high voice she affected to sound like a teenager grating even over the telephone. "For all of Callison, Washington and Nelson* counties." *Sherry Lynn is in Louisville, visiting Kim Beddingfield, who'd been her roommate years ago when she was attending Spencerian College, and she'd dragged poor Drew along with her. In truth, though, Riley'd been glad to have her and Drew out from under foot for the afternoon while he wrestled with the year's income tax receipts — both real and faked — spread out on the huge dining room table, gathering them up to take to their accountant. Willie Ray called him a master chef because, "he sure does know how to cook the books."*

"Thanks for letting me know."

"You need to—"

He cut her off before she could prattle on. "I have to concentrate on these taxes right now. I'll be fine."

He hangs up and turns his attention back to the papers on the table.

They'd been able to launder almost half a million dollars with last fall's music festival and he was already planning an even bigger one for this year.

Three days of music — the best bands money could buy — out on a carefully constructed stage in the middle of a field. The idea had been Willie Ray's. Of course.

"So we have us a festival — which'll generate legitimate, verifiable expenses." *He'd ticked them off.* "Materials and labor to build a stage, sound equipment, lighting, food booths — all kinda stuff. Ought to cost a fortune. Charge ten dollars a head cash admission. And you're all set."

"Use little words, I'm taking notes with my crayons," *Riley'd said.*

Willie Ray was often frustrated by the fact that almost nobody in his world "got there" as fast as he did, on a multitude of topics. Sometimes Riley thought Willie Ray was, indeed, a for-real, certifiable genius. Or maybe a marijuana-growing idiot savant.

"Ain't no way to track cash admissions. Ain't no way to count noses in a field full of drunk teenagers in the dark. Say a thousand *people actually come and pony up their ten dollars. You just made ten thousand dollars. Likely spent forty-five thousand to make it, but that don't matter. You claim gate receipts of fifty thousand, maybe seventy-five every night for three nights. Who could prove it ain't the way you reported it? You could clean up two hundred fifty, maybe five hundred thousand dollars in legitimate earnings. And if it gets rained out — no problem. You can declare a whopping loss."*

That'd all sounded good when Willie Ray'd explained it and got it blessed by their master-chef accountant. But as Riley sits amid the pile of actual receipts for actual expenses, he feels totally overwhelmed.

The phone rings again and he is tempted not to answer it.

"Riley! They spotted a twister on the ground out by Harper's Mill."

Riley's heart freezes.

"Moving what direction?"

"Oh, not toward the house, the other way. It's headed northeast toward the county line, but they're saying there's hail in that storm the size of golf balls and if the Corvette is still sitting in the driveway, you need to—"

Riley didn't care that the sports car wasn't in the garage. He did care that a tornado was headed north from Harper's Mill. Jessie was out there! She and a crew of half a dozen workers were in that old barn off Booker Road trimming buds.

Surely, they'd gone home when the weather got nasty. But in a windowless barn, how would they know what was bubbling and boiling in the sky on the other side of King's Crown Knob? Unless somebody had a transistor radio — which nobody would because reception was lousy out there.

"We got a crew working—" He doesn't finish the sentence, is up and running, doesn't even bother to grab a jacket off the hook by the door, catches a fragment of Sherry Lynn's voice coming from the receiver he'd dropped on the floor.

"You're not going out there! Riley Hannacker, you stay—"

Racing out to the Stingray, he leaps in, grateful that it's the fastest car they own, and peels rubber out of the driveway.

It's probably at least ten miles, maybe more, as the crow flies, from Harper's Mill to the barn off Booker Road. That's a long way in tornado miles.

Riley'd always been fascinated with twisters — such powerful juggernauts of destruction. He's almost sure he'd read that only a handful of tornados in history had stayed on the ground more than about ten miles. And he is certain that the fastest forward speed ever documented was fifty miles an hour. So the twister that'd been spotted would suck back up into the thunderstorm before it even got to King's Crown Knob, let alone the other side of it.

And if it does, it couldn't possibly make it before he does, approaching from the west. He has time. He knows he's not behaving rationally, flying off into a storm — the cavalry to the rescue.

Jessie and the crew probably aren't even there. They could be done by now. Or they'd heard the warnings and left.

Still, he can't shake the awful feeling in his gut.

He hasn't gone two miles before the rain hits — so thick it blinds him, and he's reduced to a crawl. Leaning forward, he tries to see, but the windshield wipers can't wipe the deluge off fast enough, and he doesn't dare do more than inch forward.

A three-minute lifetime later, the rain stops like he's turned off a spigot but the wind has ripped limbs off trees and scattered them over the road. He dodges the big ones and clatters over the little ones, probably doing some kind of damage to the low-slung undercarriage of the Corvette.

What he sees in the sky as he rounds the final corner is a horrifying sight. The boiling mass of supercell thunderstorm, black on top, and on the bottom, it's the sick greenish-purple color of a day-old bruise. Careening off the road he almost loses control of the vehicle as he pulls down the old gravel road leading back to the barn. The wind whipping the trees stills almost as suddenly as the rain turned off and he knows he's imagining it — must be imagining it — but the air feels heavy and his ears pop.

In the awful stillness, he can hear the sound of an approaching freight train.

There are no train tracks for twenty miles in every direction.

The blinding rain slams back into his car, scoots it sideways in the gravel, reducing visibility to zero. He can see nothing out the windshield, has to stop and sit while wind and hail attack. He can hear nothing above the hammering of hail on the roof and hood.

The rain lets off enough that he can see to drive, and Riley continues down the gravel road to the barn. When he finally passes the last of the weeds and bushes, what he sees ahead horrifies him. The roof over the front part of the barn is gone, leaving a gaping hole with dangling, broken boards. Debris is scattered on the ground all around, pieces of roof, tree limbs, chunks of wall ripped off the side of the barn. Jessie's pickup truck, half covered by a gigantic piece of tin — from somewhere — is parked outside the closed door of the barn.

When the other workers left, she left with them! Surely, she left with them.

Leaping out of the car, he runs through the drenching rain, dodging debris, mud and puddles to the barn door, calling her name.

"Jessie! Jessie, are you in there? Jessie!"

Grabbing the bay door on the left, he drags it open enough to enter. It's raining as hard in here as it is outside, cascading down from the gaping hole in the roof above. The interior is in disarray. The table is turned over, chairs scattered, marijuana buds lying in the mud.

"Jessie!" he cries, panic in his voice. "Are you—?"

He hears a sound from the far side of the barn where a metal water trough lies upside down in a pile of hay. As he runs toward it, the edge of the trough lifts up off the ground and a small voice cries, "Riley?"

He lifts up the side of the heavy trough and finds Jessie crouched beneath it.

"Jessie," he breathes.

"I was ... the wind and the rain ... and then I heard a roaring sound and I knew what it was—"

She continues to babble as he takes her hands and pulls her to her feet. "But I didn't know what to do, where I should go, and the building was shaking."

He grabs her and hugs her to his chest and they stand in the drenching rain like that for Riley doesn't know how long, with Jessie clinging to him and babbling out her story and him glorying in the feel of her in his arms and the knowledge that she is all right.

He comes back to himself and looks around for somewhere to get out of the rain. He spots a door that likely leads to a tack room in the back of the barn, where a large part of the roof remains intact. Grabbing her hand, he leads/ drags her toward it, shoves open the door and is rewarded with a room that's only damage is the broken-out window on the far wall, where rain is flying sideways into the interior. Best of all, there's a big pile of horse blankets and he steps to it, takes off the top one and drapes it over Jessie's shoulders.

She is trembling so violently — shock and cold combined — that her teeth are chattering, chopping her words into hiccupping sounds.

"You got to get out of these wet clothes," he says and without ceremony reaches out and starts unbuttoning her blouse.

She clamps her jaw tight to quell the chattering, pushes words out between gritted teeth. "It's okay. I'm fine now. Really. I'm—"

He grabs her by the shoulders and speaks intensely into her face.

"Stop it! You don't have to be tough and strong all the time. You almost got carried away by a tornado. You're entitled to be upset about it."

His words freeze her face as if he'd slapped her. Then her expression ... melts. Her lip begins to tremble, her eyes well with tears and she throws herself into his arms, clutching him tightly, sobbing — long, gulping, wrenching sobs that go on and on.

Rain blows in through the broken window. The hammering wind batters the building and it groans and shifts. The room smells like hay and manure and horses.

Riley eases Jessie down to the floor on her knees beside the pile of horse blankets, manages to peel her arms from around his neck so he can unbutton her blouse. He strips it off, and quickly wraps the horse blanket back around her shoulders. The great heaving sobs have exhausted her and she is slumped forward on her knees, crying, the sound almost childlike.

"So scared," she says, and looks at him, actually makes eye contact for the first time. "I heard the rumble and then I realized … and I didn't know what to do."

He pushes her wet hair back off her forehead. "So'kay now." His voice is gentle, kind. "You're safe, didn't blow away." He takes a breath. "But you really need to get out of the rest of those wet clothes."

"Your clothes are as wet as mine."

Their eyes meet and lock and a thousand words of communication pass between them in a single heartbeat. Riley can't look away. He falls into the beauty of her eyes, becoming aware as if discovering it for the first time, that she has no shirt on under the blanket wrapped around her shoulders.

They remain locked together with fierce gazes tangled up together, braided together into a single cord.

He finds himself brushing his lips tenderly across hers. Then she pulls him toward her, leans into the kiss, hungry for it, and a lightning bolt of pent-up passion strikes them both and they are consumed by it, powerless to resist. But neither of them tries. This is right and good and they both give themselves unreservedly to it, the storm of their desire as powerful as the wind hammering rain against the barn roof.

Chapter Fifteen

"YOU'RE STARING AT ME," Jessie said.

"I always stare at you. When we're in public, I try not to drool at the same time, though."

The rumble of thunder came again, and Jessie cut her eyes anxiously toward the window.

"I need to get home before the storm hits."

He stood, took both her hands in his and held them to his lips.

"That storm's a long way off. Don't go. I want to talk—"

"About what? What is it we haven't already said?"

There was, of course, nothing they hadn't already said. And said. And said again. He'd called to ask how she was doing the day after the storm, of course, said he wanted to see her. But he could hear the constraint in her voice even when she said hello.

"I'm fine, really. You don't need to come—" She'd stopped. "No games. You don't want to see me to make sure I don't have a broken neck we didn't notice yesterday. You want to see me because ... and no."

"No?"

"Lots of nos. No, I'm not sorry about what happened yesterday. No, I don't regret a single second of it. And no … I can't … we're not … it's not going to happen again. Ever."

"Jessie, listen—"

"Final answer. Full stop."

"But Jessie—"

"There are yeses, too. Yes, I do" — she grabbed a breath — "love you." She'd said it yesterday, had confirmed that the link they'd forged was real. The words had sunk deep into him, through him, transformed the very nature of who Riley Hannacker was, and even if she'd denied it now, he couldn't change back. The words had been sweet cream spreading out into black coffee and it couldn't be undone. Her voice broke then and the next words were tear-clotted. "Yes, I do want you. Yes, I wish it could be different. But it is what it is. I am who I am. You are who you are. Not. No."

And she had hung up. He'd called again. And again. He didn't know how many times, desperate to change her mind and sickeningly certain he would not be able to. He'd hoped seeing her in person … She'd finally agreed, but he'd known what she'd say as soon as she saw his face.

She gently pulled her hands out of his.

"Riley, we've already had this conversation."

"I want to have it again."

"It's just beating a dead horse."

"The horse isn't dead. It's on life support."

That made the two of them think of Davie and the banter fell apart.

"I need to go."

"Jessie, don't *do* this."

She caught his eyes with hers and echoed his words. "*You* don't do this."

"I want to marry you, Jessie. We could have a home, a life."

"We both already have homes and lives."

"You can't possibly believe I owe any loyalty to Sherry Lynn. She's slept with half the men in the county and is working her way through the other half. I turn the other way because I genuinely don't care, but she won't fight a divorce, wouldn't dare. It would get ugly."

"Divorce is ugly."

"Says who?"

"Says God."

"No, says Father Donavan." He held up his hand. "I, for one, don't think he speaks for God. This is 1978. People get divorced. It happens all the time. The Hardestys and the Malones and … others, you know there are lots of others. There's a big stink in the beginning, everybody twittering with gossip, and then people find something else to talk about. I don't care what anybody thinks of me, Jessie. I love you and I want you to be my wife."

He paused, then said into the silence between them, his voice defeated.

"It's not about Sherry Lynn, though, is it?" It wasn't a question. "It's about Davie."

"Please, Riley, don't …"

"I understand that you still love him — of course you do. And we'll both take care of him until …"

The *until* was inching closer but he didn't know for sure whether Jessie had accepted the reality of that yet. People in a Permanent Vegetative State didn't have a normal life-span. Jessie had gotten Davie the best of everything to help him — the best medical care, the best equipment to deal with his physical needs, the best therapy. Spared no expense. But you didn't have to be a medical professional to see that Davie Monaghan was slowly slipping away. His heart would give out eventually. Sooner rather than later. The very best Jessie could do for him still left him an emaciated shadow of the man he'd been, who had made no connection to anybody or anything in his environment in the almost a decade since Jackson McClusky fired an RPG into their bunker in Vietnam. Riley hated himself for wishing — often — that Davie had been killed outright by the blast like Andy Taggart had been. Jessie could have mourned his passing ... and moved on.

Thunder rattled the windows, clearly much closer, and Jessie stepped around him to where she had left her purse on the countertop. With her back still to him, she said, "I'm sorry, Riley."

She did turn to him then, her lower lip quivering.

"I do love you, Riley. I really do. I just ... *can't.* I'm sorry." Her eyes glimmered as if she'd repressed so many tears for so long that behind her eyes were pent-up oceans.

Taking big strides out the back door, she let the screen slam shut. He heard her truck engine start and listened to the sound of it dwindle into silence as she drove away.

Only then did he sag into the chair and put his head in his hands. What else could he do to convince her? Better question: did he have the right to keep ripping her heart out by trying?

JESSIE WAS CRYING, not making a sound, just shaking shoulders and tears. She never wore makeup and often thought in the last ten years that it was good thing she didn't because she cried so often it would always be smeared.

Riley had been staring at her. She had caught him doing that a dozen times, and wondered often why the rest of the world couldn't see what was written all over his face. But it was only apparent to her, she supposed.

Davie had never looked at her the way Riley did, with unrequited longing. He didn't have to. They fell in love, got married, had a glorious life together … until.

She didn't often look back on that early time, the beginning, when the permanence hadn't yet sunk in, when grief and despair fought with hope every day for … years.

It was easier when the hope died. There weren't so many tears then.

For a while after that, she'd still had Davie's mother to care for, who'd had a stroke and occupied a "hospital room" in her renovated house next to Davie's. His mother had died in her sleep, peacefully, three years ago. Jessie liked to think that Ruth finally made it to the royal wedding she'd talked about ever since she had her first stroke.

Then, it was just her and Davie. And after a while, she had trouble conjuring up in her mind what the "old Davie" had been like, what his face looked like when he smiled … without drooling. The excitement and passion and intelligence in eyes that were as vacant now as a window on an empty house.

She had loved that Davie, adored that Davie. And when she accepted that he was gone, she found that she loved the Davie in the bed, too. In a different, maternal way.

She had never meant to … with Riley. Except some part of her *did* mean to. She hadn't orchestrated the circumstances that made it possible, but it didn't just *happen*. She let it happen. She welcomed it, and when it did, for a brief bubble in time she felt like spring had come to her soul after a very cold, snowy winter and she merely basked in the warmth. Didn't think about the past or the future, just reveled in the right now of being in Riley's arms and listening to him tell her he loved her, expressing emotions she had felt for years but had kept locked up inside.

Funny thing, she never once felt "guilty" about what the two of them had done. She probably should have, probably should have felt like she had betrayed Davie. But guilt was never part of the equation. The Davie who had been her husband, who'd ridden a magic carpet with her and promised he'd come home from war without a scratch — she'd never have betrayed the promises she made to him. But that Davie had died. And she had made no sacred vows to the Davie in the bed. She cared for him, made sure he wanted for absolutely nothing, got him the best medical attention money could buy. But that was as far as her obligation extended. She didn't owe him the rest of her life. She wasn't responsible for sacrificing herself on the altar of their long-ago love. She had a right to a life. And she knew, was one hundred percent certain, that her loving Davie would want her to be happy.

So why wouldn't she marry Riley?

It made no sense, was totally irrational. His marriage was a joke, a sham, her marriage was dead. The sensible thing to do was to get divorced and marry each other, make a life and a home — and *raise a family*.

But she couldn't. And she understood with profound certainty that she never would. She'd never *divorce* Davie.

Chapter Sixteen

Jackson McClusky's silver limo with the tinted windows drove down between the stately oak trees on either side of the Dawson house property, around the curved driveway to the back of the house, where a black cargo van and a nondescript black sedan car were parked in front of a three-bay garage. He got out, stretched and looked around.

He'd always admired this place — who wouldn't, it was one of the finest homes in the county. Maybe not the most expensive, the flashiest and most opulent, but it had class. Dignity. It was a beautiful woman in a fine formal gown — instead of fishnet hose and a tank top.

After instructing his men to take his things inside, he wandered out to the gazebo, surrounded by azalea bushes in the backyard. Stood looking out over the acreage, inhaling the sweet smell of the fragrant blossoms.

It was good to be home. In truth, it surprised Jackson just how good it felt to be … where he belonged. That was something couldn't nobody take away from you, something you couldn't never lose. You could lose your job, you could lose your wife or your dog or your wallet … or your mind.

But you couldn't never lose where you was from. That was yours, belonged to you no matter where you wandered over the wide world.

He didn't think he'd remain in the Dawson house. For one thing, it would always be that — the Dawson place. And wouldn't matter how much money he put into it or how he fixed it up, wouldn't nobody ever call it the McClusky place. He wanted that. Might be he'd need to build his own place to get it — somewhere hadn't nobody ever lived before. Well, if he did, he wasn't gonna build one of them mansions with fifteen dozen rooms and fountains out front. He'd been in houses like that all over Central and South America — Colombia, Nicaragua, Paraguay, Belize. The drug lords he'd come across, and he figured they was all just about the same, didn't have a whole lot of taste and style.

He heard the rumble of a motorcycle in the driveway and watched the Harley Davidson curl around the house and come to a stop beside the other Harley and the limo in front of the garage. Alejandro lifted his leg over the bike and stepped off, and then spotted Jackson in the gazebo.

"You git'er done?" Jackson asked.

"He turned and went off down some winding road up into the hills, but I found a straight stretch with an embankment on the right side. I roared around him and *nudged* him off down it."

"He dead?"

"Wreck didn't kill him, but he did smash into a tree. He hadn't got the seatbelt off before I got to him." Alejandro held his hands out as if he were holding something, then snapped his right hand out and his left hand back. "No marks. It'll look like he broke his neck in the wreck."

Jackson nodded his approval and the man went into the house with the others. He'd send both the bikers and the limo back to Nashville tonight. He'd enjoyed driving into town in the big silver car with the bike escort. It'd been fun, but his plan required that he remain unseen until he chose to reveal himself — at a time and place of his choosing. He had the element of surprise on his side and he wouldn't give that up because some dumb farmer recognized him. Maybe he didn't, of course. Maybe he was just waving to be friendly. Well, Jackson couldn't take the chance, couldn't mess this up or the prayer he'd prayed as he lay in his own piss in the trunk of a car a month ago would be answered — he'd be dead.

JACKSON IS PRAYING AS FERVENTLY *as he ever prayed. He isn't begging, pleading for his life, though. He is begging God to make it quick. No torture, oh dear God please, no torture. He had heard stories about what El Escorpión — the scorpion — did to people. Cutting them into little pieces, while they were still alive. Toes, fingers, arms, feet, ears, tongue … until they bled to death.*

When Los Asesinos soldiers snatched somebody off the streets, threw them into a car trunk with a black bag over their head and drove out into the countryside, nobody ever saw that person again.

Please, God, no torture. If Jackson had any way to do it, he would slit his wrists, or cut his own throat before they came back to get him out of the dark room where they'd dumped him. But he is lying on a filthy floor with his hands behind his back. Not like before, when they were taped with duct tape and he could peel it off … with his skin … to escape. This time, he is handcuffed.

And the thing is, Jackson has no idea what he's done to earn the displeasure of El Escorpión. He'd been running his own operation, small, not the grand international drug cartel he'd dreamed about five years ago. Still, he makes enough money to live in style in Guatemala. He stays out of the way of the big cartels and they ignore him because he isn't big-time enough to concern them.

And then, two days ago, he went to Colombia on business. He was eating at a sidewalk cafe in a little town outside the city of Bogotá when a car skidded to a stop in the street, three men got out of it, pointing their guns at the crowd. Two of the men ran to his table, yanked him to his feet and dragged him away.

The door on the other side of the room suddenly opens and the lights come on, blinding him. Two men, not the same two who had kidnapped him, but two others, pull him to his feet and haul him out of the room and down the hallway. He has no black bag over his head now and he can see that he's in some kind of prison. They pass many locked cells, where emaciated men with dead eyes stare vacantly at them, and then down another hallway to a door.

Jackson smells his own urine then. He'd wet himself in the trunk of the car. Fear, yes, but they'd kept him for hours and he couldn't hold it. The two men throw the door open and Jackson sees that it's a room that's mostly empty. There is a table, a couple of straight-back chairs, and ... chains. He sees chains attached to the table. Is this where they interrogate people? What does he know that anybody would possibly care about?

They haul him to the chair, drop him down into it, and affix the chains to his wrists, then they leave. He looks around, now seeing details. Brown spots and smears everywhere. Dried blood. He'd thought the table was reddish brown. No, it's a wood table that has been smeared with blood. Lots of blood. He's afraid he's going to be sick, swallows hard, then jumps when the door opens again and a tall, slender man limps into the room. Not El Escorpión himself but one of his lieutenants — a man called Daga — which means dagger. His head is shaved bare, but he has a full beard halfway down his chest and his eyes are small and cruel.

"I have three words to say to you, Mr. McClusky, that I understand mean something to you."

The other two thugs enter behind him. One of them has brass knuckles, not brass-colored, though — brown, the color of dried blood.

Then Daga speaks the words: "Callison County, Kentucky."

His Spanish accent is thick, but the words are clear. Jackson reels. What … how …?

"You know the place, yes?"

"That's my … I grew up there," he stammers.

Where is the man going with this? Nobody in South America knows where Jackson is from, he's never told … No. They couldn't possibly have brought Jackson here because of what he'd done the night he arrived in Bogotá — got roaring drunk and challenged the men in the bar to a shooting contest. He vaguely recalled standing up on a chair and bragging that he could shoot the eye out of a squirrel at a hundred yards, that every furry critter "in Callison County, Kentucky" ran and hid when they seen him coming.

"So you know the people in this place, too, yes?"

"Yeah, it's a small place. Everybody knows everybody."

That seems to confirm something for Daga because he nods.

"So I heard. All of you are … close knit. So you might say to an outsider …" He stops, and adopts a mangled Kentucky accent. "We take care of our own. Outsiders come against one of us, you come against all of us. And won't a one of you live to see another sunrise if you do."

Who is Daga quoting?

"… uh … everybody knows everybody else, but they ain't all friends, if you know what I mean."

"Explain to me what you mean."

"They's big families. And some of 'em is the enemies of others of 'em."

The man says nothing, clearly wanting Jackson to continue.

"Take, for instance, the McCluskys. We been fighting for years, generations, with the Hannackers."

"Hannackers? Nate Hannacker?"

Jackson sucks in a breath. How does Daga know Nate Hannacker?

"You grew up in Callison County … you're in the marijuana

business. You were a part of the organization, yes? Maybe you were even there that day."

"What organization? What day?"

Jackson hadn't seen the blackjack in Daga's hand until he slaps it down on the table with a sound as loud as a gunshot.

"The Cornbread Mafia."

The words are colored with loathing, hang in the air between them while Jackson scrambles to figure out what's going on.

"I heard of the Cornbread Mafia, yeah, sure, but I wasn't never part of it."

"I know all about them," Daga says. Then he begins to tell an amazing story about a drug dealer who had to be Willie Ray Taggart, with that red hair, and freckles — as the front man for the organization that stole their biggest customer. How five men were sent to teach the Cornbread Mafia, who were "just a bunch of dumb hill-billies," a lesson. How the men limped home wounded — all but one. And the one who come home dead — Little Jimmy — had been related to some New York mafia boss.

What he describes is so far above and beyond the Hannackers, Willie Ray and Jessie Monaghan it is laughable. An army of armed men? Sentries and guards … and walkie-talkies.

Then Daga lifts his right foot up onto the chair, pulls his pants leg up and his sock down. His ankle is a mass of scars, not even an ankle, really, just a lump, in the wrong place. No wonder he limps.

"Your Cornbread Mafia did this to me. Today, I will return the favor — to you." He pauses, thinks. "How is it you say … yes, with interest."

Chapter Seventeen

WINONA MCCLUSKY LOOKED across the table at Kentucky State Police Detective Booth Graham and wondered how she had ever allowed herself to get involved with the man. It wasn't just that he was as homely as a mud fence … not that she had a lot going for her in the looks department. He reminded her of Quasimodo, but really he looked more like the gargoyles on the roof of Notre Dame than he did the hunchback lurking inside it.

The cratered pock marks on his skin looked like the surface of the moon. She couldn't imagine being Booth Graham as a teenager — with his face covered in the acne that had produced the lunar landscape.

She almost shuddered.

"Are you sure you can get her to bite?" he asked, and then did just that — took a big bite out of a yeast roll and chewed with his mouth open.

Had she been drunk that first time? No, she couldn't even claim inebriation. She'd been stone cold sober the evening when the two of them were working late on a case — not the one they both cared about, the Hannacker case.

This was the case of two punks who'd stuck a gun in the face of poor Mrs. Carlisle at Carlisle's General Store and made off with a whopping $210 and change. The stupidity of most criminals always astounded Winona. It had when she was defending them and it did even more so when she was prosecuting them. Two kids, who'd been in that store buying Moon Pies and RC Colas just about every day of their lives ... and they think Mrs. Carlisle can't identify them if they wear ski masks. Seriously?

Winona had offered to work late on the case in the privacy of her office, hoping for an opening to ask Booth about the Smith & Wesson .38 snub nose revolver he'd mentioned that afternoon. He'd dropped that little nugget earlier in the sheriff's office — when the sheriff had pointed out with a snarky smile that a .38 revolver was the kind of gun that'd killed Nate Hannacker. Well, duh, Winona knew that. It was the same kind of gun she had, the untraceable gun she thought of as the Hannacker Pistol even after somebody beat her to the punch and killed the man before she had a chance. *Somebody* who had a Smith & Wesson .38 snub nose revolver.

She might even have been talking about the gun, wondering where Booth got it or saying something to that effect when he'd dropped a file on the floor and both of them reached down at the same time to pick it up. Their hands had brushed, they'd both looked into each other's faces, and then she saw it ... she actually watched his eyes travel down her face and her neck and smack down into her cleavage.

And she did have cleavage!

The good Lord had seen fit in his infinite wisdom to deny her all the other components of female beauty. Her hair was somewhere in the transition from blonde back to brown. After years of bleaching it herself she had pretty much fried the hair follicles — or that's what the hair-dresser told her — leaving her with the options of frizzy brown hair or frizzy blonde. She'd picked brown. To match her eyes, that were the color of mud, looking out at the world from the shaded area beneath her protruding brow ridge.

Think Neanderthal.

Her body was nothing to set off fireworks about — bird legs, a too-long neck and no ass whatsoever. But cleav-age. Oh, my yes, Winona McClusky possessed two over-large breasts that required the elastic power of an industrial-strength bra to hold in place.

He'd noticed that.

And she'd … what had she done, exactly? Acquiesced was the most accurate description. He clearly was aroused and wanted her and she hadn't had sex in waaaaay too long to be picky. So they had … mated. Yeah, that was less feral than copulated.

They started meeting regularly after that and she had gradually gone from warm anticipation to something like dread every couple of weeks when the day loomed nearer. They'd agreed to meet in Louisville for dinner tonight and then get a hotel room.

Well, she just had to suck it up, buttercup and soldier through it. She needed Booth Graham. He was her — she didn't like the phrase "partner in crime." Business partner, that was better. It had been like pushing a rope to get him to the same emotional space she occupied. Yeah, yeah, yeah, all that uphold-the-law stuff, she understood. But where had it ever gotten either one of them? Defend, protect and serve was a nice slogan to put on the door of a squad car, but in their own personal game of cops and robbers, the score now stood at robbers everything, cops nothing. But they could change the score by changing the game. Since they couldn't *beat* the Cornbread Mafia, they should *join* them. Oh, not in raising weed. Join them in the enjoyment of the spoils of their enterprise.

Bleed them dry.

Make them pay.

It was time they looked to their own futures, she'd told him — find a way to feather a nest of their own by plucking the Cornbread Mafia chickens.

Winona'd had her own exit strategy figured out long before she mentioned her plan to Booth. She'd informed the county clerk earlier today that she was withdrawing from the Commonwealth's Attorney's race only a few weeks away — citing "health reasons." She was … *sick*, she'd told him. Very sick. Sounded ominous, made it clear it was something serious — and *private* — so it would be rude to ask her about it. He didn't ask.

She'd had her little house on Booker Street on the market, trying to sell it for almost two years because she couldn't stand listening to the little neighborhood kids yelling and squealing all the time, particularly when she wanted to sleep in on Saturday mornings. If it didn't sell before she set the ball rolling … she'd get a real estate agency to rent it out for her. And after a while, when the agency couldn't get in touch with her at the address she'd provide them … well, it would be their problem to decide what to do with the house and the mortgage.

She already had a passport, had been checking out resort areas in Central America where they said you could live like a queen on a few thousand a month. She knew investment bankers, and eventually, she would launder the money so they could invest it for her, and if she planned right, she could live in style for the rest of her life without having to defend or prosecute a drunk driver ever again.

Winona wouldn't be investing the whole million, of

course, just her half. Once they had the money, she'd break it off with Booth, give him his share and be done with him. It was tempting to figure out a way to stiff him so she could keep the whole amount, but if you did a thing like that, you'd spend the rest of your life looking over your shoulder.

"If she gets wise and figures out what we're doing we'll have more than egg on our faces," Booth said … with egg on his face.

Stop it! The way you think about him affects how you feel about him and how you act toward him, and you've come too far to screw the whole thing up now. The man sitting across from her in the fancy Louisville restaurant did *not* have egg on his face. It was something else. Smack in the middle of Booth Graham's chin was a piece of … well, something edible that'd bailed off his fork on the way to his mouth. Little piece of roast beef had made a break for it. She shook her head.

"You brought the recording equipment, right?" she asked, trying to drag her eyes away from the roast beef escapee on his chin. "I want to test it out."

As soon as she'd decided to take what she thought of now as "her cut" from the Cornbread Mafia, she'd known she'd have to have help to pull it off. She wasn't what you'd call handy with any kind of electronic … gadget. How many people could screw up an electric toothbrush, for crying out loud! It had taken her an hour to figure out how to operate the answering machine on her phone and half the time she ended up erasing messages before she had a chance to listen to them.

Booth Graham was not only a master at electronic surveillance, but could lay hands on the exact equipment they needed for the job. Half a million dollars was better than none, and if Winona tried to do the job by herself and botched it, she would end up with a handful of nothing.

"It's in the car. I'll take it to the room tonight and demonstrate how to use it."

He smiled what she was sure was intended to be a flirtatious smile, but the mutinous roast beef totally destroyed the effect. Clearly, Booth Graham was still smitten with their relationship.

BOOTH GRAHAM HUNG what he hoped was a seductive smile on his face, like draping a surgeon's mask between his ears. He was determined to stay the course with Winona McClusky because once he'd gone over to her side, there was no turning back. He was a lawman breaking the law. A police officer risking prison. The juice had to be worth the squeeze.

If shacking up with the ugliest woman he'd ever met was part of that bargain, well he'd signed on for it and it appeared to be moving the ball down the field. Though by now, their mutual … call it what it was, greed … might have been enough to elicit her ongoing interest and determination without resorting to regular sessions of bump and tickle. The affair pre-dated the Cornbread Mafia case, of course, but it still had its roots in the Hannackers, courtesy of the identical pistols he and Winona shared.

The Nate Hannacker murder weapon. She had one and he had one. Now, if two people couldn't bond over a coincidence like that, what could they bond over? She'd acted like she was curious about his weapon though he'd feigned disinterest in hers. They'd sounded like a couple of kids on a playground: I'll show you mine if you'll show me yours. In truth, he was dying to get a look at her pistol, to hold in his hand the gun that had killed Nate Hannacker. Maybe someday she'd tell him the whole story, the part that came after she figured out Nate had killed her father and her brother — the good part. Maybe if he got her drunk … naaaa, Winona McClusky was hard enough to take when she was sober. The thought of her slobbering drunk made his skin crawl. Besides, he didn't expect them to be together for long after the deed was done. She'd be heartbroken when he dumped her, of course, but it was hard to stay sad with half a million dollars in your pocket.

One thing was clear — when the two of them left town, the mystery of who killed Nate Hannacker would never be solved.

Chapter Eighteen

MAMA BERT HUNG up the phone and sat quiet, thinking. Wondering if it'd been the right thing to do, backing down like she done. She hadn't never seen the man she'd been talking to but she knew what he looked like. Well, what he musta looked like. She'd heard his voice over the phone often enough — with his New York I-talian accent — that soon's she seen that Godfather movie, she knew. Big Mike Genovesi looked like Don Corleone. Acted like Don Corleone, too. Oh, he wasn't the boss or nothing like that, but he was one of them high-up lieutenants and she could close her eyes and imagine him kissing the ring of some dude in a three-piece suit, bein' that respectful. Or that scared.

She thought about that scene in *The Godfather* where the movie director wakes up with a horse head in his bed. Half awake, feeling something sticky, reaching over and turning on the light and there the thing is right there in the bed beside him and blood everywhere and he screams and screams.

She had to hand it to Nate Hannacker. What he done

to them Colombians five years ago was dang nigh as good as a horse head in the bed — convincing them fellas he was gonna throw them into a pigpen and let the hogs eat them alive.

Who-eee! *Brilliant.*

He'd bamboozled them South Americans so total they went running back to they boss with they tails 'tween they legs, telling him how the Cornbread Mafia was the meanest dogs in the junkyard. That reputation had kept the lot of them safe long enough to become what they'd pretended to be — a huge organization with enough guns to stage a right sizable war with anybody, if it was to come to that. It never did, of course, 'cause of them pigs.

She shook her head. It was a straight-up shame for a fact that the doin' of it had cost Nate Hannacker his life.

If they just hadn't *killed* that fella. If they'd just sent all five of 'em home with crap in they pants and bullet holes in 'em, the I-talians woulda let it lie. But they kilt the one fella who mattered and they'd had to pay for that. He'd likely looked just like them other South Americans. Anybody'd a'mistook that black hair and them brown eyes as Hispanic. 'Parently Nate and his crew didn't know he wasn't, but they wouldn't have killed him 'less they had to, so it didn't make no never mind whether they knew or not. Wouldn't have changed nothing.

They shot James "Little Jimmy" Defazio and next thing she knows her phone's ringing and it's Big Mike and he is one pissed I-talian. 'Parently this Little Jimmy dude was his nephew, his "baby sister's baby boy." Big Mike's organization bought weed from the Colombians, though what his nephew'd been doing with the squad of goons who come down to Callison County to kick ass and take names was a mystery to her and Big Mike never bothered to explain. His organization was gonna be buying weed from her, too — which was to say from her *and* the Corn-bread Mafia, but that sticky eye-for-an-eye thing just about crapped in everybody's punchbowl.

MAMA BERT AIN'T USTA BEIN talked down to like this and she has to bite her tongue to keep from sayin' something she'll regret. He assumes she knows exactly what he's talking about when in truth she ain't got no idea whatsoever. She'd got wind that something went down at the Hannacker place on Thursday, but hadn't had time to dig out the specifics.

Big Mike blows off steam all over her, disrespecting who she is, but she has to let it go. She may be the biggest frog in this pond but they's ponds waaaay bigger'n this one and them ponds got frogs with teeth.

"I got no interest in starting a war, you know what I'm sayin' to you," he says, then says something in Italian she supposes must be profanity. "This Cornbread Mafia bunch — they got too much fire power and it would get ugly."

Fire power? Nate, Willie Ray, Riley and Jessie Monaghan? Seriously?

When you don't know what to say you's always better off not sayin' nothing at all, so she kept her lip zipped and just listened.

"And what would be the point in that? We kill a bunch of them, they kill a bunch of us — who wins at that game?"

She did venture to point out then that "you'd be cuttin' off your nose to spite your face if you's to take the whole bunch of 'em down. They's the ones gonna be supplying me the weed I promised you."

Getting connected to Big Mike had been grabbing the brass ring for Mama Bert, or so she figured. She'd been buying narcotics on a small scale from various dealers, working her way up the food chain, intent on getting connected to an operation that could supply her hard drugs in volume, which she intended to supply to her dealers all over the state. She'd mentioned she could lay her hands on some weed, if they's to want to purchase any, and the next thing she knows they's on her like white on milk — offering way more than she'd ever intended to charge for all the weed she could supply. So she'd got dollar signs in her eyes and the next thing she knows she's guaranteeing them an amount of product she ain't got. So she'd gone to Nate Hannacker.

"You do business with the Cornbread Mafia?"

"Uh huh."

"So you know this … Nate Hannacker, yes?"

"I do."

Then he goes off in I-talian again for awhile 'fore he settles down and repeats the description of Nate that'd been told to him. Only the man he's describing ain't Nate Hannacker! Not even close. Couldn't be any other human being on planet Earth but Big-un McClusky. Why does this fella think Big-un is Nate … or that Nate is Big-un?

"And this Nate Hannacker — he's in charge, yes?"

She chooses her words carefully. "Far's I know, Nate's runnin' the show."

"Alright then. I will eliminate this Hannacker man. Not a full-scale war, just one man — vendetta." She looks that word up later and finds out it means vengeance. "Vendetta to even the score. You know where my man can find him, yes?"

Who? Nate or Big-un?

Mama Bert's thoughts are spinning around in her head so fast they might catch her hair on fire. Must be that Nate and his bunch used some kind of smoke and mirrors to convince a bunch of Colombian henchmen that the Cornbread Mafia was Sherman marching on Atlanta, something that involved Big-un McClusky. How'd they pull that off? If she outs them, tells Big Mike the Cornbread Mafia ain't but four farmers, one of 'em a girl, he's likely to decide to take them all out — come in here blasting away. Mama Bert needs the Cornbread Mafia alive and well to grow the weed that's gonna make her a fortune.

But if he's gonna send a lone hitman, who is she going to finger

as the guy's target — Big-un or Nate? Either way, soon's the dude
starts sniffing around he's gonna find the load of crap they dumped.

"You ain't got to send nobody," she hears herself say. "I'll handle
it myself — I'll send you the obituary out of the newspaper when
I'm done."

"A bullet in his forehead, yes?"

"I'll slice and dice him any way you want."

He grunts his approval. She can tell he's impressed with the offer,
that her stock in the company just went up. Soon's she hangs up she
decides she'd do just what she'd said she would. She'd handle it
personally. *She figures she owes Nate that much.*

MAMA BERT DRUMMED her fingers on the table as she
thought. Big Mike was almost as mad today as he'd been
five years ago about his dead nephew, made it clear he
was *not* going to pay a whopping thirty percent more for
this year's marijuana than he'd paid last year. Trouble
was, last year had been the final year in her five-year deal
with Riley to purchase weed at two-thirds the market
value. This year's crop would cost Mama Bert thirty
percent more than last year's. But when she'd tried to pass
that price increase on to her customers, Big Mike had
thrown a world-class conniption fit. So she'd backed off
the price increase, would have to eat the loss herself —
and Mama Bert didn't *never* lose money on a business
deal.

Unless … What if she could figure out some way to get
Riley to cut *his* price? He'd told her five years ago that she
didn't have no leverage 'cause she didn't have nothing to
hold over his head. Looked like now she was gonna have to
find something, and she had an idea. Might be she knew
something Riley Hannacker wouldn't want the whole
county to know about — just a guess, little things Mama

Bert'd observed. She wasn't usually wrong about such things.

There was a knock at her door and her man Floyd, one of the bouncers, stuck his head in and announced, "They's a man here says his buddy wants to talk to you, but wants to come in the back way, not through the bar."

"And who might this fella be?"

"Says his name's Jackson McClusky."

Chapter Nineteen

As MAMA BERT sat in her office in the back room of the tavern, waiting for Floyd to escort Jackson McClusky into her office, she scratched around in her mind for everything she knew about the man. What she knew and what she'd heard.

He'd been in that massacred National Guard unit, come home wounded, burned, she thought, instead of shot. She'd seen him on the street in Brewster one time and he'd looked like a little sample size of Big-un — dirty, bearded, bedraggled. And he'd had a wild, crazy look in this eyes that was about way more than whatever pharmaceutical product he might have been taking. Then he'd got arrested in Louisville and gone off to prison. He'd got out five or six years ago and was growing weed on the back of his daddy's farm. Then he'd just vanished.

She made a *humph* sound in her throat. There'd been a lot of that going around among the McCluskys at the time so maybe it was hereditary. Or something in the water.

Jackson had been living with Big-un out on his farm, was laying low, keeping his nose clean, and then he went missing. Nobody knew where he went. The hands that'd been helping him with the crop took it upon themselves to harvest the crop and divvy up the proceeds. She'd bought some of it off'a them, that's how she knew. And then nobody heard from Jackson McClusky again.

Now, he was coming in through the back entrance of the tavern to have a sit-down with her. Maybe he was coming back here, go back to raising weed. But October was a peculiar time to show up if you's plannin' on raisin' a crop! If he was planning on growing pot next season, might be he had some kind of business arrangement he wanted to propose to her. Well, she didn't do business with nobody but the big dogs, the ones that could provide her weed by the ton to ship off to her customers. She didn't have time to fool with some guy just starting out.

There was a perfunctory knock on the door before Floyd opened it and ushered a man into her office. He did take after his daddy, she thought, though Big-un McClusky had so much hair on his face it was hard to see his features. She knew him from way back and this boy favored him some. Smaller, of course, *waaaay* smaller. But he had a presence. Didn't exactly swagger into the room, but he wasn't intimidated, neither, wasn't the skinny runt she'd been expecting.

The man standing before her had spent a considerable amount of time working out, and he had the sculpted body to prove it. His shoulders were so broad and thick that his shirt didn't even fit over the bulk right. His arms bulged in his shirt sleeves. He had his father's blocky face and a shock of black hair, couldn't tell his eye color in this faint light but if she was to guess she'd have said something light — blue or gray. He had a mustache, neatly trimmed, and an equally neat beard.

Then she noticed the black ... *something* on his left arm.

It was some kind of leather contraption that extended from just below his elbow to the top of his hand. A brace or cast or something like that.

"I don't believe we've ever met, officially," he said. "I'm Jackson McClusky, Big-un's oldest."

"I know who you are, same's you know who I am. I'm a busy woman — cut to the chase. What is it you want?"

She'd packed as much wallop as she could into the words but it didn't appear to bother him. He didn't drop a beat.

"I ain't been back long, come in Monday evening, brought my bikes."

Was *this* who'd rolled down Main Street in a silver limousine trailing two Harley Davidsons? The whole town'd been talking about it.

"I just bought the Dawson place. I come home to put the Cornbread Mafia out of business and take over. I was wondering if you'd like a piece of that."

There hadn't been a whole lot of times in Mama Bert's life that she'd been totally surprised, what they called speechless surprised. This here was one of them. Oh, didn't cost much to rent a limo ... the bikes would be harder, though. And if he really had bought the Dawson place, he hadn't used Monopoly money for that. He'd made hisself a fortune doin' *something*, wasn't no big-shot wannabe just blowing smoke.

She acted like what he'd said didn't make no impression on her. She had learned long ago by bitter experience that if you let folks know what you's thinking — friends and enemies alike — you was setting yourself up for a world of hurt down the road. If you wasn't able to hold onto your own emotional responses, they was two things you had better avoid — playing poker and being in charge.

You run something, didn't matter what it was, you'd best play every interaction close to the vest.

"And what makes you think I'd be interested in that kind of proposition?"

"'Cause you been buying weed from the Cornbread Mafia for a right smart while at a reduced rate and that rate done run out. You're gonna have to pay full price now and I know for a fact your customers ain't happy with the price hike. I can offer you the same amount of weed you was getting from Riley and his bunch. I'll charge you the same price you paid them last year — but without no expiration date on the deal."

How could Jackson McClusky have found out about her arrangement with the Cornbread Mafia?

"You in the weed bidness, are you?"

"Yes, ma'am."

"Where you grow it?"

"Central and South America mostly — Nicaragua, Guatemala, Colombia, some in Brazil. But I'm looking to branch out and get into *domestic* production. Smuggling large amounts of drugs across the border can be … problematic."

"Your weed ain't good as theirs."

That'd be the rub. She'd been providing her customers the best. Well, almost the best — she'd cut it with some B-grade to make it go further, but they couldn't tell. They wouldn't likely be happy with anything less.

"No, it ain't. My weed's better'n most, but ain't nobody's weed good as theirs." He paused. "But what I plant next spring will be."

She sat back. "You're right sure of yourself, ain't you, son."

"I am."

"Uh huh." She didn't say nothing else, just studied

him. Let the silence get uncomfortable. He didn't fidget, just sat still, looking at her until she finally spoke.

"I wanna make sure we both singing from the same sheet of music. You offering to sell me good weed at a better price than Riley's charging me now — right? And in exchange for this low-priced weed you want … what? What is it *I* got that you want?"

"Information."

That right there almost toppled Mama Bert. The deja vu of it. Five years ago, Riley Hannacker had stood right in the same spot this fella was standing now and said the same thing. He'd give her a special price for weed in exchange for information. He'd wanted to know what it was she'd known about Nate Hannacker that'd give her an opportunity to blackmail him.

"What information might that be?"

"Ain't nobody but the Cornbread Mafia grows Right-eous Weed."

"Baby Bear's bed," Mama Bert said, and he nodded.

She wasn't no expert, but she made it her business to know about the products she bought and sold. If there'd been some kinda chart — like a bestseller list or the top ten songs list — for marijuana, Righteous Weed'd be at the top, the undisputed gold standard for domestic marijuana. Smoked smooth, with a real intense, long-lasting high that didn't have no side effects whatsoever.

True, there was international brands as good — some folks'd say a whole lot better — than Righteous Weed. The Brazilian weed called La Linda, which was Portuguese for "beautiful," Marah from the Middle East — which she understood meant joy in Arabic — Happy Smoke from the Bahamas and Golden Journey from Thailand. Those were exotic, provided a whole different experience, one that was more attuned to foreign tastes than to the sensibilities of

American buyers. Golden Journey was mildly hallucino-
genic, sometimes more than mildly, though the trips was
mostly pleasant ones and wasn't the kind of flashback reactions that hard drugs like acid produced. La Linda was so
relaxing it was almost impossible to smoke a joint without
taking a nap afterward. Happy Smoke was supposedly an
aphrodisiac, at least it had that effect on some people.
Marah produced a super-alert high that lead to long,
meandering philosophical conversations that started
nowhere, ended nowhere and went nowhere in between.

But Righteous Weed was Baby Bear's bed.

"I ain't gonna grow no knock-off. To grow the real
thing, I gotta get my hands on their *seed*. I figure you might
know where they store it, and if you don't know, I 'spect
you can find out."

"Riley and them others don't grow much local no
more, took they operation out of state."

"Yeah, but Callison County's where they come up with
Righteous Weed. I don't know nothing about hybrids and
the like, but 'parently they do and I'm bettin' they ain't
stopped tinkering around with it. And they'd do that here,
at home. Commercial sinsemilla ain't got no seeds in it, but a
pound of *fertilized* weed's got enough seeds to grow an acre.
Tell me where I can lay hands on a jar of seed … find me
a field with fertilized weed … or a barn where they got it
drying."

He showed his own cards then, made her glad she
hadn't shown hers. He let his guard down and she got just
a glimpse, but that was enough. She saw that there was
more emotion wrapped up in his offer than he was
letting on.

"They got what I want and I mean to take it. And take
them *out.* It's a two-fer."

It was clear as the nose on her face that planting them

three people in the ground was way more important to Jackson McClusky than planting the seed he was plannin' on taking from 'em.

So what was it Jackson McClusky had against Riley Hannacker, Willie Ray Taggart and Jessica Monaghan? Sure, there was the whole Hannacker/McClusky thing going on but this was way bigger than that. The little glimpse she got of what was behind the curtain of Jackson McClusky's soul — it was *hate*, as violent and fiery a hatred as she'd ever seen. Hate and something else, too. Might be it was fear.

He hated them, but he was afraid of them, too.

Now why was that?

Chapter Twenty

JACKSON LEFT the tavern the way he'd come in, the back door in the dark of the back parking lot. It hadn't been a dark parking lot until José had shot out the bulb in the big lamp on the tall pole. Maybe he should have mentioned that to Mama Bert, told her she had a light out that she might ought to get fixed.

His smile broadened. The meeting had gone well, better than he'd expected, in fact. She'd bought what he was selling. His bluff had panned out. He'd known that first night — when Daga's men had dragged him back to the room with the roaches and he'd spent the night coming up with a scheme — that he had to have help. He'd need somebody local on his side. Not none of the McCluskys, they didn't know nothing. There was only one "local" with what he needed — power, influence, connections, a network of spies … and a heart as black as a lump of coal. The trick would be coming up with the right bait for that hook.

He'd spent a considerable amount of his preparation time in the past few weeks nosing around, finding out who was selling what, who was buyin' it and what they was paying for it. That's how he'd found out Mama Bert had suddenly raised her prices. The rest … that'd just been an educated guess. And he'd scored. Twice. Once with Mama Bert and once with El Escorpión.

DAGA LOOKS *at the biggest of the two henchmen and tells him to unlock Jackson's handcuffs.*

"Take him to la sala fiesta," he says. "That's the 'party room.' A special place with thick walls."

Jackson is desperate.

"You kill me, you're doing the Cornbread Mafia a favor. They been trying to kill me for five years."

"And why is that?"

"Because I" — *Jackson scrambles, spits out the first thing that comes to mind* — *"killed their leader, Nate Hannacker, the big man in charge. I put a bullet in the middle of his forehead."*

Jackson had heard what'd happened to Nate the same night Riley, Jessie and Willie Ray had tried to kill Jackson.

"Why should I believe you?"

"It ain't hard to find out. Call and ask."

"Call who?"

"Call … the newspaper and ask if they run an obituary for Nate Hannacker. It's been five years but they'll remember. They'll tell you I ain't lying."

"So he's dead. Why should I believe you killed him? And why should I care?"

"Ask them who done it. They'll tell you the crime ain't never been solved, 'cause I got away with it. Law don't know it was me, but the rest of the Cornbread Mafia knew and they come after me."

He lifts up his left arm as high as the chains will allow, nods at the black brace. "Broke my arm getting away, hid in a cattle car to get out of the county … but I swore I'd be back someday to even the score."

The man not wearing brass knuckles steps forward with a key and unlocks the cuffs holding Jackson's hands to the table.

"I wanna make 'em pay what they done to me," Jackson says as the man starts pulling him to his feet. He nods toward Daga's ankle. "You just gonna let it slide what they done to you?"

Daga pauses, holds up his hand and the man lets go of Jackson and he sinks back into the chair.

"El Escorpión does not have the men to waste fighting their army, and to what end? Some of them die, some of us die, and what do I have to show for it?"

The man takes hold of Jackson's arm again, pulls him out of the chair and starts to drag him toward the door.

"What if he didn't have to send an army? I could do the job myself. I could kill all the leaders of the Cornbread Mafia."

"How could you do this thing?"

Jackson has one shot and he'd better be convincing.

"I grew up in Callison County. I know every holler, creek, back road, abandoned barn and unlocked building between Taylor and Nelson Counties. What's left of the Cornbread Mafia after I planted Nate Hannacker is his grandson Riley Hannacker, Willie Ray Taggart and Jessie Monaghan. I know where to find them all."

Daga nods and the man releases his hold on Jackson's arm.

"This Riley, he has blond hair and Willie Ray — red hair and freckles?"

"And a big ole scar on the side of his face. I was the one done that to him."

"And Jesse is a black man."

Black? Wasn't none of the Cornbread Mafia black, but Jackson wasn't about to argue with Daga. Two out of three would get it so he nodded.

"Jesse, the black man who shot me and two of my compadres, sliced open another's face, he has an artificial leg." Ace! The guy was *talking about Ace, had to be. How did Ace get involved in all this? "I would very much like to see this Jesse dead."*

Daga was wavering, Jackson saw a chance, but he still needed something, one final something to push him over the edge.

"I could do more than just kill the leaders."

"What more?"

"I could lay my hands on what every grower in the country'd like to have."

"And that is?"

"Seed. What if I could get you seed so you could grow the Righteous Weed they sell? Wouldn't El Escorpión like to get more money — ten, twenty percent more per pound than he's getting now?"

Daga snaps his fingers and says to the man with brass knuckles, "Go. Make some calls. Find out if he's lying."

The man leaves the room and Daga turns his back on Jackson and walks — limps — to the lone barred window and stares out. Jackson grabs hold of himself tight. Either Daga fell for his rap or he didn't. Jackson'd said his piece and jabbering now would look weak. He holds his tongue and waits.

After a few minutes, the man Daga had sent out of the room returns.

"I called the office of the Callison County Tribune *and talked to the receptionist. She said Nate Hannacker got shot five years ago, murder. I asked who did it and she said they never caught the murderer."*

Daga nods. "Take him back to the holding cell."

THE NEXT MORNING when they came for him, they took him to El Escorpión himself. Jackson had never seen him up close. Though his hair was black and his skin dark, his eyes were blue — the lifeless blue eyes of a shark cruising a polar ocean.

Jackson laid out his plan, how he would arrive in style

to show the Cornbread Mafia that his organization was as big and bad and mean as theirs. He would get Riley, Willie Ray and "Jesse" to come to a meeting — without their bodyguards — a summit, to present them a business proposition to expand into the international market, grow and sell Righteous Weed all over the world.

"And they would believe such a ridiculous story?" Daga had asked. Jackson had *not* said what he was thinking — Why not? You believed their ridiculous story. Instead, he said the three would be lured by greed, would be willing to set aside old animosities if the price was right, and once he got them all together, unguarded, he would kill them.

"And how will you get their seed?" El Escorpión had asked. It was clear *that's* what interested El Escorpión. Daga'd wanted revenge, but the boss man wanted seed.

Jackson had said that part would be easy — he'd steal it. He knew where they stored it — after all, he grew up in Callison County.

El Escorpión cut Jackson a sweet deal — land to grow weed, seed to grow, a place high up in the *Los Asesinos* organization. That was if he succeeded. If he failed, they'd kill him — slowly.

Gratefully, the South Americans didn't know that if Riley, Willie Ray and Jessie really were in the same room with him, they would kill Jackson and not the other way around. His grand entrance would be for Mama Bert's benefit — to convince her to help him find the seed. Once he had the seed, he'd take out Riley, Willie Ray and Jessie one at a time, before they ever even knew he'd come home. The element of surprise.

Chapter Twenty-One

WILLIE RAY and the other two dozen workers had the heat in the little house on the Larsson farm outside Martinsburg in northern Minnesota cranked as high as it would go. He was still cold, though. Oh, he'd brought a *jacket* with him from Kentucky, in case it got cool at night. But not a parka. He didn't *own* a parka.

"They got lots of names for 'em," said Beetle Perkins when he joined Willie Ray at the window, looking out as the trees danced and swayed in the wind.

"I could come up with a few colorful ones myself," Willie Ray said and stuck his cold fingers into his jacket pockets. Gloves. They did have work gloves in the barn, had to wear them when you was trimming buds to keep the sticky off your hands. He'd ought to go out to the barn and get some gloves. Naaaa. By the time he got back to the house with them, he'd be about froze solid.

"They mostly call 'em Clippers, for short — like a clipper ship 'cause they swoop down outta Canada without no warning."

The weather'd been fine when Willie Ray flew in, cooler than he liked, but anything less than about eighty degrees was too cool for Willie Ray. Then they'd awakened two days ago and it was freezing outside, wind blowing a gale. "Mostly they're Alberta Clippers. But the fella I talked to said they was sometimes called Manitoba Maulers, Ontario Scary-os, or Saskatchewan Screamers."

Willie Ray favored some kind of combination — Scary-o Screamers.

"He said middle of October was real early for one. I didn't mention that I bet my boys'd be swimming in the river back home today."

That was one reason Beetle was one of the guys designated to shop for supplies in the little towns around the farm — 'cause he wasn't real chatty, didn't have much to say. The less the locals knew about what was going on at the Larsson farm, the better. Planting and tending the marijuana crop only needed a handful of men. But harvest was another thing altogether. That was *labor intensive* — cutting it and hanging it in the barns to dry, then trimming the buds one at a time, by hand. An ordinary farm operation wouldn't require more than two dozen workers to bring in the corn crop. And that's what appeared to be growing on the farm. They'd planted six rows of corn around the outside edges of all three of the fields to hide the weed from view — three football field-sized plots laid out end to end. From the air, Willie Ray could tell the difference in the green color, but his was a practiced eye. Most folks wouldn't notice, and it wasn't like the farm was on the glide path of a major airport. Willie Ray'd had to fly into Amhurst, a bigger town twenty miles south that had a small landing strip and one hangar.

The work crew never went anywhere as a group, so the

locals didn't have no idea how many men they was; just one did the shopping in each of several little towns around and didn't buy food like he was feeding an army. The men was from small towns in Kentucky and knew something as odd as a farmer comin' in every week and buying ten times as much food as he could eat would get round.

Willie Ray could feel the cold through the window panes and shivered.

"That fella say how long these clipper things last?"

"Couple of days ... sometimes as long as a week."

"A week!" Willie Ray swallowed the rest of what he was going to say. The other guys knew well as he did that they needed to be out there in the fields *right now*. Jammed together into this little three-bedroom house with nothing to do but smoke cigarettes, watch television and play cards was already beginning to wear on everybody's nerves.

If there was one thing Willie Ray Taggart was not good at was doin' nothing. He was impatient by nature, always had been, never wanted to have to wait. As a kid, he'd had every present under the tree unwrapped, inspected and re-wrapped long before Christmas morning. And since he got back from 'Nam, waiting left his mind too unoccupied to keep memories from creeping in. Visitations increased when he had nothing to do.

He often wondered if he would still see the vision of his dead brother now, if they'd been able to kill Jackson McClusky five years ago. At the time, some part of him was convinced that killing the man who had murdered Andy would somehow free his spirit. Or free Willie Ray from his spirit. But Jackson had got away, and after all this time Willie Ray was beginning to wonder if they'd ever get a shot at him again. Visitations were no longer frequent. Andy would suddenly appear ... just appear ... on Willie

Ray anytime, anywhere in those first few years. But after Jackson got away, it didn't happen as often.

Still …

Almost all the men had families, but weren't allowed to contact them. That was the agreement they'd made when they signed on to harvest a weed crop out of state — no phone calls, letters, visits. Complete radio silence. That was hard on the men, and every day they were stuck in the farm house was a day longer they'd be away from home. Willie Ray was glad he didn't have a wife and kids on account of that, knew he'd always be one who didn't have nobody to go rushing back home to. He was certain he would never marry — though he had lotsa girlfriends. He was fun to be around, showed his dates a good time. Most folks knowing he was a millionaire many times over attracted a lot of the wrong kinda girls, though. Riley was all the time saying "never say never," told Willie Ray that one of these days a special girl was gonna come along … But Willie Ray knew things, just knew them, in a way Riley never had. He knew he would never get married. And he knew he would die young. He was okay with both those things, intended to jam as much living into his days as he could because he understood they were numbered.

The next morning, Willie Ray awakened about dawn to silence. It was quiet, still. The raging wind that had whistled in the eaves, battered at the shutters and made the old house creak and groan was gone. The Clipper had sailed on.

He dressed and went quietly into the kitchen where he found Beetle, nursing a cup of coffee, his face downcast.

"You look like your wife left you and your dog died," Willie Ray said. "Ain't you looked outside? The storm's gone."

"Yeah, but it left this behind."

Beetle gestured to a marijuana bud lying on the table in a puddle of water.

"It's mostly melted off now. Go on out and see the rest of 'em. The whole crop is coated in ice. Every man Jack of them plants is froze to death."

Chapter Twenty-Two

ELI BRADIGAN LIKED the little town of Bardstown, Kentucky. It reminded him a little bit of his hometown, Sellersburg, about fifteen miles up Interstate 65 from Louisville, but it was older, more quaint, and had that indefinable quality known as Southern charm going for it. He hadn't stopped to see My Old Kentucky Home, had passed it on his way to Callison County for his first drive-around. He'd driven slowly up and down the winding roads in Callison County, thinking, marveling at how beautiful it was, with a whole crayon box full of bright autumn colors splashed on the hillsides, and fields lush and green with crops ripe for harvest. It had become clear quick why marijuana was so hard to locate here. No limit to what you could hide back up in those hollows.

The first Virgin Mary statue enshrined in half a bathtub had struck him as odd. Then he saw another, and another. There were dozens, maybe hundreds of them scattered in yards all over the rural part of the county. Agent Peterson told him later they were called "Bathtub Marys."

The place was seriously Catholic, as was neighboring Nelson County, where he'd set up a small office on a side street called Mulberry Alley a couple blocks from the center of town. There were many "alleys" in Bardstown, Gooseberry and Raspberry, too. They were renting space for "a law office," which it technically was. You certainly didn't want to advertise that the FBI had moved into town, but folks would figure it out pretty quick when they started asking questions.

He'd rented a couple of rooms for himself and agents Thomas, Peterson, Lincoln, Zucarelli and Beddingfield in one of the big old houses that lined the major streets leading to the town square, where he could literally walk to work. He was doing that for the first time today, the sidewalks empty on Stephen Foster Boulevard so early on an October morning, the dew still glistening on the thick grass in the yards he passed. Most of the handful of people he met smiled and nodded. A couple didn't smile, were clearly wondering why a black man was walking down the sidewalk in *their* neighborhood — even if he was presentable in a suit and tie. He could tell by the tightening of the lips, and the stiffened posture when he'd offended some white person's delicate sensibilities by daring to breathe air in their world. His good looks served him well on such occasions, but he doubted those people would have been welcoming even if he had been Sidney Poitier.

The lady who owned the house where he rented rooms had said there was a coffeeshop named Cupa Java right off the court square and he planned to stop by for coffee before he went into the office. He'd burned the night oil there last night, going over papers — copies of land transfers, Property Valuation office records on the houses on certain farms. One in particular caught his eye — the house belonging to Riley and Sherry Lynn Hannacker's tax value on the roll was a hundred thousand dollars. Clearly Hannacker had some kind of deal going with the PVA's office because Eli had driven past the home and it was an overdone mansion/castle that'd been built by somebody with a flair for tacky. It was garish and overdone, and ridiculously opulent, all the way down to the concrete lions that sat on either side of the grilled archway and wrought iron gate that defended the driveway. He noted surveillance cameras mounted in each lion's right eye.

Eli could see the courthouse ahead in the center of a traffic circle. Then he stopped cold. Set inside the circle were two granite monuments. One was white, larger than the other. Crossing the street, he stood in front of the monuments. The white one listed the names of local soldiers killed in Vietnam. It was a big list for such a small town. The smaller pink monument beside it had a bronze plaque that read: "In Memoriam, Dedicated to these men who gave their lives in Vietnam in 1969 for the preservation of freedom." Below those words was a list of names.

Andrew Taggart

Ben Higgs

Kenny Taylor

Ronnie Benson

Jude Boone

Caleb McAllister

Randy Nickel

"Erected on 30 May, 1970 by fellow members of Charlie Company of the 151st Infantry Battalion, Kentucky National Guard."

An old black man ambled past, leaning heavily on a cane. Eli asked, "Excuse me, I'm not from around here. This monument—"

"That's them that was killed in the massacre."

"Massacre?"

"Don't know if the military calls it that, but that's what it was. National Guard unit was headquartered here and got called up, went to Vietnam and wasn't there six months before them seven got killed on one night, one battle, some place called Fire Base Eagle's Nest."

"And they were all from Bardstown."

"The headquarters of the guard unit was in Nelson County, but the boys in it come from all the counties around. Ever one of them seven was from Callison County. A whole bunch more got wounded real bad but survived."

The old man ambled away but Eli stood where he was in front of the monument.

Eli's files on the Cornbread Mafia members noted that some of them had served in the military, nothing more specific than that. Andrew Taggart. Related to Willie Ray Taggart, maybe? Had they been in that battle, watched their buddies dying all around them?

Something subtle shifted in Eli. The connection was automatic. He'd been to 'Nam, 1960 to 1962, just an eighteen-year-old kid. He never let himself think about it. Had never talked about it, hadn't even told Juliette what happened to him there.

When he stepped into his office half an hour later, he intended to dig into the military records of Taggart, Hannacker and Monaghan first thing. But Agent Peterson waggled a sheaf of papers in front of him, grinning his gums dry.

"Good news or bad news first," Pete said.

"Bad."

"Wouldn't give us a court order for the pay phones."

It'd been a shot in the dark anyway.

Eli had petitioned the U.S. District Court in Louisville for permission to install wire taps on the home phones of Riley Hannacker, Willie Ray Taggart and Jessica

Monaghan. Since those petitions were still pending, he'd set his sights on three public pay phones in locations near the homes of the Cornbread Mafia members. He'd found criminals often used pay phones for "work conversations" rather than their own land lines. The 1967 Supreme Court ruling in Katz v. the United States had overturned the more law-enforcement friendly Olmstead ruling so he was required to get a court order to tap the pay phones.

"And the good news?"

"We got all the others! Taggart's, Monaghan's and Hannacker's." Eli smiled broadly. Now they were getting somewhere.

"You won't see me jumping up in the air and clicking my heels together. I tried that once when Juliette and I were on vacation." He didn't say why he had wanted to click his heels together. *That* was none of Pete's business. "And I ruptured my Achilles tendon. I actually heard the thing snap."

"Ouch." Pete cringed in empathy.

They'd packed all the techie equipment to Bardstown. Now came the task of setting it all up, hooking in the proper lines, making sure the recording equipment functioned properly — none of which was Eli's strong suit. But Agent Tony Zucarelli was something of a techno whiz kid — though his size and build would have cast him in the role of a professional football lineman. Jed Lincoln looked the geek part — small frame and rimless glasses, had a law degree from Yale, but had worked his way through school as a plumber. Agent Beddingfield was quiet and soft-spoken — with a mind like a steel trap. When he did say something, everyone listened. Bill Thomas had told Eli that Peterson was the most versatile of the group. His boy-next-door face got witnesses to trust him and perps to underestimate him. He had a degree is criminal psychology, was a sharp-shooter in the military and was fluent in Spanish, French, German and Russian.

Wire taps were a lot like panning for gold. Every now and then you actually found a gold nugget. But the other ninety percent of the time, you listened to giggling teenage girls talking to their boyfriends, women gossiping — occasionally something mildly titillating like men lying about where they were when they couldn't make it home for dinner.

Eli left the others to get the bugs out of the equipment, while he paid a visit to the National Guard armory, wanted to find out more about the Callison County boys' short-lived tour of duty in Vietnam.

Chapter Twenty-Three

WILLIE RAY STOOD with the rest of the crew, watching the sun slowly melt the ice off the field of marijuana.

"It's all dead," Beetle moaned.

"Naw, it ain't," Willie Ray said stubbornly.

"You think these plants gonna live through this?"

"I do."

"I know you bred weed to grow in places that wasn't hot, not like that South American weed. But ain't no plant gonna survive being froze like a fly in a ice cube."

"They ain't dead. Not all of 'em. I 'spect some of them are, but the rest is gonna do just fine." Willie Ray's face brightened. "In fact, I bet this here's gonna be the best crop we ever raised."

"How you figger that?" Beetle asked.

Willie Ray didn't give the kinda explanation he coulda given. He'd studied cannabis down to the molecular level, understood how the plant reacted to stress.

"We top the plants so they'll grow out big and fat instead of tall. What happens to the colas after we cut off the top of the plants?"

"They get bigger."

"Bigger than they ever woulda got if we'd left them be."

"'Cause the whole plant gets more sunshine."

"Uh huh. But that ain't the only reason. Cuttin' off the top shocks the plant, and it responds by producing even better seed in them colas, with even higher levels of THC."

The other men looked at him like he'd just grown a third eye.

A worker Willie Ray knew only as "Pepper" tapped him on the shoulder. "Uh … Willie Ray. You need to come see this."

Pepper led Willie Ray toward the edge of the field facing the road, as Willie Ray continued his reassuring monologue that the weed would, indeed, survive, that the crop wasn't lost.

"Even if it is dead, which it ain't, but even if it is, we can harvest it right now—"

"I 'spect we'd better get after it, then, start cuttin' it fast as we can."

"But it *ain't* dead!"

Pepper pointed toward the road. "Maybe the weed ain't, but the corn is."

Willie Ray looked toward the road where a concealing wall of corn had been planted to hide the weed crop. The curtain of corn still stood, but it wasn't green anymore. The freeze had killed the plants and drained all their color, leaving brittle stalks to form a pale yellow-white wall that wasn't hidin' nothin'.

He'd planted the corn late, so its twelve-week lifespan would serve as cover until the weed had been harvested. Though he'd bred the pot to thrive in lower temperatures, he'd just planted plain old corn to fence it in. Now that corn was dead as a post. And any fool driving down the road could see the marijuana still standing tall and green behind it.

"Let's get cuttin'!" Willie Ray said, and they did, chopping the plants down with long-bladed corn knives and hauling them into the barn to wet-trim them. The crew worked around the clock, fearful every time a vehicle drove down the road. It wasn't likely these Minnesotans had ever seen any marijuana on the hoof, but they didn't have to know what it was to figure out that something out of the ordinary was going on. And sooner or later …

He grabbed a few minutes later that day and called Jessie, told her what was going on.

"WHERE'D the call come in from?" Eli asked. Agent Bradigan had come back from the National Guard armory to find the office buzzing. A call had come in through the tap on the phone line of Jessica Monaghan while they were still setting up their equipment. They scrambled to connect everything quickly, but only got bits and pieces. And the call had been a gold nugget.

Agent Zucarelli shook his head.

"We never got a bead on an exact location, just area code 218."

"Where's that?"

"Minnesota."

"*Minnesota?*"

"From south of Duluth all the way to Canada."

"I'm betting it was Willie Ray Taggart," said Bill Thomas. "Heavy Kentucky accent."

"So what is Willie Ray Taggart doing in Minnesota?"

"Apparently, he's … growing weed," Zucarelli said.

Eli struggled to get his head around that. There'd been fewer and fewer marijuana busts, fewer and fewer sightings in Callison County in the past couple of years — though the supply of Righteous Weed dealers were selling hadn't decreased. Instead, it had steadily *in*creased. The Cornbread Mafia was growing it somewhere, and Eli assumed they'd branched out into neighboring counties in Kentucky. But Minnesota?

"Play the tape again," Eli said. "And fill in any gaps you can."

The tape was garbled, words missing and bad reception, but the agents who'd been working on the equipment when the call came in had heard a couple of things through the wire tap that the equipment hadn't been able to record.

"... *IT WAS A SCARY-O SCREAMER* ..." said the male voice Thomas thought was Willie Ray Taggart's.

"Stop the tape," Eli said. "What's he saying?"

"Sounds like 'scary ice creamer,' to me," said Zucarelli. "Or maybe creamer, like coffee creamer. I've played the tape over a couple of times, slowed it down, and those are the words."

"Anybody know what scary ice cream means?"

They all shrugged. Eli nodded and Agent Peterson started the tape where it'd left off. There was static, then a woman's voice — Jessica Monaghan.

"... *whole three acres?*"

Three *acres* of weed. That was a huge crop.

There was more static, unintelligible words, then—

"... *real pretty ... sunrise lit up the ice.*"

"... *every plant?*"

"... *and every bush, tree ...*"

"I think he's talking about an ice storm," Agent Peterson said.

"Find out if there was an ice storm in Minnesota today," Eli said, and Peterson went to his desk and picked up the phone.

"... *Beetle ... all dead.*" More unintelligible words. "*... just plain old corn ...*"

Then just words, both Taggart's and Monaghan's — a few understandable.

Taggart said, "*... there nekkid ... anybody drivin' by ... twenty-four-seven ...*"

Monaghan said, "*... careful ... cut and run ...*"

Eli couldn't make out any other words. They played the tape through three times, and by then Peterson had reported that a storm had struck in North Dakota, northern Minnesota and a small part of the upper peninsula of Michigan the last couple of days, said they called it a "Canada Clipper." In some places it was just wind and snow, in others, ice.

Eli leaned back against Zucarelli's desk and asked the group. "Thoughts?"

"I heard Taggart say— It's not on the tape, but I'm sure he said 'pale yellow, not green,'" Thomas said.

"Sounds like an ice storm hit their crop, froze it but maybe didn't kill it," said Agent Lincoln, speaking up for the first time. He was an exceedingly quiet man, but astute and observant and a crack shot, had been a Marine Corps sniper in Vietnam. "Maybe that's the twenty-four-seven. They're working around the clock to harvest it. "

"If the storm didn't kill it, why are they in such a hurry to harvest it?" asked Agent Peterson.

"'... just plain old corn,'" Agent Lincoln repeated. "'... there naked.'"

"Anybody driving by ..." Eli said, and he got it at the same time Bill Thomas did and they spoke in unison.

"The storm didn't kill the marijuana—" Bill began.

"But it *did* kill the 'plain old corn — pale yellow, not green' — which was concealing the marijuana from view," Eli said.

Corn was the go-to crop in which to hide weed — sometimes planted between the corn rows, sometimes behind it, though marijuana that hadn't been topped would grow taller than corn. Eli'd seen corn fields where each marijuana plant in it was bent over and tied by twine to a stake in the ground.

"So 'anybody driving by' can see it now," Bill finished.

"They have to get it harvested, in the barn and out of sight quick, before somebody spots it behind the dead corn." Eli walked to the map of the United States on the wall.

"Minnesota ..." he said thoughtfully, tapping the state with his pen and shaking his head.

"Why Minnesota?" Bill asked, but Eli went on.

"And somewhere between here," Eli indicated an area south of Duluth, "and here," he indicated the rest of the state to the north, "there's a *three-acre* crop of marijuana sitting 'nekkid' in a field, in plain sight."

"And we have to find it," Agent Peterson said, and Eli nodded.

"We need to start working the phones to the locals." Eli remembered that one of the great wake-up calls of his career with the FBI had been when he figured out that agents spent way more time on grunt-work, on the phone or doing paperwork, than they did arresting bad guys. He was consigning them all to hours talking to local law enforcement officers, many of whom ... probably *most* of whom ... were not fans of the FBI.

"*Hey, could you go out and drive around in the countryside, checking out farms to see if there's dead corn and live marijuana growing on one of them?*"

Then his mind went back to the question Bill had asked. Yeah, why Minnesota? It was six, maybe seven hundred miles, a twelve-hour drive, from northern Minnesota to central Kentucky — a four- or five-hour flight in Willie Ray's plane. And it was cold there — as evidenced by the freak ice storm. Why would they plant marijuana that far north, and oh by the way, why didn't the weed freeze just like the corn did?

Then another thought struck him and his stomach tightened. If the Cornbread Mafia was raising three acres of marijuana in Minnesota … where *else* might they be raising it? How big was this organization anyway?

Chapter Twenty-Four

WINONA MCCLUSKY PUT the bait on her hook and dropped the sinker into the water Sunday morning. It made a satisfying plunk sound.

Everything worked according to the plan she'd laid out. The day was beautiful, Father Donavan's homily was palatable and not overly long, St. Augustine Church in Brewster was packed with all the usual suspects — with one addition — the strikingly handsome man sitting beside Winona. His name was Steve Kaiser.

The man was a perfect specimen — *literally* tall, dark and handsome. Probably topped six feet four inches, with thick black hair hanging over his golden tanned forehead in a widow's peak. His eyes were a light gray that was magnetic. Decked out in a suit coat that strained around his broad shoulders, and a sweet smile that revealed piano key teeth, he was as good as it got. If Steve couldn't make it work, Winona would have to go back to the drawing board and come up with some other way to find out what she had to know.

Steve Kaiser owed her big time. He had been arrested

for armed robbery a decade ago, when he was barely eighteen, was looking at spending the best years of his life behind bars when his court-appointed attorney, Winona McClusky, came to the rescue, courtesy of a chain-of-evidence flaw she discovered in the prosecution's case that got the weapon Steve had used thrown out. Then she badgered the poor Indian woman whose husband owned the convenience store, got her so confused she was near tears when she left the stand, walking away from a jury who'd determined she was way too fragile and flighty to make a positive identification. So Steve had walked.

Steve's debt grew beyond gratitude for an acquittal when he sat across the desk from her not six months later, desperate for her to get his older sister out of a prostitution charge. Clearly, the girl was a hooker and even if Steve's vision was clouded by adoration for the only mother figure in his life, the prosecution had a case she couldn't budge and Steve would accept no kind of plea bargain unless it kept his sister from going to jail. The case went to trial and Winona got lucky. She spotted a guy on the jury who'd been the uncharged accomplice of a drug dealer she'd gotten off. She caught his eye, held it, and then bet the farm that he'd convince the jury to find the girl not guilty. He had.

After that, Winona had found Steve a job as a courier — ferrying legal documents all over Louisville, got him off the streets and away from the influence of his lowlife older sister who died in an alley from an overdose less than a year after she'd been in the courtroom.

Winona'd urged Steve to go to college, and he made it through a couple of years before the job she'd gotten him as a tour guide at Churchill Downs lead to a career working for the racetrack. When she'd called him a month ago, told him what she needed and asked for his help, he had fallen all over himself to oblige.

Now, her eyes scanned the crowd of people leaving the church until they landed on one of her cousins, and she bulldozed her way through the crowd, then pretended to "bump into her" in the aisle.

"Why Sherry Lynn, how are you doing?" Winona gushed, grateful that her husband, Riley, had left the church with their little boy as soon as the priest said amen. Winona'd noticed that before, how Riley took the boy out as soon as the service was over, but Sherry Lynn usually hung around for a while, chatting.

Sherry Lynn's eyes flashed over Winona's face and went to Steve. Hung there. Her mouth didn't exactly drop open, but if she had smiled any wider when Winona introduced them, the ends of the smile would have met in the back and the top of her head would have fallen off.

"So what brings you to Brewster, Mr. Kaiser?" Sherry Lynn asked, batting her long eyelashes to make sure he noticed her beautiful blue eyes, a dark shade that was almost purple.

"Steve, call me Steve."

"Then I'm Sherry Lynn."

If Steve's smile had been plugged into the electrical system of the church, he'd have blown every fuse in the building.

"Okay … Sherry Lynn … I'm going to be doing some legal work for Winona's old law firm. Traveling back and forth from Louisville a couple of times a week."

"You live in Louisville?"

"Uh huh, I'm a native — never been out in the country, though. What are the sights a city boy like me ought to see?"

At that point, Winona happened to see someone she absolutely *had* to speak to, so she excused herself.

"Keep Steve entertained for me, will you, Sherry Lynn? I'll be right back."

She wasn't right back, of course, stayed away as long as she could, hung around talking to anybody who'd give her the time of day for what felt like half an hour — the church was almost empty, when she returned to Steve's side to whisk him away.

He and Sherry Lynn were laughing gaily when she approached, and Winona imagined she heard an inaudible sound, something like the snap a trap makes before it squeezes out a mouse's guts.

"I was just telling Steve that he should go out to Double Springs Distillery, get a personalized bottle of bourbon with his name on the label. I've seen how much the tourists love them — I volunteer at the gift shop there on Thursdays."

"So they'd put my name on it?"

"'Brewed especially for Steve Kaiser' is what the label will say."

"Well, I absolutely have to get me one of those." There was a pregnant pause that Winona pretended not to notice. "Maybe I'll see you there."

"Oh, I'd be glad to give you a tour of the distillery. It's on the National Register of Historic Places, you know. There are lots of pretty things to see."

"I'm sure there are."

Winona grabbed Steve by the arm and piloted him out of the sanctuary before Riley showed up to collect his wife, made it all the way out to her car before she started laughing.

"What, you think I laid it on too thick?" Steve asked.

"Any thicker than that and you'd need a shovel."

"You didn't tell me that she was pretty. This is going to be fun."

"Do you put notches in a gun belt or something to keep track?"

"Oh, I never forget a pretty face. I told her I was getting an apartment in Bardstown, cut down on the commute from Louisville."

A permanent place instead of motel rooms offered all manner of opportunities.

"I've already signed the lease on a place. I need to move some stuff in so it looks like I live there … before Thursday."

They both smiled.

Chapter Twenty-Five

AGENT BILL THOMAS stuck his head into Eli's office after his shift on the headphones.

"You missed a biggie," Thomas said. "I got to hear a blow-by-blow of some pimple-faced adolescent boy's first date with his 'main squeeze.'"

"Interesting?"

"Agonizing. That boy ever comes anywhere near my daughter I'll strangle him with his jockstrap. Don't you think it's about time to pack it in?"

Eli looked up from the papers on his desk.

"It happened July 5, 1968." He lifted one of the papers and read from it. "A force of several thousand Viet Cong regular army soldiers swarmed over an artillery base called Fire Base Eagle's Nest."

He looked up from the sheet. "A company of National Guardsmen, farm kids who'd been milking cows six months before, had come in off patrol that afternoon and happened to be there when the Cong sprang the ambush."

Agent Thomas came the rest of the way into the room and sat down in a chair.

"The fellow I talked to read me a first-person account." Eli shook his head. "Part of it didn't make a whole lot of sense, something about how a soldier named Hannacker warned the camp, woke them up or they'd all have been murdered in their sleep. Said he used some kind of ... moonshiner's yell."

"Hannacker. Can't be more than one of those."

"Our Riley Hannacker, alright. He was injured, got a good head-knocking and a back full of shrapnel. Taggart got—"

"Willie Ray Taggart was there, too?"

"Uh huh. A bunch of Callison County boys joined the National Guard to keep from being sent to Vietnam. That's where Taggart got that scar on his face. His brother Andy was killed in the battle. And Jessica Monaghan's husband, David, suffered a head injury. Left him just short of brain dead."

"That's why the three of them are hooked so tight."

"Give the man a kewpie doll." Eli leaned back in his chair and rubbed his eyes.

Bill shook his head. "Maybe that's where they got interested in weed. I hear every soldier there smoked it."

"Not *every* soldier," Eli said.

"You were there?"

Eli nodded.

"And didn't partake? Why not?"

"Truth?"

"No, I like to be lied to."

"I've known all my life the answer to the question 'What do you want to be when you grow up?' I never even considered anything but law enforcement. By the time I was in 'Nam, I'd figured out if I made it back home, I wanted to become an FBI agent." He shook his head. "Shoot, I was just a kid, eighteen, but I figured even then that there'd be questions on some official form somewhere someday about 'prior drug use.' I wanted to be able to put down 'none.'"

"So that song and dance you did when we had that first meeting in Indy, the part where you said 'I may or may not have smoked a couple of joints when I was in college'—"

"I wasn't conning anybody," Eli said and grinned. "The answer was 'may not.'"

Later that night on the phone, Juliette picked up on something in his voice when he told her what he'd discovered about the Callison County boys in Vietnam.

"You're making some kind of connection here," she said. "What is it?"

"The first evidence we have, following the paper trail of expenditures unexplainable by their income, was in 1973 — a renovation of a house belonging to Ruth Monaghan, David's mother. I thought it was odd when I read about it, what was added. They didn't put in a swimming pool or a new deck. Now it makes sense. They turned that house into a nursing facility for her son."

"For Jessie Monaghan's husband, who was wounded in Vietnam?"

"Uh huh."

"So you're saying the Cornbread Mafia spent the money from their first marijuana crop making a nursing home for their injured buddy?"

"The dates line up."

"And that bothers you. Why?"

"I'm just trying to make it fit in my head how the Cornbread Mafia went from helping out an injured veteran to feeding live people to pigs."

"*What?*"

Eli hadn't meant to say that.

"You mean they did that, fed people to pigs?"

"That's what our informant told us. He said he'd seen evidence … like skulls and shoes by the pigpen." He could almost hear Juliette shudder over the phone. "Anybody who'd do that — you'd have to be more than a little psycho."

"Dangerous."

"So I'm told. I'll be careful."

After he hung up, he thought about what his grandmother used to say when he relayed to her someone's outlandish tale. "Consider the source," she'd say. The source of his information about the Cornbread Mafia had been a South American drug dealer who would have sold out his old granny to save his own skin.

But everything he'd told them had panned out so far. It just … didn't fit. Was 'off' somehow. Eli would be glad to apprehend the trio, talk to them face to face. It didn't matter one way or the other. They'd broken the law in a big way, had been living the high life on illegal profits for almost a decade. They could nudge Mother Teresa out as candidates for sainthood and it still wouldn't matter. They deserved whatever they got and Elijah Bradigan was eager to put the criminals behind bars. That's where they belonged.

Chapter Twenty-Six

"Mrs. Maxwell, this is Sherry Lynn Hannacker — how you doin' today?" She sounded ridiculously sweet, even in her own ears, but this mattered.

"Tolerable, I guess. You?"

Mauvine Maxwell had taught piano lessons when Sherry Lynn was a little girl and her best friend, Gloria Mattingly, had been one of the woman's students. Oh, how Sherry Lynn had wanted to learn to play, too, but there was no money in the budget of a family with nine kids for such frivolous things as piano lessons.

"Fine, just fine."

"My arthur-itis is givin' me fits but I get by better'n most. Wilma Tuttle told me a week ago Sunday that she couldn't use her thumbs hardly at all anymore and mine ain't that bad. They's stiff, got them big ole lumps on 'em, but it don't matter how they look long's they work."

Lumpy hands. Brown spots. Gray hair. Wrinkles. Sagging *everything*. The ravages of age. Well put — *ravages*. Sherry Lynn hadn't given ten seconds of her life to considering the degeneration of the body with age — until physical beauty was all she had. Now, she obsessed over a single gray hair, had started planning for a facelift when she spotted that first line around her eyes.

It had all been so simple when she was a kid. People got old. But what difference did it make — two old people, their gnarled, wrinkled hands clasped as they cut into their fiftieth anniversary cake, with all their kids and grandkids gathered around. That was what life was and it just … was. Nothing to dread, it just … *was*. She and Riley would *be* that old couple. Oh, some spats and arguments along the way, sure, couldn't stay married for half a century without some disagreements, but the commitment would see them through lumps, bumps, wrinkles and brown spots. When two people loved each other, they figured out a way to stand up to whatever life threw at them.

Loved each other. Riiight. Riley Hannacker and Sherry Lynn Bennett — two people who'd love each other to the end. Except not. Oh, she had loved Riley alright. Adored him. Would have done anything for him. But Riley didn't love her, never had loved her. The day that realization came home to roost in her consciousness, moved all its things in and set up housekeeping, she had spent the whole afternoon in the bathroom vomiting.

Once she looked it square in the eye, there was no denying it. He had never told her he loved her. She blew by that as a stupid teenager because it's just how guys were, didn't like to say sweet, intimate things like that. Wrong. Riley had never told her he loved her because he didn't love her. And if it hadn't been for Drew, he never would have married her.

That was the truth still in its long johns with the butt flap down.

The understanding of it had come after they'd finally moved out of Nate Hannacker's house and into their own place together. Now, it would be perfect, she thought. Now, she would have Riley's undivided attention, wouldn't have to share him with Nate. And she was sorry the old man was dead, she really was, but she was certain that as soon as Riley got over his grief, things would change between them. He would turn to her with his ideas and plans, share with her his problems and concerns. They'd grow emotionally close and with that would come physical closeness — they'd make love in the middle of the living room floor at noon if they wanted to! And then there'd be more children, the houseful of children she'd always longed for.

None of it worked out that way, of course. Riley was as cold and distant with her in the new house as he had been in the old house. He'd built a fortress around his soul — with her on the outside and him locked safe behind the walls. And it wasn't like he said something or did something that revealed the truth of his feelings, or lack thereof. There was no grand epiphany, no blinding moment of understanding. She just woke up one morning — it was a Tuesday, she recalled, and outside the first snow of winter was falling out of the dead gray sky. And she knew. Just *knew.* It was so clear and obvious it was stunning that it'd taken her five years of misery to figure it out. And the understanding had been like a week-long case of the flu. She hadn't cried, though, didn't rant and rave and mourn. She just sat, staring into empty space, as the understanding settled around her like the snow outside — a little at first, just covering the surface, then more and more until she was buried in an avalanche of it. She'd lost ten pounds that week, and that's when she'd realized that she could lose all the weight she'd gained. It hadn't even been all that hard, really. She had been stuffing food in her face for years because she was miserable, trying to fill up the empty hole in her belly where her husband's love was supposed to be.

When you love a piece of pineapple upside-down cake, it loves you *back*!

Of course, they were stuck with each other, her with him and he with her. It wasn't like there was a Get Out of Jail Free card, not in Catholic Callison County. Oh, people got divorced — of course, they did, it was 1978 for crying out loud. It would cause a stir — her family would be apoplectic — but if you were willing to brave the winds of the storm you were certainly free to launch your ship out into it. And it wasn't like she hadn't considered it. Why stay married to a man who ignored her? Who hadn't made love to her in … she didn't like to think about that. Why not just leave? One word: money. She and Riley'd struck a bargain the night after she and Drew'd cowered in a tobacco barn while gunmen shot Nate Hannacker's house full of bullets. *Shot* at Riley! They never said the words out loud, but they both understood it. Her end of the deal was to stay out of Riley's way, let him grow his weed, pretend she'd never heard the words Cornbread Mafia, though in truth she knew every intimate detail. His end of the deal was to … give her anything she wanted.

They'd both kept their bargain — though in the beginning she had no idea the enterprise would extend all over the country and bring in millions of dollars. And he had no idea the "anything" that she wanted included any man who struck her fancy.

Which was why she had called Mauvine Maxwell.

"Listen, Mauvine, I was wondering if I could take your shift at the gift shop this week. I'm not on the schedule for Thursday, but something has come up and I reeeeally need to be at Double Springs that day."

"Well, I already made plans—"

"Please! It's important or I wouldn't ask."

"All right, then. You go on ahead. It ain't like it's a paid job or nothing like that. I ain't getting nothing out of being there on Thursday."

Oh, but I am. *I* am.

Sherry Lynn didn't say that, of course, just gushed her thanks, hung up and called her hairdresser who agreed to squeeze her in early — she'd get highlights — and add in a manicure and pedicure. She'd have to settle for a new dress somewhere in Brewster, though, because she didn't have time for a trip to Louisville or Lexington. A new blouse to go with her floral skirt, something … *blue*, to bring out the color of her eyes.

She passed Riley on the stairs coming down as she was going up.

"I'm volunteering at Double Springs on Thursday, so I'll be home late," she called back over her shoulder from the second-floor landing. "And tell Drew to put on some of that zinc oxide stuff. I don't want his nose peeling at his birthday party."

Chapter Twenty-Seven

It had been three days since Willie Ray had called Jessie to tell her about the Canada Clipper and the frozen corn crop and Riley was still holding his breath. His first response had been to drop everything and go to Minnesota to help out, but one more worker wouldn't make that much difference and Riley had plenty to do at home. Even though nobody'd noticed the "nekkid" marijuana ... *yet* ... Riley couldn't seem to shake the sense that walls were closing in around them.

In that frame of mind, he had to cling to his temper with his fingernails to keep from exploding all over Sherry Lynn. She'd said yesterday she'd be volunteering at Double Springs on Thursday and that usually put her in a good mood, but she'd acted this morning like she'd suddenly had ten items added to her to-do list. It was maddening. He hated how he had to plan and connive and orchestrate even the most mundane circumstances to get around the absolute rock wall of his wife's negativity. It was almost comical to watch the predictable scenes play out.

"What do you think about building an arboretum in

that meadow behind the house, make a stone walkway from the swimming pool to it?" Sherry Lynn would say.

Translate that: I have decided to build the thing, something else we can add onto the massive Hannacker mansion to make it even more ridiculously opulent.

"I think it's a good idea," he'd say, and watch disappointment spread across her face that she couldn't turn the decision into a conquest.

"If we build one, what color should we paint it?"

Translate that: Pick a color so I can say I don't like it.

"How about the same color as the bath house by the pool?"

"Pale blue? That's *awful*. I've already decided to have the bath house repainted — sage green."

Mission accomplished.

What he was doing for Drew's birthday would be the biggest, most complete manipulation he'd ever attempted. But if it made Drew happy, if it did anything to lift the black cloud from around the boy's countenance, it would be worth any sacrifice.

Riley had decided to get the boy a horse.

Not a pony, a *foal* Drew could raise. That ticked several boxes. Sherry Lynn would blow the top off the house if Riley tried to give the boy a full-grown horse — or even a small pony. Drew had admired the beautiful horses at Land's End every time they drove past the paddocks, moaned in little-kid desire to have one. Sherry Lynn had been apoplectic. Drew would *not* have a horse, would *never* even ride a horse. Why, they threw their riders every time they had a chance and getting thrown from a horse was catastrophic, it could kill you. If he recalled correctly, at that point in the conversation, she had begun describing the scenes from *Gone With The Wind* where Scarlet O'Hara's father and then her little girl are killed falling off horses. As if the fact that a movie had depicted such a situation was all the argument anybody needed to hear.

But a foal was different. Drew wouldn't be able to ride it for two years, so a foal presented no immediate danger. That made it harder to rail against. And he'd hatched a plot to have Jessie bring the foal to Drew's party. Jessie, because she was always a calming influence on Sherry Lynn, and the party because Sherry Lynn couldn't send it back or anything like that — not right in the middle of his party.

Raising the foal would be good for Drew, give him something to care for, to pour himself into, to bond to. There'd be something out there in the future to anticipate and look forward to — and there'd be plenty of time for Drew to take riding lessons. They'd just put an addition on the side of the stupid arboretum out back with a stall and fenced-in paddock. Maybe more than one stall. Riley'd always wanted to ride. His grandfather would have gotten him his own horse if he'd ever asked for one, but Riley's attention was focused on the farm animals he raised and showed in competitions. He'd somehow never gotten around to fitting a horse fantasy into his real life.

He'd had long talks with Brady Garrison, the foreman in charge of the stables at Land's End. Of course, Riley wouldn't get Drew a thoroughbred. Though maybe Sherry Lynn would sign on for that — an expensive thoroughbred would give her one more charm to hang on her opulence bracelet. But thoroughbreds were bred to race — their bloodlines went back generations, each mating calculated to get a horse that could make it from the starting gate to the finish line at any racetrack ahead of all the other horses. They were often temperamental animals, and were certainly too fragile — with those slender legs and ankles — for a kid to ride over the fields and in the woods.

No, Riley would get Drew a "pony horse," and there was a herd of them at Land's End. The word "pony" was deceptive, since the horses that were used to help care for the thoroughbreds were full-sized horses. The practice of "ponying" meant using a rider on one horse to lead a riderless horse. Trainers used pony horses to exercise a thoroughbred too young to be ridden, or an injured horse or one recovering from illness or surgery. A pony horse had to have a calm and steady disposition, and the herd of them at Land's End had been bred for those characteristics — which was exactly the kind of horse Riley wanted for Drew.

Riley had gone back and forth about how best to present the gift to Drew. Of course, he wanted to allow the foal to totally surprise the boy, spring it on him out of nowhere in front of all his friends.

But it was always hard to predict how Drew would behave in a crowd, and Riley wanted to get Drew the perfect foal, the one *Drew* wanted. There were four of them now the right age at Land's End, very different in color, size and personality. Drew really ought to pick it out for himself, select the exact one he wanted and fall in love with it on the spot.

Surprise him?

Let the boy pick?

Back and forth.

Then Jessie gave her gentle counsel.

"Wouldn't it be better for the two of them to get acquainted calm and slow? Can Drew keep a secret, not let on that he knows he's getting the foal?"

Riley almost laughed at the question. That kid had been keeping secrets from his mother his whole life. He was a master at zipping his lip. And he wouldn't have to hide his anticipation and excitement after he picked the foal. Sherry Lynn would just think he was actually looking forward to his birthday party a week from Saturday instead of dreading it.

And he *was* dreading it. Any fool could see him tense at the very mention of the event. Why couldn't Sherry Lynn see that? It wasn't that she didn't love her son — she adored him, but hers was a clinging kind of smother-love. Truth, Sherry Lynn was so self-centered and self-absorbed that she seldom noticed the feelings of others around her. And besides, the birthday party was "an event," an opportunity for Sherry Lynn to preen and show off all the things she'd bought with the vast fortune Riley was making selling weed. She didn't have an opportunity like that very often. He'd put his foot down early on, after the Christmas party she threw the first Christmas they lived in the new house. Totally tone deaf to the emotional states of her husband and her son, still grieving Nate's recent death, she'd had more than a hundred people to dinner. Drew had hidden in his room, refused to come out. Riley had made it clear — *never again.* So she'd had to make do with small gatherings of women — tea parties, bridge, bunco. Drew's party wasn't ideal from her perspective — parents dropping their kids off instead of coming inside to ogle the splendor — but she'd make the best of what she had.

Riley decided to heed Jessie's counsel. School would let out before noon next Wednesday for some kind of teacher's meeting. He'd make up an excuse to pick Drew up and they'd go to Land's End.

Riley was determined to make that day one Drew would remember for the rest of his life.

And as it turned out, it was.

Chapter Twenty-Eight

Winona McClusky looked up at the big black ape standing in front of her desk and somehow managed to hold onto her legendary temper.

He had waltzed into her office pretty as you please, flashed a badge with one hand while he handed her a business card with the other.

"I'm Special Agent Elijah Bradigan, with the Federal Bureau of Investigation." He'd extended his hand to shake hers and when he did she realized who he reminded her of, that black actor, what was his name. Sidney Poitier. She'd seen him in *In the Heat of the Night*, and this guy could be his twin brother. She resisted the urge to comment on it, since she was sure such comments fell into the category of tall-guy how's-the-weather-up-there lines. Instead, she stood and took his hand.

"Winona McClusky." She clipped off the title, Commonwealth's Attorney, since it was clear he knew who she was or he wouldn't be here.

God, how she loathed the FBI.

They pranced around in suits and ties and knew everything there was to know about all things related to law enforcement, thank you very much, and would deign to allow other legal peons to aid in an investigation so long as they stayed appropriately in the background and let the spotlight land squarely on them.

But the sudden hole in the middle of her belly wasn't because she disliked the FBI, it was there because she was sure she knew why he was here.

"McClusky?" he said. "Same last name as the sheriff."

Well, give the man a kewpie doll.

"Yes, he's my uncle. You'll find a lot of big families in this county. Now, what can I do for you, Agent Bradigan?"

She let him stand there for a few beats too long, hoping it would make him uncomfortable before she offered a seat.

"Oh, forgive me. Please sit down."

He sat comfortably in the chair opposite her desk and she could feel him assessing her, like little bat wings beating against her skin. She'd be curious to know what conclusions he'd reached after his examination, but admitted she probably wouldn't like to hear them and it didn't matter.

"How can my little office offer assistance to the FBI?" She tried to keep the sneer out of her voice, but it sneaked in on its own. Bradigan ignored it.

"We're investigating an organization of drug wholesalers operating out of Callison County. We'll be pursuing charges based on the Kingpin Statute."

"Pretty weighty charge. Who is it you're looking for?"

He laid it out for her, telling her nothing she didn't already know, but surprising her with what they'd been able to find out on their own. And they'd been *on their own*. She knew her homies.

He opened a file and placed it on her desk. She left it there while he told her that it was a report from the U.S. Attorney's Office in Louisville about the Cornbread Mafia, with her listed as the primary source. She supposed it summarized the more than half dozen attempts she'd made to get them interested in the case, before she gave up.

"It's clear you've known about this organization longer than we have, and I'd like to enlist your cooperation in the case."

"Oh, I know about all the weed growers in this county. You'd be hard-pressed to find anybody who doesn't. I've been trying to take all of them down for years."

"I wasn't aware it was that pervasive."

"Even if the FBI manages to take down the big dogs, the little dogs will still be barking in my backyard."

"We plan to scoop up as many as we can and try them in federal court."

"Good luck with that."

He gave her a look that was somewhere between condescending and petulant.

"Maybe you'll get lucky and catch some of them with their hands in the cookie jar, but the Kingpin Statute's for the ringleaders. Now, you and I may know it's Hannacker, Taggart and Monaghan, but knowing it and proving it are two different things entirely. You're going to have to get somebody to roll over on them, and like I said — good luck with that."

He kept talking but she blew a fuse somewhere inside, didn't even wait for him to pause to take a breath.

"Well, it's clear you already know how to make your case and you don't need help from little old me to prove it."

"I'd like copies of previous cases you've brought—"

"I've never had the three of them up on charges because they're too smart to get caught. All I ever get is the little guys, and I can't even get a conviction on them.

You're welcome to those case files but they won't tell you squat."

He just sat there in his pressed suit, so un-ruffled and confident. God how she hated that.

"I'll be glad to have my assistant get you the case files. You got a truck, because I've got three file cabinets full."

"I was hoping I could talk to you about the three leaders, get your input on the best approach—"

"There is no good approach. There are only bad approaches. And you don't need my help for those." She hung the most unconvincing smile she could muster on her face. "Anything else I can help you with?"

He finally got the message and rose.

"Thank you for your time, Miss McClusky." When he turned without another word and walked out it was all she could do not to reach down and grab a paperweight and throw it at him. Instead, she grabbed hold of her temper.

As soon as he was safely out of her office she placed a call to Detective Booth Graham at the Kentucky State Police Post in Columbia. Tonight was scheduled to be one of their "date nights" but she couldn't wait that long to talk to him.

"We got problems," she told him when he answered the phone, then waited until he could take the call in his private office.

"What kind of problems?"

"Tall, black and looks like Sidney Poitier."

"Wha—?"

"The FBI. They're investigating the Cornbread Mafia. The agent just left my office. They're going after Riley, Willie Ray and Jessie with the Kingpin Statute."

She waited impatiently while he reeled off a litany of obscenities. When he'd blown off steam, he said despondently, "We're screwed."

"How you figure that?"

"The FBI will freeze their assets, for starters, and—"

"Not until they bust them. And right now, they don't have enough evidence to make an arrest, or they wouldn't have come crawling in here asking for my help."

"Are you suggesting—?"

"We get in, get ours, and get out quick — before the feds lock them up."

"But—"

Winona brightened. "In fact, I can use this, tell Jessie the FBI is nosing around, that with one phone call I can land the whole lot of them in the iron house."

"What are you going to threaten to tell the feds? We don't *know* anything, can't prove—"

"Not yet we don't. Steve's going to see Sherry Lynn on Thursday. After that, we'll—"

"You think in *one* date—?"

"It's all we've got time for."

"If we pull it off, they'll tell the feds we blackmailed them! I'd prefer not to end up in a cell next to Hannacker's."

"Let them squawk. They got no proof. It'd be their word against ours. Who're the feds going to believe?"

Winona thought about it for a moment, then added slowly, "Besides, I don't think they'll talk to the law. I don't think they'll say a word. They're … hardcore."

ELI WENT from the Commonwealth's Attorney's office to the sheriff's office in the courthouse and walked into a circus. Two farmers were about to come to blows over a squash. It became clear the vegetable was special in some way and when Eli got a look at it he could see why. It was as big as a watermelon. State fair prize-winning size, which it was clear both farmers knew.

"Them vines grow wild and this 'un come over into my garden and I watered it and fertilized it *on my land* which makes it my squash — and I'm showing it," said a man in an Allis-Chalmers hat, with a belly that hung out over the top of his jeans so far you couldn't see his belt buckle.

"The hell it is!" Farmer number two was a bald scarecrow of a man, skinny arms and legs sticking out of his coveralls, and a bony face with a chin that looked like the knob on a femur. "I planted that squash. I bought the seed and paid for it. Wherever that plant grows a squash, the squash b'longs to me."

The sheriff bore a noticeable family resemblance to his niece, or cousin or whatever — the ugly woman Eli'd just spoken to. He stood behind the counter where the squash lay. The farmers stood in front of it. The sheriff finally had enough of the bickering.

"Here's what we're gonna do, boys." He pulled out a vicious-looking knife and before either farmer could protest, he brought it down on the gourd on the counter, cleaving it into two reasonably sized pieces and completely ruining it as a fair competitor. He shoved the cleaved pieces off the counter and onto the floor and told the farmers, "Get that thing outta here. Herman, you cut your squash vines and keep them from growing out into Bob's garden. Bob, you keep your hands off Herman's squash."

The sheriff then turned his considerable girth and lumbered back into his office.

"May I help you?" The receptionist, her attention no longer riveted on the gourd in front of her had finally noticed Eli standing there.

Eli shook his head. "I'm good, thanks," and he left by

the same door he'd entered, while Bob and Herman argued over the pieces of squash scattered on the floor.

There had actually been a couple of classes at Quantico about how to liaison with local law enforcement, how to make them feel included and necessary, how to establish the proper parameters of authority.

Nothing in either of the classes had prepared Eli for a gourd war. The sheriff was clearly as dumb as a brick. His cousin/niece/whatever was not. She was shrewd and clever and she had some kind of side game going here. It could be as simple as hurt pride over the big, mean FBI showing up and hogging all the glory for solving the case. But in her cagey eyes, Eli saw more than that. It wasn't just that she didn't want to help him. She would do everything in her power to hinder his investigation.

Why might that be?

What interest did Commonwealth's Attorney Winona McClusky have in the Cornbread Mafia? Were they buying her off? Possible. Maybe the payoff extended to her Neanderthal uncle and others in local law enforcement.

No way to tell. But his trip to the courthouse hadn't been a total waste. The adventure made it clear that Eli could not share the results of his investigation with Winona McClusky or anyone else in law enforcement in Callison County — and Eli needed to watch his back.

Chapter Twenty-Nine

"WHY, THIS PLACE IS LOVELY!" Sherry Lynn gushed. "You said it was a dump."

Breezing through the living room of the small apartment and into the tiny kitchen and breakfast nook, she calculated that the sunroom she'd added to the house three years ago was bigger than this.

"Correction," Steve said. "I didn't say this place was a dump, I merely said it wasn't a whole lot better than the roach motel where I stayed when I got here."

Steve. Sherry Lynn loved that name. It sounded so tough and masculine and ... sexy. She glanced down the short hallway to the bedroom and was glad to see it had a king-sized bed. But, in truth, the connection, the chemistry, the lust she felt for him, they might not make it off the living room couch.

"Please, sit down. Make yourself at home, such as it is," he said and turned toward the kitchen. "I'll make us a drink."

"None for me, thanks. I'm not much of a drinker."

"That's only because you've never tasted one of Steve Kaiser's strawberry daiquiris. I guarantee you'll like it."

"Maybe just a small one, then. I have to drive home from the distillery."

He stopped and looked at her and she felt a shiver go down her spine.

"Not for a while, you don't. The evening's young."

As he made the drinks, Sherry Lynn wandered around the room, looking at nothing, just too nervous to sit down. She was glad she'd taken the time to dash up to Lexington and back after all, not for a new dress but for new lingerie. It would be worth it. The white lace of the bra against her tanned bronze skin was, if she did say so herself, positively delicious. She'd spent the whole way out to Double Springs Distillery this afternoon imagining him inching her lace panties slowly down her tanned legs.

She could see black chest hair in the open collar of Steve's shirt and she positively ached to see him with the shirt off. Some men were so covered in body hair they looked like apes. Bud Peters had been like that, but she should have suspected it. He had black hair on the tops of his fingers and it was thick on his arms. Still, she had not been prepared for a hairy back!

Steve would have sculpted chest hair, she was sure of it. Just the right amount in all the right places. Rubbing her face in downy soft chest hair was gloriously arousing.

She noted the standard lighthouse picture on the apartment wall. She was sure apartment complexes bought them in bulk and put one in every apartment — though she did have to admit this apartment was nicer than she'd expected, certainly way better, and more private, than some anonymous motel room. The picture was crooked and she reached up and straightened it and felt something stuck to the back of the frame. Something small and round—

"Planning on getting new curtains, too?" Steve said from the kitchen doorway. "Maybe put up a wallpaper chair rail?"

"I'm not redecorating — it's just that crooked pictures drive me nuts." He came to her and took her hand, the one she'd been straightening the picture with, and led her to the couch. "But I do admit I like to decorate. Getting it all to match, the curtains, the carpet, the furniture coverings is a lot harder than you'd think it would be."

He had a drink in his other hand and handed it to her, standing tall, looking down at her.

"You're going to love this drink." He paused for a beat. "I promise you've never had anything like it."

"Where's yours?"

"I just made one — for you. If you like it, we'll both have a second one."

"Oh, I doubt that. One drink and I get positively loopy." She patted the couch next to her. "Sit with me."

"I bet you're cute as a button when you're … loopy."

He sat beside her, close enough so their thighs touched, and she sipped the drink. It didn't taste strongly of alcohol. She liked that, though it had a bit of an odd flavor underneath the strawberry taste.

"I bet you're a mint julep girl. All beautiful girls in Kentucky love mint juleps." He paused and looked deep into her eyes. She felt giddy from the attention. "You're definitely a beautiful girl. Woman. A strikingly beautiful woman. But you know that, don't you, Sherry Lynn."

She took another swallow of the drink and it was smoother going down than the first had been.

"What a sweet thing to say." She moved to set the drink on the table but he stopped her hand.

"You don't like it? Because if you don't, I'd be glad to make you—"

"No, no. I do like it. I do."

She took a big swallow and sighed.

"You smell like strawberries." He leaned his face next to her. "Smells … good enough to eat."

She drained the glass so she could set it down. She had better things to do with her hands than hold a drink. Reaching up to trace his jawline with her fingertip, she fell back on the couch cushion. A bit of a clumsy movement, actually, like she'd tripped. But lying back like this gave him a glorious view of her cleavage.

Her head felt momentarily foggy and she shook it to clear it. When she did, the room tilted slightly and she couldn't seem to focus her eyes. But then he kissed her, and she closed her eyes and forgot about everything else in the world.

When she opened her eyes again, she was lying on her back on the couch, with her skirt wrinkled and hiked up almost to her waist. Her blouse was buttoned, and still tucked in. She closed her eyes again, uncertain where she was and how she'd gotten here. She felt a thudding headache in her temples.

But she couldn't remember much of anything after Steve had kissed her. Why were her thoughts so fuzzy?

"Awake now, sleepyhead," said a voice above her and she opened her eyes again to see Steve standing beside the couch. Random thoughts were pinging around in her head? Did he take his clothes off? He didn't look like he'd gotten undressed. Had she? If she took her blouse off … how/why was it neatly tucked into her skirt now? She tried to sit up but a wave of dizziness swept over her and she collapsed back down.

"Lie still and you'll feel better in a few minutes. I'll get you some coffee?"

What had happened? Had she … passed out? From *one* drink? She heard Steve banging around in the kitchen and sat up carefully. Her panties were on a little crooked and she felt the unmistakable sensation between her legs that told her she'd just had sex, but she couldn't remember it. She could remember little bits of things. They'd talked — about all sorts of things. Pieces of sentences floated by her consciousness and were gone.

"… in old barns that look abandoned …"

She'd told him about her swimming pool, that she was lousy at tennis, about the puppy she'd had as a little girl, offshore accounts in the Cayman Islands and how to make banana pudding.

What in the world—?

Steve returned to the room with a cup of coffee and handed it to her.

"Just a couple of sips and you'll feel better."

"I … I don't remember …"

"Remember what?"

"Anything."

He sat down beside her and touched her bare thigh where her skirt was hiked up.

"Well, I remember enough for both of us. You were *incredible*."

He touched her neck, tracing his fingers down it to her breast, ran it under the lace of her bra and stroked lightly. The catch on the new bra was stiff and hard to fasten, but it felt snug now… almost like she never took it off. But of course, she did. Or he did.

"You'll remember next time," he said and nuzzled her cheek. "I will make it memorable."

She wanted to be excited by that, to be eager. She

wanted to feel … something, anything. But she felt like she was wrapped in cotton, numb.

"Please tell me you'll see me again."

"Of course I will," she heard herself say. But the words were disconnected somehow, didn't have any meaning.

"Next week?"

She hesitated.

"What night are you free?"

Monday? What was she doing Monday night? She had no idea, her thoughts were too jumbled to recall.

"I'll call you and we'll set up a day and time. Please say yes. I want you so bad."

"Yes, I'm sure I'm free next week … sometime. Or I can be."

"We'll have a night together you'll never forget."

She certainly hoped so.

Chapter Thirty

WINONA, Steve Kaiser and Booth Graham gathered around Winona's kitchen table, listening to the recording of Steve's — what should she call it? Tryst. Now, there was a word you didn't get a chance to use every day.

Winona had to admit Steve had done a masterful job of seducing Riley Hannacker's wife. Seated across from Steve now at the table, Winona couldn't help conjuring up some fantasies of her own. It didn't help that Booth was sitting next to him, and Booth had the charm and sex appeal of a Coke machine. He had been taking notes, and after they played the tape through for the third time, he said, "You can turn it off now. We don't need to hear the heavy breathing again."

That had been Winona's favorite part.

"She's a beautiful woman so that part wasn't hard." He grinned. "Well, actually it was *hard*."

He laughed at his own joke but the other two didn't.

"I got as much information from her as I could, but we're supposed to meet again next week and I'm going to concentrate on finding out—"

"Forget next week," Winona said. "We'll run with what we have."

"But I know I can get more out of her."

"This will have to be enough. We're out of time."

"I didn't know there was a ticking clock."

"There wasn't before, there is now. We have to get our money while the Cornbread Mafia still has money, and while they're still free to get their hands on it."

"You know something I don't."

"I got a visit on Tuesday from the FBI."

She watched the color drain out of Steve's face.

"The feds are building a case under the Kingpin Statute. They'll seize all their assets. If we don't get ours quick there will be nothing to get."

"How did the FBI get wind of the Cornbread Mafia?" Steve asked.

"What difference does it make how they found out? They know. I don't know how close they are to an arrest, but we need to move fast."

Looking down at the notes he'd made, Booth pointed to the names of offshore banks in the Cayman Islands. "I sure wish we knew more about these accounts."

"I'd be surprised if Sherry Lynn Hannacker has access to the account numbers, if that's what you're suggesting, and it'd be an awkward subject to chat about during foreplay. Actually, I'm impressed she knew as much as she did."

Sherry Lynn, once plied with booze and drugs, had given them all manner of information about the trips her husband made to the Caribbean, and the ones Willie Ray Taggart made to Arkansas, Minnesota, Iowa, Missouri and other states. And poor Sherry Lynn got soooo lonely when he was gone.

It seemed Willie Ray and some college professor

named Wooly or Fuzzy or something like that had made hybrid marijuana that grew well in the U.S., unlike the South American strains that needed a longer growing season. In fact, they'd developed weed that would grow as far north as Canada — Righteous Weed, which was the hottest product on the market.

"We don't have to have the account numbers, but we can bluff, say we have them — how would Jessie know whether we actually did or not? In fact, my little visit from Special Agent Elijah Bradigan is going to build a fire under her. I bet she has no idea they're closing in on her."

They had decided that they'd approach the "weakest link" — Jessica Monaghan. Winona would make her an offer. Winona would remain silent about the Cornbread Mafia's weed fields all over the country, about who they'd hired to help them, an impressive list of names, and how they were stashing money in numbered accounts in OFCs, offshore financial centres in the Cayman Islands. The cost of Winona's silence would be a nice, round number — one million dollars — or $330,000 and change from each of the Cornbread Mafia leaders.

Booth had balked at such a high figure; Winona didn't think it was high enough. Steve was getting a flat fee of twenty thousand dollars so he didn't care one way or the other.

"They turn around millions of dollars in profits every season. They're getting off light with just a million," Winona said.

"How are they going to arrange that kind of payment on short notice?" Steve asked.

"That's their problem," Booth said.

"It doesn't take but a couple of seconds to make a wire transfer," Winona said.

"Or they could pay cash," Booth scoffed. "Just make a withdrawal from Willie Ray's stash — a tanker full of hundred-dollar bills buried somewhere in a field."

"Does he really—?"

"Yeah, Bigfoot and the Tooth Fairy take turns guarding the place." Winona shook her head. "Even if they really did have that much cash ... where would *we* put it?"

When Special Agent Elijah Bradigan came rolling into her office two days ago, he had turned her world upside down, changed everything. She had put all her plans on hold. First priority was getting the money before the government froze the Cornbread Mafia's assets. But afterwards ... she'd had all her ducks beak to tail feathers for a leisurely exit, and now ... she'd just have to play it by ear. She'd likely have to hang around longer than she'd intended so's not to look suspicious.

A lot of it depended on what the Cornbread Mafia members did when they got busted. As Booth had pointed out earlier, maybe when the feds started squeezing them, they'd finger her for blackmail. She really didn't think they would — that code of silence thing. But if they did, well — good luck with that. Winona would be sure not to leave a trace of their business transaction behind. No witnesses. No paper trail, everything verbal. Then it would be Jessie Monaghan's word against hers, and with the charges they were going to throw at that woman, she wouldn't be in any position to throw rocks at anybody else.

"So you're just going to *leap* into this?" Steve asked, looking from one to the other. "Get in before they get arrested. Isn't that kind of ... dangerous?"

"It's a little like a smash-and-grab robbery," Booth said. "You break the glass, you grab as much loot as you can and then you run like hell."

"I'll give her one week," Winona said. "Next Saturday, the twenty-eighth. They'll just have to make it work. Now, if you gentlemen will get out from under foot, I'll call Jessica Monaghan and tell her we need to talk."

Chapter Thirty-One

"Is this Jessie Monaghan?" asked a voice that sounded familiar, but Jessie couldn't place it.

"Who wants to know?"

The voice chuckled. "This is Winona McClusky, and we need to talk."

Just like that — we need to talk.

What on earth could Winona McClusky want to talk to Jessie about? Not just Winona McClusky. *Commonwealth's Attorney* Winona McClusky.

"Hello, Winona," Jessie stammered. She did, after all, know the woman. Winona'd been in Louisville when Jessie was typing up depositions and filing cases at Tanner, McClusky and Fowler, but she'd come into the law office sometimes. They spoke. Probably exchanged half a dozen sentences. That was almost a decade ago. "How can I help you?"

"What we need to talk about we need to say face to face. How about I meet you in the park tomorrow — that picnic table by the tennis courts."

"I don't understand—"

"This isn't complicated. We need to talk. You need to hear what I have to say. Be there at noon."

The line went dead.

When Jessie replaced the receiver, she felt a wave of dizziness and her stomach rolled. She'd been feeling punk for a couple of weeks now and was being careful to stay out of Davie's face. She couldn't let him catch whatever stomach virus she had. He was so fragile.

Sitting down on the sofa beside the telephone, she gritted her teeth and concentrated and the dizziness passed. But not the awful feeling in the pit of her stomach. That kicked-in-the-belly feeling. She had to call Riley. She didn't want to do that. She tried never to call him. She made that rule for herself a long time ago because if she ever called him one time just to hear his voice, the temptation would be stronger the next time. At night, when she was so lonely she'd pat the bed beside her and Magic would jump up on it and curl up by her feet.

She really did need to talk to him, though. This was business.

"'Lo, Hannackers," said Sherry Lynn's chirpy voice and Jessie cringed.

"Hi, Sherry Lynn. How you doin'?"

"Jessie! It's so good to hear from you. We really need to get together more often but with all that's going on ..."

Jessie's throat constricted.

"All *what* that's going on?"

"Drew's birthday party, silly," she chirped. "There's just so much to do to get ready for it." She lowered her voice to a conspiratorial whisper. "And Riley wouldn't let me set up hot-air balloon rides. Can you believe that? What kid wouldn't like a ride in a hot-air balloon? The other children would have been talking about Drew's party for months afterward."

"I'm sure they will be even without the hot-air balloon rides." She paused, tried to sound off-handed. "So, how is Drew?"

"He'd be a lot better if his father took better care of him! I let him out of my sight and there's no telling what Riley'll let him do. He got Drew a banana split the other day and he knows Drew has a delicate stomach — IBS, that's Irritable Bowel Syndrome. The poor kid had ... you know, the runs."

"Maybe it's some kind of stomach bug," Jessie said. "I've been feeling kinda punk myself lately."

"Well, I rushed him right into town to see Dr. Callahan — he took over Dr. Dawson's practice, you know."

"You took Drew to the doctor because he got sick on ice cream?" Jessie couldn't hide the incredulity, but Sherry Lynn blew right by it.

"Drew's been looking awfully pale ever since and I think there may be something Dr. Callahan isn't telling me. So I'm keeping an eye on him." Like she didn't always helicopter over Drew. "And if I see anything peculiar, anything at all, I'm going to take him to a specialist in Louisville or Lexington."

She stopped to draw a breath and Jessie seized the opportunity.

"Is Riley around? I need to talk to him about ... Willie Ray."

"Sure. I'll go get him. Just a sec." Jessie heard the receiver clunk down on the table and Sherry Lynn's voice calling Riley. Summoning Riley, that's what it always sounded like to Jessie.

"'Lo Jess, what's goin' on?" Riley said, with practiced impersonality.

"I got a call from Winona McClusky and she wants to talk to me."

"What about?"

"She wouldn't say, but she wants to meet in the park at noon tomorrow."

"And you think that's because she doesn't want anybody to overhear you?"

"You got a better explanation?"

There was silence on the other end of the line.

"I don't like it," Riley said quietly.

"Copy that."

"Don't suppose there's anything you can do except go talk to her and find out what she wants. Meet me at the house late tomorrow afternoon and we can talk about it."

"Are you worried?"

"No, I'm not worried."

"Liar." She hung up the phone.

Chapter Thirty-Two

JESSIE WAS THERE EARLY. She sat at the picnic table crunching on the ice in an almost empty cup of coke from Hardee's, remembering the times she'd brought Magic to the park with her and let him chase sticks. But the dog hadn't been a particularly playful sort. She always thought of him as a child who'd been forced to grow up too fast and was adult-serious all the time. He'd gone from a puppy to a dog the day she brought Davie home from the hospital, and he'd never been much of a frolicker afterward.

Oh, he'd obediently chase a stick and bring it back to her when she threw it, but it was her game, not his. He was content to lie on the ground at her feet watching the world go by.

As soon as she saw Winona crossing the grass to the table, Jessie imagined Magic's reaction. He wouldn't have liked her, would have raised his hackles and let out a low rumble of a growl.

Winona sat down across from Jessie, drew in a breath and draped a smile between her ears like a surgeon's mask.

"There's no reason this has to get ugly," she said. "We

can be civilized, conduct our business and go on our way. That's pretty much up to you."

Jessie didn't know what to say, so she said nothing.

"Let's get it established from the git-go that I know what you're doing, you and the 'Cornbread Mafia.'"

Jessie had no intention of contradicting her because she had been shocked into silence, but it was clear quick that any effort in that regard would be wasted.

Winona held up her hand.

"I didn't come here to listen to you deny what we both know is true, so let's not go there. I know chapter and verse about your organization, know so much that Booth Graham could clamp handcuffs on you tomorrow morning and haul all of you away for a very long time."

Booth Graham.

Jessie went from zero to sixty on the angry scale between one heartbeat and another.

"Then you need to turn your pet state police detective loose, arrest me and I will see you in court." Jessie started to rise.

Winona barked out a chuckle.

"In this county? Seriously? You know I couldn't get a conviction here."

"Then what do we have to talk about?"

"He looks just like Sidney Poitier."

Jessie knew she was supposed to ask who that was and what it had to do with their conversation but refused to play the game.

"He might even be better-looking, you know, as black men go. Name's Elijah Bradigan. Special Agent Elijah Bradigan with the Federal Bureau of Investigation."

Jessie kept her face immobile with an effort.

"He paid me a visit on Tuesday and we had quite a little chat and your ears must have been burning. He doesn't know half of what I know, what I can *prove*, but I didn't share."

"Such as?" Jessie challenged.

"I know that you have offshore accounts full of money in the Cayman Islands, numbered accounts. I know the numbers."

That was a lie. It had to be. She and Riley had memorized the numbers and other than their attorneys, *nobody* knew them. Not even Ace and he'd helped the two of them set up the accounts. If that was a lie, was all the rest of it a bluff, too?

"I know you don't grow a whole lot of weed locally anymore, got too hot here so now you grow your weed on farms out of state." Then she rattled off the locations: Minnesota, Arkansas, Nebraska, Kansas, Wisconsin, Iowa and Missouri. "Willie Ray takes care of off-site production."

How could Winona McClusky possibly find out a thing like that?

"I know there's a substantial amount of cash in a safe in Riley Hannacker's office that's behind a picture of Drew when he was a year old. The combination is right to 5, three turns left to nine, back right to six."

Jessie felt like she might actually vomit. "Why are you telling me this?"

"You and the others are growing weed and making millions. Booth and I want a cut."

Winona let that sink in, and went on. "This is a simple, straight-forward business transaction. I have accumulated enough evidence against all of you to put you away in the iron house — *if* we lived anywhere in the world except Callison County. But U.S. District Court in Louisville is *not* Callison County. It's a whole different kettle of fish. Now, I can either give what I have on you to

Mr. Poitier Lookalike or I can feed it into the paper shredder in my office."

Jessie was furious. She was also scared spitless. Did Winona McClusky really have evidence that could put them away? A few of the local farmers on whose land they grew a selected number of plants had gotten caught over the years. They'd mostly waltzed through the court system unscathed — and were richly rewarded afterward. What did Winona have to tie the Cornbread Mafia to those busts?

But how could she possibly have found out about the numbered accounts? Or the combination to the safe in Riley's office, for crying out loud.

"Here's how it goes. The FBI is nosing around your operation. Just sniffing. Right now, they got squat. But if I give them a piece of evidence I just uncovered — a game-changer piece of evidence — all the cards in the little slot machine will line up the same and the bell will start ringing *ding, ding, ding.* Added to what little they already know, what I tell them will be way more than they need to establish 'probable cause' to subpoena bank records, land transactions, execute search warrants. And what the FBI might turn up with that kind of thorough search, I don't know. But you do."

No, actually, she didn't. She personally knew very little about the financial end of the business. That was Riley's job, and the attorneys and accountants he'd hired on Ace's recommendation. They'd all said the Cornbread Mafia was safe. But from the probing of the *FBI?*

"Bottom line — without my help the FBI will buzz around for a little while, and if you're lucky, they won't be able to turn up anything on their own that'll put you away and they'll give up and go looking for low-hanging fruit somewhere else. I don't have any say over what they do with what they already have. But with my help, they won't go looking for nectar in a more likely flower. They will stay right here and sting you."

"What do you want?"

"A million dollars." She blew by the shocked looked on Jessie's face like she'd just asked for a five-dollar donation to the Salvation Army. "I'll take it in a wire transfer to my offshore account." Winona's fake smile had never faltered through her whole spiel, but it became real now. "Or in cash. Shoot, maybe it's not a myth. Maybe Willie Ray really does have a boxcar buried out there in the woods somewhere stuffed with hundred-dollar bills. Don't know, don't care. One million dollars — in my hand or in my account." She pulled a slip of paper out of her pocket and slid it across the table to Jessie. There was a multi-digit number on it. "By noon next Saturday or Booth and I will join forces with the FBI, put all our information and resources at their disposal, and act as consultants, providing local, on-the-ground expertise to help put the Cornbread Mafia away for a good chunk of the rest of your lives."

All Jessie could say was, "A *week?* Seriously? You can't possibly expect—"

"Can and do. Put up or shut up. A certain … business deal I have in the works has a hard deadline so there's no wiggle room. October 28, or I become Sidney Poitier's new best friend."

Winona stood, looked down at Jessie, and the cold calculation in her eyes was impossible to miss. "I would have put a bullet hole in Nate *Hannacker* myself for killing my father and brother if somebody hadn't beaten me to it." She spit the words out. "There's nothing in life I'd like more than to crush the rest of his family. Well, one thing — a million dollars."

ELIJAH BRADIGAN and the other FBI agents sat in the conference room of their Bardstown office, listening in silence to the recording made from the bug the agents had put on the underside of the picnic table next to the tennis courts in Brewster Park early that morning.

The place names rang like a Chinese gong in Eli's head.

Minnesota.

Arkansas.

Nebraska.

Kansas.

Wisconsin.

Iowa.

Missouri.

Seven states. *Seven!*

Finally, Bill Thomas spoke into the silence. "You remember that scene in *Jaws* when the fisherman sees the great white for the first time?"

"Yeah." Eli knew where Bill was going. "The guy said 'I think we're gonna need a bigger boat.'"

189

Chapter Thirty-Three

RILEY ABSOLUTELY DID NOT WANT to hear what Jessie had to say about her meeting with Winona McClusky. But here he sat at the kitchen table in the house he'd grown up in, waiting for her to arrive.

He always missed Papa. Sometimes more than others, but the missing never left him and he finally accepted that that was what life was about when you lost somebody you loved unreservedly. It gave him an unwanted insight into how Jessie must feel about Davie.

Right now was one of those times when he wanted to talk to his grandfather so badly he spoke out loud into the empty house, as if Nate could hear him.

"I just want to sit out on the front porch with you, one butt cheek hanging out the hole in that stupid nylon lawn chair, and look at the stars and the fireflies." There'd been such a sense of the rightness of the world then, an innocence that … when it was gone, it was gone for good.

He heard a vehicle crunch the gravel in the driveway and sat where he was, staring off into space, thinking nothing in an effort to keep from thinking about everything, until Jessie came in the back door.

She brought light with her. He knew that was an illusion, wondered if maybe all men thought that about the women they loved, but it seemed to Riley that there was some kind of glow around Jessie. A kind of firefly light that wasn't meant to light up anything, but pulsed off the glowing spirit within her.

And there was a hum. When she sat quiet and looked at him, he could hear a humming sound, almost like a transformer. No, like disturbed bees settling back on the hive.

"It's bad, isn't it?" Riley said.

"Yup. It's I-need-coffee bad."

She began to rummage around in his cabinets looking for the coffee, talked while she made it, and he knew the coffee was a ruse to keep her back to him so the heavy words wouldn't be so hard to say.

Winona McClusky was blackmailing them.

Just like Mama Bert had blackmailed Papa.

The offshore accounts. The fields in other states and who was working them. Winona knew about all of it.

Jessie turned and sat a cup of coffee in front of him.

"Riley, she even knows the combination to the safe in your living room."

"*What?*" That could not be, absolutely could not be. Only he and Sherry Lynn—

"What's the combination?"

"I don't remember. I wasn't exactly tracking on all cylinders when she told me. R5, then a nine and something, a six or seven. I don't remember."

"She was bluffing. Made up a combination out of thin air."

"You think? But everything else was right on." She

paused. "There's more. An FBI agent came to her office earlier in the week, said he was working on a case ... *against us.*" She almost choked on the words.

"What does she want?"

"A million dollars!"

He'd have choked if he'd taken a sip of coffee before she said the words.

"That was pretty much my reaction, too."

"And by next Saturday."

Riley couldn't speak, could only shake his head.

"Why just a week? What's her hurry?"

"She said she had some kind of business deal with a deadline."

"I don't buy that. You don't extort a million dollars from somebody so you can buy a McDonald's franchise. There's some other reason for the hurry."

Riley didn't like the conclusion he came to.

"Maybe she wants her money quick ... because she thinks the FBI is about to ..." He couldn't even say the words.

"She said they didn't have enough evidence without her help."

"Another bluff. Maybe she made up the whole FBI agent thing to scare us."

"I suppose that's possible. Where could she possibly have gotten information like that?"

"I don't know."

But he did know, some part of him did anyway. He just wouldn't let himself listen to it because the scenario was too horrifying to countenance.

"We can't decide what to do until Willie Ray gets back."

"It's either pay her or kill her."

"Right," Jessie said. She clearly didn't think he meant

it. He'd been dead serious. "What guarantee do we have that if we pay, she'll keep her end of the deal?"

"None that I can see." That sense he'd had of the walls closing in, it struck him now and made it hard to breathe.

"Next time Willie Ray calls, tell him to high-tail it back home. We need him here. It's time to circle the wagons."

"Meaning?"

"Either pay Winona or … not." He didn't say "kill her" but that's what he was thinking. "And then get ourselves so lawyered up, we'll be wrapped in Teflon."

"What can lawyers do at this stage?"

"Depends on what the law has — the law, not Winona. And what they can *prove*."

Jessie let out a breath and shook her head, spoke softly, maybe wasn't talking to Riley at all.

"How could she possibly know all that? How could she find out?"

Riley was afraid he knew.

Chapter Thirty-Four

SHERRY LYNN HAD SPOTTED Jessie in church and gone running up to her, babbling about Drew's upcoming birthday party. Riley hated it when she did that. It was torture to stand in polite silence, not looking at Jessie, and pretending to be interested in what his wife was saying.

Drew looked equally pained. He didn't like to hear his mother go on and on about the party, it was embarrassing. And anything that kept them in the building after the service made Drew nervous. He wanted to get out of the crowd and go home, stood close to his father, looking around, searching the crowd for ... what? Most kids were afraid the Boogeyman was hiding in their closets or under their beds. Drew expected to encounter the monster of his nightmares in any crowd of grownups.

Riley was wondering for the umpteen billionth time what had Drew so spooked when he saw Jessie's eyes widen in a look that was hard to read. Surprise/shock. Sure. But something else, and it wasn't a look anybody saw often in Jessica Monaghan's eyes — rage.

Riley and Sherry Lynn were facing Jessie, who was

focused on something, somebody behind them. Sherry Lynn turned to follow her gaze and looked shocked, too, though not nearly as affected by whoever was standing behind Riley. He turned around then, and stared into the cold shark eyes of Jackson McClusky.

"Hello there, Riley, Jessie. You doin' alright?" Jackson asked, a picture of polite, casual interest.

He was dressed for church, suit and tie. As were the muscle-bound hunks who stood on either side and back a couple of steps from him. Jackson looked fit — tanned, healthy and strong. Riley had noticed in his brief encounter with Jackson five years ago that he was no longer the skinny runt of the litter he had always been. But Riley hadn't been paying attention to such things at the time. He took in Jackson's appearance now, though. He had completely re-sculpted his body. His shoulders were so broad his suit jacket pulled just a little too tight over them. Even under a coat, Riley could see the muscle in his upper arms, his chest was broad, his belly flat. This was a man who worked out, who had worked out every day for years. His shock of black hair was stylishly long, with a bit of a wind-blown look — Robert Redford in *Butch Cassidy and the Sundance Kid*. He had a neatly trimmed mustache and beard, and came as close as any McClusky ever did to good looks.

The calculated, surprise encounter had been designed to shock Riley and Jessie, upset and disorient them. He had selected the neutral ground of St. Augustine Catholic Church on a Sunday morning to rub their noses in his return, was sending a message loud and clear — I'm back now and ready to rumble.

Jessie's feelings were written all over her face — always were. She didn't know how to be anything but real. Should take lessons from Sherry Lynn, whose "pretty girl" facade was always firmly in place, with no hint of what might be going on beneath the mask.

Riley kept his own face unreadable, wouldn't give Jackson the satisfaction of seeing the impotent rage he felt.

"Hello, Jackson," he said, his voice level and even.

Sherry Lynn took her cue from him. She knew there was "bad blood" between her husband and Jackson, that it had something to do with what'd happened in Vietnam. But he'd never revealed to her what he remembered about her cousin. He didn't share things that important and intimate with his wife. She looked from Riley to Jackson and was too self-absorbed to notice the animosity sparking between them.

"Why Jackson, it's good to see you." Then she actually stepped forward and gave him a little hug. "Where you been for so long?"

Jackson took a long, appraising look at Sherry Lynn and said, "You've certainly changed in the past five years."

She preened like a rooster.

"I hope it's for the better." The angling for a compliment was sickening.

"You look lovely," Jackson said, and while she giggled a faux protest, he turned his attention back to Riley.

"These are my friends Mañuel and José." He flicked a gesture in their direction.

"I'm sure you take them everywhere, faithful as dogs."

"Yes, guard dogs."

Jackson stepped in it when he turned to Jessie and asked innocently, "How's Davie? Better, I hope."

She took two steps toward him and punched him in the face!

Not some delicate female slap. She hit him in the jaw with her fist and all the strength she could muster. His head snapped to the side and he went down, falling backwards into the arms of his bodyguards, who clearly didn't know what they were supposed to do about an attack by a woman.

Riley grabbed her as she went after Jackson, blood in her eye, yelling at him, "Davie's just the way *you* left him, staring at the ceiling and drooling."

Gratefully, most of the congregation had already left and were chatting on the front steps, but the ones who remained were treated to quite a show. Father Donavan appeared out of nowhere, like a genie out of a bottle, and stood gawking at Jessie and the prostrate Jackson, who was being helped to his feet by his crew.

"What on earth is going on here?" The priest was clearly horrified, and shocked. That kind of outburst was not the sort of thing anybody expected from Jessie Monaghan. "This is a house of God."

Riley had an iron grip on Jessie's arm and he pulled her close and whispered urgently in her ear. "Later! We'll *take care of* Jackson. You're playing right into his hands."

And she was. As Jackson was helped to his feet he had a gloating, gotcha look on his face as bright as a lighthouse lantern.

"It's alright, Father," he said, rubbing his jaw. The beard would hide the swelling and bruise. Riley wished she'd hit him in the nose. She'd have broken it and blacked both of his eyes. "It's my fault." The magnanimity slathering his words so thick you could cut it with a butter knife. "I said something … inappropriate." He looked at Jessie innocently. "I am really sorry. Do you forgive me?"

Jessie got it now, was onto Jackson's game.

"It's not *my* forgiveness you need." Her voice was as cold as a shark in a polar ocean. "It's Davie's. You're welcome to come by the house anytime — well, not in the middle of the night like your last visit, but any other time — and ask him for it. See what he *says*."

She glared hatred at him as pure and bright as the first rays of sunrise.

"I don't know what's going on here," Father Donavan said, "but clearly the two of you have … issues. I'd be glad to talk to you both, offer counseling—"

Jackson burst out laughing. It was such a loud, inappropriate sound that it stunned everybody.

"Save your counseling for somebody who needs it, Father," he said, his voice full of mirth and his eyes full of murder. "Jessie and I will … work out our own problems, won't we, Jessie?"

"Count on it."

Chapter Thirty-Five

JESSICA MONAGHAN HAD NEVER in her life felt a wave of emotion as powerful as what rose up from the center of her being when Jackson McClusky said Davie's name. That word was *pure* and his mouth was *filthy*. She let the wave carry her forward, was barely aware of hitting him, only knew that she wanted to wrap her hands around his neck and squeeze the life out of him. No, not that civilized. She wanted to rip his throat out with her teeth.

Everything that followed was colored in red mist, fog that stole the clarity of images, blurred the edges and obscured. Mist that fell from the sky, but you could see through it. It didn't distort, it cast what mattered in the world in harsh relief, stark and centered. And clear. Absolutely clear.

In that frozen moment of time, the image of the bearded, mustached face was burned into her soul. Every line and plane, every detail. She had hated him before, when he tried to kill Davie, smother him with a pillow. She had voted to kill him, would have killed him. But then he was gone and the opportunity was lost and the hatred grew bigger every day, year after year. It settled down deep in her, a sleeping panther, curled up with its tail covering its nose. Waiting. If she hadn't been restrained, she would have tried to tear him apart with her bare hands.

Riley had whispered into her ear. "Later! We'll *take care of* Jackson. You're playing right into his hands."

And the red mist vanished as quickly as it had come. It was replaced by a chill wind that she felt ruffling her hair as it passed.

She would kill him, make no mistake about it. Nothing in her life mattered as much as killing Jackson McClusky. She'd been unable to sleep last night, obsessing over Winona McClusky's blackmail threat, and now that faded into the back recesses of her mind. She and Willie Ray and Riley would kill Jackson — *that's* what mattered. They would hurt him first, though. She couldn't imagine how or in what way, only knew he must leave this world on his journey to hell with a scream of agony on his lips.

"… with me into the bathroom and put something cool on your temples," a squeaky voice she couldn't place at first — Sherry Lynn — was saying. Jackson had turned on his heel and left the church, and now the planet was struggling to climb back into its orbit around the sun. Gravity worked again, and she could hear her own pulse thundering in her ears. She came all the way back as Sherry Lynn shoved her in front of her into the ladies' room, saying something in the squeaky voice she had affected after she'd "shed the lard" was how Riley put it. Maybe she thought the voice made her sound younger. It didn't. It made her sound like she'd just inhaled helium and it grated on the nerves of everyone who heard it. Ripping off a piece of paper towel, Sherry Lynn turned the water on and wet it. "… grandmother said the cool of the water would go right from your temples to your brain."

She let herself be led and ministered to. Tolerated water dripping out of the paper towel — and Sherry Lynn — because she had to. Managed not to sound rude with "I don't want to talk about it right now" when Sherry Lynn poked and prodded to find out whatever in the world had possessed Jessie to do such a thing!

Riley was waiting outside the bathroom when she and Sherry Lynn came out.

"Where's Drew?" Sherry Lynn asked.

"He didn't want to stay in here. He's waiting in the car."

"All by himself?"

Sherry Lynn couldn't see that Riley wasn't paying attention to her, was focused on Jessie, his eyes conveying a wealth of meaning and feeling.

"Why, he must be burning up in that hot car."

"He knows how to roll the windows down."

"Give me the car keys," Sherry Lynn said, "and I'll start the car, get the air conditioner running to cool it. I bet that boy's about to melt."

Then she turned to Jessie and did what she so often did — handed her Riley on a silver platter. Had for years sent him over to Jessie's to help out, told Riley long ago that she and Jessie were "soul mates" from the bond they'd forged driving back from Texas to Kentucky after the guard unit left for Vietnam. Sherry Lynn had gotten her Riley back, Jessie had ... well. In a display of rare unselfishness, Sherry Lynn always did anything she could to help Jessie out.

Maybe that part ought to have made Jessie feel guilty. It didn't.

"Riley's going to walk you out to your car," she said, "make sure you're okay. And if you need anything ... anything at all ..."

As soon as they got out of earshot, Jessie said, "You

shouldn't have pulled me off him."

"We'll get him. I promise." The steely determination in his voice calmed her.

Jessie looked down at her hand and her knuckles were red and swollen. She was now able to feel surprise at what she'd done — surprise, not regret.

"I … don't know what … I'm kinda out on the edge right now."

"You don't have to explain yourself to *me*! I get it. But truth is, Jackson won this round. He got what he wanted, to shock and surprise us."

"What for? What's he doing here, back in Callison County with his … goons?"

"Good question. Is he going to stay? Move back and live here—?"

"The Dawson place," Jessie said. "I drove by there a couple of weeks ago and there was all kinda activity. They were putting in surveillance cameras. Do you think maybe Jackson …?"

"It would mean he's planning to stay, didn't just stop by for a howdy and shake."

They had gotten to Jessie's car.

"What are we going to do? How are we going to get past Tweedledum and Tweedledee?"

"We'll figure it out, but we need Willie Ray."

As she opened the car door, he took her arm.

"He's coming after us, too, you know." Riley's eyes were full of concern. "The best defense is a good offense. He's got some kind of plan—"

"Think he's got a whole army of Tweedles?"

Riley shook his head. "Sneaking and ambushes are more Jackson's style." He stopped, then plunged ahead. "I think you need to hire an armed guard—"

"Don't be silly. I have an alarm system — an expensive

one."

It didn't summon the law — who would take fifteen minutes to get there, if they showed up at all, and wouldn't be on her side when they did. Besides making a god-awful noise, the alarm would sound in the homes of her four closest neighbors — one of whom was her brother, Lanny, who had two strapping teenage sons. They could and *would* come to her aid immediately — half a dozen or more men who would definitely be on her side.

"That's not enough—"

"It'll have to do. No guard, but I'll be packing everywhere I go." She looked full into his eyes. "You do the same — be careful."

JACKSON WALKED TO HIS CAR, sandwiched in between Mañuel and José.

He refused to allow his hand to move to his jaw, his fingers to probe the ache, the swelling and bruise he was sure was there, hidden by his beard.

Coming down off the coke high, the sense of invulnerability fading, Jackson was just beginning to grasp what a monumental mistake this had been. Oh, he'd managed to convince himself it was a good idea, told himself it would fit into his plan. He'd go to the church and startle them, rattle them, shock and frighten them. He'd given in to the craving, sniffed a line of coke this morning, and all his careful planning fell apart. Coming here was *not* part of the grand plan. He'd come because he was frustrated, had been sitting around waiting for word from Mama Bert for almost two weeks. He'd lost his patience, lost his cool, traded in the element of surprise for the satisfaction of seeing the impotent rage on their faces.

And he would pay for that. You always paid for it when you screwed up. He might have doomed his whole plan, maybe doomed himself — all because he had lost control. He had disciplined himself for years not to take action in response to some momentary impulse. He'd lost everything five years ago for not thinking ahead.

Then he got up this morning despondent, depressed — sniffed a little happy juice to make himself feel better, and had thrown everything he'd learned out the—

Stop it!

The only thing worse than making a mistake was obsessing over it, focusing all your energy regretting it. Okay, he'd messed up. *Move on!* Stop overdramatizing. He hadn't doomed his whole plan to failure. He'd been in Callison County so long, word about him was bound to leak out soon, and at least this way he didn't have to wonder if they'd found out, and he got to see their reactions.

He hadn't expected Jessie to punch him, though. Riley maybe, but not Jessie. He didn't know her very well, she'd just been Davie's girlfriend in high school and his wife after but he and Davie weren't exactly chummy. The blow galled him more than he wanted to admit. Jessica Monaghan was taller than he was, not bigger and stronger, but the woman had three or four inches on him. And he'd always hated to be around tall women. They made him feel inferior. And the loathing in her eyes. Surely someone filled with that much rage would be controlled by it, would let their anger lead them to places cold reasoning would never take them. Jackson had to be better than that.

Seated alone in the back seat of the van, Jackson reached up and touched his face, allowed himself to feel the pain and the rage and the humiliation. Jessica Monaghan would pay for this! They all would.

Chapter Thirty-Six

WILLIE RAY HATED to leave Minnesota, was dreadful worried about the crops outside Martinsburg, exposed like they was with crews working around the clock to get the weed into the barn 'fore somebody spotted it. He didn't like leaving that job to Beetle and the others, but he'd worked with them non-stop for ten days — with no problems *yet* — and he had six more sites to see to and was already almost a week overdue.

It'd be a sight warmer in Missouri than it'd been in Minnesota, though the sunshine wasn't the only reason Willie Ray liked flying into Empire Township. He'd become friends with the man who operated the little airport. Oh, he got to know all the folks who ran the little airports in Kansas and Iowa, Wisconsin and Nebraska and Arkansas. Making friends was just how Willie Ray rolled. Since he always had to hang out for awhile after he landed waiting for one of his men to come to the airport to fetch him, he usually had time to chitchat.

But Jack Broczkowski was a rung above all the others. Willie Ray glanced over into the co-pilot's empty seat occupied now by a gold box with a big red bow on it. Inside was a bottle of Double Springs bourbon, with a special label "Brewed especially for Jack Broczkowski." He knew Jack would take one look at it and feel like he'd won the lottery.

Willie Ray was flying VFR, low because he didn't really want to show up on anybody's radar — literal as well as figurative — and he spotted the big steeple of the Empire Township Methodist Church off to his left. He banked, did a wing-around on the steeple and headed toward the outskirts of the little town where a strip of pavement, two corrugated tin hangars and a gas pump marked the Richland County Airport that Jack managed.

From the air, Willie Ray could see the little trailer house office, positioned at the midway point of the lone runway on the north side. And he could also see the little building to the east of the other structures, set far back in the woods that housed Jack's treasure, hidden from prying eyes. The bottle of Double Springs was a thank you gift from Willie Ray, expressing his gratitude for Jack allowing Willie Ray to share it.

It'd been one of the coolest things Willie Ray'd ever done.

WILLIE RAY SITS *in the overstuffed chair in the trailer house office of the Richland County Airport watching Jack Broczkowski light a cigar.*

"Can't smoke 'em at home — the wife, you know," Jack says, taking a big puff and blowing the smoke out in little rings into the room.

"How'd you do that, them rings?" Willie Ray asks. "I always wanted to do that, tried and tried with cigarettes. Reckon cigar smoke is thicker or something?"

"A good friend, a good man taught me how. He could blow rings inside of rings!"

"Would he teach me how?"

Jack's face stiffens.

"He's dead."

"I'm sorry."

"Killed in a fire fight."

Now it's Willie Ray's turn to stiffen. "You was in 'Nam?"

"First Brigade, 3rd Infantry Division. Stationed just south of the DMZ."

He indicates the scar that slices across Willie Ray's cheek like a bolt of lightning.

"I had you pegged for a vet. Figured 'Nam's where you got that." *He pauses for a beat. "My brother got killed there. He was in the 101st Airborne Division, perimeter security for a New Hampshire National Guard artillery battery in a place called Fire Base Eagle's Nest."*

The room suddenly seems too small. There's not quite enough air to breathe.

"My brother got killed there, too. Only we called it Tweety Bird because—"

Jack's eyes widen.

"You was **there?**"

Willie Ray nods and continues because he has to, is compelled to. Whenever he talks about that time the words come out like he's vomiting and he can't seem to stop. "See ... an eagle builds a nest high up in a tree so it can see everything, locate its prey. But Tweety Bird's in a cage with a cat prowling around right outside."

"Charlie wrote home that the place was a massacre waiting to happen. He was due to ship out in less than a week."

They sit in silence for a time while their relationship settles into its new shape, takes on more substance.

Jack blows another circle ring of smoke, sets the front legs of his chair back down on the floor and says, "I got something I wanna show you."

He takes Willie Ray out of the office building around the back of the two hangars into the woods. Ain't even a trail to follow, but Jack knows where he's going and finally Willie Ray sees a small, corrugated metal building nestled in the trees about half a mile from Jack's office. Though it's surrounded by woods, there's an open area in front of the bay doors. When they get to the building, Willie Ray lets his eye travel down the length of the smooth area and can see it leads to the far end of the airport's single runway.

Jack picks up a rock that isn't a rock next to the building, takes a key from it to unlock the padlock on the bay doors, opens them and Willie Ray's jaw drops. Sitting before him is a ... no, it can't be ...

"Is that a—?"

"A Boeing-Stearman Model 75 Kadet, built in 1942."

Willie Ray had never seen a vintage biplane before, not up close anyway, just at airshows, performing acrobatics. It was in mint condition, painted bright yellow — a color Willie Ray thought of as school-bus yellow, with a red stripe down the length of the fuselage and a blue tail.

"My father bought it surplus after World War II and used it as a crop duster for fifteen or twenty years, then stuck it in a barn. It sat there gathering dust until Charlie was a teenager. Me and him restored it, took us three years."

Willie Ray walks slowly around the biplane in awe.

"Wanna take her up?" Jack asks.

While Jack moves the chocks from in front of the wheels and performs the preflight inspection of the aircraft, Willie Ray goes back to the little office and tapes a note on the front door.

"Earl, go into town and have dinner at that steak house — on me. I'll be back before dark."

When he returns to the small hangar and starts to climb carefully up into the cockpit, Jack says, "You do know, don't you, that the pilot sits in the backseat *of a biplane."*

"How come?"

"Center of gravity. The pilot's weight is aligned with the weight of the fuel tanks and counterbalancing the weight of the engine." Jack grins. "And it helps to be sitting right over the landing gear, keeps the tail down so the prop don't cut a hole in the runway."

Jack gestures toward the backseat pilot's position. "Have at it."

The following couple of hours in the air were by far and away the best time Willie Ray had ever spent flying. Jack takes him sight-seeing all over the county, urges him to fly low — like Willie Ray loves to do in Callison County.

"That there's the high school," he yells from the seat in the front. "'Bout got kicked out of there half a dozen times."

Over the town square, Jack points out the old courthouse. Willie Ray doesn't say nothing about the courthouse in Brewster, which was set on fire by Union soldiers during the Civil War. ... 'cause it might be some of Jack's forbearers had been holding the torches. Willie Ray wasn't right sure which side Missouri'd been on.

"Empire Township Lake," Jack calls out. "There's at least half a dozen lakes within thirty miles of here, but wouldn't nothing do but for the city to build another one!"

"You fish there?"

"Naaa, got a better place to fish."

He tells Willie Ray to take the plane up off tree-top level and to fly north from there over woods and farms until Jack points to a pond, a barn with faded red paint and an old house below.

"My parents' farm. Couldn't bring myself to sell it when they passed. Best fishing in the county is in that pond. That barn's where me and Charlie worked on the plane. I hid it there so's my first wife couldn't lay claim to it in the divorce settlement."

As they're pushing the plane backwards into its little hangar, Willie Ray nods to the word painted on the nose — "Rabbit," with the top of the two b's made into bunny ears and a nose painted beneath them.

"Where'd the name come from? I'd have called it something cool like the Red Baron."

Jack reaches up and touches the painted word.

"I didn't name it. Charlie did. This was his *plane. Daddy gave it to him and he paid for all the restoration. I come into the barn one day while the paint was still wet."* His eyes take on a thousand-yard stare. *"Charlie put his arm around my shoulders and said, 'I named it after you, Jack Rabbit.'"* He clears his throat. *"My big brother was like that."*

And Willie Ray says, "So was mine."

WILLIE RAY LOOKED at the windsock next to the office of the little airport, banked and turned to land into the wind. He parked the Skylane in the wide piece of asphalt that served as a parking lot for aircraft. Willie Ray'd only ever seen one other airplane here, and today he had the whole space to himself.

Jack was on the phone when Willie Ray entered, wrangling with somebody about the truck that was supposed to have delivered aviation fuel to service his pump three days ago. He motioned Willie Ray to sit down and ended the call, but didn't favor Willie Ray with his lopsided grin.

Willie Ray held out the gold box with the red bow, but Jack still didn't smile.

"Might be there's some trouble about," Jack said. "The state police come out here a couple of days ago asking all kinda questions about the planes that landed and who was flying 'em."

Willie Ray's stomach dropped through his body to the floor. He had never told Jack what occasioned his trips to Missouri, and Jack had never asked. He was a smart man, though, figured out that whatever Willie Ray was doing was *private* business.

"I played dumb, said I didn't know none of the pilots. Just filled up they tanks and they left. Didn't say who they was looking for specific, or what for, but said it was confidential, that I wasn't s'posed to tell anybody they'd been asking around. They took my log books, though, so they got all the names."

As soon as Earl picked Willie Ray up at the airport, Willie Ray told him the state police had been at the airport, asking nosey questions. Earl turned white.

"You seen anything peculiar, anything at all?" Willie Ray asked.

Earl shook his head. "Nope." Then he changed his tune. "Well, there was the one thing … this county-mounty, deputy sheriff come rolling up to the house and said he was looking for some cows that'd got out of a field down the road, wanted to know had I seen them. I told him I hadn't seen no cows. I was scared to death he was gonna ask did I mind if he looked around, because he was scoping everything out while he was sitting there. But he didn't, just thanked me and drove away."

"You think he really was just looking for lost cows?"

"Well, at the time I did."

"Who calls the sheriff when their cows get out?"

Earl shook his head. "I didn't think of that. Maybe they was out on the road or something."

"Let's get out to the farm. I wanna talk to the other hands."

About half the weed here was still in the field, the other half in the barn drying. It was a really good-looking crop. Though everybody on the crew knew how to do it, Willie Ray had personally sexed the plants, getting rid of the males. Had instructed the hands to check the females every couple of days for hermaphrodites.

What should Willie Ray do? The law had come

snooping around! Not some random farmer who might wonder about that green stuff growing behind six rows of dead corn — the *law*! Should he keep fishing or cut bait? The thought of just bailing out, walking away from millions of dollars' worth of weed made him physically sick. But he couldn't ask these men to keep working if he believed it was too dangerous. The marijuana laws varied from state to state, but considering the amount of weed they'd have on their hands if they got busted, they were looking at manufacturing marijuana charges, which he thought would draw prison time in just about every state.

Willie Ray didn't like knowing the fate of this crew of men was in his hands. If he said to stay, they'd stick. Then, if they got caught, it'd be on him.

Soon's he got to the farm, he was gonna call in, talk to Jessie.

Chapter Thirty-Seven

ELI HAPPENED to be working his shift at the headphones when the call to Jessica Monaghan's phone number came through. In the world of panning for gold in wiretapping, it was a nugget big enough to pay off the mortgage on Eli's house. It came in from the 314 area code.

CALLER: *We got ourselves a problem.*
    Monaghan: You don't know the half of it.
    Caller: What—?
    Monaghan: You go first. Did somebody see through the dead corn?

"WILLIE RAY TAGGART," Eli said to Zucarelli, who was tracking all incoming calls. Zucarelli was exceptionally proficient at tracing calls, but it was hopeless if the call was short.

. . .

TAGGART: *Nope. Ten days around-the-clock work and the guys are ready to drop, but so far, so good.*

Monaghan: So what is the problem?

Taggart: Later. Your turn now. What is it I don't know about?

Monaghan: Winona McClusky wants a million dollars or she's going to tell the FBI all about us.

ZUCARELLI GAVE ELI A THUMBS-UP. "It's a rural line in area code 314. Nearest town's Empire Township, Missouri."

Well, now they could scratch Missouri off their list.

After Commonwealth's Attorney Winona McClusky unloaded on Jessica Monaghan on Saturday — sealing her own felony extortion charge — Eli had called in and unloaded on his superiors that one case in one state had just become eight cases in eight states.

"We need to subpoena phone records on the Monaghans', Taggarts' and Hannackers' numbers going back two years," he advised, "track down the exact location of every long-distance call to those numbers from anywhere in Minnesota, Arkansas, Nebraska, Kansas, Wisconsin, or Iowa."

Eli spent the next three hours on the phone, a lumberjack hopping from one log to another to prevent a log jam, as resources to take on this suddenly-expanded case were allocated.

"I worked Operation South Bend Fence two years ago," Agent Peterson told him during a break between calls. "This is shaping up to be that — just with marijuana."

Eli swallowed hard.

In Operation South Bend Fence, undercover operatives made more than four hundred buys of nearly a million dollars' worth of goods from thieves at a South Bend, Indiana warehouse. Forty FBI agents and 140 state and local officers arrested more than 150 subjects, clearing almost six hundred local cases.

Eli Bradigan had signed on to ride one bucking bronco; now he found himself in charge of the whole rodeo.

TAGGART: *Seriously?*
   Monaghan: It gets worse.
   Taggart: What could be worse than that?
   Monaghan: Jackson's back.

THERE WAS silence on the other end of the line, then a single word: "Jackson" slathered in so much loathing it was more growl than word.

Who's Jackson? Eli wondered.

TAGGART: *You seen him?*
   Monaghan: At church on Sunday. I punched him in the face.
   Taggart: At church?
   Monaghan: Uh huh.
   Taggart: Break his nose?
   Monaghan: Tried.
   Taggart: We're gonna break more than his nose. I'll be home soon's I can get there, help out in the barn tomorrow morning, fly out about noon. I'll be home before suppertime.
   Monaghan: Now it's your turn. What was the trouble you called about?
   Taggart: We got ourselves a nosey sheriff here.
   Monaghan: Nosey how?
   Taggart: Nosey as in coming to the house, saying there were some

cattle got loose on the farm down the road, wanted to know had we seen 'em.

Monaghan: Who calls the sheriff when their cattle get out?

Taggart: That's what I said.

Monaghan: The sheriff just left, then, didn't ask to look around the property?

Taggart: Nope. Never even got out of his cruiser. My buddy at the airport said the state police had come looking to find out who was flying planes in and out. Of course, they coulda been looking for all kinda stuff.

Monaghan: What do you think we should do?

Taggart: That's what I called to ask you.

Monaghan: The sheriff and the state police ... I say we pack it in, harvest what's already in the barn, load up everything and—

Taggart: And leave the rest in the field? That there's some serious coin.

Monaghan: Yeah ... but we got bigger fish to fry.

THERE WAS A PAUSE.

TAGGART: *Uh huh — Jackson. See you tomorrow.*

Monaghan: I'll make a pot of beans.

Taggart: And cornbread.

THE LINE WENT DEAD.

Eli leaned back in the chair and took off the headphones. His mind was spinning, but he wouldn't allow himself to go running down some rabbit trail — *Jackson.* Why was the guy so important? But Eli, too, had bigger fish to fry.

"Phone number belongs to Clara Westford. Called the

courthouse and they said the 'Westford estate' owns a farm on Rural Route 3, a mile past Dunston Pike," Zucarelli reported.

"This is our chance to catch Willie Ray Taggart with his hands in the cookie jar. We've got to move on that operation tomorrow morning."

"If the county-mounties don't beat us to it," Bill Thomas said. "They sniff something."

"Just got to hold them off a day … I want to know why the state police and sheriff's department are snooping around." Eli turned to Agent Peterson — he was the kind of people-person who could grease skids. "Contact the St. Louis office — talk to Special Agent Winston Spencer, he's a friend of mine. Tell him we need the locals to back off so they don't blow our bust."

He looked at Bill Thomas. "Your go-bag ready? I intend to be standing outside that barn tomorrow morning. I want to put the cuffs on Mr. Willie Ray Taggart personally."

Chapter Thirty-Eight

RILEY HANNACKER WOULD HAVE SAID that nothing in the world was powerful enough to distract his racing mind from thoughts of the FBI, blackmail ... and Jackson McClusky.

But he was wrong.

Once he'd called Brady Garrison at Land's End to set up a time to take Drew to the horse farm to select a foal, Riley had trouble holding onto his own excitement. Part of it was living a childhood fantasy vicariously through his son. He wished he'd taken the time to have a horse as a kid. But mostly it was because the more he thought about it, the more he became convinced that a foal was just the thing to drag Drew out of his depressive funk and back into the world of light and sunshine again. What nine-year-old boy could resist falling in love with a toothpick-legged, gangly baby horse? And love was the thing to rescue Drew. Falling in love with something else might prove to be the thing to move the boy beyond his grief over the grandfather he'd lost.

Drew was surprised to see Riley waiting outside his school when class let out before the lunch bell.

"Where are we going?" The apprehension Riley heard in his voice broke Riley's heart.

"To Land's End. There's a horse there I need to talk to."

As he climbed into Riley's truck, tossing his books on the floorboard, Riley watched anticipation war with fear on the boy's features, and they appeared to come to a truce because a flicker of anticipation lit the boy's face.

"What is it you need to talk to a horse about?" Drew asked. Riley cast a sideways glance in his direction, surprised that he could still be struck speechless by how much he loved the boy, and what a perfect little boy he was. His good looks could have made him a fortune as a model, not that Drew needed anything to make him a fortune. With sun-bleached blond hair and tanned skin, coupled with Sherry Lynn's almost-purple eyes, the boy would have graced the front of any magazine cover. Eyelashes and eyebrows so pale they were almost invisible — just like his namesake, Willie Ray's older brother, Andy.

Thoughts of Jackson threatened to break free and invade Riley's mind like a swarm of locusts, but he fought them off. Other than Drew's coloring, however, the boy no longer was the "spitting image" of the young man who'd been blown apart in Vietnam. As Drew'd grown older, he looked more and more like his grandfather, Nate. Might be that was wishful thinking on Riley's part, but others had commented on the similarity, too.

"Okay, joke. Truth is I need to talk to Brady Garrison. I thought since you got out of school early today, you'd enjoy going with me to look at the horses. But if you'd rather not — your mommy will be in Louisville shopping all day but I could take you to—"

"No, no. I want to see the horses, but—"

Riley heard the question coming and headed it off at the pass.

"It'll just be you, me and Brady. The other hands will be busy with the thoroughbreds and I doubt that mayor-for-life Malcolm Murdock is even home. I know his wife and kids are on the Baptist church's trip to Washington, D.C. this week." In the four years the Cornbread Mafia had spent doing their processing in the fancy horse barns at Land's End, Riley had only caught sight of Mr. Murdock half a dozen times.

Riley resolutely grabbed the conversational ball and dribbled it in another direction.

"So…. tell me which of the things your mom has planned for your party do you hate most?"

Drew grinned and relaxed.

"The bouncy castle."

"Really? I figured it'd be the clown."

Drew rolled his eyes.

"I forgot about the stupid clown. I got to pick and I asked for a hobo clown because those are usually sad clowns, aren't they? Not like the ones with red hair and big shoes that squirt water out of a flower at you."

"A hobo clown was probably the best choice, but who knows what this bozo—?"

"That's his name, Bozo the Clown."

"Not a good sign. Sounds like red hair, big shoes and squirting flower to me."

Riley didn't pass by the front entrance to the farm this time, as was his custom. Instead, he drove beneath the big archway that proclaimed "Land's End" in letters five feet tall, made from wrought iron to match the ornate gate and the fencing along the driveway up to the house.

Normally, Riley would have driven to an unnamed

gravel road a mile beyond the front entrance. The gravel road ended at an old barn, but behind the barn, a dirt road lead through a tangle of weeds and bushes into the woods, where it was little more than an animal track. That road ended in a barbed wire fence with No Trespassing signs on the posts. You had to get out of your truck and go to the farthest post. It appeared to be stuck in the ground like the other posts but it wasn't, and you could move it and the barbed wire fence back out of the way, and drive through the opening. There appeared to be no road at all beyond there, but if you drove along the fence line out of the woods into a grassy field where black angus cattle grazed, then up a small rise and down the back side of it, you'd come to a huge building that looked like all the other horse barns at Land's End. It wasn't. For the past five growing seasons, the not-a-barn had served as a "safe spot" for Cornbread Mafia workers to process their crops for market.

You couldn't see the Murdock mansion from the road. It was set back behind stately oak trees that stood sentinel, soldiers at attention all the way down the lane to the drive-way. They turned aside when the driveway forked and drove around to the back of the house, past a grape arbor trellis so thick with vines it extended like a tunnel all the way from a side door to the driveway.

Riley pulled up into a parking area beyond the house. There were a couple of vehicles parked there already, but nobody was in sight. The berm of bushes that formed a fence for the backyard of the Murdock house was about fifty yards away.

Brady Garrison came out of the barn as Riley and Drew got out of the truck.

"Brady, this here's my boy, Drew."

Brady held out his hand and Drew did as he'd been

taught. Riley had instructed him on the fine art of hand-shaking, told him to grab a man's hand in a firm grip and look him in the eye. That's how Nate had said it ought to be done.

"Glad to meet you, Mr. Garrison," Drew said, and didn't sound the least bit glad at all, but he said the words and that in itself was pretty good for a nine-year-old.

"Good to meet you, too, son. Your daddy here says you like horses."

"I'd *like* to like horses," Drew amended, "but I've never spent any time around them."

"Well, I got something you need to see. Got me four brand new foals, born this spring, ain't but a few months old, cuter'n puppies and even more playful."

Drew's face actually lit up then and he favored them both with a genuine smile.

"Foals — *baby* horses?"

"Follow me."

Brady led them into the barn, which was a huge, well-ventilated area with doors on the front, both ends and the back.

"This here's the pony barn. Them others out there," he gestured to the clump of buildings farther down, "them's for the thoroughbreds, the money horses. Though my ponies have a lot of sleep-overs in the show barns." He explained the uses of pony horses as "besties" for the thoroughbreds as they passed stall after stall. Some horses stuck their heads out over the stall gates as they passed, others nickered, all of them appeared glad to see Brady.

They came to a pen by the north side door to the barn. It was bigger than a stall and enclosed by boards spaced far apart so it was easy to see in. All four of the foals in the pen came to stick their soft velvet noses out through the slats when they saw the people gathered outside.

The look on Drew's face when he saw them — his smile would have melted frost off a windowpane on a snowy morning.

"Them two's fillies." Brady indicated a small foal, a paint — mostly brown but with a wide splotch of white around her belly, and a white mane and tail. "I call her Jelly Bean, and that there one is Pumpkin." The one called Pumpkin was slightly larger, her coat a rich russet color with a black mane and tail. "Them two bruisers is Bagel and Coco — short for Coconut." The colts he indicated were slightly larger than the fillies, but not much. Coco was an appaloosa. His head and neck were a chocolate brown, though his mane and tail were black and he had a white mask on his face. From his shoulders back was white with gray, black and brown splotches and spots. His front legs were brown, like his neck. His back legs were brown, too, from the rump down. The one called Bagel was the biggest of the lot — a shiny black horse, dark as coal, with a white marking down his face that looked like a lightning strike, and white feet — looked like he was wearing white gym socks.

"You know much about horses?" Brady asked Drew, knowing the answer, but kindly trying to draw the boy out. Drew absolutely did not like strangers, but he took immediately to Brady.

"No sir, not hardly nothing at all."

"Well then, let me give you a brief education. Horses stay pregnant for eleven months and we try to breed them so the foals are born in the spring — that way they got the whole summer outside to grow and develop. Foals are almost always born at night, and it don't take long at all. Takes a human mama hours, sometimes days to give birth, but a horse don't usually take but a few minutes. Many's the time I've been sitting outside a stall, waiting. I go take a leak, come back and the mama's in there licking her newborn. Being born quick and at night — that's how horses in the wild keep their babies away from predators. A foal can walk two hours after it's born."

"Their legs are so … long," Drew marveled.

"That they are, son. A horse is born with legs about as long as they'll ever be. They'll grow another ten or twenty percent, but it ain't hard to estimate how big the adult's gonna be by looking at the baby. These here is weanlings, just got weaned from they mamas. You got to keep them away from they mamas for at least a month so's her milk'll dry up, but the foals need to be around other horses. Horses is social creatures, don't do well at all by themselves. You need to put the foals with other horses and not just other foals — adults, some barren mares, maybe, or geldings. The mares will teach them manners."

"He ain't talking about not talking with their mouths full," Riley put in.

"Foals will make this noise — sounds like baby talk, when they first meet an adult horse. It's their way of saying, 'I'm just a little fella, and I ain't gonna hurt nobody.'"

Brady reached into his pocket, pulled out a carrot, broke it into pieces and held the pieces out to Drew.

"You're about to become their new best friend."

"Can I?" Drew was awed.

Brady reached for the latch of the gate. "Go on in. Hold the pieces of carrot on your palm, so they can use their lips to pick 'em up. Hold a carrot in your fingers and you might get bit."

He pushed the tall gate inward and Drew went into the pen. Then Brady closed the gate behind him.

"Let's you and me have a talk," Brady said and drew Riley back away from the pen, where Drew was giggling as the little horses jostled him and each other to get at the treats.

He kept his voice low.

"Might want to know that they's folks asking around about you."

"What folks? And what are they asking about?"

"Nosey questions — the kind that start with w's — where, what and who. Wanting to know about … seed."

Chapter Thirty-Nine

Willie Ray didn't get a whole lot of sleep after he talked to Jessie last night, but he figured she and Riley was prob'ly starin' up at the ceiling, too.

Jackson.

The name bounced around like a bowling ball in Willie Ray's head, crashing into every other thought and plan and emotion, knocking every other thing out of the way.

Sure, Willie Ray was still scared some Minnesota farmer driving down the road by the Larsson farm was gonna see that green stuff growing behind the stalks of dead corn and decide maybe he'd ought to tell somebody about it.

Sure, he was still worried about the state police checking the airport logs and the deputy sheriff out looking for lost cows.

And yeah … blackmailed for a million dollars! Oh, Willie Ray s'posed he could lay hands on that kinda money and wouldn't miss it, but blackmail was nasty business, and what was to guarantee Winona McClusky wouldn't wanna keep sucking on that teat?

But Jackson …

Everything in life paled in the white-hot glare of Willie Ray's loathing, his … oh, call it what it was … his *obsession* with revenge.

Nothing in Willie Ray's life mattered to him as much as making Jackson McClusky pay for what he'd done to Andy. He was itching to get to the airport and fly home so the three of them who'd voted — three black rocks — to kill Jackson five years ago could figure out how they was going to do it.

At the same time, he needed to make sure this operation could close up shop and get the hell outta Dodge before the sheriff come looking for more livestock. There was one barn almost full of drying weed now, and Willie Ray figured to put everybody to work in it. Trimming weed was long, tedious business.

The crew had started soon's they got the word from Jessie last night. Didn't take a whole lot of equipment to harvest weed — sharp scissors for trimming buds, pruners for big branches, tables, rubbing alcohol, rags, gloves and a big bowl to put the buds in. Some of the men had got hold of silk aprons. The resin didn't stick to silk. Those that didn't have gloves rubbed olive or vegetable oil on their hands to keep the sticky resin from building up.

They had set up tables inside the old barn, running from one end to the other — long tables they'd bought out of a church basement where they was used for food during socials, wedding cake and punch, that kinda thing. They'd got the folding chairs separate, hadn't bought cushions for them yet so they was all gonna have sore backsides from sitting hour after hour on the hard metal. The workers would swap out jobs to move around some — taking the plants off the drying rails, cutting off the fan leaves to create piles of buds for those seated at the tables to trim.

The barn backed up on the woods and had only the two bay doors in front. When they took their first break before lunch — a ten-minute cigarette break for the smokers — Willie Ray sat down, leaned back against the back wall and lit up. After the break, it'd be his turn at trimming buds and he was figuring how he was going to get the sticky cleaned off his clothes so he could fly out at noon when he glanced at the ceiling and noticed a good-sized hole in the barn roof above him. He'd have swore there wasn't no holes in the barn roof when they'd come for a look-see before they rented it.

He looked up at Phil Adams, who'd just come over to bum a light for his cigarette.

"Was there always a hole in the roof up there — I never seen it."

Phil looked where Willie Ray pointed. "Must be a couple shingles got tore loose from the roof. We had a lotta wind the other day."

Willie Ray stood, stomped out his just-lit cigarette. "I'm gonna climb up there and see if there's any way to patch that thing. All we need is for a storm to come up and get all this dry weed wet."

Jessie'd said once that Davie was "a little hinky" about heights so she and her brother had taken turns working on the top rail when they were housing tobacco. Willie Ray was like a squirrel climbing trees. Using the ladder to the empty hay loft, he reached up, grabbed a roof strut and hauled himself up onto it. Bent over at the waist beneath the slanted roof, he edged his way out on the strut until the hole was directly above him. It was probably eighteen inches across, but not that wide. Almost looked like some-thing'd come crashing down through it because all the roof boards was jagged there, like they'd broke. He'd need to go outside and climb up on the roof to see—

Suddenly, a loud voice called out from beyond the front bay doors, like somebody talking through a megaphone. Everyone froze.

Ever after that, Willie Ray was never able to say exactly what the voice had said. Something like, "You inside the barn. I'm Special Agent—" … something that sounded like Bradley. The next words was clear, though. "—with the Federal Bureau of Investigation."

The words "under arrest," Willie Ray thought, but maybe he imagined that part. He thought he heard "surrounded" and "hands over your heads" too, but his heart was pounding so loud in his ears he couldn't be sure. When both big bay doors began to open from outside, instinct and panic joined hands and the two of them grabbed hold of Willie Ray Taggart and took his body for a ride.

Chapter Forty

It happened after Drew and his father started back to their pickup truck. Daddy'd parked beside some other pickup trucks behind the hedge that hid the Murdocks' backyard from view.

Drew felt like he was going to jump right out of his skin.

Coco, the appaloosa — though Daddy said Drew could change the name, call the horse anything he wanted. After all, Coco was Drew's *very own horse.*

Drew didn't know if he'd change the name or not. That was too big a decision to make on the spot and Mr. Garrison said he could take his time, wasn't no hurry. He liked Coco, but maybe after he took the time to think about it, he would come up with a better name — one *he* had given to *his own horse.* Yeah, he'd change his name. He'd come up with something amazing!

He'd listened to Mr. Garrison's descriptions of what it would be like to raise a foal, he'd listened and tried to concentrate but his excitement had made concentrating hard. That was okay, though, he told himself. He had plenty of time to learn. The foal would need to stay with its buddies and the rest of the herd until he was a lot older. But Daddy would take him to visit his foal often, he'd promised, and once his mother got used to the idea that Daddy had given Drew a horse without asking her in advance, he figured his mother would take him as well.

She'd only be mad about the part where she wasn't consulted. The actual fact of him having the little horse ... even his mom couldn't come up with a sensible reason why that was dangerous.

Drew had so many thoughts to think he really didn't have room in his mind for all of them. There were fantasies to conjure up and enjoy, about the day he was finally able to take Coco out for a ride. Put a saddle on him and get up on his back and ride him, ride him all over the farm. And even get him to gallop, as soon as he got out of sight of the house, of course.

And taking care of her. Once she was his horse, Daddy had made it very clear that the horse would be Drew's responsibility. Daddy would help, guide and show him how, but the actual doing of things, from trimming his hooves to combing his mane, would all fall to Drew.

As they got near the truck, Mr. Garrison called out to Daddy.

"I got one more thing you need to know."

"I'll be right back," Daddy said and walked back to the barn. Drew continued toward the truck and when he got there, he sat down on the huge front bumper, his mind spinning.

He was so concentrated on what was going on inside his head, he didn't even pay attention to when the cramping started. He'd felt a twinge or two when he was in the barn but there was far too much going on then to be bothered by a little thing like stomach cramps.

Drew shouldn't have ignored them. When they struck, you needed to pay attention. Now, they were so strong they took his breath away.

Mommy took him to Dr. Callahan in town, wanted to take him to some other doctors in Louisville, but Daddy wouldn't let her. Dr. Callahan had said Drew had a "delicate stomach," which was why he'd thrown up often as a baby and when he was little. But when the vomiting stopped, diarrhea took its place. Dr. Callahan said it might be a sign that he had a thing … it was initials, an I and a B, irritable bowel syndrome. Daddy and Mommy'd argued about it a bunch of times, with Daddy saying it was an emotional response to "all he's been through," saying he never had it "before." Drew knew before what. Mommy worried he had something like cancer and yelled that if anything happened to Drew it would be Daddy's fault.

All Drew knew was that sometimes he would get awful stomach cramps and if he didn't get to the bathroom quick … He had only messed his pants one time and it had been the most awful experience of his life. He'd been outside playing and wouldn't go inside until it was too late. But nobody knew about that time. He had cleaned up the mess, cleaned himself and cleaned it out of his pants, washed his pants in the bathroom sink, and then sneaked them into the laundry basket for Mommy to wash. He threw his underwear away. After that, he vowed to be more careful.

Another cramp hit him like a lightning bolt and he looked frantically around for Daddy. He had gone back into the horse barn to talk to Mr. Garrison. What could Drew do? And he better come up with something *quick*.

There was a bathroom in the barn where Daddy

worked sometimes because he'd mentioned it. But Drew didn't know if any of the other barns had bathrooms. He didn't think they would. Who puts a bathroom in a barn?

A cramp struck hard and didn't go away. That meant it'd be soon, real soon.

Where could he—?

He could go in the Murdocks' house. Daddy'd said Mrs. Murdock, Katie and Darren were gone on that trip to Washington and maybe Mr. Murdock wasn't home either. Go through the hedge, across the backyard, in the back door — there was a bathroom right inside the back door. He knew that because Mommy had made Daddy get the builders to tear out a coat closet beside the back door of their house and turn it into a bathroom because Mommy had been in the Murdocks' house and they had one like that and it'd be so handy to have one there.

Daddy had argued a little bit, pointed out that if anybody had to go bad, there were bathrooms and showers in the bath house around the pool, but that wasn't good enough for Mommy. He remembered hearing Daddy grumble, "If the Murdocks had a dead horse, you would want one, too."

Drew'd never been inside the Murdock house, but …

The decision was made for him when the urgency took hold of his belly and he had to go *somewhere*. Diving through the shrubbery on the back of the backyard, he ran as fast as he was able to run, kinda doubled over in pain and holding his butt cheeks tight together. He couldn't make a mess in his pants here, on the day he got a new horse!

He ran up onto the back porch and just barged in the back door. That was unthinkably rude, but the alternative was worse — he'd just explain to whoever he ran into that he had to go.

Sure enough, right inside the back door was a smaller door on the right and when he shoved it open, he found what he was looking for. He wouldn't have lasted another thirty seconds. As it was he almost couldn't wait until he got his pants unbuckled and down.

He squeezed his eyes shut as relief washed over him, though the cramping continued. The stink was awful and he looked around and found candles on the back of the toilet. Mommy kept candles in the bathroom to make it smell better. As the cramping eased off, he took a match out of the little box of them, and lit the candles, smelled cinnamon and vanilla — but mostly, he could just smell poop.

Daddy was going to wonder where he'd run off to when he went back to the truck and Drew was missing. But he'd understand as soon as he found out the reason.

The whole thing didn't take very long and the cramping stopped, which usually meant the episode was over, though sometimes there were what Daddy called "encores" and he had to go again. But Drew was in some-body else's house and all he wanted was to get out of there. It might be he would be lucky enough to get out the back door without anybody even knowing he'd been there.

With his tummy still feeling "iffy" he stood and pulled his pants back up, flipped the switch beside the light switch on the wall and a bathroom fan came on. He buckled his belt, stood for a moment, listening, but he couldn't hear anything because of the fan. He'd just have to make a run for it, bolt out of the house and hope nobody saw. Yanking the door open, he plowed right into somebody, someone who was standing just outside. He kinda bounced off and hit the wall beside the door.

"Whoa there, partner," the person said, who'd been

knocked a little off balance by the blow. "What's your hurry?"

The voice.

Drew recognized the voice.

And then his worst nightmare came true. Lifting his eyes, he looked into the face of the Thing.

Chapter Forty-One

WILLIE RAY DIDN'T *DECIDE* to stand up into the hole in the roof. He just did it. But the opening wasn't near big enough. Grabbing a piece of wood along the edge, he wrenched it free to make the open space wider, but it was still too small. Muscling another loose board aside with his shoulder, he got his head and right arm out, then pushed upward with all the strength in his legs. Boards bowed upward as he shoved and wiggled frantically, feeling the jagged end of one board gouging a furrow through the flesh on his left side. That hurt so bad he didn't even feel the nail — had to have been a nail — slice his chest open from his collarbone to his belly button.

Finally, he wiggled and squirmed the top half of his body out onto the roof on his back and yanked his legs up out of the hole like they was dangling over a pit full of crocodiles. Lying flat beside the hole, he listened to the pandemonium in the barn below, cops yelling orders as they rounded up the men who'd been working there. Willie Ray realized he was lying on a good-sized broken shingle. Rolling off it, he wrenched it free and placed it over the hole, found another piece of shingle, smaller, to put beside it. With those shingles in place, the hole wouldn't be so noticeable from below. Might not even be visible.

Then he lay beside the hole, panting, listening to the awful sounds from below, not letting himself feel his injuries, not yet. He could see several police cruisers, red lights flashing, in front of the barn and assumed if he could see the cars, anybody inside the cars could see him. So he commando-crawled up toward the peak of the building, leaving a bloody snail trail on the shingles. The higher he went, the more he could see below, which meant those below could see more of him. By the time he got to the peak, the first of his crew was being led out into the area in front of the barn by what looked like an army of officers. If any of them happened to look up at the top of the barn at that moment, he was a bug on a pin there. Then he slid up and over the peak and down on the other side of it. That side of the barn was snuggled up into the woods. All he could see below the roof there were trees.

He lay panting, listening, maybe crying softly, he couldn't tell, so horrified and scared he felt like throwing up. The sounds of voices moved from inside the barn to outside it. If he stuck his head up and peeked over the peak of the roof, he coulda seen what was going on, but he didn't want to know that bad. He could imagine what he'd see from what he could hear and that was bad enough. Where he lay, longways beside the barn peak on the far side, he couldn't be seen from the front of the barn. He lifted his head and turned to look the other way — just trees, but if anybody cared to go wandering out into 'em, he might be visible from some point there.

When he turned his face back toward the front side, Andy was sitting on the peak of the roof beside him. Torn-up Andy, the horror visage.

It no longer shocked Willie Ray to see his brother. Just the same. Frozen in time on the day he died at age eighteen a decade ago. Blond hair that was almost white — just like Drew Hannacker's — eyebrows and eyelashes so light they were almost invisible. Startling blue eyes. His little girl, Andrea, had got his blue eyes. She looked more like her mama, Emily, with dark hair. But her eyes were pure Andy.

Andy never spoke to Willie Ray. Had only ever spoken the night when they captured Jackson, told Willie Ray it was okay, everything was going to be alright. Willie Ray didn't know what he meant at the time and he had never been able to puzzle it out.

Now, he just sat looking out at the police officers arresting Willie Ray's crew, the whole front of his body ripped open and his oozing guts hanging down between his legs onto the barn roof.

"Andy, *get down!*" Willie Ray hissed and Andy turned to him, but the expression on his face didn't change. It never changed — always a little confused and surprised, the look that probably froze on his features in the moment he died. Even when he'd spoken to Willie Ray that one time, the expression on his face stayed the same. "They'll see you, get *down*."

Andy turned slowly around, lifted his legs up over the peak of the barn, dragging his guts behind him. He stretched out flat onto his belly on the other side where Willie Ray cowered. Now, all Willie Ray could see without lifting his head were the soles of Andy's combat boots. They were caked in mud. It'd been raining that night at Tweety Bird.

~

DREW HANNACKER COULDN'T DRAW in another breath, was shocked so suddenly out of the world where the sun shone and birds tweeted — and he had a new *horse*! — back down into the dark shadowy world where he hid in corners of his mind, careful, always careful.

Never sat with his back to a door. Always looked for ways to get out of a room, Willie Ray called them escape routes.

And never, never, never let anybody sneak up on you.

He was frozen as hard as a piece of stone for a moment, could do nothing but cringe away against the wall, his eyes glued to the face in abject terror. Terror like he'd felt that night. Only bigger. The terror ate a hole in his belly and let all the air out so he couldn't breathe. He stared, shaking his head, pleading "don't hurt me" with his eyes. But pleading wouldn't work. He could tell the Thing recognized him, knew who he was. The Thing that had killed Pop Pop, stood over his body and pointed the pistol at his face. Pulled the trigger. Put a hole in his forehead.

The Thing knew Drew had seen and it would have to kill him, too.

"Please don't ..." — he cringed away toward the wall — "... *kill me*," he heard himself whisper, but he wasn't sure if he said the words out loud or just in his head until the Thing answered.

"*Kill* you? Why on earth would I—?"

"I ain't told nobody I seen you, I swear I ain't!" He heard his voice, a whimper like a baby rabbit that'd got run over by a hay rake. "I won't never tell ... promise I won't ..."

Then the terror exploded in his chest, went off like a bomb.

Run!

The Thing was between him and the back door, so he

turned and ran the other way, into the house, flew away on feet with wings, away, away as fast as his pumping legs would carry him. He seemed at once to be slogging through tar that grabbed at his feet and sucked him down to the floor, not letting him move forward. At the same time it felt like he was, indeed, flying. That his feet didn't even touch the floor as he ran, faster than any deer, away from the Thing.

Into a kitchen …

He heard his heart hammering in his ears.

Across the kitchen.

Around the cabinets.

Bam!

The world went black.

Chapter Forty-Two

WHEN A LITTLE BOY come barreling out of the bathroom and crashed into her, looked at Mama Bert's face, mumbled crazy stuff and then ran away in terror, she 'bout wet herself in surprise.

'Fore she had a chance to figure out what in the wor— she heard a kinda crash, a loud thump, and she followed where the kid had run into the kitchen. She found him sprawled out on the floor, unconscious, a great big ole lump in the middle of his forehead. He'd gone running through the kitchen and around that corner, must have collided head-on with that open cabinet door. Woulda been the right height to smack him a good one in the head.

She'd a'got down on her knees to see to the boy if she could have, but sitting down on the floor at her age and size was a commitment she never made lightly. Malcolm come into the kitchen then and saved her the trouble. Musta been coming down the stairs when he heard the ruckus, 'cause he couldn't a'heard nothing up there in his second floor office where the two of them'd been talking.

She'd cut a deal with Jackson McClusky, though she

wasn't at all convinced he could hold up his end of the bargain. She'd checked, found out he'd moved into the Dawson place all right, but hadn't no papers been signed yet. Some corporation, she supposed it was his, had put in the bid that'd been accepted. Thing was, she wasn't never gonna find out if Jackson was good as his word unless she held up her end of the deal, and she hadn't counted on that being as hard as it was. Find out where Riley kept his marijuana seed — easy enough. 'Cept Mama Bert'd called in every favor from every informer she had and had come up snake eyes. So she'd come here to have a sit-down with Malcolm Murdock and pick his brains, such as they were. Riley'd been processing his weed in one of Malcolm's horse barns for five years — surely Brewster's Mayor for Life or one of his men knew something.

"I thought I heard—" Malcolm saw the boy on the floor and sucked in a gasp. "What—?"

"Run into that door, I 'spect," she said, indicating the cabinet door standing open. "Knocked him cold."

"What's he doing in …?"

"I ain't got no idea."

"Well, we gotta … *do* something …" He blustered and looked around, frantic. "Ice, get some ice for his head." The man stepped past the boy to the cabinet, yanked open a couple of drawers until he found a dish towel, then went to the freezer and grabbed some ice cubes, dropped most of them. He put the ice in the dish towel and knelt down beside the boy, putting the icepack on his forehead.

"What's Drew Hannacker doing in my kitchen?" Malcolm asked. "Where'd he come from?"

Drew Hannacker.

That's why the kid'd looked familiar.

"Musta come out here with Riley and — yeah, that foal. My foreman mentioned Riley was thinking about getting a pony horse for his boy." He lifted the ice pack off the boy's head to look at the lump and might be it'd stopped swelling so he put the ice pack back on. "Riley's around here somewhere. You need to go get him, tell him his boy's ... maybe we'd ought to call an ambulance."

Mama Bert didn't move.

She could think a lot faster than Malcolm could talk and things was beginning to connect up she didn't like one bit.

Drew *Hannacker* had taken one look at her and was scared spit-less. So scared he run off and crashed into a cabinet door. Powerful scart. Thought she was gonna *kill* him. Why would he think a thing like that?

"*Ain't told nobody I seen you.*"

What had Riley Hannacker's boy seen her—?

Her heart shifted into a gallop in her chest.

Might be the proper question to ask was what had *Nate Hannacker's grandson* seen that made him scared Mama Bert was gonna kill him?

His words reverberated inside her skull and her galloping heart burst into a full-on run.

"I won't never tell ... promise I won't ..."

Was it possible ... could the boy have been in the barn that night?

A niggling little memory surfaced about the Callison County Burley Festival a couple of years ago. The kid had gone missing then for awhile, she remembered; the whole crowd had been looking for him. He'd got in line for a funnel cake, they said, and then just run off. *She'd* been in that funnel cake line. Did he see her and—?

Mama Bert downshifted through surprise to shock to fear between heartbeats.

"You gonna go get Riley?" Malcolm prodded.

She had about fifteen seconds to make the decision, might have three minutes, no more'n five to pull it off.

Soon's that boy come to, they'd ask why he'd run off, what'd scared him, and when they did, he'd start babbling.

Stepping to one of the drawers Malcolm had pulled open, she took out a roll of duct tape she'd spotted there, pulled out a piece and ripped it off.

"Ain't no use to tape it on," Malcolm said when she leaned over the boy's head with the tape. "I'll just hold it here while you go get—"

He stopped talking when she didn't use the tape in a futile attempt to hold the ice pack in place. Instead, she stretched it across the boy's mouth, then smoothed it down tight.

"What are you doing?" Malcolm was horrified.

Grunting as she straightened up, she pointed to the small rug in front of the sink.

"Need to roll him up in that," she said.

"What …?" Malcolm didn't have the air to finish.

"We ain't got but a minute or two, so ain't no time for jabbering or arguing. Unless you want me to give Jim Bingham them pictures of you fiddling with them little girls" — he gasped when she said the newspaper editor's name — "you best do what I say!"

"But what—?"

"Ain't no time, now!" she barked.

She leaned over and dragged the rug next to the unconscious boy.

"Roll him up in it," she said.

"I … *no!* I'm not gonna roll a *little kid* up—"

"Him being a little kid wouldn't bother you if he was a girl. You'd likely be dropping your pants right now to get you some!"

His head snapped back like she'd slapped him.

Leaning over as best she could, she moved Drew's arms down to his sides and began to roll him over onto the rug.

"Help me!" she roared and Malcolm, took it from there, rolled the boy over, wrapped the rug around him, then rolled him over again a couple of times until his body was invisible.

"This here's how it's gonna be. I'm gonna go get in my truck parked out back and drive away. Only I'm just gonna come around to the side door — and you're gonna carry the boy and the rug out and put it in the back of my pickup."

Malcolm's face was the color of chalk.

"This is … *kidnapping*. This boy may be hurt—"

"You think you ain't gonna do no such thing, but you are. I done said ain't no time for jabbering. You be waiting for me with the boy at the side door, or as God is my witness, I swear I will have them pictures hand-delivered to your house — eight by tens — make sure your kids is home to see 'em."

Malcolm said nothing, probably couldn't talk.

"And I'll make a hundred copies, get a couple of fellas to stand outside the door at church on Sunday, handing them out to everybody who walks by. The one where that little girl's a-crying while you do her — what was she, maybe twelve years old? Your face is real clear in that one. Now do what I told you!"

She paused again. "Best not be getting any ideas about trying to stop me." She wagged her finger. "Five packets of pictures, sealed up, addressed and stamped — ready to be mailed."

She'd told him a long time ago that he better hope she lived to a ripe old age because if anything ever happened to her, she'd left instructions that packets of pictures would be mailed out on the day of her funeral. She hadn't, of course. Wasn't but three people even knew them pictures existed — the Mexican photographer, her man, Floyd, and herself. Well, and Malcolm. Didn't but one set of the pictures exist. They was only good for blackmail if she was the only one had 'em. Let a whole bunch of other folks see 'em and sooner or later one of two things would happen: whoever seen them would hit Malcolm up for money, or the pictures would get out and wouldn't be no good to her no more.

Mama Bert hurried as fast as she could to the back porch, out the door and across the yard to the back gate. She could hear Riley's voice calling Drew's name before she got to where she'd parked her truck. His truck was parked right next to hers.

He looked upset, somewhere between annoyed and scared, still figured the kid'd come running up any minute. He was surprised to see her there — reasonable reaction. Mama Bert didn't get out much, made the people she wanted to see come to her.

"You seen Drew?" he asked before she had a chance to say anything.

"Your boy? Nope. He lost?"

She could tell he didn't want to talk to her. The two of them probably hadn't exchanged a dozen words in the whole five years they'd had business dealings. Didn't hurt her feelings none that he didn't like her. Life wasn't no popularity contest.

"I don't know where he is. He was supposed to wait for me here at the truck." He started calling again, "Drew! It's time to go now. Drew!"

"He's 'round here somewhere," she said, "He'll turn up."

Then she got into her truck and drove away.

Chapter Forty-Three

AT FIRST, Riley was just annoyed.

Where had Drew got off to?

He didn't need this, not right now.

His mind was spinning, trying to figure out what it all meant. Brady said that a couple of his men had reported seeing Away-From-Here's in town, suit-and-tie types, who was asking questions. Didn't take a rocket scientist to figure out they was police of some kind, but what particular flavor that might be Riley couldn't guess.

Might be some special unit working with the state police. He'd heard rumblings that they were going to beef up their efforts. And locals, too. Lowlifes. Brady'd said they was nosey-ing around, wanting to know what they didn't have no right to know.

"Drew!" he called, loud. "We gotta get home. Come on!"

He looked around at the barns he could see and no little blond boy came running out of any of them.

Right now was a bad time, a really bad time to have a swarm of cops nosing around. He wouldn't be processing large quantities at Land's End this year, for the first time, but there were multiple small operations all over the county. He couldn't imagine how anybody could find and identify half a dozen small processing sites. A couple maybe, but not all of them.

Cops … and Jackson.

He balled his hands into fists. His insides were still torn up over the sight of him in church on Sunday. Obviously, Jackson had some kind of elaborate plan in mind to kill him, Jessie and Willie Ray before they could get to him. He'd probably spent a very long time plotting out the whole thing. Riley could feel the crosshairs of a sight on the back of his neck every time he went outside. Willie Ray would be home later today, though, and then the three of them would have to come up with a plan of their own.

They'd have to talk about Winona McClusky, too, oh by the way. Blackmail. It was just like a McClusky to come up with a pond-scum scheme to steal what they couldn't earn. They were all like that. *Jackson* was a McClusky.

"Drew!" Looking around, he called out at the top of his lungs, "Drew!"

Nothing.

He heard someone approach from the Murdocks' backyard, turned around and discovered it was Mama Bert!

Now that was a surprise. She stayed to herself, safe in the shadowy confines of the tavern, only ever ventured forth for church. Every couple of months or so there was a Mama Bert sighting in town but it was rare.

She moved slowly, her ponderous girth swaying with each step. It was hard to see in the dim light of her office — which was surely Mama Bert's intention — but out here in the sun, he could see all the folds and bulges. She had, indeed, gained weight since he saw her last.

"You seen Drew?" he asked her before she had a chance to say anything.

"Your boy? Nope. He lost?"

He didn't want to talk to her, didn't trust her any farther than he could throw a grand piano.

"I don't know where he is. He was supposed to wait for me here at the truck." He started calling again, "Drew! It's time to go now. Drew!"

"He's 'round here somewhere." Mama Bert got into her truck. "He'll turn up." She pulled out of the parking space and drove away toward the road.

Riley kept hollering, with concern spreading out in a flower into his chest. The boy hadn't come back to the barn with the foals — which was the only conceivable place he'd want to go. Riley would have seen him if he'd come back there.

"Drew!" he cried out, and could hear the growing fear in his own voice. "You're about to be in a world of hurt, young man! Drew!"

He turned slowly around in the dirt. Nothing. The other barns, then. Drew must have gone to one of the other barns. Which one? The line of them stretched out for over half a mile in both directions. He'd have gone toward the barns near the horse paddocks, wouldn't he? That was south. Riley started to run toward the nearest barn, then thought better of it and jumped into his truck, pulled out of the parking space too fast and sprayed dirt out behind the back tires as he flew off toward the barn.

When Riley banged on the back door of Malcolm Murdock's house half an hour later, he was holding onto his growing meltdown with his fingernails.

He didn't wait for an answer to his knock, just opened the door, stepped inside and cried, "Drew! Are you in here?"

He threw open the first door he came to, a bathroom that vanilla and cinnamon candles filled with a cloying sweet smell. Stepping into the kitchen, he heard footsteps coming down the stairs.

"Who's down here?" a voice called tentatively.

Mayor-for-Life Malcolm Murdock.

"It's me, Malcolm, Riley Hannacker. I'm looking for my little boy." Riley continued across the kitchen, pulling open the pantry door, the broom closet.

Malcolm appeared on the other side of the dining room.

"Riley? What—?"

"I told you. My boy's lost." *Lost.* He hated the word as soon as it passed his lips, hated the lonely, frightened sound of it.

"Why are you looking for him … *here*?"

Incipient hysteria dragged the old joke into Riley's mind. *Drunk is looking around on the ground in the glow of a streetlight. Stranger comes along — "Lose something?" Drunk answers, "Yeah, my car keys" and he points off into the darkness. "Dropped them over there." Stranger asks, "If you lost them over there, why are you looking for them here?" Drunk says, "It's too dark to look over there."*

"I've searched outside. I thought maybe … he came in the house."

Even in his present state, Riley couldn't help noticing that Malcolm looked awful. His face was some shade of gray. He stood with his head hanging low, shoulders slumped. Wouldn't look at Riley.

As if answering the question Riley didn't ask, he said, "I'm … ill. Not feeling well at all." He made a sort of vague, all-encompassing gesture. "You're welcome to look around for him if you like."

Malcolm definitely looked sick, certainly didn't respond

the way the men who worked for him had responded when Riley'd said Drew was missing. They all dropped whatever they were doing and helped him look. Must have been two dozen of them and their combined efforts turned up not a single trace of the boy.

Where could he have gone? How could a little kid just … *vanish* like that?

Mumbling thanks, Riley hurriedly searched the house — closets, storage rooms, attic and basement. He'd already called Drew's name so long and loud his voice was hoarse, but he didn't call for him here. If Drew were in this house, he was hiding. For what reason, Riley couldn't fathom, but it would do no good to call out for him.

Coming down the center stairs into the grand foyer, Riley found Malcolm just standing there beside the ridiculous fountain. A porpoise standing on its tail, its body twisted in a pose of jumping spewed water out of its mouth into a pond that must have been three feet deep.

Malcolm didn't look at him. His eyes reminded Riley of Davie's eyes — they focused on the spot you occupied in space but never really looked at you.

Jessie!

God, how he wanted to call her, wanted her here beside him, wanted her comfort.

He hadn't called Sherry Lynn yet.

Malcolm didn't say anything. Just stood there. Didn't ask if Drew'd ever run off like this before, or suggest Riley call the law — which others had suggested and he'd refused — or speculate where the boy might be.

He just stood there.

"Don't suppose somebody took him, do ya?" Malcolm said softly, then was clearly horrified that he'd made such a suggestion.

And it was, indeed, a horrible speculation — one that

Riley'd built a wall around, until he heard the words come out of somebody else's mouth. Then the wall crumbled.

Drew couldn't/wouldn't have gone wandering off and then just not come back. If he left this farm, he'd been forced to.

"Jackson."

The name was so slathered in layers of rage and loathing it almost didn't sound like a word at all. Jackson McClusky was the only person on the planet who had a motive to … *kidnap* Drew. To get at Riley, of course. Riley couldn't imagine how on earth he'd managed to pull it off, but Jackson was the only reasonable explanation for Drew's disappearance.

Riley would find Jackson McClusky. He would kill the man with his bare hands and get his son back.

Without speaking another word, he turned and ran out to his truck. Men were standing around outside the barns now, all of them disturbed and confused by Drew's disappearance and Riley's desperate attempts to find his little boy.

Brady came toward his truck and called out, "Want us to spread out, start searching the woods?"

"I know where he is."

Riley roared past them all, headed for Bald Knob. The back side of Bald Knob.

Chapter Forty-Four

MAMA BERT TURNED off the lane leading out to the road
and pulled into the driveway of the huge Murdock house,
drove around it to the far side where an arbor trellis
stretched from the door to the end of the sidewalk.

Leaving the front door open and the engine running,
she stopped to let down the tailgate and then run fast as
she could up through the tunnel of morning glory vines to
the door. The door was standing open and Malcolm was
standing just inside, cradling the rolled-up rug in his arms.

"Bert, what's wrong with you? What do you want to do
a thing like this for—?"

"Come on!" she growled the words, looking around.
"Get that kid into the back of my truck!"

She rushed long beside him. Couldn't nobody see them
through the morning glories and when they got to the end
of the arbor, she stopped him and peered out, looking
around. Anybody coming up to the house from the barns
would see, or somebody driving down the lane from the
road.

But nobody was. She shoved Malcolm toward the

looked almost genuine. But it morphed quick into a rage that might have equaled his own.

"You come roarin' in here, pull a gun on me. You best lower that rifle or you ain't gonna leave here alive."

Riley didn't lower the weapon, but he did lower his cheek toward the stock so he could sight down the barrel.

"You tell me what you done with my boy or I will blow a hole in your chest big enough to drive a tractor through."

"Your … boy? The little kid? Why would you think the kid's here?"

"*My* son is here because *your* son brought him here. If you don't—"

"My son?"

"Jackson!" He spit the name out like the taste of it in his mouth made him sick.

"I ain't seen Jackson in five years!"

"Liar! He was at St. Augustine in Brewster on Sunday.

"News to me."

"I'm ain't gonna ask again. Where—?"

He heard a click behind him, the sound of a pistol cocking, felt the barrel jam into the base of his skull.

"Drop that there rifle in the dirt or I'll blow your face off the front of your head." It was a woman's voice, but deep and husky.

Riley froze.

"You got to the count of *one.*"

Big-un spoke then, his voice a low rumble.

"If your boy's missin', who you figger's gonna go find him after Dottie blows your head off?"

Riley dropped the rifle.

Big-un nodded at it and a teenage boy Riley hadn't seen, who was standing off to the left and also had the drop on him, came forward and picked the rifle up out of the dirt. He pitched it to another teenager *who looked just like him.* Seeing double — Big-un's twins. Papa'd said he couldn't tell them apart.

Big-un spoke to the boys.

"He so much as farts, both of you blow him away."

The matched set of boys fit the stocks of rifles into the crooks of their shoulders.

"S'okay now, Dottie." The pistol barrel that'd been jammed into the back of Riley's skull was gone. "You go on in the house. We got this."

The woman must have turned and gone back toward the house. Riley never even got a glimpse of her.

"Sit down," Big-un said. "Plant your butt right there in the dirt."

Riley sat, glaring at Big-un.

"If looks could kill, you wouldn't a'needed that rifle." He lumbered toward Riley, still holding the hoe. He'd been mucking out the barn because the hoe-head was covered in manure. He came to within about ten feet of Riley and stopped.

Looking up at Big-un McClusky was intimidating enough if you were on your feet. From the ground, the mountain of a man looked ten feet tall. But Riley wasn't afraid. He was still too mad to be afraid, though when the compulsion drained out of his chest, he understood more than most what a dumb thing he'd just done. He realized he'd been wrong as well as stupid. Though Big-un was likely a good liar — all the McCluskys were — he wouldn't have bothered lying to Riley. If Jackson'd been here, Riley would already be dead.

Jackson wasn't here. Which meant Drew wasn't here, either. That realization took all the air out of Riley's lungs and he slumped where he sat.

"Now tell me how come you come roarin' in here like yore hair was on fire."

"My son, Drew. He's missing." He paused. "He's ... nine years old," and was horrified by how tear-clotted his voice sounded.

"And you come looking for him here because ...?"

A light of rage jolted energy back into Riley's body like a bolt of lightning.

"Jackson took him!" He ground out the words through a clenched jaw. "Kidnapped him!"

"And why would Jackson do a thing like that?"

Riley sat back. Why bother?

"It's a long story and you ain't gonna b'lieve it anyway."

Big-un gestured to the boy on the left.

"Bring me my barrel," he said, then looked down at Riley. "You got that right — I ain't gonna b'lieve it. But tell me anyway."

Chapter Forty-Six

RILEY SQUINTED in the glare of sunlight shining over Big-un's shoulder, and thought to wonder if he'd planned it that way. Not likely. The boy had rolled half a whiskey barrel out of the barn and set it upright behind Big-un. The big man had sat back on it. Good thing it was made out of oak.

"So you're saying it wasn't really Jackson's fault that the man got burnt alive?" Big-un asked.

Riley had decided if he was going to explain why Jackson had kidnapped Drew, he was going to start at the beginning, or as close to the beginning as he could get. He had nowhere else to go, no other place to look for Drew and if there was even the thinnest strand of hope that Big-un knew something that might help, Riley's only chance to find out was to come completely clean.

"Hard to say it wasn't his fault when he poured gasoline on the guy's head," Riley snapped. He paused. "Okay, no, I don't think Jackson intended to *kill* the guy for singing a Christmas carol. Me and Ben and Davie told the sergeant that. But him dying was Jackson's fault and he needed to answer for that."

"Nothin' come of it, though, right?"

"Right."

"How come?"

"Well, see, we was *busy* that night — we got a little distracted. Gettin' massacred'll take your eye off the ball."

"Sergeant didn't say nothing?"

"Sergeant got killed and so did Ben Higgs. And Davie ..." The image of the rest of it filled Riley's mind with red mist and his chest with such rage he couldn't even speak. Big-un was saying something when he finally found his voice.

"And then the VC—?"

"No, not the Cong! *Jackson!* Jackson did it! Jackson picked up a Cong RPG off the ground and fired it in the door of our bunker — to shut me and Davie up. It worked, too. Davie Monaghan hasn't said a word since, hasn't thought a thought, neither. Besides a back full of shrapnel, my brains got scrambled so it was three years after the war before I remembered what Jackson done."

Riley hadn't been looking at Big-un when he spoke, but he lifted his chin and stared the big man right in the eye as he said the rest, his voice quiet because he didn't seem to have enough air to talk any louder. "The blast killed Andy Taggart, ripped him open so his guts was hanging out. Willie Ray wanted me to help him stuff 'em back in."

Hard to read the reaction of a man like Big-un. He didn't show much, and with his face covered up in that bird's-nest beard, you couldn't see whatever look might be on it. But his eyes grew huge and he stopped breathing. Just stopped, tried to stare a hole through Riley, stare into his soul to burn the words and images away, but Riley held his stare until he dropped his eyes.

"That's why Jackson run off five years ago. I'd been having flashbacks, nightmares … and one night, it all came back, like watching a movie. A horror movie."

Riley shook his head.

"I ain't got no idea how Jackson found out I'd remembered what he done, but he come after me and Davie. Shot at me and missed. Tried to smother Davie in his bed."

"Smother." Big-un repeated the word in an emotionless voice.

"Put a pillow over his face … me and Willie Ray caught him in the act."

Now Riley found he was glaring at Big-un, but he didn't care.

"We was gonna *kill* Jackson. Would have killed him … but he got away from us before we had a chance. Never seen him again until he comes walking up to me in church on Sunday, that smirky smile on his face." Riley ground his teeth. "Me and Jessie's waitin' for Willie Ray to get back home tonight before we go after Jackson. We will catch him eventually, and when we do, we *will* kill him."

And then the reality of the past couple of hours flowed back into Riley's mind with a force that left him feeling like he'd been slapped.

"Jackson took Drew." He said the words quiet, didn't paint them in the raging fury he felt. Just said them. "I never figured out how he knew I'd remembered what he done, and I don't know how he got to Drew, neither. But he's got my boy and—"

"Why? Why would he kidnap Drew?" Big-un's voice wasn't so much challenging as it was curious. "What does that get him? Jackson don't do nothing 'less they's somethin' in it for him."

Riley hadn't thought to reason that out. He knew

Jackson was back in Callison County and Jackson hated him so of course, Jackson did it. But what if …?

"To get at you somehow so's he could kill you? That don't make no sense. If he got close enough to you to snatch your boy, he coulda kilt you right then. So why didn't he?"

Yeah, why didn't he?

Papa had told Riley that Big-un was smart, had said people didn't realize how quick and shrewd he was. Maybe …

"Where was you when your boy went missin'? Who else was around?"

Motive *and* opportunity.

"'Pears to me if you wanna find that boy you gonna have to use your head 'stead of runnin' off half-cocked …" He gave Riley a hard look. "This here's a dead end. You need to *b'lieve* that and go look somewhere's else."

He nodded to the boy holding Riley's rifle. "Unload it and put it in his truck."

Then he spit out a plug of brown tobacco juice that came within an inch of where Riley sat. "Now, *you* — git off my land!"

The big man turned his back on Riley and lumbered off toward the barn. He never looked back.

As Riley drove slowly away from Big-un's farm, he tried to look at the situation as dispassionately and objectively as Big-un had done.

Somebody had to have both motive and opportunity.

He couldn't think of anyone who'd have a motive to kidnap Drew. Nobody.

Okay, opportunity, then.

Who had been at Land's End when Drew went missing?

Probably two dozen people!

All the farm hands — how many of them? Twenty, maybe more. Trainers and groomers and … Jackson got to one of them! Brady had said people were nosing around, asking questions about Riley and the others. Jackson had gotten to one of them. Somebody knew Jackson would pay big bucks to have Riley Hannacker at his mercy, stumbled upon Drew alone — *Riley never should have left the boy alone!* — saw an opportunity and took it.

But what had they done with Drew? Riley and the others had searched everywhere … but maybe one of the searchers was only pretending to help.

Not just the farm hands, though.

Mama Bert was there, too.

Mama Bert was undoubtedly capable of such a thing but she had no reason to kidnap Drew, no motive. Malcolm Murdock had been there, too — who also had no reason to kidnap Drew.

But unlike Mama Bert, who'd strode past Riley normal as you please, Malcolm had been … *something.* He'd said he was sick and he certainly looked the part. Maybe there was more to it than that.

Riley grabbed hold of his emotions and refused to allow himself to go roaring back to Land's End like he'd gone roaring off to Big-un McClusky's. He needed to *think* what to do.

He needed Jessie.

Chapter Forty-Seven

BLEEDING from gouges and cuts on his sides and chest, Willie Ray lay with his dead brother on the top of the barn outside Empire Township, Missouri for the rest of the day. The sun climbed up high in the sky and started sliding down in the west before the last of the police officers left the area.

Willie Ray listened, caught pieces of conversation, knew they were asking the men questions, and the men weren't answering. They searched all around the barn, whether looking for Willie Ray or just looking around in general he didn't know. They probed around in the woods behind the barn and beside it, but the foliage was thick on the trees. He could hear the officers' voices but couldn't see them, so assumed they couldn't see him either, or that they hadn't looked up where he was hiding.

Eventually, he heard car doors slam. Listened as one vehicle after another pulled away from the area in front of the barn and drove down the dirt road toward the highway. Finally it was silent and gradually he could hear the birdsong return to the woods. He stayed where he was.

They had left a guard, of course. Prob'ly more than one. There was a fortune in marijuana in the barn and they wouldn't just leave it there. Besides, it was … *evidence.* A chill went down his spine, like ice water dripping from one vertebra to the next.

When the sun began to sink down below the tree line to the west, he knew it was time to move. He'd had lots of time to think what he ought to do. He had to get off the roof while there was still enough light to keep from breaking his fool neck, enough light to see what he was doing so he could do it quietly so's not to alert whoever was babysitting the weed. He certainly couldn't go back down through the hole where he'd come up. He'd spotted a couple of trees with limbs that extended out to the barn and figured to make it to one of them and down. And he had to have some light to make it through the woods to the other side. He hadn't been here but a handful of times, but he searched every memory he had and the best he could recall, the woods climbed up and over a hillside and there was another farm in the valley below it. When he finally moved, stiff from lying in one position for so long, he didn't stand, just crawled to the edge of the roof and along it until he found a limb he figured would hold his weight. He could grab it, swing down off the roof on it and drop to the ground, which was still far enough to break an ankle, but it was the best he could do. Before he reached for the limb, he looked up toward the peak of the roof. Andy had stayed there with Willie Ray all day and Willie Ray wasn't sure he could leave his brother behind if Andy was still lying there. But he was gone.

It took what felt like three hours but was probably less — or more — for Willie Ray to make it through the woods, follow the fence line of the field to the next field and the next, making his way north toward the airport. It was a full-moon night and he could see well enough at first. But as the moon rose higher in the sky, the light grew dimmer. He had to get to the airport before dawn.

For about half a mile, there was no cover at all and Willie Ray'd had to risk running down the side of the road. Sprinting full out, he made it to a stand of bushes before there were any headlights on the road. He sat in the bushes, gasping and coughing, cursing his cigarettes … and wishing he had one now, but he'd left them on the floor of the barn. Running had bounced the gouge on his side, made it hurt worse, and he tried to be careful to walk gently after that.

He didn't wear a watch so he had no idea what time it was when he finally made it to the airport. The windows in the trailer house office were dark. Jack's car wasn't parked out front. The place looked deserted. On the other side of the lone runway from the airport office building was a heavily wooded area and Willie Ray stood in the trees there, looking out across the stretch of tarmac at Kiwi, sitting in a puddle of bright light from the big light on a pole above it. His was the only plane parked in front of the trailer house office. Maybe there were more lights to turn on if there were more airplanes, or maybe there was only the one. The moonlight had been failing for a while now as clouds moved in to cover it. Now it was overcast and almost totally dark … and Kiwi was as tempting as the cherry on the top of a hot fudge sundae, sitting there waiting for him to start her up and fly away. But it might be like biting into Snow White's apple to try it — and he thought that in English class that'd been called mixing metaphors.

His mind kept hopscotching around like that, burping out random thoughts — keeping him from attending to the growing pain in his side and chest. When he kept his right hand tight against his gouged left side it kept the wound from pulling open if he made a sudden movement. That didn't stop the blood flow. He wasn't bleeding bad enough to bleed to death, he didn't think, but maybe enough to make him lightheaded. Maybe if his head had been clearer, he wouldn't have taken the chance. But it wasn't and he did. Stepping out of the trees, he started walking slowly across the dark runway toward his airplane.

～

DREW HAD A HEADACHE.

Right in front. Why would he wake up with a headache?

He opened his eyes and the world was crazy, blurry, moving and he was dizzy. So he closed them again. Tried to figure out if he was awake or still dreaming.

He was afraid, scared to death. Sometimes nightmares seemed so real the scared he felt when he was asleep was still there when he woke up. That was happening now.

He opened his eyes again, searching for the familiar lights and shadows of his bedroom, where Revolutionary War redcoats marched across the wallpaper border while armed colonists waited in the trees to pick them off. Marching in a line to get shot at. He'd always thought that was dumb.

But his blurry vision couldn't locate the border up by the ceiling. He couldn't locate anything familiar and ...

He wasn't in his bed. He didn't feel sheets under him, or his soft mattress. He was lying on something hard, like a rug on the floor. Did he fall out of bed? His bedroom floor was carpeted.

And what had he been dreaming that had scared him so badly?

Suddenly bright light shone all around and he squinted, couldn't open his eyes looking at it.

"You's faking, son, just pretending you's still out. Ain't never a good idea to try to fool old Mama Bert."

Who said that? Who was in his bedroom …?

He forced his eyes open, squinting, and what he saw made him dizzy again but not because his head hurt. He wasn't at home in his bed at all. He was on the floor in a room … It smelled dusty, like in the attic of the old house on the farm. The air smelled stale.

"You, boy."

The toe of a shoe nudged him not gently in the side.

"I'm talking to you, Drew Hannacker. Open up them eyes and look at me."

Drew opened his eyes. He looked. It was the Thing, right here in his bedroom except he wasn't in his bedroom. She leaned over him, close to his face, and his bladder let go and he wet himself.

"Answer me. Can you hear what I'm sayin to you?"

She poked him again with her shoe in the side, harder this time.

"Answer me!"

"Yes ma'am," he heard his lips say and was amazed that he'd spoken because he didn't think he had meant to. It had just happened. A reflex.

"You know who I am."

"Yes ma'am … you're … the Thing."

"The what?"

Somehow his mouth was functioning. She was saying things and he heard them and he was answering. But the deeper part of himself was so scared he couldn't talk. How could he be too scared to talk, but talk anyway?

"I'm Mama Bert. Everybody knows me. What'd you call me a ... *thing* for?"

He stammered again, "I didn't know your name."

"When was it you didn't know my name? You seen me somewhere and you didn't know my name so you called me a thing — that right?"

He nodded.

She kicked him again, not nudged, kicked.

"Sit up!"

He tried to sit up but the room spun so he froze, was still and the spinning stopped and he sat all the way up, looking up at her. With the light behind her head, her frizzy hair was a black halo with a gold outline and her face was mostly in shadow.

"Now, tell me when it was you seen me but you didn't know my name."

Drew's mouth locked up. It had been answering her, sort of on its own, but now he was suddenly in control again and he couldn't make his jaw move.

"You seen me this afternoon and it scared you spitless, why was that?"

He had no voice.

"You was scared because you'd seen me *before* — but you didn't know my name, then so you called me a thing — that's right, ain't it, son?"

He managed to nod. Without even realizing it, he was scooting backward on the floor away from her, but she was following. When he felt the wall at his back, he felt panic spread through him.

"You can't go running out of here like a jackrabbit so don't try."

He looked down and realized for the first time that his ankles were tied together, taped together with duct tape.

"I ain't gonna ask this but one more time. When was it you seen me and it scared you?"

He was terrified to say anything, but the look on her face made him scared more to be silent.

"… in the barn," he whispered.

"What'd you say? The barn?"

He nodded.

"What barn?"

"… my Pop Pop's barn." The words were so soft he barely heard them himself, but she heard him.

"Your Pop Pop being Nate Hannacker, that right?"

He nodded again.

"So you seen me there with your Pop Pop. Where was you at because I didn't see you."

She *didn't see him.* She didn't know Drew had seen what she did. No, she was lying. She knew.

"In the playroom Pop Pop made for me."

"Playroom? Where?"

"Behind the tack room."

She nodded. "But you could see out into the barn — through a hole or a crack or something?"

"A crack."

"So you was watching?"

He couldn't speak so he nodded.

"You seen me shoot your Pop Pop?"

He tried to cringe away into the wall behind him.

"Answer me!"

He nodded.

She kicked him then, hard, in the leg. It hurt bad enough to cry but he didn't.

"Talk."

"Yes ma'am. I saw."

"Saw me what …?"

"Shoot Pop Pop."

"How many times you see me shoot him?"

"Twice."

"Once in the chest. When was the second time?"

"In the forehead. You put the gun down real close to his face and you pulled the trigger and there was a hole in his forehead."

Chapter Forty-Eight

THE FAT DEPUTY was the one who spotted him. Crouched back from the window on the side of the airport office that faced the runway, he had a line of sight across the tarmac.

"Somethin's moving out there on the runway." He spoke in a whisper loud enough for Eli, who was positioned behind the gasoline pump, to hear. Bill Thomas and another deputy were covering the parking lot area behind the building. Two additional deputies knelt in the shadows, one at each end of the building.

The unidentifiable blob of greater darkness moving toward them gradually resolved into a man walking across the center of the runway, not headed toward the building but angled toward the lone airplane parked in front of it.

Eli held his SIG SAUER .45 in a two-hand grip, pointed at the ground. He would wait until the figure was clearly visible in the splash of light before he demanded that he halt. None of the other Callison County men were armed, though there were various firearms in their vehicles — mostly rifles and shotguns. There was no reason to believe Willie Ray Taggart had a weapon on him. His gait was odd, though, bent over. Then he stumbled, reached his hand up to his side, and the deputy stationed at the far end of the building stepped out of hiding with his gun pointed at Taggart.

"Drop that weapon," the deputy cried. "Drop it or I'll shoot."

Taggart's head snapped up, his shocked face made white by the light. Then he turned and ran. The deputy opened fire.

DREW SAID it all in one shuddering breath — told the Thing he'd seen her shoot Pop Pop — then, as if he'd only just heard the words himself, he clamped his hands over his mouth.

"And when you told folks what you seen — what'd they do? Why didn't they b'lieve you?"

"I didn't tell nobody."

"You watched me shoot your Pop Pop and you didn't tell nobody?"

He shook his head, remembered that she'd kicked him for nodding and said, "No, ma'am. I didn't tell nobody."

"And why was that?"

"I'd … get in trouble?"

"What for?"

"I wasn't s'posed to get out of bed at night. Mommy said. But I followed Pop Pop because I wanted my GI Joe doll."

"And what would your mama do if she found out you'd got out of bed without permission and went out to the barn?"

"She'd spank me. She said."

The Thing … Mama Bert … burst out laughing, a full belly laugh that seemed to echo in the small room.

"So you watched me shoot your grandfather, but you never told anybody about it because you were afraid you'd get a spanking?"

She was laughing as she asked the question.

"Yes, ma'am."

She stood looking down at him, shaking her head.

"Can you beat that?" She paused. "And you ain't never told nobody since?"

"No, ma'am.

She continued shaking her head as she looked down at him. Then she wrinkled up her nose.

"Did you piss your pants?"

He was so horrified he couldn't speak now, no matter how hard she kicked him. He merely nodded.

"Well, you're just gonna have to sit in it."

She turned around and went out the door and closed it behind her, kind of waddled because she was so fat. Fat like Mommy used to be but wasn't anymore.

Mommy. And Daddy.

He wanted his mommy and daddy so bad he started to cry, couldn't help it. But he cried as quiet as he could because he didn't want the Thing to open the door and come back in.

Reaching up to his forehead, he touched a big lump there and winced from the pain. It hurt. His whole head hurt. But his heart hurt worse. It was a mix of scared and sad. Scared of what was going to happen to him. And sad because he knew he was never going to see his mommy and daddy again.

Or the foal, Coco.

He would never get to ride Coco.

He put his face in his hands and sobbed, didn't try to

be quiet, couldn't help how noisy it was. He kept crying because he couldn't stop.

A BULLET FLEW by Willie Ray's head close enough for him to hear the buzz.

Contrary to every cop show and western movie you've ever seen, it is seriously difficult to hit a moving target.

The sergeant's words from basic training rang in Willie Ray's head and he zigzagged off into the darkness, hunkered over, staying low.

He heard more gunfire, a bullet ricocheted off the tarmac at his feet. What felt like a bee sting lit up his left forearm just below the elbow.

Then a voice yelled, "Cease fire. Stop shooting, you idiot."

There was more yelling and sounded like somebody was chasing him, more than one somebody. Willie Ray kept running. He only glanced back once, saw a couple of flashlight beams moving off into the darkness toward the trees on the other side of the runway where Willie Ray'd been hiding. But he didn't run back the way he'd come. He circled around and doubled back, angling to come out near the trees on the same side of the runway as the office building. Then he ran along beside the woods. It was too dark to run through them and he couldn't have found his way in daylight. But he knew that the trees had been cleared away in front of the small corrugated metal building maybe half a mile from the airport office and when he got to the open area, he ran down it toward the structure he could only barely make out in the darkness. Willie Ray got to the building panting, drenched in sweat, blood flowing freely from the wound on his side. Reaching into his pocket, he pulled out his lighter and "flicked his Bic." With the bright flame illuminating the ground, he found the rock with the key to the padlock, slid the bay doors open, and went into the coal-mine dark of the building where Rabbit was nothing more than a bigger puddle of shadow before him.

His lighter provided enough light so he could see to remove the chocks in front of the wheels. There was no time and not enough light for a proper pre-flight. He'd just have to trust everything was in working order. The small biplane's engine wasn't loud, but as soon as he started it, the hounds would come running.

Climbing into the back seat of the plane, he almost wished Andy was in the seat in front of him. He'd never before wished for the presence of the horrifying apparition of his brother but he did now. He could wish all he wanted, of course, and Andy wouldn't show up. Andy hated to fly.

Willie Ray sucked in a big breath, whispered a heartfelt "Hail Mary," and started the engine. He only allowed it to idle for maybe thirty seconds, but it seemed like a lifetime, then he turned up the throttle and the plane moved slowly out of the building. Once the wings had cleared, he cranked the throttle and raced across the flat ground in front of the building. The little biplane needed only about a third of the runway to take off and he held his breath, sure that any second the fuselage would be ripped apart by gunfire.

It wasn't.

Seconds later, he was airborne, soaring up into the night sky.

Chapter Forty-Nine

"You have to call the sheriff!" Jessie said, as Riley knew she would. Knew it would be her first response. "You have to let the law handle it."

He suddenly felt so very tired. Being here with Jessie had given him renewed strength, but the effort to get the two of them on the same page was draining it out again.

They sat at Jessie's kitchen table, didn't have to speak quietly because Harriet Porter wasn't home. The live-in nurse who looked after Davie had gone on the Baptist church trip to Washington D.C. — would be gone a week.

"Listen to yourself, Jessie. This is all about Jackson *McClusky*, who has the *same last name* as the sheriff."

"You don't know for sure it's Jackson."

"Yes, I do, and so do you if you'll let yourself know it. Jackson shows up in the county on Sunday and two days later Drew goes missing. Who else could it be?"

"But … why? Why would Jackson take Drew? What does he get out of it?"

"That's what Big-un said. I didn't have an answer for him and I don't have one for you. But if it's not Jackson, who is it? It has to be about me, someone with a grudge against me, somebody who wants something from me. It's not like a nine-year-old kid has *enemies*."

Nine years old. Though he'd turned nine two weeks ago, the big-bash celebration party was set for this Saturday afternoon. Would Drew be there?

It hit Riley then. All the pent-up fear crashed through his defenses, a raging river washing away a dam, and he was powerless to fight it off. Putting his elbows on the table, he dropped his face into his hands and … broke down. It was the first time in five years he had allowed himself to express powerful emotions. He had cried when Papa died — was murdered! — and he'd come to Jessie then, too, as his safe harbor.

He made no sound as his shoulders shook and tears wet his hands. Jessie got up and came around the table. She didn't sit, though, just stood beside his chair and pulled him over against her, holding him against her body. She wasn't crying with him, as she had done about Papa, but she was making some kind of sound. Something like whimpering, small moaning sounds that spoke of emotion from a place that was already scarred and bruised.

"Jessie, if something has happened to Drew …!" The words rode a strangled sob out of his throat.

"Nothing's happened to Drew!" She spoke with such confidence he could almost believe she was right on the basis of the strength of her words. "He's just fine now and he's going to stay just fine."

She reached down and lifted his face up toward hers, held his chin. Looking into the full-on beauty of Jessie always made it hard for him to breathe. She had tears running down her cheeks, but her jaw was set, resolute.

"I am soooo sorry, Riley. Seeing you hurt like this …" She let the sentence trail off. "I'm sorry for you but I'm not afraid. Sweetheart, if somebody took Drew to get at you, they're not going *to hurt him*. They're going to make some attempt to contact you. Use him to get you to … do something, or give them something. Right now, the best thing you can do is not panic. Hard as it is, all you can do is wait."

He buried his face in her warm body, wrapped his arms around her so tight it surely must have hurt but she didn't complain. He allowed himself to let it all out, the pain and the fear, express it here, now, this one time. When he finally lifted his head and wiped his face, the crying part was done. He'd emptied himself out. Nothing left inside but grit and determination, and the boiling rage that was banked in his chest, waiting to roar out of him like the fire of a dragon and consume everything in his path.

When he had his voice under control, he called Brady Garrison.

At the sound of Riley's voice, Brady began peppering him with questions about Drew.

"Did you find him? Where was he at? Is he all right?"

"Brady, I need your help."

The tone of Riley's voice silenced him.

"Anything. Name it."

"Give me a list of every man who was at Land's End this afternoon… and don't ask me why I want it."

There was silence on the other end of the line.

Then Brady said quietly, "Call me back in five minutes."

He called back and Brady read off names as Riley wrote them down. Riley asked questions about the names he didn't know, Brady told him everything he could think of. There were a couple of people neither one of them knew well, so Riley put a mark beside those names, figured to come back to them after they'd exhausted all the other options. Half an hour later, they had narrowed the list down to only two names they couldn't be completely certain about. Brady had only a mailing address, a rural route number, for one of them; Riley was pretty sure he knew where the other man lived, or could make a couple of calls and find out.

Riley hung up the phone and looked helplessly at Jessie.

"All I can do is track down—"

Jessie turned at a sound, a distant phone ringing.

"That's Harriet's phone," she said. "She's on that trip to D.C., won't be back until Saturday."

Riley turned back to the list.

"This is the fourth time her phone has rung while you were on the phone to Brady."

"Answer it."

Jessie rushed to Harriet's apartment and lifted the receiver. Riley figured she'd made it just in time to hear a click in her ear.

"Hello."

"Figured if I kept calling Harriet's number, you'd pick up eventually." Jessie held the phone so Riley could hear what was said. "Must be somethin' wrong with your phone. I been callin' and callin' and gettin' nothin' but a busy signal."

"Who is—?"

Riley knew.

"Give the phone to Riley." There was a pause. "And you might want to consider how it is I knew where to find him when he wasn't home," Mama Bert said. "And what else I might know about the two of you, *Mrs.* Monaghan."

Riley was so startled, he didn't know how to respond.

"I'm calling about your boy so you need to sit down, shut up and listen." Riley couldn't have spoken even if she hadn't told him to keep silent. "I'm only ever gonna say this one time."

There was a shuffling sound and another voice came on the line — Drew!

"Daddy …"

"Drew! Are you all right? Are—?"

Mama Bert was back on the line.

"He's just fine." She turned away from the phone. "You tell him, Drew. Did I hurt you? Don't you lie to your Daddy — tell him the truth."

"She didn't hurt me," Drew said, but he sounded so terrified it broke Riley's heart.

"See, I told you—"

"If you so much as touch a hair on his head, I'll—"

"You ain't in no position to be making threats so shut your mouth!"

The menace in her voice rumbled through the phone lines.

"You say one more word less'n I tell you to, and … it'll get ugly."

Riley said nothing.

"That's better. 'Thout you buttin' in, this ain't gonna take long. I got something you want, you got something I want. And we gonna trade. Just like we done before. Simple as that."

"Wha—" Riley started to ask, but caught himself.

"What have you got that I want — that's what you was gonna ask, wasn't it? Real simple answer, one word. Seed."

Seed?

Riley was holding the phone so Jessie could hear and they looked at each other in astonishment.

"You heard right. I said seed. Marijuana seed. Righteous Weed seed."

Again, he started to speak, but this time Jessie shook her head and he remained silent.

"You cut me off that good price and my customers was reeal unhappy this year. I been trying to figure out what to do about that when it come to me that I'd ought to grow my own weed so I wouldn't have to depend on nobody else. Trouble is, I can't just grow any old weed. My customers is used to the best. Baby Bear's bed. Didn't figure you'd *sell* me the seed … and then, lo and behold, this afternoon the answer to all my problems literally fell into my lap. And I took it."

She paused and Riley wondered if he was supposed to say something, but before he had a chance, she spoke.

"I's just giving you a minute to digest all that, and to think what it means — logically, using your head and not your gut. *It means don't nobody got to get hurt here*. This here's a business deal, plain and simple. You get what you want and I get what I want. Now if you was to … oh, I don't know … come to the trade armed, say. Or bring along some others with guns. Then it wouldn't be business no more. It'd be personal. And when I get in a personal fight, I don't never fight fair and I *always* win. Them kinda fights is ugly, and somebody *always* gets hurt.

"Or let's say somewhere down the line you was to decide you didn't like the deal we done. Next week, next month, next year. Get yore panties all in a wad about it and decide to … even the score. Just remember I been around a lot longer than you and faced down men way smarter and meaner than you are. You come after me, you's picking a fight with a predator. Predators always go after the weakest prey, always find the *young*, defenseless ones that even a big herd *can't protect every minute of every day*."

He got her message. She paused again.

"All right, you can talk now."

"What do you want?" The words were without intonation or emotion, floating up in the smoke above the molten lava of his rage.

"You gonna bring me two quart jars of seed, collect your boy and take him home. *Meet me* at the home of Brewster's own Mayor for Life Malcolm Murdock. *You got one hour, starting now.*"

He digested that — Malcom was mixed up in this! — as she continued.

"You come all by your lonesome — *un-armed*. That means not even a pair of fingernail clippers. You do *anything* … even the tiniest little thing that raises the hackles on my neck … and your boy won't be in attendance at his ninth birthday party on Saturday. Won't take you and me five minutes to do our bidness, then you can take your boy home." She paused. "He's got a little bump on his forehead — I didn't do *nothin'*, just ask him — so you might want to put some ice on it 'fore you tuck him into his bed and read him a bedtime story." She paused again. "What do you say?"

"An hour's not enough time."

"It's all the time you got."

There was a beat of silence. Two.

"Deal," Riley said. The phone clicked and the receiver went dead in his hand.

Chapter Fifty

Riley stood with the silent telephone receiver in his hand. Stood for five, maybe ten seconds without moving. Didn't breathe, didn't think, his head as empty as the spot in his belly where the wind blew through, the place where he mourned his grandfather.

Jessie took the receiver from him and hung it up and the motion reanimated him, like putting his batteries back in. They both spoke at the same time, garbling each other's words.

Riley said, "I think I could use pinto beans."

Jessie said, "Now, we can call the sheriff."

Riley caught the one word, "sheriff."

"Beans?" Jessie asked. "What for?"

"You know I can't get to the Tree House and back to Malcolm's house in an hour! Cannabis seeds are all shapes and sizes and dried beans look the most like Righteous Weed seeds. Besides, she's never seen any to know the difference."

Jessie put her hand on Riley's arm.

"We have to call the sheriff now." He opened his

mouth to protest but she waved him off. "Use your head, Riley. You know where she'll be and when — with Drew. The sheriff and his deputies could surround—"

"The house of Malcolm Murdock, Mayor for Life, on the word of Riley Hannacker? Seriously?"

"But they're ... police officers and this is *kidnapping*!"

"No, they're McCluskys and this is family."

"Call the state police, then—"

He didn't have time for an argument and he needed Jessie's support. Putting his hands on her shoulders he looked earnestly into her face.

"Even if the police would actually do something — and they won't — but if they did they're so inept they'd get Drew killed. Clyde McClusky. Put Drew's *life* in the hands of that bumbling fool. His deputies are a bunch of untrained bozos who'd screw up a one-car funeral."

"The FBI, then." A half-hearted effort.

"Where's the nearest FBI agent? Louisville? Cincinnati? Indianapolis, maybe. That's why she only gave me an hour — so I wouldn't have time to summon help.

Riley was on the hook for this one. He saw that realization settle around Jessie.

"Fine, then. It's just us."

"Just *me*."

"You planning on duct-taping me to the bedpost because that's the only way you can keep me from going with you."

"It has to be me, *alone*." He put his fingers to her lips before she could speak. "There's Davie." The live-in nurse wasn't here to look after him. "I'm glad Willie Ray's not here because he'd be even harder to handle than you are. I have to go in there alone and bring Drew out. And you have to let me."

"*She's* not going to be alone — she'll have half a dozen

armed guards. Riley, if you go in there by yourself, unarmed, neither one of you is ever coming back out."

"Why would Mama Bert kill me? Or Drew? What for? Like we said about Jackson, what's in it for her? Two dead bodies … after she got what she wanted, or thinks she did."

"About what she wants, what she *says* she wants. What's with her sudden interest in marijuana seeds? What's up with that? She's never shown any interest in growing weed. Why now?"

"When we were selling it to her at a bargain price, there was no need for her to grow it herself. Now there is. I believe she's telling the truth about her customers being pissed off about her price hike. She's got enterprises all over the country — maybe she doesn't plan to grow the weed herself — she going to get somebody else to …"

He let the words trail off, ran his hands through his hair in fear and frustration.

"Let's stop focusing on what we don't know and focus on what we do know."

"And that is?"

"The only thing that makes any sense is that she was mostly telling the truth. She wants seed, and suddenly she sees Drew at Land's End all by himself and she snatches him, an impulsive crime — the teller left the cash drawer open. Which means she's as anxious for this 'business transaction' to go smooth as we are."

"And when she figures out she's got two jars of pinto beans?"

"Once I get Drew out of harm's way … Bertha Calhoun is gonna pay for what she's done. For traumatizing …"

The word caught in his throat. Poor Drew, so scared. Yeah, Mama Bert was gonna pay dearly for that! He gritted his teeth. "I will take that *witch* on and we'll see who's predator and who's prey!"

He realized his words were upsetting Jessie.

"Hey, there's no sense in getting out there ahead of our headlights. One step at a time. We'll worry about what to do about Mama Bert when the dust settles."

"I'm scared, Riley."

He put his arms around her and found her trembling. Kissing the top of her head, he crooned. "It's gonna be okay. You'll see." He pulled out of her embrace and stood looking down at her. "We got to keep the main thing the main thing. Concentrate on what we're certain of. We *know* Mama Bert took Drew as a means to an end. She won't hurt him — has no reason to. We know there's nothing in it for Mama Bert to kill me, either. Only a fool commits two murders when she doesn't have to and Mama Bert is nobody's fool. Drew and I are safe."

Chapter Fifty-One

THE FEDERAL BUREAU OF INVESTIGATION had helicopters. Surely, they did. Of course they did. And maybe the Missouri State Police had choppers, too. Shoot, might be the Richland County Sheriff's Department had a helicopter. One or the other of them, or maybe all of them, would be dispatched to chase after Willie Ray as soon as somebody could put in a call.

He hadn't flipped on the running lights — remembered Harold Tobin's instruction "red light on the right, coming *at* you in the night" or some such as that. Small aircraft had a red light on the left wing and a green light on the right wing so other aircraft could tell their direction of flight by the positions of the different colors. Rabbit the biplane wasn't white, thank goodness. Its school-bus yellow color wouldn't reflect light. It'd be a shadow passing above the houses and barns and fields. He figured that out here in the country there weren't a whole lot of folks who'd decide to take an airplane ride at four o'clock in the morning, but if any had, he would see them coming even if they couldn't see him

He had no idea how much time he had. State Police might have a chopper fueled and ready to go in ... what was the capital of Missouri, anyway? Joplin? No, somewhere else. Jefferson City? Didn't matter. Willie Ray didn't know how far either one of them was from Empire Township, and maybe there was one closer they'd send after him. When he'd first staggered out of the woods at the edge of the airport, he'd wondered if he had delusions of grandeur. Would they *really* go to the trouble to stake out his airplane to catch him? Did they want him *that* bad? Well, apparently they did.

He flew maybe a hundred feet above the treetops, grateful that the sky had cleared and there was a dim glow of moon to light his way. Skirting the little town, he headed due north by the compass. Given how he'd spent the day — hiding from the FBI on the roof of a barn with his dead brother — he should not be enjoying himself. But he was! It was impossible to fly an amazing aircraft like Rabbit and not feel something akin to euphoria.

I gotta get me one of these!

Yeah, right. Copy that. Like you're ever gonna get to spend any more of the money stashed in the Tree House. He bet there was two million dollars there, at least. Maybe less. Maybe *more*. He'd ought to count it. But if the FBI was fixing to haul him off to the iron house, he might be making his last flight for a good long time. He and the others were apparently in deep, deep doodoo. He shouldn't be surprised. They'd talked about it half a hundred times. With Sherry Lynn Hannacker spending money like it was burning a hole in her pocket, it wasn't like Riley was flying below the radar. Over the past nine years, they'd probably employed a hundred different men to work in their fields, had rented a little piece of some farmer's back forty from a couple of dozen different farmers. Paid cash for everything. Gave money away. People knew what they were doing. Local people. But the locals wouldn't talk to the law. So how did the FBI find Willie Ray?

That was one of a whole herd of questions that'd buzzed like gnats in his head as he lay on the barn roof looking at the red mud on Andy's boots. He couldn't imagine what'd given him away, but that was the problem with growing weed out of state. To these folks, Willie Ray and his men were the outsiders. They didn't have a home court advantage here.

Passing over Empire Township's manmade lake, he continued north. The minutes crawled by. He was beginning to believe he'd missed his destination when he saw a shiny spot on the ground up ahead, a small round pond glowing in the scant moonlight. He circled it a couple of times, wishing there was a windsock to tell him the direction so he could land into the wind. With its dual wings, the biplane was more susceptible to cross winds than his Cessna. The field in front of the barn sure looked short! Jack had taken off from there and landed, hadn't he? How long ago? Maybe the field used to be longer. Well, it was too late to worry about that now. The barn was on the west side of the field. He came in from the east so he could taxi into the barn. Slowed the craft until he was afraid it'd fall out of the sky, brushed the tallest of the trees in the woods beyond the barn with the landing gear, pulled the nose up and cut the throttle … and eased down into the dirt like a swan on a pond.

For a horrifying few moments he feared he was coming in too hot — there were no brakes on a biplane! — and would ram the barn at the end of the field. If Jack had just been bragging that Rabbit's low stall speed made it possible to "land the thing almost lake a parachute," then Willie Ray and the aircraft were both about to come to an abrupt and untimely end. But as soon as the wheels hit the soft dirt, the drag slowed the forward motion. Though the biplane only came to a complete stop a horrifying fifty feet in front of the barn doors, it did make maneuvering the aircraft into the building a simpler task. He couldn't get the whole plane inside, and maybe Jack hadn't been able to either. The bay doors wouldn't close all the way, but far enough that from the outside you couldn't see the tail of the plane that was blocking them.

Leaning back against the doors, panting, Willie Ray saw with dismay that the eastern sky was dark blue instead of black. It would be daylight soon.

He hated to break into the old farm house by the road, and might be he wouldn't find any food or water there if he did, but he'd see to it Jack Broczkowski got paid hand-somely for "borrowing his airplane" and the rest — enough money to buy a "Jill" Rabbit to keep Jack Rabbit company.

All that was out there in an unknown future, though, a scary future. Willie Ray Taggart was likely on a fast track to jail. They hadn't busted the operation in Minnesota — not that he knew of, anyway. He didn't know if they'd got close enough to identify him on that dark runway. But shoot, if the FBI was trying to take the whole thing down, he'd go crashing down right along with it. Prison. For how long? Hard to think about that as a real possibility — prob-ability — without the kind of sick feeling in his gut he'd had every morning after they called up the guard unit.

He reached up and touched the scar that ran down his cheek from the corner of his eye to his jaw. He'd survived what come after the guard call-up and he'd survive what-ever come after this, too. Or not. And really, either way was fine with Willie Ray.

Chapter Fifty-Two

WHEN RILEY DROVE up the driveway to the big colonial house that was the centerpiece for the Land's End horse farm, there were no other cars parked out front. The upstairs of the house was bright, the downstairs lights were off, on the inside anyway. The spotlights were located strategically behind flowers and bushes, lit up the outside like it was centerstage in an opera. Sherry Lynn had wanted those and had been surprised when Riley didn't put up a fight. She wanted them for ornamentation; he figured it was hard to sneak up on a place that's lit up like a Christmas tree.

He looked around as he walked up the sidewalk to the porch, but if Mama Bert had armed men stationed out here, they were hidden so well Riley couldn't see them. He ignored the doorbell — that he knew would produce a melodic chime inside. It felt good to raise his fist and bang hard on the door.

"Who's there?" called a voice from within. Malcolm.

"Riley Hannacker."

"You alone?" That was Mama Bert.

"I'm alone."

"You and your boy gone be reel sorry if you ain't."

"I said I was alone!"

Silence.

"You bring the seed?"

"Two jars, just like you said."

"Open the door and push it in, set the jars down inside, then you walk in with your hands raised up high as a Penny-costal in church."

Riley opened the door and placed the two jars full of dried pinto beans on the floor, then walked around them into the foyer and stood in front of the ridiculous porpoise fountain with his hands in the air. The chandelier that hung down from the ceiling two floors up was glittering brightly, casting prisms of light to dance on the walls and the hardwood floor. The regal staircase that swept down from high above was on his left, the archways on both sides of the foyer, one leading into the dining room and one into the formal living room, were dark.

"Close the door, fool — you born in a barn?"

Riley took a step back, reached out to the door and slammed it shut with a bang, then lifted his hand back into the air.

"You just stand where you are until I get an all-clear that you didn't bring along any party crashers."

A minute or two went by, then Mama Bert called out from the depths of the dark living room. "You stand where you are and Malcolm here is gonna make sure you ain't packing."

A few seconds later, Malcolm Murdock shambled out of the darkness, looked like a zombie, his eyes on the floor, his shoulders hunched.

"Frisk him," Mama Bert said.

Malcolm didn't seem to hear her, just stood where he was.

"I told you to—"

He moved to Riley then, stood before him, looking helpless.

"How do you—?" he began and his voice was soft and dry, scratchy and eerie, as if he were, indeed, dead and was speaking to them out of his crypt.

"Pat him down. Make sure he ain't got no gun stuck down in the back of his pants. Feel of his ankles."

Clearly, Malcolm did not want to touch Riley. He reached out a tentative hand and Riley turned his back so Malcolm could see there was no gun.

Malcolm got down on his knees carefully, an old man. He had aged twenty years since Riley saw him this afternoon. He half-heartedly felt of Riley's ankles, then started getting slowly to his feet. Riley did not reach down a hand to help him up.

"I said I'd come alone and unarmed and I did. Now where's my boy!"

"Steady, there. I'm the one's in charge here and we gone do this my way. You brung my seed?"

Gesturing with his chin, Riley said, "Right there. Two quarts like you said. I want to see Drew."

"How do I know that there's the seed I want? How do I know you didn't fill them jars up with rocks?"

"Look for yourself."

The light from the chandelier was way brighter than Riley remembered, from the one occasion when Sherry Lynn insisted they attend the Murdocks' Christmas party. The light must have been dimmed that night for effect. She might not know what a Righteous Weed seed looked like but at least she could tell the jars weren't filled with rocks.

"Malcolm ... check."

298

Malcolm shuffled over to the nearest jar, picked it up, put it in the crook of his arm and unscrewed the lid. Sticking his hand down through the opening, he withdrew a handful of the contents, examined it.

"It's seed."

"Marijuana seed?"

It occurred to Riley that Malcolm might not know what a marijuana seed looked like, but he sounded convincing.

"Yeah, marijuana seed."

"I want to see my son. I kept my end of the bargain. It's time for you to keep yours."

"Malcolm, get the lights."

Malcolm went back into the darkened living room, flipped a switch and four table lamps snapped on. Not bright light like in the foyer, dimmer and golden glowing through the shades.

Mama Bert stood in the center of the room with Drew. She had what looked like a Colt .45 in one hand and the collar of Drew's shirt in the other, holding him tight up against her side.

"Drew!" Riley gasped. He took one step forward.

"Hold it right there," Mama Bert said, and cocked the pistol.

Riley froze. Drew's hands and feet were not tied, but there was a piece of duct tape across his mouth, and a huge purple bruise on his forehead. Before Riley could say a word, Mama Bert said, "Wasn't my fault. He run into a cabinet door." She looked down at Drew. "Didn't you?"

Drew nodded, his eyes huge with terror.

Malcolm had put the jar back down on the floor and began shuffling back into the living room.

"Let him go. I brought you the seeds. The trade's done."

"First, you step into the fountain."

"What!" Riley was outraged, didn't try to keep the anger and menace out of his voice. "I'm not going to—"

"Yeah, you are. Soon's you're standing in that water, I'll send out your boy."

Why the fountain?

Like she'd heard the question, she said, "Hard to jump somebody when you up to your knees in water."

The explanation didn't ring true and Riley felt unease spread like the opening of an oleander blossom in his chest. Malcolm shuffled up to Mama Bert but didn't stop next to her, just kept walking. Riley took two steps and lifted his foot up over the three-foot-tall edge of the fountain, staying near the rim where the spray of the water out the porpoise's mouth didn't reach.

He turned to face Mama Bert. She took a couple of steps toward him, then let go of Drew's shirt and shoved him at Riley. Drew raced across the marble floor of the foyer, jumped over the edge of the bowl and grabbed his father in a vice-like hug, his face hurried in Riley's chest. Riley hugged the boy to him, could feel his shoulders shaking as he cried but he made no sound because of the tape over his mouth.

Rage burned in the back of his throat. Mama Bert would pay for this, for what she'd done to this poor little boy. Why would she ever believe Riley wouldn't make her sorry one day?

Yeah, why would she believe he'd let it slide? He got a sick feeling in his stomach then.

He needed to get out of here with Drew — now!

Reaching down with his right hand, he gently peeled the duct tape off Drew's mouth and sobs erupted from Drew's throat. He smoothed the boy's hair back, crooning, "It's okay now, Daddy's here. I gotcha."

But the boy didn't calm, was still utterly terrified.

Riley hugged him tight, and when the boy's face was buried in his father's chest, Drew whispered, "She killed Pop Pop. I *saw*."

Riley's mind went totally white, like those films of the moment after the detonation of a nuclear warhead. Pure white light and heat burned all thought and meaning away.

But it all returned in the next heartbeat and his eyes snapped to Mama Bert.

She had moved closer to the fountain while he was hugging Drew, stood only about ten feet away. She had the Colt .45 out in front of her in a two-hand grip, aimed at his chest.

"I hated to do it, I really did, but there was nothing for it after Nate killed that I-talian. They'd a sent a army in here and killed you all if I didn't."

Riley had no idea what she was talking about and didn't care.

"The boy was in the barn, seen it all," she said, her voice even and the hand holding the gun totally level and steady. "Didn't never tell nobody because he was a'feared his momma'd give him a spanking for getting out of bed."

She shook her head.

"Can you beat that?"

Every muscle in Riley's body coiled tight, ready to spring. But she was right. It *was* hard to jump somebody when you were standing in a fountain.

As if she could read his mind again, she said, "Yeah … and ain't nearly as big a mess to clean up, neither."

He knew then she meant to kill them both.

Bam!

The gunshot filled up the world.

Chapter Fifty-Three

ELI BRADIGAN HATED working with amateurs!

Putting up with hotshot county-mounties excited to actually have a real live crime to investigate was more than just annoying. It was dangerous. Willie Ray Taggart had gotten away because they'd wanted to play cops and robbers. That deputy had opened fire without any justification for deadly force. There was no reason to believe Taggart was armed — Eli hadn't found a gun of any kind on the other Callison County men they'd arrested. Taggart was lucky they didn't kill him, though they did wound him — not badly. There was only a small blood splatter on the spot where he'd been standing, and a few drips of trail leading away from it.

Eli hadn't even known the other deputy *had* a rifle until he hauled it out and started to sight in on the little airplane that took off at the end of the runway. Eli'd wanted to throttle him.

Shoving the gun barrel to the side, Eli'd hissed, "You got X-ray vision or something, because *I* can't tell from here who's piloting that aircraft."

"It's Taggart," the deputy had protested. "Who else could it be?"

Eli had been incredulous. "Who *else* could it be? Seriously? You'd shoot a plane out of the air in the dark because … well, the suspect *must* be the pilot? What were you planning to say to the widow or the mother of some poor schmuck who decided he wanted to go flying in the moonlight … '*Oops*'?"

When Eli went after the rest of them in Callison County, he'd be in charge of a team of trained agents. With the Kentucky State Police as *backup*. And that moronic county sheriff and his imbecilic deputies directing traffic — somewhere out on the interstate.

Eli waited with Bill Thomas until they finally found a judge to get a search warrant for Taggart's plane. Without ripping up the seats and removing the door side panels, there was nothing of interest, and he'd let a forensics team handle that part later. The local yokels got in touch with the proper authorities about the aircraft that'd flown away into the darkness — the one he knew Willie Ray Taggart was piloting — but they'd have to wait until dawn to start looking and Taggart would be long gone by then. He was no fool — knew he'd never be able fly all the way back to Kentucky in that little biplane. He'd get out of the sky quick, set it down somewhere, get on the telephone and call one of the others to come get him. Eli's agents would be listening to the call, and Eli would get there first — bag Taggart and whoever came to rescue him.

Eli'd been convinced he'd catch Taggart with his hand in the cookie jar … but *somehow* he'd eluded capture. Now he was out there somewhere, in the wind. Forensics would turn up evidence that Taggart had been in that barn, of course — though maybe not. The workers were all wearing gloves when they were arrested, to keep the sticky resin off their hands. But if Eli could catch Willie Ray while he was a still a fugitive, he could tack on other federal charges — like fleeing across state lines to avoid prosecution. He'd hit him with every charge he could think of in hopes that Taggart would be willing to make a deal.

But in truth, Eli didn't hold out much hope for that — regardless of the charges. Not much hope at all.

"I'M Special Agent Elijah Bradigan with the FBI," he says to the handcuffed man seated in a chair on the other side of the table. He's a small man with a crooked harelip scar on his upper lip. Maybe he speaks with a nasal twang because of it, but Eli never finds out.

"So you're …" He looks at the man's Kentucky driver's license. "Phillip Adams, is that right?"

The man looks back at him and says nothing.

"You live at 384 Sulphur Springs Road in Callison County, Kentucky?"

The man just looks at him.

"This is your driver's license, isn't it?" He holds it out in front of the man's face but he doesn't look at it. Just sits, says nothing.

"You know what the charge against you is, right? Manufacturing with intent to distribute marijuana. For fifty to ninety-nine plants, the penalty is up to twenty years in prison and a fine of up to a million dollars. A hundred plants to nine-hundred ninety-nine plants carries a penalty of five to forty years in prison and a fine of two to five million dollars. We haven't counted them yet, but I figure there was somewhere between a hundred and a thousand plants in that barn. Do you understand what that means?"

Silence.

"Even as a first offense, you're looking at a significant prison sentence. But I might be able to help you out with that. In exchange for your testimony—"

He only gets that far when the man yawns broadly, leans back in his chair and closes his eyes.

Another half hour of questioning is met with fake sleep, never opens his eyes a single time.

He gets marginally more out of Hudson Watkins. When asked if the driver's license in Eli's hand is his, he grunts, "Uh huh."

He follows that up with an equally enlightening "Yup," when asked about his address, and a shoulder shrug when asked if he understood that he was in serious trouble. Eli wonders if the group had actually practiced in advance, because the second man performs the same yawn-eye-close routine as the first as soon as Eli tells him he can help him out with the charges against him if he'll cooperate.

But the third man doesn't yawn and pretend to nod off. He's more hostile than the others, belligerently silent, a big man with a broad chest, a head of unruly black hair that falls into his eyes, and significant body odor. Eli asks him about Willie Ray Taggart.

"What happened to your boss? You don't have to play dumb, we know Willie Ray Taggart is running the show. He ran off and left the rest of you holding the bag, you know?"

The black-haired man named Phelps glares at him from under a single black unibrow that resembles a wooly worm over his eyes.

"He flew in here in his fancy airplane, then bailed out on the rest of you when the heat was on. Saved his own butt. Why would you want to protect a man like that? He obviously doesn't give a Fig Newton about you."

The man leans his head back and hawks a wad of spit at Eli, which falls short and lands with a splat on the table separating them.

THE ONLY WORDS any of them spoke during hours of interviews were polite requests to go to the bathroom. Only Phelps had been belligerent so far. Maybe some of the men slated for later interrogation would be more forthcoming, but Eli didn't think so. He'd decided he'd try to make them angry, see if that would pry something out of them. Maybe after they'd spent some time behind bars, they'd rethink their reticence. But he didn't really believe that would matter, either. That kind of stubborn loyalty was unique and Eli couldn't help a grudging admiration for the men, and an unconscious recalibrating of his assessment of their leaders. The kind of monsters he'd been looking for didn't generate this kind of loyalty. And not fear loyalty. Steadfast *allegiance*.

If it held up, that did not bode well for Eli's case against the ringleaders. Somebody was going to have to open up and finger the leaders. Without someone's testimony, he couldn't make the Kingpin Statute charges against Hannacker, Taggart and Monaghan stick.

And they were in charge. He was certain of it.

Riley Hannacker. Willie Ray Taggart. Jessica Monaghan.

If they really weren't the ruthless monsters he'd had them pegged to be … what kind of people were they?

Chapter Fifty-Four

MAMA BERT STOOD with the Colt .45 leveled at Riley's chest, her hand steady. But an odd look took over her face, like she was confused. Surprised.

Then her grip on the pistol loosened and it clattered to the tile floor. She stood a moment longer, like she was about to turn around and rush off to attend to something important that she'd forgot. Her knees buckled then, and her huge body tumbled to the floor, her head smacking the tiles with a sickening cracking sound before she rolled over onto her back.

She lay perfectly still.

Malcolm Murdock stood in the archway from the living room, slowly lowering the pistol in his hand.

"Is she dead?" he asked, in a voice that sounded like he was the one who was dead.

Riley cut his eyes toward the door and the stairs, had to get Drew away before her men—

"She's alone," Malcolm said. "All happened so fast, I don't think she told anybody."

Riley got out of the fountain and stepped up to the

body, water pooling around his shoes. He couldn't tell if she was breathing, but her eyes were open. Reaching down, he picked up the pistol she'd dropped, pointed it and pulled the trigger, shooting her in the center of the forehead, made a neat little hole, looked just like Papa's.

Drew stood beside him, watching.

Malcolm looked at Riley and Drew and told them, "You need to get out of here." Then he walked back into the living room and picked up the receiver of the telephone sitting on the side table.

Riley seemed to be tracking too slowly, like the words were a beat or two behind the movement of Malcolm's lips. But his meaning was clear, and he was right.

"Malcolm, what … why—?"

Malcolm paused with the receiver halfway to his ear.

"She's been blackmailing me for years." He cocked his head to the side, musing. "She must have planned the whole thing out in advance, but I don't know how she could have …" He glanced at Drew, then into Riley's eyes. "In El Paso for a Thoroughbred Breeders Association Convention. Her man Floyd got me drunk, maybe drugged me, I don't know. Took me across the border into Mexico and …" He stopped, took a breath. "There were … *pictures*."

He reached down and dialed 911.

Looking at Drew, Malcolm's eyes filled with tears. "I am so sorry, son. So sorry. I shouldn't have let her …"

Then he spoke into the receiver.

"This is Malcolm Murdock and I want to report a murder."

"It wasn't *murder* — you saved our lives," Riley hissed.

Holding the receiver against his chest, Malcolm whispered, "This is on *me* … I … she set it up so pictures would be … disclosed in the event of her death." He nodded at

Mama Bert's pistol still in Riley's hand. "You were never here. I'll clean the prints — go!"

Riley stood frozen for a moment, heard Malcolm speak into the receiver.

"I just shot Bertha Calhoun. Twice."

Riley set the pistol down on the floor carefully, took Drew's hand and started for the door. He stopped to pick up the quart jars of seeds, listening to Malcolm's calm voice tell the dispatcher there was no hurry, no need to send an ambulance. Mama Bert was dead.

Without looking back, Riley closed the door behind him and ran with Drew out to his truck. He had just gotten behind the wheel when he heard the sound of a single gunshot from inside Malcolm's house. Then it was quiet.

RILEY DIDN'T MAKE it all the way home from Land's End before he pulled over. Just drove far enough away, found a dirt road he could angle his truck into. Drew had been sitting beside him as rigid as a mannequin. The boy was in shock and maybe worse. When he was just four years old, Drew had seen Mama Bert kill Papa, had sneaked out of bed for whatever reason, went to the barn and saw the whole thing. And for five years, the little boy told no one.

It explained everything. His sudden shyness, not wanting to go out among strangers. Maybe even explained what happened at the Burley Festival. He must have seen Mama Bert in the crowd. In fact, Riley remembered seeing here there. She had been in the line to buy a funnel cake. He'd given Drew money to go by himself to get a funnel cake.

Then he was kidnapped, watched his father put a bullet in Mama Bert's forehead.

Could a *child* ever get over that kind of emotional trauma?

Riley turned off the truck lights and sat in silence for a little while, listening to the crickets in the grass beside the road, the tree frogs, and nearer, the clicking and ticking of the truck's engine cooling. He needed to say something, had to say something. But he didn't know what.

Then he just let go, reached out to Drew and pulled him into his arms and hugged him fiercely. He babbled then, spoke words into the boy's hair. "I love you, Drew. I am so sorry … about all of it. So sorry you watched Pop Pop die. So sorry I left you alone. If I'd stayed with you, Mama Bert couldn't have …"

He said other things too, about how he would be a better father from now on, would look after Drew better, would never let anybody or anything hurt or scare him again.

At some point in his ramblings Drew started to cry, soft, as if he was trying not to.

"Cry, Drew!" Riley finally said. "You don't have to hold back the tears."

And that opened the flood gates. Then boy cried hard, hugging his father in a strangle hold, great wrenching sobs that tore out of his chest and ripped open Riley's heart. He sobbed as if his heart would break. Cried and cried until he finally wound down and was silent, just sniffling, breathing in that hitching way little kids breathe when they've been crying for a long time.

He seemed to be trying to pull himself together, but Riley didn't want him to stop until he was ready to stop.

"It's alright, Drew. You can cry some more if you need to. Scream, yell, kick things, break things … whatever you want to do. You're entitled. After what you've been through, you're entitled to break every lamp in your mama's living room."

He thought that hit home with the boy.

"And you can talk about it if you want to. You can tell me or" — He didn't even bother to say "your mommy." Drew could never tell his mother about what'd happened to him — "or that counselor, or Father Donavan, or Uncle Willie Ray ... or nobody at all. You don't have to say a word to anybody ... right now. You don't have to talk about it until you're ready. One day, you will need to tack words onto what has happened to you, but not tonight or tomorrow or next week. When you're *ready*."

The boy's voice was ragged. Riley barely heard what he said.

"I ... wet my pants, Daddy. I ... I'm sorry."

Riley squeezed his hug tighter.

"It's nothing to be embarrassed about ... listen ... if it'll make you feel any better ... I'll pee in my pants, too, and we can both go home with wet pants."

Maybe Drew laughed softly.

"It's dry now. But it stinks." He paused. "I don't want Mommy to ... be mad at me."

A wave of unreasoning rage washed over Riley and he could barely control himself. Drew was so afraid his airheaded mother would give him a spanking that he harbored a horrible secret for five years.

What would Riley say to Sherry Lynn when he came in with Drew an emotional wreck and a lump on his forehead? When she got home and found both of them gone, she'd probably been apoplectic — and that was hours ago.

He'd make up some kind of excuse — tell her he'd taken Drew to Land's End to play with the foals while he talked to Brady, they'd spent the day there, where Drew fell in the barn and hit his head. Then something bad happened at the Murdocks' and the police came and that upset him. End of story.

Of course, she'd demand to rush Drew to the hospital emergency room the instant she saw him but Riley would … he'd just tell her no! Let her explode and throw a tantrum. He didn't give a rip what she thought, he was going to take his son home, get him cleaned up and put him to bed and sit by his bed until he fell asleep. She could take Drew into town to see the doctor tomorrow, but *not* tonight.

Drew stayed snuggled up against Riley's side as he drove home and Riley reveled in the sheer joy of the boy's nearness. He'd stop and use the payphone at the 7-Eleven, give Jessie a quick call to tell her what'd happened, that Drew was safe. *Safe* — everything else in life paled by comparison. Winona McClusky. Jackson. Yeah, even Jackson. All that mattered to Riley Hannacker right now was Drew—

Willie Ray.

He was supposed to be home today, said he'd be there by suppertime.

Where was Willie Ray?

Chapter Fifty-Five

THE BODYGUARD NAMED José woke Jackson shortly after dawn Thursday morning with the news.

"The woman you went to see at that tavern the day after we got here, that Mama Bert — she got shot dead last night," he said.

Staggering bleary-eyed out of bed, unbelieving, Jackson dispatched all four of his men to town to find out everything they could about the shooting. By the time they returned, Jackson was up, dressed, drinking coffee, *planning*.

Seemed Malcolm Murdock killed Mama Bert, then committed suicide. The gory details weren't hard to find out because the whole town was talking about nothing else. The mayor-for-life owner of Land's End thoroughbred horse farm had shot Bertha Calhoun in cold blood, called the police dispatcher and confessed, and when the law arrived, they found Murdock dead, too — self-inflicted gunshot wound.

The whole town was spinning around in circles trying to figure out why Malcolm Murdock would do a thing like that. Jackson didn't care why. The deed was done and the doing of it left Jackson McClusky up a creek without a paddle. He paced for the rest of the morning around the big old Dawson house, out to the gazebo and back, couldn't sit down, couldn't be still. He was clinging to his resolve with his fingernails, only about three spineless seconds away from giving in and snorting a line of coke. Or worse.

He couldn't steal what he couldn't find.

And he couldn't find what he was looking for without Mama Bert's help! It wasn't like he really could *negotiate* with the Cornbread Mafia, as he'd suggested to El Escorpión — get together over coffee and make some kind of deal. It was three against one.

Unless he evened up the odds.

How about two against one — one who had an edge.

Yeah, he could make that work. Not here, of course. Had to have someplace private. And he knew just the place.

He strode back into the house where his four henchmen were sitting at the kitchen table playing cards. They didn't think he understood Spanish so they said all kinda nasty things about him to each other. They were nothing more than hired help, and he was finally gonna be able to put them to good use. But one day … one day soon, he would be el jéfe.

"I'm going home," he announced. "Gonna go pay a visit to my mama."

Jackson had grown up on the far side of Bald Knob same as the other kids, and the fact that his father had never approved of him didn't somehow excommunicate him from the family. His mama'd been different, though. She had never sided with Daddy about their oldest son, always tried to take up for him whenever she could. She was his mama, after all, and she was the one person in the whole world who would ever love him unconditionally. He was sure his father was no more anxious to see him than Jackson was to see his father, so he would leave mother and son alone to have a nice little visit.

But that was not to be. Jackson's heart sank when he got out of his rented van just as his father was pulling out of the barn on a tractor. He hoped his father would just drive on, go plow that field or whatever and leave Jackson be, but he didn't. He stopped, killed the engine on the tractor and climbed down off of it and headed Jackson's way.

Well, it was what it was. At least Jackson looked good. He had filled out in the five years he'd been away, his shoulders were even broader than when he'd got out of prison, his arms more muscled. He was no Big-un McClusky, but Big-un was one of a kind. Jackson could take any of his brothers now, though, take them down without getting a hair out of place. Take them down with one eye tied behind his back.

"Heard you's back in town," Big-un said as he approached. Jackson wasn't surprised he'd heard. After the scene at St. Augustine Sunday, the whole county knew he'd come back.

His father didn't offer to embrace, of course, they'd never done that even when he was a kid. He didn't hold out his hand to shake. Didn't smile either.

"Been here for awhile," Jackson said.

"Where you at?"

Jackson didn't see that that was any of his father's business.

"Here and there." He knew his father had wanted an answer to his question or he wouldn't have asked it. He wasn't one for chitchat. And he liked the fact that his response had irritated the big man, though he certainly showed no sign of irritation — or any other emotion on his big face.

"I come to see Mama," Jackson said and turned toward the gate in the fence.

"She ain't here. Gone to the grocery." Big-un looked at his watch. "Oughta be back any minute now."

Jackson did not want to hang around waiting for his mother. He turned back toward the van.

"Tell her I stopped by."

He hadn't taken a step before his father asked, "What's that there contraption on your arm? Covers up them burn scars you got over there in 'Nam?"

Jackson nodded and kept walking.

"… when you was beating at the flames on that fella you set on fire — that the way of it?"

Jackson stopped, stood dead still for a moment, then turned slowly to face his father. The man's face was as impassive as a body in a casket.

"Now, where'd you hear a thing like that?"

"Smitty tole me. He worked for the Cornbread Mafia, said Riley got drunk one night and was telling war stories."

"And Riley said that? Said I set the Jingle Bell Man on fire and got burned putting out the flames?"

"The *Jingle Bell Man* …" Big-un considered the name, then continued. "Yeah, that's what he said." Spitting a plug of tobacco juice into the dirt, his father grumbled, "Course, don't nobody b'lieve a word them lying Hannackers say."

"You got *that* right."

Big-un hated the Hannackers about as much as Jackson did, so it didn't matter what he'd heard, he hadn't bought it. "Only way to tell when they're lying is if their lips is moving."

Big-un nodded and Jackson couldn't help feeling a

bond of kinship. Not so much because the old man was his father but because they did, at least, share the same hatred for the Hannackers. But what else his father'd said rose up in bright letters in his mind. Smitty Wilson worked for the Cornbread Mafia. Maybe he knew …

"Shame Ben Higgs got kilt," Big-un said before Jackson could ask about Smitty, "and ain't around to call Riley out on the lie."

"Ben was a good guy.

"Got his head blown clean off is what I heard. Wish Riley'd got his head blowed off 'stead of Ben."

"I *tried*."

Soon's the words left his mouth, Jackson regretted saying them, but they seemed to find a soft landing on his father's face.

"Really? How so?"

He really did *not* want to talk about this. How did they get here? His father had never said hi, bye or kiss my foot about the war to Jackson when he got back. Why was he so chatty about it now?

Then it occurred to Jackson that maybe … maybe his father had come to regret the way he'd treated his oldest son. Might even be he was proud of Jackson for going to war.

"My buddies was getting killed all around and him, a *Hannacker*, was still standing. Wasn't right. When I got the chance, I tried to take him out."

"It's always a good idea to kill a Hannacker any time the opportunity presents itself."

He never would have supposed his father would react this way.

"Best I could do was cut him up some."

"Give him a back full of shrapnel, didja?"

"Wish I coulda done worse."

His father nodded, then seemed like he was done with the subject because he asked, "You gonna be here long?"

Now was Jackson's opportunity to ask about Smitty.

"Depends. I got … business to attend to. You say Smitty's working for the Cornbread Mafia?"

"*Was*. Ain't no more. They didn't treat him right, got rich and he didn't get squat."

"Ain't surprised. It was them run me out of the county five years ago."

His father's eyebrows went up.

"Did they now?"

"They come after me soon's I got out of Eddyville, ganged up on me, was gonna kill me for what I done in 'Nam." He paused. "But I'm 'bout to return the favor, make them *pay* for what they done to me."

"Pay?"

"They got the best weed around and I figure to take it — get me some of their seed to grow in South America."

"How you figure to lay hands on their seed?"

"I'm gonna make a trade. What they want for what I want. Fair and square."

Big-un spit in the dirt. "Ain't no Hannacker plays fair. He'll sneak around, try to trick—"

"He's the one gonna get tricked. My men hid in the rocks gonna cut 'im down."

They both looked up as a car approached on the lane, Jackson's mother home from the grocery store.

"There's your ma," Big-un said. "You take care, now."

He shoulda turned around and walked away then, but he didn't. Just stood looking at Jackson, and Jackson couldn't a'said what kind of look it was. Then Big-un headed back to the tractor, started it up and chugged out into the field while Jackson carried the groceries into the house for his mother. Had a nice little chat. She give him a glass of ice-cold lemonade and he snatched what he had come for off a nail when her back was turned. She tried to get him to stay for supper, but he said he had business, that he'd stop by some other time.

Jackson drove away pondering the interaction with his father. He couldn't escape a feeling that there was something … *off* about it. His father'd acted like Jackson had just gone off to town instead of disappearing for five years. And all that business about the war. What was that all about?

Something was *wrong*, but he couldn't put his finger on what it was. Soon's he had his business taken care of, he'd come back out to the house and see could he figure out why his father'd acted like he done.

He dismissed the thoughts then. He had things to do, an ambush to plan!

Chapter Fifty-Six

WILLIE RAY HOLED up all day in the old farm house next to the barn where he'd parked the biplane, fearing any minute the air would fill with the sound of screeching sirens. There had been water in the house, it hadn't been turned off but the electricity had. Still, he was able to clean up his wounds — tore up some curtains to make bandages. The nail slash was particularly troubling. If it was a nail, it was bound to be rusty. When had Willie Ray last had a tetanus shot? And that "bee sting" he'd felt had been a *bullet* — went clean through his forearm and apparently didn't hit nothing important before it come back out the other side. Oh, it hurt, but the gouge and the slash hurt so bad he hardly noticed the bullet wound at all.

There was nothing in the cupboards to eat but he hit the jackpot when he went down into the root cellar. That's where his grandmother had put all the vegetables from the garden she put up in Mason jars and the homemade jams, jellies and preserves. At first look, he thought the shelves were empty. They were big, deep shelves and in the light coming in through the slit window on the ground outside, they appeared bare. But he flicked his Bic lighter and leaned over, and sure enough, pushed way to the back was a trove of food somebody'd missed.

He dined on green beans, peas, carrots and a single bite of okra — which he thought he could eat because he loved fresh okra cut up, dipped in cornmeal and fried, but discovered that canned okra was as slimy as fish guts.

There was strawberry jam, blackberry preserves, and a couple of big quart jars of pickles. Sour pickles. But beggars couldn't be choosers.

There'd been nothing to do as the daylight grew outside, noon came and went and the sun slid down the western sky but see to his wounds, take stock of his resources and come up with a plan. He would not allow his mind to stray to Jackson! If he let himself consider that Jackson was within his grasp, he'd do something wildly foolish to get at him. He couldn't do that. And the million-dollar blackmail. Willie Ray smiled at how little he cared about that. Long's they had some guarantee this was a one-off, it was worth a million dollars to get rid of her. It was only money, after all.

Willie Ray's most pressing need was to get in touch with Riley and tell him what'd happened. Warn him, so maybe he could pull the other crews out if he thought they was in danger of getting busted. That'd be huge, walking away from that much weed. Riley and Jessie weren't in the immediate personal danger Willie Ray'd been in. He had come within a hair's breadth of getting *caught* in a barn full of marijuana.

The raid was explainable. That sheriff asking about the cattle musta seen somethin' Earl didn't think he seen, got suspicious, and come back with reinforcements. Maybe that's what the law in other states done — called the FBI when they thought somebody was growing weed. Right now, there was really no reason to believe that anything bigger was going on than just the one crew. Yeah, one crew … men rotting in a Missouri jail. Oh, how he hated that! He should have packed it in right from the git-go, left it all. It was his fault they got busted. He and Riley and Jessie would take care of them, hire the best attorneys money could buy, make sure their families wouldn't want for nothing, but that didn't make them being in jail any easier to take.

Still, the workers they'd hired for the other fields in Kansas, Iowa, Arkansas, Wisconsin and Nebraska was all right. They'd harvest their weed and get paid handsomely for their work — more money in a couple of months than any of them could earn in a year at a regular job — two if they was just farmers. He had no reason to believe the sky was falling … other than a gut reaction. But he couldn't shake a sinking feeling deep in his belly that some major, major guano was about to come into contact with the air-conditioning. Willie Ray'd learned his lesson, though, would tell Riley to get that crew out of Minnesota right now … *exposed* like they was. Trying to harvest the rest of the weed wasn't worth the risk.

Taking stock of his resources, Willie Ray was dismayed to realize that he only had a couple of five-dollar bills in his wallet, and a handful of credit cards he was afraid to use. He had to get out of here tonight. He had no idea what kind of manhunt was underway, but he needed to get more than thirty miles away from that barn full of weed! He had to find a phone somewhere and call in, tell Riley and Jessie what'd happened and get one of them to come get him. He cleaned himself up the best he could in a cold-water bath with no soap, tried to clean his clothes, got the big hunks of mud off, cleaned his boots. But his clothes were still filthy, and a man who looked like a bum usually got treated like one. It'd be harder to see his filthy clothes in the dark, and he'd travel at night, but still he wouldn't risk trying to hail a ride. A phone and a place to hide until the cavalry arrived — that was the only way out of this.

When it was good and dark outside, Willie Ray set out east. Callison County was probably five hundred miles from here and he certainly couldn't walk all that way but east was the only direction that made sense. He'd flown over this area half a dozen times, driven through it twice and he called every one of those memories to mind. He knew how to tell your direction —in the daytime and at night. Night was easier, all you had to do was find the Big Dipper and the North Star. In daylight you had to find a perfectly straight stick and put it absolutely upright in the ground in bright sunlight. Mark with a rock where the shadow on the left of the stick ended. Come back in half an hour and mark where the shadow was then. The space in between them two shadows was north.

He followed the edges of fields, traced around fences, went around woods when he could 'cause he couldn't see the star through the trees.

Musta been about midnight when it happened.

He was hot and tired and itchy from being dirty — and hungry and thirsty, too. He had spotted a farm house about half a mile ahead, all the lights out, dark. From where he was, he couldn't see if there were any vehicles parked near it, but he did see there was a livestock barn back from it. They'd have a water hose in that barn to fill up the water troughs for the cattle. There was a fenced-in field between him and the barn. He climbed the rails, hopped down into the field and started across it, grateful for the open area. Sticking to the shadows of trees and bushes where he couldn't see where he was putting his feet, he'd been tripping and falling like a drunk. In his dark tee-shirt and pants, wasn't likely anybody who chanced to get up and go to the bathroom would look out a window in that farm house and see him in the middle of the field. But he hurried along anyway, looking forward to some water—

There was a snorting sound behind him and Willie Ray stopped moving. He knew that sound. Didn't want to know it. Oh, my no he didn't want to know it, but it was clear. He didn't move, just looked back over his shoulder. The big bull looked like it was the size of his pickup truck. It was a mottled color, mostly white but with black spots mixed in like an appaloosa pony. Its horns were at least two feet long, curved around its head and tilted slightly upwards — the better to impale you with, my dear.

It weighed a thousand pounds if it weighed an ounce and even in the dark Willie Ray could see that the animal was *not* happy.

Chapter Fifty-Seven

WHEN JESSIE MONAGHAN'S eyes suddenly snapped open to peer into the black night of her bedroom, real terror was still several minutes away, tucked securely into the back pocket of the future, snug there in the darkness.

Now, she was just anxious. No, not anxious, anxiety was nameless fear and Jessie knew exactly what she was afraid of, could recite the whole long list.

But none of that was what had awakened her. What had?

She shook her head to dislodge the tattered, gauzy remnants of sleep so she could focus, relaxing back onto pillows with cases that smelled of sunshine as gusts of a warm night breeze swirled the white lace curtains in a fitful dance. The digital display on the clock informed her it was 3:30 a.m. — too early to get up and claim that starting now would give her a good jump on the day; too late to go back to sleep and get any real rest tonight.

She wouldn't be able to go back to sleep anyway, not with her mind in turmoil. Life and the world had puttered along in a leisurely fashion for so long, Jessie was lulled into some kind of belief that "the worst was over." Whatever the worst was. Stupid thinking. The world was full of monsters and tragedy could strike anybody anywhere without warning.

She lay in the darkness of her bedroom, her thoughts spinning around and around, touching on every one of the horrors in her life only lightly before moving on to the next.

Drew — poor little Drew. She'd only talked to Riley briefly, and he'd said the boy was all right. But how could he be after what he'd seen? The whole town was a-twitter with talk of what'd happened at Land's End last night, and that nine-year-old had had a front row seat.

Jackson.

The sight of him in church, a devil-in-a-human-being-suit come back home to … yeah, to what?

Remembering clutched at her belly and she felt nauseous. She'd been feeling sick to her stomach a lot lately — no big surprise there, either. What with the threat of blackmail — Winona McClusky saying "a million dollars" as effortlessly as "pass the salt." And, oh by the way, *the law* nosing around … the *FBI.*

She shivered, even though the night was warm.

What had she gotten herself into that it had come to this?

What had *they* gotten into, because whatever was about to happen to her was about to happen to Riley, too. And Willie Ray. Where was Willie Ray? He'd told her when he called Tuesday that he'd be home before supper the next day. But he never showed up. She'd expected a call all day today, hovered near the phone, but nothing. What had hap—?

Thump.

The sound. *Again.* Yes, it had been a thump that had roused her.

Her mind instantly reconnected to the night Jackson had come to kill Davie, had been holding a pillow over his face — stop it! *This* wasn't *that* and irrational fear would not a good bedfellow make. Though her house wasn't wired the way wacked-out Sherry Lynn had decked out her mansion — with every alarm, surveillance camera, even a safe room — Jessie *did* have an alarm system, an electronic one that would summon help immediately if it went off. Not as good as the alarm system Magic had provided when he slept every night by Davie's bed. Jessie still missed the beautiful black dog she'd found as a puppy on the roadside on a cold winter day when Davie was still Davie, even though he was on the other side of the planet. Until Magic, Jessie hadn't even known dogs could get cancer.

So what was the thump?

Davie was asleep. She'd tucked him in hours ago and he always slept long and deep. Once she'd decided to put a baby monitor beside his bed, she didn't feel the need to get up every couple of hours to check on—

The sound of the thump had come from downstairs, but *not* through the baby monitor. She looked at the receiving unit on the bedside table on the other side of the bed. The little red light indicated it was on, but no sound issued from the speaker. *No sound at all.* There was always a background of light grinding static whenever the unit was on. Now it was silent.

Her heart kicked into a gallop, even as a voice from that maddeningly reasonable part of her mind began to plead its case before the High Court of Common Sense. *This old house creaks, moans, groans and thumps all the time, the security system is engaged and you have a pistol in the top drawer of the nightstand.*

She let out the breath she'd been holding as sweet relief washed over her.

No, it's not!

The gun wasn't in the nightstand.

She'd promised Riley as they stood together in the church parking lot after their encounter with Jackson that she'd pack a weapon everywhere she went. She had taken it downstairs with her while she bathed Davie tonight. *It was still there.* She could picture it lying on the table beside her copy of Stephen King's novel *The Shining* that she was reading aloud to Davie. The book was scarier than she'd thought it'd be, was scaring *her* — so she needed to pick something else. She could read the phone book to Davie and he wouldn't care — she just wanted him to hear her voice.

Come on Jessie, the voice in her head cajoled. *You're overreacting. The security system, remember.*

Security systems could be disabled. Cat burglars in movies did it all the time. But cat burglars broke into houses to steal the family jewels. If someone had broken into Jessie's house, it wasn't to make off with her two diamond stud earrings, the ones Davie'd given her for Christmas that constituted all the jewelry she owned. He'd given them to her under a sprig of mistletoe, kissed her—

Kissed. KISS. The same company that'd just installed a security system at the Dawson place, had installed the one for her house years ago.

Another sound. Not a thump, just a … sound. She gasped, the intake of air so abrupt and urgent she almost started coughing. Instead, she stopped breathing altogether. It was just a small sound, really, but a noise even one of those mindless idiots in horror movies would consider sinister. Jessie certainly did since she'd made a Note to Self only a few hours earlier that she needed to fix the hinge on the door from the kitchen into the foyer, put some WD-40 on it or something because it squeaked.

That was the sound. That squeak.

She grabbed the telephone on the nightstand beside the bed, wrestled the receiver off the cradle with shaking hands — her brother Lanny could be here in less than five minutes. She put the receiver to her ear. No dial tone. She stifled a small sob.

He was here.

It was absurd. Totally ridiculous. Couldn't be. But it was true. This time, he hadn't come to kill Davie. Davie was no threat to him. Jackson McClusky had come to kill her.

Chapter Fifty-Eight

THE BULL TOOK a step or two, turning to display his whole body. He arched his neck.

Every alarm bell inside Willie Ray was singing ding! Ding! Ding! When a bull done that, he was showing off his largest profile because he thinks you're challenging him.

Willie Ray had got *too close* before he seen it! He was inside the bull's threat zone and it would defend that territory.

Moving as slowly as possible, Willie Ray turned to face the creature. You didn't *never* turn your back on a bull. And you didn't never run from one neither, not if you intended to live to see another sunrise. He took a step backward, trying to inch away, but the bull wasn't buying it. He pawed the ground in front of him and snorted. Willie Ray's breath caught in his throat. He was as scared as he'd ever been in 'Nam, with mortars ripping up the world and Cong soldiers shooting at him. He was in as much danger now, maybe more. He'd seen what a bull could do to a man.

. . .

WILLIE RAY, *Andy, Riley and Wallace Beckley are playing king of the mountain on a mound of dirt in front of the chicken house next to the tobacco barn at Bucky's. That's what they call Wallace — Bucky — because he has the biggest front teeth Willie Ray has ever seen. His mama always says, "Oh, he'll grow into 'em. They just look big now 'cause his head's small." Willie Ray stared at him once when he wasn't looking, calculating, and he figured Bucky's head would have to be the size of a pumpkin for them teeth to look right.*

Bucky's mother had asked Jean Taggart to help her finish up a quilt for the little Lightner baby, and she'd brought two of the boys along … and Riley, too, of course. He was one of the family. They're all about ten or eleven years old.

Willie Ray is the only one who sees the whole thing. He's the king and up on top of the mound of dirt, looking right into the field where Bucky's daddy keeps their bull. Ain't no bull that's sociable, but that bull is an exceptionally foul-natured creature.

He sees the bull paw the ground, looking at something off to its left, and Willie Ray freezes, stops playing the game to follow the bull's line of sight. There's a man coming toward them across the pasture with a fishing pole slung over one shoulder and a couple of small fish on a string in his other hand. He's way, way too close to the bull. Willie Ray doesn't recognize the man, but he must be Bucky's uncle, his mama's brother, visiting from Cincinnati.

It hits Willie Ray all in a rush that the man doesn't know—

He opens his mouth to yell, "Don't run!" but he's too late. When the man sees the bull, he drops the pole and the fish and takes out running for the fence. The bull catches him before he's even halfway. Willie Ray watches in horror as one horn stabs into the man's back and the beast lifts him off the ground and throws him into the air.

Someone's screaming now. Willie Ray doesn't even realize the voice is his, but the man is screaming, too, and the other two boys turn to look. They all see the next part, the part where the bull tramples the man, ripping at him with its horns.

When the bull's done, it wanders off, but can't nobody go out into the field to help the man until Bucky's daddy comes with the tractor. Don't matter. Ain't no help for him now.

WILLIE RAY HAD nightmares about that bull for years after, swore he'd never get anywhere near another bull as long as he lived. Now he stood in a moonlit field with a bull that could see way better than he could in the dim light. Like dogs and cats and such, there was some kinda light-reflecting thing in their eyes that amplified the light — the thing that made the eye-shine of a deer in the headlights. Willie Ray'd got too close to the bull before he knew it was there, had got inside the area around itself that any bull would fight to defend. This bull was in full-on fight-or-flight mode, and wasn't no way this monster was planning on *running* from little ole Willie Ray.

Wasn't but one thing to do, and Willie Ray would have to wait until it charged to do it.

He didn't have to wait long.

Chapter Fifty-Nine

RUN!

Hide!

Fight!

Which? Only seconds to decide.

Fight?

With what? Her gun was downstairs. She'd only been able to clock Jackson in church on Sunday because he was surprised. He was shorter than Jessie, but no longer puny. He was surely stronger, and besides, *he* wasn't unarmed. He had come with a gun or a knife.

A knife. He meant to slit her throat in her sleep.

Hide, then?

Her bed was unmade, her sheets still warm. He'd know she'd just left—hiding was futile. She had to run.

She flew to the door of her room in bare feet with her long, white nightgown whipping around her legs.

Calm down.

Jackson didn't know which bedroom was hers; he'd have to look in them all and hers was the last one, at the end of the hall across from the back staircase. If she could

333

get to the back stairs before he appeared in the hallway from the front stairs …

She peeked around the door jamb.

The night light at the base of the stairs cast a pale yellow glow up the steps — backlighting a grotesquely pointed shadow moving slowly up the wall, its edges as jagged as a shard of glass. She watched, spellbound, like a mouse staring into the eyes of a cobra, as the shadow reached the top step and spread out thick as tar on the hallway floor. She knew the man who owned it was only a step or two behind.

The fine down of blond hair on her arms instantly stood on end, popped upright by goosebumps. She flattened herself against the wall by the door, panting, her face wet. Was she crying? No, it was sweat, fear sweat! She heard a faint squeak, the familiar carpetmuffled cry of the top stair tread. She pressed herself tighter against the wall and held her breath, afraid Jackson could hear her ragged, shuddery breathing.

He'd search each room as he came to it, wouldn't he? He'd stop first at the room at the top of the stairs, take two or three steps into the room to see the bed was empty. That was all the time she'd have to dash across the hall and disappear down the back stairs.

She visualized where he must be. Top of the stairs now. Crossing the hall. She counted the seconds — one Mississippi, two Mississippi, three Mississippi. He should be inside the room … now.

Jessie leapt out the door.

And slammed into a man standing outside in the hallway. He was huge, muscular and tall. Not Jackson.

She couldn't stifle a scream as she flattened herself against the wall opposite the man. There was a soft chuckle from the darkness behind him. Jackson. Light blinded her from the overhead light in the hallway and she saw a third man — the other one who'd been with Jackson at church, standing by the switch. It dawned on her ponderously, like picking up something huge, that there was no one to rescue her.

"I'm so sorry, Jessie," Jackson said, faux concern oozing from his voice. "I didn't mean to startle you. It's awful when you get blindsided by a surprise attack."

He hit her in the face with his fist. The blow slammed her head back against the wall behind her and the world began to gray out. She fought it, though, clung with all her strength to consciousness as pain exploded in her cheek and jaw. Her knees began to buckle under her but the man grabbed her forearm and held her upright.

"Hurts, doesn't it?" Jackson said, rubbing his own bearded jaw. "You'll be happy to know I didn't hurt poor, helpless Davie."

The flood of warm relief told her how terrified she'd been about Davie's safety. He'd be fine because Jackson had no reason to kill Davie. Not anymore.

"He didn't feel a thing when I smothered him with a pillow."

She tried to cry out, but couldn't, tried to make some kind of sound to express the awful blow that had just hammered into her belly. She could only gasp and look at Jackson with wide eyes.

"Oh, don't give me the grieving wife routine. You been caring for the guy, feeding him and changing his diaper for years. You're glad he's finally dead."

She tried to hit him, but he was ready and blocked the blow. He wasn't ready for her other hand, though, her other *claw*. She gouged her fingernails into his right cheek and ripped downward. He howled and hurled her to the floor and started kicking her. Curling into a ball, she tried to avoid the blows but they kept coming, her back, her hips and legs, her neck.

He drew his foot back to slam his shoe into her face, but the man beside him cautioned with only mild interest, "She gotta be able to talk, doesn't she?"

Jackson halted the motion. He reached down and grabbed a handful of her hair and lifted her upward by it. She scrambled to get her knees under her to hold her weight before the hunk of hair came out in his hand.

He nodded to one of the men and he grabbed her by the upper arm and lifted her to her feet.

"Ohhh, how very much I'm looking forward to messing up that pretty face," Jackson said, leaning close.

She spit at him, mostly the blood in her mouth from the split lip, but he dodged it, drew back to slap her again, but didn't. He ran a lascivious look up and down her body and she became aware of the flimsy nature of the white cotton nightgown.

Jackson grinned at the man holding her upright.

"We'll get us some," he said, but the man showed no emotion at all.

Jackson grabbed her arm and yanked her out of his grasp into her bedroom and threw her on the floor.

"Make up that bed," he said.

She stared up at him uncomprehendingly.

"You heard me. It's gonna look like you left of your own free will. Keep folks confused for a little while anyway."

"Make it yourself," she said.

She watched him grab hold of his temper.

"I can make this real ugly, Jessie. Real, real ugly. You will still be able to talk on the phone after the three of us get finished with you. We'll share you with the others, too. Can't be selfish with a dish as tasty as you."

She wanted to remain defiant, wanted to refuse everything …

She looked at the two men with Jackson. One's face was immobile. But the look on the other one's face was as readable as a billboard. Rolling over on her side, she used the bed to help herself stand up, the pain of the blows where Jackson had kicked her washing over her. He might have broken a rib. Maybe more than one.

None of the men moved to help her as she slowly smoothed the sheets and pulled up the bedspread.

She finished and stood looking at Jackson.

"You think I'm some kinda idiot?" he raged. "Them frilly pillows goes on that bed when it's made. You best make it look right, or I will make you very sorry you didn't."

Jessie arranged the pillows, made sure not to place them where they were supposed to go. Not that it mattered. Who would notice a thing like that?

"Get dressed, clothes and shoes," Jackson said, and she just stood, looking at him. "Behind the screen." He indicated the Japanese standing screen that'd been in Ruth's room years ago, then grinned. "We ain't got time for what'd happen if you's to drop that nightie right here in front of us."

She picked up the shirt and jeans she'd worn today and tossed on a chair, stepped behind the screen and dressed as quickly as she could, trying to ignore the tearing pain in her side. When she stepped out, he grabbed her purse off the dresser and fished out her car keys, tossed them to the taller man.

"You drive."

Without another word, Jackson grabbed her arm and led the way down the hall to the stairs. Jessie tried to look over her shoulder into Davie's room when they passed the door.

Davie! Davie … dead.

Jackson must have seen her craning her neck. He didn't stop, didn't even slow down, just said, "He's better off and you know it. All I done was finish what I started nine years ago."

Chapter Sixty

WILLIE RAY KEPT BACKING AWAY SLOWLY from the bull. Wasn't gonna do no good, but if he just stood still there, soon's the bull charged, Willie Ray was like to turn and run from instinct. Maybe movin' would quell his terror.

It didn't.

The bull charged.

A Sherman tank roaring across the field at him.

Panic welled up in his chest and he was starting to turn his body for flight when his mind grabbed hold, made him be still.

He had to time it just right. If he done it too soon, the bull would see and he would be dead meat. If he done it too late, the bull would be on him and he'd die beneath its trampling hooves.

Wait …

Closer …

Wait …

The only sound in the world was the rumble of the beast's hooves as it came at him in a fright-train rush.

Wait …

Now!

Willie Ray suddenly dropped to the ground and rolled out of the beast's path. The bull roared by him, carried forward by its own momentum, and Willie Ray scrambled up to his knees, but stayed low to the ground and as close as he dared to the bull.

A bull did not recognize anything below a certain height as an enemy worth attacking.

The bull turned, looked around trying to find him. It didn't look down at the ground right in front of it where Willie Ray cowered in terror. He could smell the dusky stench of the beast, the manure on its hooves.

The bull snorted, took a few steps forward, with Willie Ray just below its line of sight, scuttling away from its approach like a sand crab.

He'd never heard of anybody escaping from a bull like this, feared any second the creature would look down at him and stab him with one of those hooked horns. It didn't.

It snorted, grunted.

Now what?

If the bull lost interest in the attack, it would just wander off. *Theoretically,* it would wander off.

What was Willie Ray supposed to do then? As long as the bull was in attack mode, it would tear him apart if he ever lifted up into its line of sight. And he had to stay snuggled up pretty close to the beast to stay below its line of sight. Once it got far enough away from him, it would be able to see him without looking down.

He couldn't spend the rest of the night crawling around on the ground a few feet away from a bull.

The bull kept circling, searching. When it found nothing, it finally turned and started to trot back toward the end of the field where it'd been before it spotted Willie Ray.

What should Willie Ray do?

He curled up into a fetal position on the ground and just lay there.

He thought the bull had continued toward the other end of the field, but he was so afraid to move he didn't dare lift his head where he could see.

Was it just standing there, *out of Willie Ray's line of sight*, waiting for him to show some sign of life? Was it like a cougar, waiting to pounce?

He lifted his head by millimeters … and discovered that there was a splat of manure, still soft and certainly pungent, inches from his face. He lifted his head and looked over it. The bull was about fifty feet away, with its head down, grazing.

Cattle could sleep standing up; well, they could doze. But all myths about cow-tipping aside, to really go to sleep, cattle lay down on the ground. For creatures with such bulk, getting down and getting back up could be a challenge, but they managed.

Should Willie Ray stay where he was until the bull lay down, if it ever did? He wasn't sure how much sleep a bull needed, but if it was only a couple of hours, maybe it was done sleeping for the night.

Lying there curled up, he considered his dilemma from a different angle, examining what he *couldn't* do.

He couldn't lie here until the farmer came out in the morning and found him.

He also couldn't stand up and walk out of the field before morning.

There was only one option, not a particularly pleasant one in a field full of cow patties, but it was better than getting gored. Willie Ray began to roll over and over, slowly, watching the bull for any sign of interest. Surely the animal could see him. Apparently, it just didn't care.

Through the grass and over the cow patties he went, registering as he did that smearing crap all over his wounds would surely put him on a fast track to infection. Probably took half an hour to roll all the way to the fence. Then he did stand, got to his feet as fast as he could and climbed over it and out of the field. He stood on the other side of the wooden fence, realizing it was nothing more than a psychological barrier. That bull could slam through that fence with one eye tied behind its back. But it'd need a good reason to do a thing like that and right now, it didn't have one. As Willie Ray stood there, the animal went to its knees and down to the ground to sleep.

Chapter Sixty-One

THEY DUMPED Jessie into the trunk of a car. The pain in her side screamed but she didn't have enough air to voice the pain ... broken or cracked ribs. The other blows made their presence known now, here in the dark, where she couldn't wall off the physical anymore. She could feel the pain. But she didn't care, flat out didn't care. She could hear the men talking, could perhaps have figured out what they were saying if she concentrated, but she didn't. She couldn't concentrate on anything, couldn't breathe, think ... *be.*

Davie was dead.

Davie. Was. Dead.

No matter how much she focused her attention on the words, they skittered away from her, leaves blown by a fall wind, just ahead of her grasping their meaning.

Both Davies were dead now. The Davie who only lived in her memories of him, the dashingly handsome man who made passionate love to her once on the kitchen table in that little trailer house down the road from his mother, the Davie who'd taken her on a magic carpet ride out into the future on the last night they spent together. The Davie who'd promised he would come home without a mark on him. That Davie was dead.

So was the other one, the shell, the husk of a person who lay immobile in his bed, day after day, after week, after year, wasting away. Couldn't focus his eyes on your face, smiled because of the random firing of synapses deep in his damaged brain. He had given nothing back for all the love she showered on him, but still she mourned his death.

She shuddered at the memory of Jackson's words.

She wasn't *glad* Davie was dead. Because when he died, he took the other Davie with him.

And Jackson McClusky had killed them both, years ago in Vietnam and only a little while ago in his own bed.

Smothered with a pillow.

Can't breathe, fighting, frantic, then the world growing gray and dark.

Jackson had murdered Davie, and what was Jessie going to do without him? She had loved him half her life, since the day he'd slipped her a note during American History class when they were seniors — and the hand-writing was so precise and beautiful she'd suspected he got some girl to write it for him.

I can't stop thinking about you, Jessie, and I'm tired of just thinking.

What would Jessie do, now that he was gone?

Reality felt cold, stark and unyielding against the hazy sadness of her grief, but reality *was* cold and unyielding. Jackson planned to kill her.

He'd kill Riley, too.

That thought struck another staggering blow to her heart and she might have cried out, grunted some kind of sound at the realization that Jackson had tried to kill Davie and Riley when they were in Vietnam, but he'd failed. He was back again now, had murdered Davie, and would murder Riley, too.

Riley.

She loved him.

Not the way she'd loved Davie. It was different, but just as strong. And Riley was still alive, still breathing, and in terrible danger. And Jessie could do nothing about that. She was a leaf in a stream, carried along by circumstances, unable to determine her own fate, let alone Riley's.

She started to cry then. Softly, because she didn't want to be heard, though sealed up here in the trunk she doubted anybody would, or would care if they did. But the thing was, she wasn't even sure what she was crying about.

For the loss of Davie, of both the Davies, because she had loved them both. Crying about what Jackson meant to do to Riley. There seemed to be no place inside her to put the kind of hate, the loathing she felt for him. It was too big, would fill her to bursting if she tried.

Jackson had to pay for what he'd done. Jackson had to die. At her hand. The only way for her to release the power of the emotion in her heart was to kill the man who'd put it there. She would kill him, somehow. If she had to die in the attempt that was fine with her. All that mattered was Jackson — *dead*. That was all Jessica Monaghan was about, as she lay in the dark of the car trunk. Every other thought, feeling or intention had been burned away.

She lay in the dusty car trunk for an hour or five minutes or a lifetime. Jessie couldn't tell. When the car stopped, she relaxed back against the floorboard, glad that the jostling was no longer playing notes of pain on the keys of her ribs.

A bright light suddenly shined on her, blinded her.

Hands grabbed her and yanked her up out of the trunk and over the edge onto the ground, but she couldn't have stood even if they'd let go of her. They didn't. They were somewhere in the woods. The headlights of the car shone on the outside of a hunting cabin that looked like any of a dozen other cabins snuggled up in secluded valleys and remote hollows in Callison County. It was rectangular, with a wide porch stretching all the way across the front of the building. Jessie could imagine that when people were using it, the porch would have a rocking chair or two sitting there. The front door was thick and sturdy, held shut by a heavy-duty hasp and padlock. Jackson inserted a key into the padlock, had to wiggle it around before the lock came open.

The interior had the smell of a room long closed up. A breath of fresh air wafted in when the men dragged her inside. The single room was almost bare. The frames for four sets of bunk beds, two on either side of the room, sat empty, no mattresses. There was a sink and stove on the back wall of the cabin, a space where a big table likely sat once, and probably a couch and some comfortable armchairs. There was a big stag trophy on one wall, so old the hide had been eaten away and the big rack was home to a lacy accumulation of dusty spiderwebs.

The room's only furnishings now were a table, three straight-backed wooden chairs, an army cot and one of those stand-up screens in the corner that probably concealed whatever passed for a bathroom. She noticed then that there were no windows in the structure.

"Over there," Jackson told the men who were hauling her along, one with each arm. The men dragged her another couple of steps and tossed her to the floor and the explosion of pain was so stunning it took her breath away so she couldn't even scream.

"Get comfy," Jackson said, standing over her as she doubled up in pain. "You're gonna be here awhile."

Then he and the other men walked out of the door and shut it firmly behind them, plunging the room into utter darkness. She heard the sound of Jackson slamming the hasp home on the other side of the door. She heard the padlock click.

Chapter Sixty-Two

WILLIE RAY FIGURED he had a fever, though he couldn't have said which of his wounds was the infected one causing the problem. Actually, he couldn't have said much of anything clearly by Friday morning. Lack of food, water, sleep, medical care and well ... other things, could do that to a man.

But at least he was comfortable, stretched out as he was on somebody's fancy couch in the back of a moving van. Had a plastic cover on it so he wasn't messing nothing up. And he was cleaner now than he had been before.

Images flitted across his consciousness and were gone.

The dairy farm where he'd sneaked into the milking shed and got cleaned off, using the pressurized, *sanitized,* spray mechanism dairy farmers used to clean their cows' udders before milking. He remembered that there were a lot of dairy farms in Minnesota, or was that Wisconsin? One or the other of them was famous for cheese but Willie Ray couldn't remember which.

And he wasn't real sure what state he was in. Illinois. Or

Indiana. Maybe he'd made it all the way to Kentucky. Couldn't be Tennessee, could it? Depended on what route the trucker took. He'd heard the driver say all this stuff b'longed to a family moving from Oklahoma City to Washington D.C., but he might pick up other stuff along the way. Willie Ray would have to abandon this ship at the next port. The trick was going to be getting off at the right time. The fella might not even stop in Kentucky, might drive straight through and stop for fuel farther east. Well, soon's he did stop, Willie Ray was gonna bail — no matter where he was, it was closer to Callison County than Empire Township, in southwest Missouri. He still had money … some. He could call from wherever he was, get somebody to come get him.

The rhythm of the big tires humming beneath the trailer was soothing, but every bump in the road that jarred him sent spikes of pain through him.

It was too dark in here to see for sure, but right now he'd have bet it was the nail slash that was making him sick. A couple of hours ago, he'd thought it was the gouges in his side. All depended on which one hurt the worst at the time.

Or maybe it wasn't neither one. Maybe he'd got food poisoning from dumpster diving behind that little grocery store for something to eat. He still didn't know where he lost his wallet out of his back pocket, but figured it was probably when he was rolling across that field to get away from the bull. The only money he had was some change in the pocket of his jeans, a couple dimes, nickels and three quarters. He'd need those to make a phone call, couldn't blow his whole fortune on a candy bar. He'd found a plastic bag full of frozen-but-thawing-out ham sandwiches in the dumpster, like a half a dozen of them, and he couldn't imagine what somebody's froze them for in the first place. But them being frozen, they couldn't have made him sick … could they?

No, he hadn't been puking, didn't have the trots, so it must be them cuts he'd smeared cow manure in.

He nodded off to sleep and jerked wide-eyed awake from the lack of movement. The truck was stopped. Where? Danged if Willie Ray wasn't gonna get hisself a watch. He didn't wear one and it sure would have been handy to know what time it was. He wished he could figure how far they'd traveled.

If wishes was eagles, turkeys could fly.

His granny'd always said that and it never had made a lick of sense to him.

He tried to lift himself carefully off the couch, but wasn't no way to move without hurting something. He went to the door, listened, couldn't hear anything. He could open the door and peek out, but the driver might be standing right there beside it. And he'd … what?

Willie Ray wasn't sure whether or not he'd broken any laws. Was it illegal to hitch a ride in the back of a truck? He didn't think so. But maybe it was if the driver didn't give you permission. Opening the door a crack, he looked out into daylight. Morning, he thought. He could only see a couple of inches of the world through the opening, but what he could see told him everything he needed to know. A parking lot, a truck stop. Beyond the lot he could see part of a sign. A gold-colored blob on top of a white background. He could make out the letters "ker" and below them the letters "rel."

Cracker Barrel.

He smiled and his dry lips cracked. He didn't know for sure what states had Cracker Barrel restaurants, but he didn't think they was any north of Kentucky.

He opened the door wide enough to see the rest of the sign.

Cracker Barrel Restaurant, Franklin, Tennessee, 55 miles.

He was somewhere in Kentucky, between Louisville and Nashville.

He slipped the sweatshirt he'd stole off somebody's clothesline over his body to cover up what he could of how awful he looked. Then he got out of the back of the truck carefully. They was some folks seen him, but didn't nobody say nothing. He went around the side of the building to the men's room. When he came out a few minutes later he looked a little better and certainly felt better. When he got a good look around, he knew *exactly* where he was, confirmed another axiom of his grandmother's that he *did* understand — *I'd rather be lucky than smart.* There was a pay phone on the outside wall of the convenience store door. Fishing in his pocket for the change, he pulled the coins out and looked at them. This conversation was gonna have to be brief.

Chapter Sixty-Three

THE PHONE RANG as Riley was coming back into the house after putting Drew on the school bus — over Sherry Lynn's angry protests. Riley was exhausted, had slept little, sat up beside Drew's bed most of the night last night just as he'd done the night before when he'd brought the distraught child home. Just sat watching over him — like he *should* have been doing Wednesday afternoon. If Riley hadn't left the child alone … oh, he understood that he was beating himself up over something that wasn't his fault, but he was so sorry for what'd happened to Drew it felt good to whale away at himself. There wasn't anybody else to kick. Mama Bert was dead.

And, oh by the way, Willie Ray was AWOL.

And Jackson was out there in the wind.

Riley had managed to rein in Sherry Lynn when he brought Drew home, kept her from snatching him up on the spot and hauling him to the hospital emergency room. But as soon as her feet hit the floor yesterday morning, she'd made a beeline for Drew, determined to have him checked out for what was surely a life-threatening injury.

Riley didn't object — he was glad to have a doctor take a look at that lump and bruise.

Drew had jerked suddenly awake, terrified, in the grip of a nightmare, as soon as Sherry Lynn came into his room. Riley had managed to whisper in the boy's ear as his mother shooed him out of the house to the car.

"Remember what's waiting for you on the other side of Saturday's flower-squirting clown and the bouncy castle — Coco!"

The boy's face had lit with joy.

"You got your very own horse, son — remember that." The boy's smile had been tenuous, but real.

Sherry Lynn hadn't returned until after noon because she'd insisted that Dr. Callahan perform a second head X-ray when the first one revealed no concussion. She had hovered over the boy all day, would only allow him to eat soft foods — for reasons that made absolutely no sense, wouldn't allow him to play outside "in the heat!" and wanted to keep him home from school today so he'd be "rested" for tomorrow's birthday extravaganza. Riley could tell Drew would rather go to school than suffer through his mother's clinging.

"'Lo, Hannackers," Riley said when he lifted the receiver to his ear.

A voice spoke without preamble.

"Jackson come by yesterday to see his mama." It was Big-un McClusky. He barked out a grunt that might have been a bleat of laughter. "Thinks I don't know he's planning on stealin' my guns — took the ring with the keys to the gun cabinet and the hunting cabin off the peg by the back door."

Riley sat down heavily on the couch beside the phone, didn't speak because he didn't know what to say. Was Big-un calling to try to talk him out of killing Jackson? No, Big-un wasn't stupid.

"You told the truth of it, what happened in Vietnam. Jackson said."

Riley was absolutely flabbergasted. Jackson went home and confessed to his father that he'd killed Andy Taggart and destroyed Davie Monaghan? Why would he do a thing like that? The only reason Riley could come up with was he did it to impress his old man, to make Big-un proud of his kick-ass son.

"Bet you clapped him on the back and told him, 'Good job,' probably bought him a beer."

"You in a war and you turn on the soldiers fighting alongside ya — ain't nothing be proud of in that."

"Yeah, but he was a McClusky trying to kill a Hannacker so ain't no rules. Andy and Davie was just collateral damage. A McClusky can be a lowlife coward, but long's he offs a Hannacker, all the rest of the clan'll be cheering."

"Not all of 'em."

That was an odd thing to say.

"You know I don't want to talk to you but you called anyway so you musta had a good reason," Riley said. "What is it?"

There was a beat of silence.

"I said the same thing to your grandpa when he come driving up to my house almost ten years ago." It was almost like Riley could hear a smile in the words. "He did have a good reason, and so do I."

"I'm listening."

"Jackson's gonna come after you and them others — Willie Ray and Jessie. He's planning on killing you—"

Riley barked out a sardonic laugh. "You think I don't know that? Listen, you tell that miserable excuse for a human being that I'll take him on anytime anywhere. And if you and the rest of your kin line up with him, you'll get what he gets. He didn't care about collateral damage and neither do I."

"I ain't gonna line up with Jackson after what he done. He's on his own."

That was a conversation stopper.

All kind of implications there that didn't square with what Big-un McClusky was all about. Then Riley remembered the day five years ago when four South American drug dealers lay tied up in Papa's barn and Big-un McClusky came lumbering in. He could remember the looks on the guys' faces. He imagined the look on his own face was pretty similar — not the fear, but certainly the surprise. Big-un had towered over them, glowering, then he'd spit in the dirt and said, "Kill 'em," and lumbered back out. It might be that one thing that convinced them the Cornbread Mafia was the meanest dogs in the junkyard. They weren't then, but they were now — or had the manpower to be if they had to. Big-un McClusky had come to *help*, because Papa'd asked him to. Papa'd hinted at it and Riley'd caught a glimpse of it himself when he'd gone to Big-un's looking for Jackson. Big-un was a lot more complicated than anybody knew.

"Wise choice," was all Riley could think to say.

"Ain't just you he's after. He come to take your seed."

"Seed?" *Jackson* was after seed?

"Said it'd be payment for you runnin' him out of the county."

Jackson was in cahoots somehow with Mama Bert. He *was* in on kidnapping Drew! The little boy's terrified face flashed across Riley's mind and was gone.

"I don't know how he plans to lay hands on my seed,

but I *do* know" — Riley ground out words between clenched teeth — "when he tries it's gonna be *ugly*."

"Might be I know how."

Riley could hear the big man's breath, a sound like maybe a bull elephant would make.

"Like I said, I'm listening."

"He's plannin' on making some kinda trade. Says he's got something you want and he's gonna trade it to you for seed."

What could Jackson possibly have that—?

"It's a trap. He's gonna have men hid in some rocks to cut you down." He paused. "But if you's *expectin'* that ... you could turn the tables on him."

It grew quiet and Riley realized Big-un had stopped talking.

Wasn't but two alternative scenarios that'd explain what Big-un had just done. Either the whole thing was some kind of elaborate trick and Big-un was in on it ... or he was setting up his own son.

"Why you tellin' me this?"

Big-un snarled, spit out two words like a plug of tobacco juice.

"*Collateral damage.* The Taggarts didn't have no dog in our fight. Neither did the Monaghans. LeRoy lost two boys — one dead and the other one all messed up. That Monaghan boy ain't got no mind left. All *Jackson*." There was a degree of cold loathing in the name that chilled Riley to the bone. "That boy never was no account, not even when he was a kid. He needs to answer for what all he's done."

The line clicked and the phone went dead. Big-un'd said what he had to say and hung up.

～

AGENT LINCOLN HAD TRACKED down the identity of the caller even before the call ended. Buford Louis McClusky, called "Big-un," had a rap sheet, but only a few charges that apparently stemmed from bar fights when he was young. In recent years, there was an assault in the third degree charge lodged against him and Nate Hannacker, who was Riley's grandfather, but the charges against both men had been dropped.

He had a son named Jackson who was in the National Guard unit that was called up and fought at Fire Base Eagle's Nest.

Eli played the tape, listened with the other agents to the conversation.

"You in a war, and you turn on the soldiers fighting alongside ya — ain't nothing be proud of in that."

He stopped the tape. "Sounds like this guy is saying Jackson went after other guardsmen instead of the Cong."

The other agents nodded and he started the tape again, played it through to the end.

"So this Big-un McClusky says his son, Jackson, was trying to kill Riley Hannacker—" began Agent Peterson.

"That McClusky/Hannacker feud business," Bill Thomas put in.

"—and the others just got in the way," Peterson continued. "That part about Andy Taggart and Davie Monaghan being 'collateral damage.'"

"So Jackson McClusky is responsible for the death of Willie Ray Taggart's brother and Davie Monaghan's brain injury," Eli said. He sat back, disgusted. "No wonder Jessie Monaghan hit him in the face when she saw him in church. I want the story on this Jackson McClusky. He's growing pot somewhere if he's after Righteous Weed seed."

"It sounds like he plans to finish what he started in Vietnam — kill the others to get it," Peterson said.

"But his father rats him out, calls Riley to warn him — which apparently wasn't news to Riley — says that Jackson's going to offer to trade … something … but it's an ambush," Bill Thomas said.

"If we could manage to catch Riley and the others while they're making this trade … we get to tie Riley to the seed, another link in the chain," Eli said.

"If he survives the ambush this Jackson fella is setting him up for," Agent Lincoln said. "These people play for keeps."

Chapter Sixty-Four

RILEY HAD JUST HUNG up the phone from talking to Jessie when it rang again. Jessie had told him Willie Ray hadn't called in yet, but she would stay by the phone.

"I need a ride, bro," said a voice on the other end of the line in what was clearly forced cheeriness.

Riley was so glad to hear from Willie Ray he wanted to cry, and so mad at him for not coming home when he'd said he would that he wanted to choke him.

Wanted-to-choke-him won the coin toss.

"Where have you been?"

"Ain't got time to chat. I'm at that little store where we stopped to clean the crap out of our pants after that run-in with Hell's Angels."

"What are you ... are you okay?"

"Absolutely not, but I'm in a whole lot better shape than Bucky's uncle was after *he* tangled with a bull."

"*You* tangled with a bull? What hap—?"

The line went dead.

Riley sat holding the silent receiver in his hand.

What was Willie Ray doing in a convenience store off Interstate 55 north of Elizabethtown?

Riley knew exactly where he was talking about. When he and Willie Ray were high school juniors, Riley had borrowed Papa's pickup truck one Saturday night to go to an away game for the Callison County's girls' basketball team. They were playing Hardin County and Willie Ray's current girlfriend was the star forward. They never made it to the game. When Riley pulled out onto the interstate, he merged with a maybe a dozen motorcycles, traveling south together. Apparently, he had cut off the lead bike, or the biker thought he had, and the guy made an obscene gesture. Willie Ray was being … well, Willie Ray. Before Riley could stop him, he dropped his drawers and mooned the biker outside his passenger window.

And the next thing they knew, the group of bikes had swarmed around the pickup truck on all sides. It was then that they saw the insignias on the backs of their jackets — Hell's Angels. The bikes began to slow down, surrounding the truck so Riley had to slow down, too. It was obvious they intended to herd the truck over to the roadside and …

It might have been the only time in Riley's life he was glad to see a police officer. Two of them, in fact. Two Kentucky State Police cruisers appeared behind the bikes, probably on their way back to the Elizabethtown KSP post, two exits ahead. When the bikers saw the cruisers, they spread out away from the truck and sped on down the interstate. Riley and Willie Ray pulled off at the next exit into the parking lot of a convenience store, waited there a few minutes to stop shaking, then pulled back onto the interstate going *north*. No basketball game was worth a run-in with their biker buddies.

Riley tried to call Jessie to tell her that Willie Ray had called, but her line was busy. He didn't have time to wait.

He and Willie Ray would go to Jessie's when they got back to town, figure out their next move.

AGENT PETERSON PULLED the headset up off one ear and shook his head at Eli. Not enough time to get a trace on the call.

"Guess Taggart made it all the way back to … well, *somewhere* nearby," said Bill Thomas.

Eli rubbed the bridge of his nose as he always did when he was tired or frustrated. Right now, he was both. He'd been counting on the phone tap to give him Taggart's location, and when Taggart called in, they could catch him and whoever went to pick him up.

He let out a long breath, chasing the recurring thought — *how had Taggart escaped from a barn that had only one door?* — out of his head and concentrated on the here and now.

No trace on the call. And nothing in the call to give him a location.

"Play the tape," he instructed Peterson, and they all listened again to Willie Ray telling Riley to pick him up at "*that store where we stopped to clean the crap out of our pants after that run-in with Hell's Angels.*"

"Is that some kind of code?" Peterson wondered out loud.

"If it is, that means they've figured out we've tapped their phones," Bill said.

If they were wise to the phone tap, Eli'd just lost his most valuable reconnaissance tool.

Walking to the window, he pulled back the curtain and looked out, watched people strolling by on the sidewalk in Bardstown, a really lovely little town. It was Eli's job to decide when to pull the trigger and round up the ringleaders. He'd spent hours on the phone with other field offices, coordinating investigations into the other locations in seven states where he suspected the Cornbread Mafia was raising weed. He'd busted the Missouri farm on Wednesday because he had hoped to catch Taggart there. But he'd missed his chance to arrest one of the ringleaders, caught red-handed. It wouldn't be more than a couple of days before other agents started busting fields — casting nets to bring in a whole lot more fish. Maybe one of *those* fish …

Maybe.

"You feeling froggy?" Bill asked.

"Getting ready to jump?" Eli said. "Not yet. I don't think they've made the wire tap … at least I choose to believe they haven't. I think that exchange was just Kentucky-speak, shorthand between best friends. I want to give it a couple more days … keep our lines in the water … hope we hear something we can use."

"DON'T BE STUPID," Riley said as he looked at Willie Ray beside him in the front seat of his truck. "I'm taking you to an emergency room *right now* — no argument."

Willie Ray looked awful. Underneath the relatively clean sweatshirt, his tee shirt was bloodstained. He'd fashioned bandages of some kind out of strips of cloth, but he obviously was wounded in the side, and chest — and had puncture wounds in his left forearm.

Pointing to the blood-stained fabric wrapped around his arm, he said, "This here's a bullet wound."

"They *shot* at—?"

"Couldn't hit the broad side of a barn." Willie Ray's voice was breathy and he was clearly in pain. "*Bullet* wound." Doctors were required by law to report all bullet wounds to the police. "I didn't steal an airplane and fight a bull to get away from the po-lice only to give up to 'em now."

Their eyes met and locked.

"Sounds like it won't matter much one way or the other," Riley said. "If they knew about that field …" The Minnesota crop, if that got busted, it was understandable, with the weed growing right out there in the open. But Missouri … unless a sheriff chasing somebody's lost cattle had seen *something* … Riley tried to keep his voice tightly controlled, but could hear the slight tremor in it. "Looks like we're busted."

"You don't know that for sure."

"Winona McClusky knew the locations of all the fields," Riley felt a flash of rage — at Winona, but even more at whoever had given her all that information.

"Which she ain't told nobody about — and won't if we pay her to keep her lip zipped."

"But *somebody* told her. So who *else* did that somebody tell?"

"Even if they raid 'em all, it's them *fields* that's busted. Ain't no lock on us. We get home, get all lawyered up, might be we can beat it."

"The sheriff and the state police … yeah, maybe. The FBI … not so much."

Both of them had slammed at a dead run into the rock wall of the unthinkable. It might just be that it was all over. The hole that opened up in Riley's belly felt like it went all the way to China. Jail … oh yeah, for awhile at least. Prison … that tasty dish was on the table, too.

Jessie!

The thought of Jessie going to jail — to *prison*. His mind stumbled over the horror of it and couldn't seem to move past it.

"Knock! Knock! Don't go south on me now," Willie Ray said, and Riley realized he was talking and Riley hadn't really been listening.

"It's the best thing to do now, so let's get at it. There's a Walmart right by the exit in E-town, and best as I recall, they's a little motel — them individual cabins, on down the road a piece."

Willie Ray was right, of course. The first order of business had to be seeing to his wounds. They'd figure out the rest after that.

Reluctantly putting the truck in gear, Riley backed out into the parking lot of the convenience store — where two teenage boys had cowered in fear a lifetime ago. As he pulled out onto the street, he dumped the rest of the load on his best friend.

"Mama Bert's dead."

"How'd *she* get dead?"

"Malcolm Murdock shot her. She kidnapped Drew because …" He'd told Jessie, of course, but was still unprepared for the twin hammer blows of rage and grief when he said the words out loud to Willie Ray. "Mama Bert killed Papa … and Drew saw her."

"Drew *saw*—?"

"He saw me put a bullet in her forehead, too. Then Malcolm dialed 911 and confessed."

"What—?"

"She'd been blackmailing him for years, had pictures he didn't want his family to see. After we left, he blew his own brains out."

Willie Ray looked at Riley with compassion. "You been a busy boy while I was gone."

Chapter Sixty-Five

WILLIE RAY LOOKED BETTER, at least mildly presentable, though he was so pale under his freckles, it looked like somebody'd spilled red sequins on his face. A shower — two big hamburgers and fries, clean bandages and new clothes hadn't exactly made a new man out of him but all of it combined did keep the old one from keeling over on the floor. Well, that and a pack of cigarettes. He smoked three in a row, lighting one off the other.

He had a low-grade fever, and you didn't have to be a doctor to see that his wounds were infected.

"Smearing open wounds in manure'll do it every time," Willie Ray said.

The probably-a-rusty-nail gash was the most concerning — angry red and filled with puss. The gouge in his side was really nasty-looking, too. And the bullet hole — a through-and-through in his arm that miraculously didn't hit anything vital in passing — was inflamed.

Riley slathered antibacterial ointment all everything and bandaged them with sterile pads and clean gauze. Whether Willie Ray liked it or not, Riley would drag him in to see Dr. Callahan as soon as they got home. Good man, had replaced Dr. Dawson who'd delivered most of the Taggart children. The young doctor knew how to keep his lip zipped as tightly as the old one had.

Riley tried to call Jessie from the motel room they'd taken in E'town to get Willie Ray cleaned up and her answering machine picked up immediately. That was strange. He left a brief message, said they needed to meet late this afternoon in the clubhouse.

And he'd called Jacob Steiner, senior partner in Steiner & Berkowitz law firm in Louisville. Ace's New York attorney had recommended him and they kept him on retainer to be available on a moment's notice in case of an emergency. This was the first time Riley'd ever used his services and he'd certainly seemed competent enough. He'd asked to speak to Willie Ray, questioned him about what'd happened in Missouri — specifically wanted to know if any of the law enforcement officers had actually *seen* him there. He thought maybe, at the airport, but it'd been dark and— Steiner said they could work with that.

He'd advised them to refuse to talk to the police. Duh. And to lock up the account books, the real ones, in a safe place. Double duh. There were two sets of books, of course, the one an accountant kept that displayed a paper trail of semi-legitimate sources of income, along with bogus expenditures. The real books ... chapter and verse, enough to hang them and all their customers. Those remained safe in a place that didn't exist.

When Riley pulled around to the back of his house, Sherry Lynn came running out the back door to greet him halfway up the sidewalk. That was not a good sign.

"Oh, Riley, where have you been? I've been calling around everywhere looking for you."

She always threw where-have-you-been questions at

him without expecting he'd answer them. He never did, which was fine with her because she didn't really care one way or the other. It was just something to say. But the look of genuine distress on her face stopped him.

"Why? What's wrong?" His heart caught in his throat. "Where's Drew?"

"He's at school, he's fine. It's …" She looked then at Willie Ray and seemed to draw strength from his presence, like maybe he could shoulder some of the load of what she was about to say.

"I don't know how to say it, how—"

He managed not to grab her shoulders and shake her, but it was an effort.

"Just say it. What?"

"I'm so sorry, sweetheart. Davie Monaghan … died."

The hammer blow landed between Riley's eyes and he just stood staring at his wife.

"When?" Willie Ray asked. "What hap—?"

"Oh, I think he just … you know… stopped breathing. I mean …"

She let it dangle and they knew what she meant. The unspoken truth in all their lives was that Davie Monaghan was fragile, that it would surprise nobody when the end finally came. But it did surprise Riley.

Jessie.

"How's Jessie? Have you talked to her?"

"Nobody's talked to her. Nobody knows where she is."

"She's not at home?"

"It was the strangest thing," Sherry Lynn said, and slipped seamlessly into gossip mode, the tone that said *I know a secret!* "You know the church trip to Washington D.C. was cut short, what with Thelma Murdock having to come home because poor Malcolm—"

"What does that have to do with Jessie?"

"Harriet Porter was on that trip so she got home early, too, and when she went into the house she found Davie … just lying there. Looked like he was asleep, but Harriet's a nurse so of course she knew—"

"Get to the point, Sherry Lynn."

The menace in his voice brooked no argument.

"When she realized he wasn't breathing, she called out for Jessie. But Jessie never came. Harriet looked all over the house, then noticed that her truck was gone, so she called 911."

Riley's head was spinning.

"So you're saying that Jessie—"

"Not me, everybody. Jessie must have just … you know — *run off*. You can't really blame her. Maybe she found him dead, or maybe he died when she was right there with him, and she couldn't handle … the rest of it. Just ran away."

No.

Jessie wouldn't have done that. She would never have walked out and left Davie … just left him there. Even if he was dead, she'd have stayed with him. And his death wouldn't so totally freak her out that she'd leap into her truck and drive away. They'd talked about it often, all of them, the inevitability of it. She wouldn't have been surprised.

Riley shot a look at Willie Ray and read the same thoughts on his face.

Jessie didn't just leave. And if she didn't … then where was she?

"I was going to go right over there as soon as I heard. Be with her and all. But when Sheila Watson called me … Cindy Tucker had called and told her … they'd already figured out Jessie wasn't there."

Her mind went on autopilot then.

"And I really didn't have time for an interruption this

morning. With all that's left to do on Drew's party tomorrow—"

Motioning for Willie Ray to follow, Riley walked away from her babble into the house.

"Something's wrong with the phone, too," she called after him. "I've already called the phone company and they said they'd send somebody right out."

He stopped and turned toward her. "What's wrong with the phone?"

"It just rings and rings and when I answer, nobody's there."

Chapter Sixty-Six

WHEN JACKSON finally heard Riley Hannacker's voice on the other end of the line, he relaxed. He'd already called half a dozen times, trying to reach him. And might be Riley'd been home, but Jackson didn't want to talk to Sherry Lynn to ask.

"Don't you never answer your own phone? I been calling and calling."

He'd been sitting in his van parked beside the pay phone on a pole out in front of the Esso Station on Chenoweth Mill Road, getting out every few minutes to put a coin in the phone and call Riley. He was getting real tired of that.

"You killed Davie." It wasn't a question.

"He shoulda died in that bunker. He'd a'been better off — I did him a favor."

"What have you done with Jessie?"

It sounded like Riley was talking through his teeth gritted. Upset, was he? Might be he should have treated Jackson better and he wouldn't be here.

"Let's skip the next part — where I tell you Jessie's snug

370

as a bug in a rug and you don't believe me and want me prove she's alright by letting you talk to her—" He stopped, let the banter drain out of his voice. "'Cause you ain't gonna talk to her. I got her and you know it and either she's alright or she ain't. You just gonna have to take my word for it that she ain't harmed."

"Jackson, if you—"

"If I hurt her you'll … what? Kill me? You think I don't know if you could get your hands on me you'd kill me right now? Woulda killed me yesterday or the day before if you could have. You best come up with a better threat."

There was silence, and when Riley spoke again, the tone was measured, calm. He was doing a pretty dadgum good job of holding onto his rage. That was a good life lesson to learn — how to hold onto your temper. You learn that and you ain't never again at the mercy of what somebody else says or does. It was a pity Riley wasn't going to have any life left to use the skill he was practicing.

"What do you want?"

"Seed."

"My seed's become real popular lately."

Jackson didn't know what that remark meant. Maybe Riley'd heard Mama Bert was sniffing around trying to find it. Malcolm'd offed her before she finished the job or Jackson wouldn't be where he was, taking the risks he was about to take to get what he had to have.

"Four gallons of seed. Put it in old moonshine jugs or quart Mason jars, don't make me no never mind which."

"I don't have that much—"

"Yeah you do."

"I only got enough—"

"You get me four gallons of seeds, real, honest-to-good-

371

ness Jack and the Beanstalk beans, or I'm gonna send Jessie Monaghan back to you in pieces!"

"I swear to God, Jackson, I only got—"

"Then you and Jessie's both in a world of hurt."

He'd considered the issue of real versus counterfeit seed long and hard, how he would know he was getting the genuine article. He didn't know exactly what Righteous Weed seed looked like. Every strain of marijuana had distinctive seeds — little black ones, bigger brown ones, tan ones, some with stripes or patterns. It finally came to him that he should ask for a ridiculous amount — gallons of it. Only way anybody could come up with gallons of seed was if they was storing it up, and why would the Cornbread Mafia store any marijuana seed except their own. He might not have the whole four gallons. He'd bring whatever he did have and try to bluff the rest and that was fine, too.

"Listen, Jackson, I don't have …"

"You shut up and listen. You gonna take that seed tomorrow out to the BMC mine entrance off Henderson Pike."

Bishop Mining Company had lost its shirt mining coal in Callison County. Oh, there was some coal, but not enough to make a profit digging it out of the ground. The big coal seams was all a hundred miles east.

"You gonna bring Willie Ray Taggart with you and only Willie Ray. I'm gonna have lookouts and if'n they see anybody else with you, I'm gonna slit Jessie Monaghan's throat — you listening to me?"

He didn't wait for Riley to respond.

"I'll have the belt line running when you get there." The belt line was a continuous loop of conveyor belt that transported coal from the face of the mine deep under the mountain out to be loaded into trucks at the entrance.

Wasn't no way Willie Ray could get the thing working, if it was even still there, hadn't been hauled off in pieces by somebody looking to sell the steel for scrap. But Riley wouldn't know that until he got there and by then it'd be too late.

"Me and Jessie's gonna be standing out of sight inside the mine. The belt line runs out and around that big slag heap in front of the entrance. So you and Willie Ray won't have to show yourselves. You set the first jug of seed down on the belt line and it'll carry the jug to me inside the mine. I'll check it out, be sure when I plant them little seeds I can grow me a stalk all the way to the sky, and I'll send Jessie out where you can see her in front of the entrance. Send me the second jug, and when I check it out, I'll let Jessie go halfway to the slag heap. You see how this is supposed to work, doncha?"

Hannacker and Taggart would think they was safe behind the slag heap, and that Jessie would come out to them slowly as they delivered the seed to Jackson.

"You two don't never have to show your faces. When I get the last jug, you got Jessie right there in front of you."

It would, indeed, be a safe way to make a dicey trade with somebody you didn't trust.

"Once you got Jessie, you and Willie Ray's gonna be tempted to come after me — get your seed back and put holes in your old friend Jackson. And I say — go on ahead, chase me through a coal mine. I'm gonna take my seed and go out one of the other mine entrances. I got me somebody knows every one of them tunnels."

Which was a lie. There were certainly people in Callison County who did know the layout of that old coal mine. He coulda found somebody if he'd looked but he didn't bother.

Jackson planned to stand with Jessie just inside the

entrance. His men'd be positioned in the rocks above the mine. Riley and Willie Ray'd come out of the trees behind that slag heap, thinking it was a shield. 'Cept they'd be sitting ducks for shooters from above. His men would mow them down.

Oh, he was sure Riley'd cheat, bring an army of armed men with him, hiding out in the woods behind him or something like that. From their position on that mountainside, his men could pick those fellas off, too. Meanwhile, he'd put a bullet in Jessie's brain, take the seed and boogie. It'd be up to Mañuel, José and the other two to get themselves back across the border.

Jackson wouldn't never look back. He'd head out south, drive straight through to Nuevo Laredo, just stopping to get gas and take a leak. Jackson would be free and clear, would raise a weed crop next year that'd make him a fortune. And most important — the three people he hated most in the world would be dead.

ELI PLAYED the whole tape of the conversation through, making sure he didn't miss anything.

"So Jackson McClusky killed Jessica Monaghan's disabled husband and kidnapped her," he said, keeping his tone unemotional and professional. Inside his belly was a cold stone of loathing for the man who used war to cover up murder.

"You pegged it," Agent Peterson said to Agent Lincoln. "These people play for keeps."

"This is the trade Jackson's father warned Riley about — an ambush," Eli said. "We'll crash his little party before he has time to celebrate."

Twenty minutes later he was looking at a topographic

map of Callison County with Nelson County Deputy Sheriff Bruce Landon pointing to the area identified as Shackleford Knob, searching for a spot where there was the entrance to an old coal mine. Agent Peterson had recruited Landon — made friends with him in the coffee shop called Cupa Java off the town square in Bardstown, where he discovered that Landon had grown up in the county next door — Callison County.

"Have you ever been to that mine?" Eli asked.

"Just drove by it is all when I was a kid, don't remember where we were going," Deputy Landon said. "They were still getting some coal out of it at the time because there was an empty coal truck in front of us and it hit a pothole and this little piece of coal popped out of the back, hit our windshield — made a big ole crack and my father was hot. He followed the truck when it pulled in to load up at the mine, got out and went after the driver. Couldn't hear what was said but you could see they were just about to come to blows, until this other fellow came out, broke up the about-to-be-a-fight — much to the disappointment of me and my little brother — and they went into this trailer that was the office of the mine. We sat there until my father came back out, had a check to get the windshield fixed in his hand."

"Tell me about the mine," Eli said.

"Like every other coal mine in Kentucky, it's just a big hole in the side of the mountain, goes back in there for miles."

"This fellow said there was more than one entrance."

"I wouldn't know about that, but it would make sense. When a coal seam peters out, sometimes you can find it somewhere else in the mountain, so you dig in there. Nobody goes in any of those abandoned mines anymore. Roofs are unstable, could fall on your head, or you could hit a pocket of CO_2 and choke to death or you could make a spark with your belt buckle and ignite some methane gas and there wouldn't be enough left of you for a DNA sample."

"Describe the front of the mine."

"The hole was cut into solid rock, something like a cliff face on the side of the knob."

"Rocks, boulders on the slope?"

"Yeah."

"And in front of it?

"Not much of anything. There are woods on both sides and the usual slag heap."

Eli raised an eyebrow.

"Stuff they dug out of the mine, rocks and the like that wasn't coal. Miners load that kind of thing on the conveyor belt and dump it in a heap out front."

After the deputy left, Eli and the agents studied the map and made plans.

"This is the smoking gun we've been waiting for. If we can catch Hannacker, Taggart and Monaghan together with four pounds of seed … the kind that produces weed like we found in Missouri …"

"Kansas and Iowa, too," Bill pointed out. "We're set up to bust those locations later today."

"The whole Cornbread Mafia in one fell swoop," Peterson said.

Jed Lincoln looked out over the top of his rimless glasses. "Jackson McClusky strikes me as the kind of man who'd roll over on his old granny to save his ass. I bet we can flip him, get him to testify against the others."

Eli figured McClusky would sing like a canary when they busted him, cheerfully throw the others under the bus. And that should have thrilled him. He wasn't sure why it didn't.

Chapter Sixty-Seven

WHEN RILEY LOOKED at Willie Ray there was color back in his cheeks. Probably didn't have as much to do with bandages and food as it did with rage.

"He's got Jessie." Riley spoke as if saying it out loud would make it real.

"He came for Jessie, all he needed was Jessie, but he stopped off long enough to murder Davie."

The look of blind fury that passed between them was as dangerous as a high-tension wire.

"Big-un told you Jackson wanted to trade something — this is it," Willie Ray said. Riley had told Willie Ray about his conversation with Big-un as he bandaged Willie Ray's wounds in a motel room in Elizabethtown.

"He also said it was a trap, an ambush."

"That mine's a good place for one. We could hunker down behind that slag heap, never stick our noses out, and somebody up in them rocks could pick us off, ducks in a washtub."

"So how do we take out the shooters?" Riley hoped Willie Ray had an idea — Riley's mind was foggy from lack of sleep, and clamped down tight with fear for Jessie. Of course, Willie Ray was in a whole lot worse shape than Riley.

"Ain't no way to take them out except to get up above them. Jackson don't know we know about the ambush … so what does that get us?"

"We're asking the wrong questions. Not how to get out of the ambush, but how to get Jessie out!"

Riley paced back and forth, nervous energy making it impossible to sit still. Sherry Lynn had flitted away to hang streamers or fill up balloons or some other idiot thing, leaving him and Willie Ray in Riley's office where they sat. The thought that Jessie was in Jackson's grasp. That right that minute he had her somewhere—

Riley stopped pacing.

"Where is Jackson *right now*?" Riley said. "Where has he got Jessie now, where's he holding her?"

"Ain't at Big-un's. Where else?"

"Jessie told me Sunday she thought maybe Jackson had moved into the old Dawson place, said she'd seen them installing surveillance equipment. He could have taken her there."

"Naaa, he knows we'll try to find her and that's the first place we'd look."

Kidnapped. Like Drew. Mama Bert had spirited him off to some place out of sight. His face bloomed in Riley's mind and burned all other images away for a moment. When he tuned back in, Willie Ray was wondering aloud about something Big-un had said.

"… can't figure why Jackson needs to sneak into his Pa's house and steal his guns. If he bought the Dawson place, showed up at church with two bodyguards, sounds to me like he could afford to buy his own weapons."

... took the ring with the keys to the gun cabinet and the hunting cabin off the peg by the back door ...

"Maybe it wasn't the key to the gun cabinet Jackson was after."

Willie Ray's eyes widened and their minds were instantly on the same track. Always had been.

"He wanted the key to the Big-un's hunting cabin so he'd have somewhere to take Jessie," Willie Ray said. "Do you know where his cabin is?"

Riley shook his head and took a deep breath. "I'll have to call Big-un and ask."

Willie Ray read the awful reluctance on his face.

"You want me to do it? My last name ain't Hannacker."

"No. It has to be me."

Identifying where his son might be hiding so Riley could go there and kill him might be a bridge too far, but Riley had to ask. It did no good. The deep-throated voice of Dottie McClusky, who'd put a pistol to Riley's skull a couple of days before, said that Big-un wasn't home, had gone to Taylor County right after lunch to look at some livestock. She didn't know when he'd be back. Riley asked as politely as he could if she knew the location of Big-un's hunting cabin and she spit out a reply.

"You think I'd tell you if I did?" Then she slammed down the receiver.

They'd have to find it for themselves.

"Lemme make a few calls," Willie Ray said. "I got cousins used to go deer hunting with some of the McCluskys."

Twenty minutes later, Willie Ray hung up the phone after talking to half a dozen relatives.

"My cousin Virgil's brother-in-law, Clayton Bussick, usta go hunting with some guys, one of them was Jackson's cousin on his mother's side, a fella named Weldon Purdy. Clay said they was a hunting cabin back in the woods there and he'd suggested once they take a look inside, maybe somebody left some beer. Weldon knew who owned it, said he wasn't nobody Clay'd want to mess with."

"He tell you where it was?"

"He didn't know for sure, somewhere on the back side of Buzzard Knob."

They exchanged a look. Buzzard Knob was off the beaten path even for Callison Countians. It lay on the Washington County line probably five miles as the crow flies from the nearest paved road.

"He said they went out Blandford Lane, then took a little dirt road about a mile north of a tree that'd been struck by lightning, left a burned-out stump."

"Would the stump still be there?"

Willie Ray shrugged.

"They went down that dirt road, then took out up a creek bed and got to a field at the top of a hill. They parked in the field and went maybe a mile through the woods to a couple of deer blinds in the trees north of there. Said you could see the cabin from the deer blinds."

"We need to find that cabin."

"And if we can't find it? Or we do find it and Jessie ain't there?"

"Then one or the other of us, I'm figuring me 'cause you're right puny, is gonna have to climb up the back side of Shackleford Knob and try to come out somewhere on top of them rocks above the mine.

"You think you could do a thing like that?"

Riley was sober. "No. But I'll try if it's the only shot we got."

The door to Riley's office opened and Drew came running in, had just gotten off the school bus. He dumped his books on the floor, turned and closed the door behind him.

"Didja tell Uncle Willie Ray about … you know?" Drew asked.

"You mean the super-secret pony that ain't nobody s'posed to know about? Naaa, he said if he told me then he'd have to shoot me."

Drew smiled and it was a relaxed smile.

"His name's Coco, only I'm not sure it's gonna stay Coco, 'cause I might think of something really cool."

"How about Fred? Or Bob. Just plain ole Bob. His middle name would be The … Bob The Horse."

Drew rolled his eyes, then turned back to his father. "I've been thinking … if you were planning on bringing Coco here, you know, surprising me at the party, I don't think that's a good idea. He won't like it, won't like all the people, or being away from the other foals and his mother."

Drew was such a thoughtful little boy.

"So I was thinking that maybe after the party, you could take me and Mommy for a ride, and end up at Land's End and you could surprise me with him there. What do you think?"

"I think that's a wonderful idea." That was all Riley could say before his throat closed up. Bad things were coming down the pike, a storm was going to slam into this little boy and knock all the underpinning out from under his life. Riley couldn't look out there beyond Jessie right now, beyond making her safe and killing Jackson. But out there beyond it was ugly, dark and scary. Riley might have to go to jail, maybe to prison, depending on how many dance steps Jacob Steiner really did know. Sherry Lynn was NOT likely to deal well with losing … everything. And she'd be all the little boy had.

"I might have to miss your party tomorrow," he said. "But I'll make sure you get Coco. I'll make sure of that."

Drew picked up on the apprehension in his father's voice but pretended he didn't.

"I wish *I* could miss my party tomorrow."

Riley grabbed his son and hugged him close. Willie Ray stood with his back turned, looking out the window.

Sherry Lynn came into the room as Riley was re-locking his gun cabinet, looked with apprehension at the rifle and pistol he'd taken out of it.

"Where are you going with that?"

"Hunting."

"Now?"

He merely nodded.

"But you … you can't …" She was sputtering. "You can't go hunting right *now*! You said you'd help me get ready for the party and there's so much left to do. I need you to—"

He took her by the shoulders and she stopped in mid-prattle.

"I won't be here for Drew's party. I've already told him and he understands."

She went off like a rocket launcher.

"*He* understands? Well, *I* don't. You have to be here. You're his father. You can't just go—"

"Shut up, Sherry Lynn," Riley said, and the contained fury in his voice stopped her in her tracks. "I have things to do. You make sure … Drew is alright."

Fear washed over her face, reminiscent of the night she'd spent hiding in a tobacco barn with the boy while Riley and the others fought off a South American drug cartel's henchmen.

"What do you mean 'all right'?"

"Just … make sure he enjoys the party."

Riley and Willie Ray rode together without speaking until Riley broke the silence.

"When did it get away from us?" Growing weed had seemed innocent in the beginning and they'd been drugged by the harmlessness, didn't see the change. When had it darkened?

Willie Ray didn't have to ask what he meant.

"Easy money breeds evil same way a fly breeds maggots." When he looked at Riley, his eyes were sad. "It's the Tar Baby. Don't look dangerous or bad, but soon's you touch it, you get stuck and ain't no way to let go."

Chapter Sixty-Eight

RILEY AND WILLIE RAY roared out toward Buzzard Knob, then down Blandford Lane looking for the spot where Willie Ray's cousin said they'd turned off into the woods. They searched the roadside for a burned-out stump but could find none. They couldn't find a dirt road either, so they finally just turned off into a creek bed and followed it up the side of the knob for half a mile before it petered out.

They left the truck there and hiked up to the top of a hill, found a meadow that might or might not have been where Clayton Bussick, Weldon Purdy and the other hunters had left their trucks.

North of there was woods ... miles and miles of woods.

"Let's see if we can find the deer blinds."

After an hour of searching, they finally found one, but no more. Maybe they were hidden by the colorful autumn foliage. Hunters would have been sighting in on deer when there were no leaves on the trees.

"North from here, then."

If the cabin was there, somewhere in the miles of woods on the north side of Buzzard Knob, there had to be another way to get to it, a road on the other side of the knob. Willie Ray's cousins had obviously come upon it from the back side.

Riley and Willie Ray made their way through the woods as afternoon drained away. Willie Ray had to be in pain, but only grim determination showed on his face. The shadows in the trees grew longer and with every step Riley's fear for Jessie grew. What had Jackson ... done to her? He wouldn't let his mind go there, wouldn't let himself think about the possibility that he and Willie Ray were on a wild goose chase that would end here in the woods with no cabin and no Jessie ... and no hope.

The sun was about to drop down behind the knob when they pushed through a stand of bushes and Willie Ray grabbed Riley's arm, pointed. Maybe seventy-five yards away, you could see the top of a roof peeking through the leaves.

It was a cabin. As they got closer to it, they saw a black van parked in front, at the end of a dirt track that might once have been a road.

Half an hour later they crouched in the undergrowth to decide what to do.

Three full circuits around the cabin had revealed that it was a windowless structure, a big shoebox with a porch that stretched the length of one side. It appeared to be a hundred years old at least, with no other entrance besides the front door. Riley's mind flashed to Big-un's farm, remembered that Papa had commented on how well the big man had kept it up. He'd done no less with the cabin. It was solid.

The door had no knob, just a handle, but a hasp on it stood open, with no padlock.

"What do you figure?" Willie Ray asked.

It was the first time Riley'd looked into Willie Ray's face in hours, and he appeared to be about to collapse. Dark circles hung like hammocks beneath his eyes, his skin was plaid.

"Let me take a look at those bandages," Riley said but Willie Ray pulled back.

"They're fine. I'm fine. They don't matter."

When Riley tried to protest, Willie Ray pointed out.

"I'm in a whole lot better shape than I was half the time we was in 'Nam. Dysentery, jungle rot, leeches, no sleep … we blew it off. Just like we're gonna blow this off."

Riley nodded.

"Van's locked up. If there's a matching hasp on the inside of that cabin door, it's got a padlock on it locked tight.

"Somebody's in there," Riley said, and as if in response to his words they heard a sound from inside.

"YOU PICKED a fine time to leave me, Lucille," Jackson crooned, his voice ordinary but he could carry a tune. "Four hungry children and a crop in the field."

Jessie watched Jackson sharpen his knife, long smooth strokes with a whetstone. She was tied up now, hands taped behind her back. She wiggled and Jackson stopped singing.

"Case you was wondering, I don't recommend trying to get out of duct tape by tearing your skin off with it. Been there, done that."

He began to sing again. "I've had some bad times, lived through some sad times, but this time …"

She hadn't eaten the cold burger and fries Jackson had brought a couple of hours ago, but she did drink the bottled water. And now she needed to go to the bathroom. She knew she'd have to do it sooner or later, go behind the little curtain and use the bucket he'd brought in for her use. But she'd hold it as long as she could.

He changed tunes.

"Once in every life, someone comes along. And you came to me, it was almost like a song."

He paused. "Ronnie Milsap — you know that song, doncha?"

What, did he think she was going to sing along with him?

She said nothing, found that her throat almost locked up every time she had to engage with him. The hatred and rage had settled in her like water seeping down into a sponge. And froze there, leaving her rigid, unable to speak.

"If you're expecting me to be a gentleman, you can forget it," he barked, nodding to the bed. "I get the cot."

He looked her up and down and then grunted in disdain. "Girls like you ain't my type."

She wanted to say, "You mean girls who are taller than you? That disqualifies half the women on the planet." But she said nothing. Couldn't.

"You get the floor. Tied to the chair leg."

He went back to his knife and his singing,

"Let's go to Luckenbach, Texas, with Waylon and Willie and the boys …"

The sound of his voice made her skin crawl.

"IF JACKSON'S IN THERE, so's Jessie," Riley whispered.

"And who else?" Willie Ray asked. "You said he had a couple of goons. They could be in there, too."

"Maybe. But his men have … things to do. If they're

gonna be up in them rocks by nine o'clock, they're gonna have to get up with the chickens."

"So what do we do?"

"Options are — go crashing in there now, or wait until Jackson comes out."

"My vote'd be Door Number Two. He'll come out in the morning to go to the mine. He'll have to bring Jessie with him to get us to show ourselves."

Riley thought about it.

"Yeah … he feels secure here, thinks nobody knows about this place. He won't expect to get jumped here. Soon's he comes out in the morning, we grab him."

Riley sat down on the ground and leaned back against a tree, beckoned for Willie Ray to do the same. Willie Ray moved carefully, obviously in pain, put his shotgun down on the ground and then sat beside it. Before he leaned back against a tree, he took out the pistol he'd shoved down the back of his pants and laid it beside the shotgun.

Willie Ray gave Riley a grim nod. "Least it ain't raining."

"And we ain't got to dig a foxhole."

Chapter Sixty-Nine

JESSIE WASN'T sure she'd be able to stand up after spending the night curled up on the hard boards of the floor. The bruised muscles and tendons where Jackson had kicked her were stiff and would only move at all with a great deal of effort, complaining with bolts of pain through the whole process.

Surprisingly, she'd actually nodded off, though. With her hands tied together and then duct taped to one leg of the table, her left cheek bruised — maybe a broken cheekbone? — left eye swollen partially shut, lip busted, a couple of ribs broken and assorted bruises all over her body, somehow she had slipped into somewhere that resembled sleep, somewhere not there on the cold floor.

She had been semi-dreaming, some strange conglomeration of twisted reality and fantasy, where she and Davie were running toward Magic across a field. Magic barked and when he opened his mouth, a hideous monster came out of it, a formless freak, part snake, part spider that had Jackson McClusky's face and—

"Wake up." Jackson kicked her in the leg to rouse her.

"No time for beauty sleep, we got things to do, places to go, people to see."

He was in a perky mood for a man who'd spent the night on a stinky cot in a hunting cabin. The air now smelled of kerosene, and she thought maybe that meant the wick on the lantern was burning out. Without the lantern, the cabin wasn't exactly coal mine dark. There were little cracks and chinks in the walls and roof, and the crack under the door admitted a half-inch sliver of light.

Had to be morning. But what time, or how long they'd been in the cabin, was information her brain refused to serve up for her viewing enjoyment.

Her throat was dry, her mouth tasted sticky. Probably wasn't going to be able to brush her teeth this morning, and it'd be a shame to die with food stuck in her gums.

Die.

Somewhere she'd shifted a kind of gear. Now, she was filled with the cold, clear certainty that she would not live to see the sun set on this day. She didn't know exactly what it was Jackson had planned, but she was sure he had set some kind of trap for Riley to walk into when he came to claim her. Some kind of trap where he'd be killed.

And she railed in the face of that. Riley was going to die this day, too, in some rigged attempt to rescue her. When it really should be Jackson McClusky who died. He deserved death, had earned death, and she yearned to give it to him with such a passion she felt herself grinding her teeth. Hatred roared through her chest like a runaway train. She wanted Jackson dead, but she wanted Riley alive a whole lot more.

When Jackson roused her, she pretended to be in much more pain than she was, pretended to be weaker, stiffer, her movements more limited than they really were.

If Jackson let his guard down, even for an instant, she would take a shot at …

She heard Jackson relieve himself into the can in the alcove beyond the corner screen. She'd had to use it once, a coffee can. She could barely stand, made a mess but didn't care. He'd been drinking Mountain Dew, one can after another, nonstop, but she'd only had the one bottle of water … however long ago, she didn't know. Her throat was parched. Gratefully, though, she didn't need to go to the bathroom.

Jackson came out from behind the screen buttoning his fly. He stepped to the table with the vicious-looking knife he'd been sharpening last night, and slit the strip of duct tape that affixed her tied hands to the table leg. Then he reached down, grabbed her upper arm and lifted her upright.

Every part of her body hurt so the moaning cry she let out was not fake. The weakness was, when she allowed her knees to buckle and she began to collapse to the floor.

He let her fall with a plop.

"I ain't playin' no game. You ain't hurt. But even if you are, don't matter. Now, you gonna stand up and you gonna walk out that door and get in that van under your own steam. Or …"

He still had the knife in his hand and he suddenly stuck the tip of it into her left nostril.

"I'm gonna split your nose, both sides. I seen a fella once in prison had been split like that, couldn't breathe right and he was really ugly." He leaned closer and she could smell the rank stench of his bad breath. "And if that don't get it …" He moved the knife. The blade was so sharp that the simple motion cut a scratch in her skin. "… I'm gonna put out one of these big blue eyes. But I'll let you pick which one."

The threatening tone left his voice, command took over.

"Now get up!"

She managed somehow, off balance with her hands immobilized, she got to her feet, swaying.

"That's more like it."

He went to the door, withdrew a key from his pocket and inserted it in the padlock holding the door shut and removed it. He pulled the door open and the color of the sunlight told Jessie it was early morning. Soft illumination filtered down through the trees in the woods, sparkling on the dew drops. The air was chilly and smelled like autumn.

Jackson stuck the knife in a sheath at his waist, grabbed Jessie by the arm and dragged her stumbling out to the van. He had the door to the van halfway open when a nearby voice told him.

"You even breathe, and I'll blow your brains all over the side of that window."

It was Riley!

Jessie collapsed to the ground out of Jackson's grasp as she cried, "He has a knife."

Jackson was moving, maybe trying to grab her or draw the knife, when an awful boom exploded off to her right and she felt blood splatter onto her face. Jackson screamed, high-pitched and wailing.

Then Riley was at her side, lifting her, speaking tenderly, pulling the tape off her wrists, and the world tilted back so she could see Jackson. He was lying on the ground beside the van door, screaming. Blood was everywhere ... then she saw.

Jackson's foot was gone. There was nothing where it had been but a ragged piece of bone.

And she thought objectively: *that's what a 12-gauge shotgun loaded double-ought buckshot at close range will do to you.*

Chapter Seventy

FBI Special Agent Elijah Bradigan stood surveying the scene. The raid that was supposed to bring in all three leaders of the Cornbread Mafia and some other fellow named Jackson McClusky — who'd be charged with kidnapping — had yielded four South American men who purported not to speak English. Bradigan's team had caught them getting into position in the rocks above the entrance to the Bishop Mining Company coal mine, had cleared the area for the nine o'clock appearance of the stars of the show, and waited. But they never came.

Where were Hannacker, Taggart and Monaghan? There was supposed to be a trade this morning — marijuana seed for Jessie Monaghan.

Bradigan turned from staring up at the rocks above the mine — it was, indeed, a perfect spot for snipers. The other agents were standing by as a couple of Kentucky State Police troopers seated the prisoners in the back of their cruisers.

Bill Thomas cocked his thumb toward the man he'd been talking to.

"No habla inglés."

Peterson hung close around the captives, not letting them know he spoke Spanish, hoping they'd say something to each other that would be helpful. But they sat mute, trying to look like they really didn't understand every word that was being said to them and around them. Once he got them separated, Eli had no doubt that he and Peterson would be able to get at least one of them to talk. But that would take time and he had a sense that time was running out.

"What'd we miss, Bill?"

The other agent shrugged, shading his eyes against the bright morning sun that'd just cleared the top of the knob.

"Riley Hannacker and Jackson McClusky made a deal to show up here this morning to make a trade … what's to miss about that?"

"You think they called it off?" Agent Zucarelli asked.

"Or changed location, maybe, not here but somewhere else?" Agent Lincoln suggested.

"How'd they do that without using the phone and why would they?" Agent Thomas said. "Seems clear to me they don't even suspect a tap."

Eli had replayed the tape of the conversation between McClusky and Hannacker again and again. Had even replayed the end of the tape that recorded the calls Willie Ray Taggart had placed after the one from McClusky.

"Those people Taggart called …" Eli said, an idea forming. "He asked all of them about when they used to go deer hunting, who they hunted with, about deer stands and hunting cabins …"

"With everything else going on, what was that all about?" Bill Thomas said.

"You remember what they said to him?" Eli asked. "Exactly?"

Agent Beddingfield did, began to spout it back, word for word — noting the roads, the landmarks, the burned-out stump. Eli hurried back to his car to retrieve a map of Callison County. He went to one of the Kentucky State troopers and spread the map out on the hood of his cruiser.

"You familiar with Callison County, the geography, I mean?"

"I've worked this county for twenty years — and what I know is there are hollows and valleys, nooks and crannies that *nobody* knows about but the locals. They used to brew a lot of moonshine here, did you know that?"

"Where's Buzzard Knob, on this map?"

The trooper looked around for a few moments, then put his finger on the spot.

"Where you going with this, Eli?" Thomas wanted to know.

"What the guy named Big-un said yesterday morning to Riley, warning him about the ambush. Remember what he said before that?"

"He said he'd talked to Jackson, that he'd come by to see his mother."

"The other part, what Jackson did while he was there."

"He stole a key to Big-un's gun cabinet."

"And his *hunting cabin*. All those calls — Taggart was trying to track down the location of a hunting cabin. Why would it be so important to him to know that *right now* — unless he and Riley think that's where Jackson is holed up?"

After Agent Beddingfield parroted for him the locations and landmarks that'd been mentioned, the trooper said, "Best bet is to go up the *front* side of Buzzard Knob. They used to log those woods pretty heavily fifty or sixty years ago, logging roads all over." He shook his head. "It's a maze."

Bradigan picked up the map off the hood and began folding it. "Sounds like a good place to look for rats."

Chapter Seventy-One

RILEY LOOKED down where Jackson was writhing in agony in the dirt, shrieking. They could just leave it at that, stand here and watch him bleed out.

"Shut up that caterwauling or I'm gonna blow off the other one," Willie Ray threatened.

Jackson kept screaming.

"Alrighty then." Willie Ray cracked open the shotgun, popped in two more shells and snapped it shut. Then he pointed it at Jackson's other foot.

Jackson's eyes were huge, his face so white his beard and mustache looked like they'd been drawn on with a Magic Marker. Coughing and choking, he managed to strangle back his screams. He still wailed, though, softer, moaning and groaning, writhing in the dirt, holding onto his bloody pants leg above the gore.

"Just shoot me, kill me," he cried, looking in agony and rage and terror into their faces. "Go ahead, do it. Get it over with."

Willie Ray unfastened the brand new leather belt Riley had bought for him yesterday at Walmart, leaned over and wrapped it around Jackson's calf halfway between his knee and the jagged piece of bone that was all that remained of his foot. He picked up the knife Jackson'd dropped in the dirt and poked a new hole in the belt that would hold it tight, then fastened the buckle.

"Had to do something or he'd bleed to death," Willie Ray said.

"So …?" said Jessie. She had pulled out of Riley's grasp and stood now looking down at Jackson, her face made of stone. Jackson had hurt her. Had hit her in the face. Her lip was swollen, her jaw bruised. And she was not standing totally upright, was slightly bent, had hugged her midsection with her arms as soon as he set her wrists free.

"Is that the way you wanna execute him?" There was a wild look in Willie Ray's eyes. "Just let him bleed to death? That good enough for you?"

That was the question, of course. Now what? How did they carry out the death sentence they'd all sworn to in Jessie's kitchen five years ago?

"No," Jessie said. "It's not good enough. He … smothered Davie with a pillow."

Rage erupted out of her then and she kicked Jackson in the face, landed a blow with the toe of her boot right in his mouth, likely broke all his front teeth, and knocked him sideways onto the ground. His cries were strangled, now, muffled.

Maybe that was it. Maybe they all ought to release their wrath in a frenzy, beat him to death. Even through the red haze of his rage, Riley didn't think that was the right thing to do. For him and Willie Ray … maybe, but not for Jessie. One day, when she could no longer feel the wrath, the animal bloodlust, that was flowing through her chest now in a freight train rush, she would remember the deed she'd committed because of it. That kind of brutality would haunt her.

"I'm gonna cut him," Willie Ray said and Riley turned to see he still held Jackson's knife.

No, that wasn't what he said. He'd said, "I'm gonna *gut* him."

"I'm gonna—" He stopped and they all turned toward a noise. It was the sound of a car engine. "What the—?"

"Somebody's coming," Jessie said, looking toward the sound of the noise, in the trees far down the hillside.

He and Willie Ray had come up on the cabin from the back side, over the knob, the way the deer hunters had come. But there was a road, obviously, that led here and it sounded like someone was coming up that road.

But maybe not. There were likely several logging roads in this vicinity.

Jessie's eyes asked the question, "What do we do?" but Riley had no answer.

"Who could ..." Willie Ray began.

Right, who could it be? Likely not somebody out deer hunting.

"If they're coming here, it's Jackson's goons. Who else could it be?"

"What do we do?" she asked. Riley didn't answer. They all strained to hear the sound above Jackson's moaning. He was no longer screaming, had his hands to his face with blood gushing out between his fingers.

The sound didn't appear to be getting any nearer, but they could still hear it. Somebody was down there. They had plenty of time to get away, vanish into the trees. But what about Jackson?

"Ain't leaving Jackson," Willie Ray said.

"Lock him in the cabin," Riley said. "We'll be in the trees waiting for whoever comes up that road."

"Meaning?" Jessie asked.

"Depends on who it is and what they want. If it's his men, we ain't lettin' them rescue him."

Riley and Willie Ray each grabbed an arm and dragged Jackson across the ground to the cabin. They opened the door and threw him inside, and slammed it behind him.

Willie Ray nodded to the blood in the dirt, the bloody snail trail to the cabin.

"Looks like we field dressed a deer," he said.

Jessie picked up the padlock off the ground. Jackson had left the key stuck into it. She snapped it into place on the hasp, stuck the key in her pocket and the three of them took to the woods.

Riley tried to help Jessie, but she brushed his aid aside. He suspected Jackson had beaten her, maybe broke some ribs from the way she was moving. She needed a doctor. They needed to put a bullet in Jackson's brain, get in that van and drive out of here, take her to the emergency room in Bardstown.

Willie Ray slipped into the trees on the south side of the cabin, Riley and Jessie went north. About fifty feet from the cabin was a stand of brush and tangled up kudzu vines and he directed her that way, tried to help her hunker down behind it. She almost cried out as she bent, said breathlessly, "kicked me," and that was all.

Then they waited. And listened.

It seemed at first like the vehicle was coming their way, up the road that led to the cabin. But then the sound began to fade, as if whoever it was had turned off on some other road and wasn't coming to the cabin at all.

Soon there was silence. Riley stood and helped Jessie to her feet, made his way through the trees back to the cabin as Willie Ray was coming out of the trees on the other side.

"Let's do this," Willie Ray said with a light in his eyes. Riley was in a hurry to get the whole thing over with for Jessie's sake — both emotional and physical.

Jessie unlocked the padlock pushed the door open. Jackson lay where they'd left him, sprawled on the floor, blood pooling all around him. She went inside, followed by Willie Ray. Riley closed the door behind them.

The three stood around Jackson, looking down. Riley held his rifle. Willie Ray had set his shotgun down by the door and stuffed his pistol in the back of his pants, but he still held Jackson's knife. Then Willie Ray said, "You say it, Riley. You say what you seen him do. You tell him about Andy, how he died."

It was an odd request and Riley definitely didn't like the fevered, wild look in Willie Ray's eyes.

"Do it," Willie Ray said, in a harsh whisper.

Chapter Seventy-Two

Andy was standing in the far corner of the cabin when Riley began to speak, tacking words again onto the horror he'd seen that day in Vietnam.

Willie Ray had wanted Riley to say it, to describe it for Andy because he didn't know what Andy'd seen that day. Andy'd been in the cabin as soon as they opened the door. It was shadowy in the corner where he stood, but that didn't matter with Andy. Andy gave off his own light, he glowed. Not like them little green men they played with as kids, the ones you left out in the sun and then when you brought them back into the house, you could go into a dark closet and see them, glowing with a green light, like a firefly. Didn't last long and then the light went out. Andy's light never went out. Willie Ray'd been seeing it now for nigh onto a decade and it was always there. But it wasn't some sickly green florescent glow. It was a white light. Well, sometimes it was golden, too. Sometimes there were little sparkles in it, all around, like what come off the end of Fourth of July sparklers — sparkles with sharp edges like swords.

Willie Ray only heard fragments, pieces of what Riley said. There had come a great roaring in his ears, a rumbling, like standing next to a waterfall. Part of it was that he had a fever, he knew that. If his mama'd laid her hand on his forehead she'd have put him to bed, wiped his face with a cool cloth and filled him up with aspirin.

"… asked Davie if he had another M16 and he showed me where there were three on the back wall. Then we both heard somebody yelling, 'Don't shoot.'"

Andy's eyes moved from Willie Ray to Riley when he said that and Willie Ray knew Andy was remembering running through the downpour, bullets plunking and spitting around him, how he dived through the door into the bunker and knocked Davie down like a bowling ball hitting pins.

"… remember how scared Andy looked. And I saw … how his eyelashes and eyebrows were so blond they were almost invisible."

Riley choked on those words, strangled back a sob.

"Then I looked out past Andy into the rain outside the bunker and saw the barrel of an RPG pointed right at the door."

Andy moved out of the shadows, slowly like he always did, his shiny guts dragging along beside him like Willie Ray's blankie used to drag on the floor behind him wherever he went. Andy stood right over Jackson, looking at him, when Riley described how a flare suddenly lit up the night and he could see through the rain, could see that the "little guy" holding the RPG to his shoulder wasn't naked like the other Cong. He was fully dressed, wearing combat fatigues.

Riley wasn't remembering anymore, he was talking to Jackson.

"*I saw you*, saw you pointing that thing at the door of the bunker, and you saw me, too — didn't you."

Riley kicked Jackson hard, the blow caught him in the shoulder. Willie Ray saw then that there was understanding and recognition in Jackson's eyes now. He was in shock from losing that foot, wouldn't live long now the way it was still bleeding, but he wasn't so ravaged by pain that he couldn't think. He was thinking, was seeing, remembering. He knew exactly what Riley was saying.

"Didn't you?" Riley demanded again, and Jackson slowly nodded his head, maybe couldn't talk the way his mouth was all messed up from where Jessie'd kicked him in the teeth.

"Say it," Riley's voice was a ragged, hoarse whisper. I want to hear you say it … or I'll cut your heart out of your chest right now and stuff it down your throat."

"… I seen …" The words were strangled, mangled coming through broken teeth and tore-up lips. "… you … and Davie."

Jessie stiffened beside him, and Willie Ray woulda looked at her but he couldn't drag his eyes off Jackson's face. The look in his eyes was unreadable, but not remorse, or regret. Like Andy always said, "He ain't sorry he done it. He's just sorry he got caught."

"When I come to, they was hauling me out of the bunker on a stretcher, past Willie Ray."

Willie Ray looked at Riley then and their eyes locked, and for an instant, just an instant, the two of them were back there together, captives of the nightmare. Then he was talking to Jackson again.

"He had Andy's head in his lap."

Riley leaned in to get closer, to spit the words in Jackson's face.

"Andy was tore open from his chest down … and his

guts was hanging out. Willie Ray was trying to put them back in." He grabbed a breath. "Begged me to *help him put them back in.*"

Riley ran out of air then, straightened back up. Likely couldn't have said another word, but that was fine because he'd done said all he needed to say.

Holding Jackson's knife, Willie Ray looked at Andy, then down at Jackson. "Ain't gonna be nobody here to put *your guts* back in."

He dropped to one knee beside Jackson, brought the knife down slowly toward his chest.

"You in there! In the cabin! This is Special Agent Elijah Bradigan with the Federal Bureau of Investigation. Put down your weapons and come out."

Chapter Seventy-Three

It was just like it'd been in Vietnam. The way time derailed — elongated and contracted — first like a slow-motion movie and then herky-jerky fast. The words that hit Riley's ears didn't match up with the mouths that spoke them, either a beat behind the lips moving or a beat ahead. Sounds from outside sounded like they were coming from inside a deep well.

Though it all happened over the course of only a couple of seconds, Riley replayed the scene in his head forever after that, slowed down the action to see every detail, what he'd seen at the time but hadn't been able to register.

The voice called from outside and they all froze.

"... *down your weapons and come out with your hands up* ..."

Then there was a motion that couldn't possibly have been real because it was as lightning fast as a striking rattlesnake and Jackson McClusky wasn't capable of that kind of movement. When Willie Ray froze, the point of the knife only inches away from Jackson's chest, Jackson lifted his left arm, like to ward Willie Ray off. But then

Jackson leaned forward and Riley saw that a … *blade*, like a sword two inches wide and pointed on both ends, had somehow erupted from the black thing, the brace on his arm, ran the whole length of it, from below his wrist almost to his elbow. He sliced with it across Willie Ray's body, opened his belly up from one side to the other, all in one motion that was almost too fast to follow with the eye.

Willie Ray didn't reel backward from the attack. He dropped the knife and collapsed, no, *lunged* down on top of Jackson, knocking his bladed arm aside. The pistol Willie Ray had stuck down in the back of his pants was knocked out. It skittered across the floor and came to rest at Jessie's feet.

Then Jackson was moving, impossibly moving. He shoved Willie Ray's body off his and began calling out, screaming, screeching, yelling words his mangled mouth couldn't possibly form.

"Help! *Help me.* They're trying to kill me. Hel—"

He didn't complete the word. A hole appeared in the center of his forehead. Looked for all the world like the one that'd been in Papa's. And in Mama Bert's. Riley never heard the gunshot, but he heard the whisper that followed — Jessie.

"That's for Davie."

She was standing over Jackson with Willie Ray's pistol in her hand. It slid out of her fingers to the floor as the door of the cabin exploded inward and armed men seemed to fill up the room all at once. Weren't there and then were, too fast to follow the process.

Riley dropped his rifle and kneeled beside Willie Ray as his best friend's insides began to ooze slowly out the wound in his belly.

One of the men, a tall black man, picked up the rifle and kicked the pistol away from where it lay beside Willie

Ray's hand. The man grabbed Riley by the arm and yanked him to his feet and then another man was on the other side of Riley, pulling both his arms behind him.

Police officers. Noise, movement and yelling. He saw another man grab Jessie where she stood staring down at Jackson and turn her around to put handcuffs on her. Riley spoke for the first time.

"She's hurt!" he yelled at the man who had grabbed her. He turned to the black man who'd yanked Riley to his feet. "Jackson kicked her and broke her ribs. You wanna puncture a lung?"

The man beside Riley said something to the man who was about to cuff Jessie, Riley heard the words but wasn't assigning meaning to the speech around him. The man stopped pulling on Jessie's arms, took hold of her by her shoulders and turned her around to march her out of the room.

"Hey you, *FBI*, I got somethin' to say."

The voice was Willie Ray's, impossibly strong, so loud it silenced everybody else.

Willie Ray lay on his back, his face ashen, blood was pooling in his mouth and he blew a fine spray of red mist out with every word.

"FBI!" he cried out again and the man who'd yanked Riley to his feet knelt beside Willie Ray as the other officer snapped the handcuffs on Riley's wrists shut.

"I'm Special Agent Eli—" the man started to say, but Willie Ray reached up with a bloody hand, grabbed his arm and pulled him closer.

"Listen up." Blood sprayed out. "I ain't got long." Willie Ray cocked his chin toward where Jackson lay sprawled on the floor beside him. "I just shot that son of a bitch for killing my brother."

Then Willie Ray's eyes shifted toward Riley. He didn't

exactly look at Riley, but at a spot in space near him. It reminded Riley of the way Davie looked at you but then didn't see you, like he was looking at somebody standing next to you. "Jackson killed Andy and Davie ... but I *got* him."

His grip on the FBI agent's arm loosened and his hand dropped to the floor, but he stared into the agent's eyes.

"You lookin' for the boss of this outfit? Well, you done found him. Name's Willie Ray Taggart." Willie Ray gasped and made a strangled sound. Every word rode out of his mouth on a spurt of blood. "I'm in charge here. Don't nobody do nothin' 'les I tell 'em." He did look at Riley then, but his eyes were starting to unfocus. "Just me, I run the Cornbread Mafia all by my lonesome."

He tried to draw in another breath to say something else, then got a confused look on his face, surprised that he couldn't breathe. He shifted his eyes away from Riley again, looked at empty air beside where Riley stood.

"Andy." It wasn't even a whisper, but Riley heard it just the same. "Comin' home, bro."

The next breath didn't come.

Chapter Seventy-Four

SHERRY LYNN GOT to the front door on the fourth chime. She'd set the doorbell so the first time someone outside pushed the button, there was a chime inside, with speakers on all the floors of the house: *ding-dong.* That was it, just the two. The second time the button was pushed, it became ding-dong ding-dong. And the third time ...

She looked at the little screen and saw two men she didn't know on the porch. Both in suits, one black, one white. She glanced out beyond them and her heart started a stuttering rhythm in her chest and she couldn't catch her breath.

There was a big black car, but there was also a Kentucky State Police cruiser and the uniformed officer was outside the car, standing by the door.

O, dear Mary Mother of Jesus this couldn't be real.

She shook her head.

It wasn't. It wasn't ... *that.*

They were here for some other reason.

She pasted her most fetching smile on her face and pulled the door open graciously.

"May I help you?"

"Are you Sherry Lynn Hannacker?" The one who asked that question was a good-looking black man who resembled some movie star, but she couldn't place which one.

"Yes, I am, and who might you be?"

The black man held out his hand and flipped open a little case that revealed a badge inside. She didn't get a very good look, because he flipped it back shut again as he spoke, putting it in his pocket.

"My name is Special Agent Elijah Bradigan with the Federal Bureau of Investigation and this is Special Agent Bill Thomas. We've come—"

She gestured at the children, the decorations, the cake. "I don't care why you've come, now is really *not* a good time. You'll have to come back later, sometime after lunch tomorrow would be best."

"I'm afraid we can't do that," the black officer said.

"Well, I'm afraid I must insist!" She heard the cold haughtiness in her voice, was hiding in terror behind it. She felt it tighten her belly like nothing she'd ever felt before. This terror was worse than the fear she'd felt when the first word came back about the battle at Tweety Bird, that there'd been casualties but nobody knew who it was, and she had imagined Riley lying dead somewhere in a stinking jungle and she'd been so afraid she couldn't catch her breath.

She couldn't catch her breath now, either, couldn't say anything else, was holding onto incipient hysteria with an iron fist. With her head high, chin thrust out, she started to close the door, but the officer shoved it backward at her and stepped over the threshold.

"How dare you—!"

"We've come for you, Mrs. Hannacker." He put out his

hand and took her upper arm, pulled her forward as he spoke. "Sherry Lynn Hannacker, you are under arrest, charged with violating the Comprehensive Drug Abuse Prevention and Control Act of 1970, Chapter 13 of Title 21—"

He kept talking as he turned her around so her back was to him, pulled her arms behind her and she felt the cold steel of … *handcuffs*.

"No!" she screamed and tried to wrench free. When she did, his grip on her arms tightened and the handcuffs snapped shut. "Take your hands off me … stop it. This is wrong, you've made a terrible mistake. What have I done?"

She threw the meaningless words at them, felt like she was tossing little bits of popcorn, light and airy and they bounced on the two men and fell off.

"… the right to remain silent. If you give up that right …"

They were pulling her away, practically dragging her across her own front porch.

"No, you can't do this."

"Come along peacefully. It'll be better for everybody if you do," said the other officer.

"I won't come … leave me alone … stop it!"

She began to struggle frantically, had to get free—

"Mommy …?" Everyone froze and looked at the doorway. Drew stood there with Anna the housekeeper. The other children formed a quiet crowd of onlookers behind him, their eyes wide.

"That's my son. Stop it. Let me *go.*" She fought desperately to get away. To get to *Drew.* "That's my little boy." She sucked in a ragged breath and cried, "It's his *birthday!*"

The black officer leaned closer and spoke into her ear.

"The boy doesn't know what's going on. He's scared and you making a scene is making it that much harder for him. You *are* coming with us, one way or another. Don't make us drag you away."

She froze and her mind took a picture of the look on Drew's face and it would flash into her mind with the horror of a returning nightmare for the rest of her life.

"Son, your mother is coming with us," he said. "She will be alright. Nobody's going to hurt her."

The two men guided her across the porch and down the front steps, one on either side. She kept looking back over her shoulder, trying to see Drew.

"Drew, honey, everything's going to be fine. This is all a big mistake."

He came out on the porch, might have followed but Anna wouldn't let him.

"Anna, look after him. And call …" Right, call who? Riley was out somewhere, she didn't have any idea where, hadn't come home last night. A lawyer? Yes, she needed a lawyer. "Call Horace Gilbert, explain what happened." She had to shout now because they were at the cars. "Tell him … I need help."

And with the word help, she broke into a thousand little pieces and started to cry.

After that, scenes and circumstances and events were all jumbled together into a single horror without beginning or end, where every moment was the most humiliating moment of her life … until the next one.

They put her into the back of the Kentucky State Police cruiser.

"Watch your head," the trooper said, and pushed her head down so she wouldn't bang it on the door frame. She'd been getting in and out of cars for her whole life and never, not one time, had she ever banged her head.

The door closed.

She felt the car pull away down the driveway. She

looked out the back window, strained to see her house —
her beautiful house. They passed between the concrete
lions on either side of the driveway and the house disap-
peared from view.

They took her to the Brewster Police station, where
they fingerprinted her. *Fingerprinted* her. They even took her
picture, front and both side views.

She refused to make eye contact with anybody, and
there were so many people around, all looking at her, she
felt like an animal in the zoo. She was so mortified, so
embarrassed for people to see this!!

More than anything else, though, Sherry Lynn
Hannacker was afraid. Terrified.

By the time she sat across the table from the two FBI
agents she was so freaked out she couldn't hear. Seriously,
couldn't hear. They said things to her, but she only heard
pieces of the sentences. She did hear "lawyer present," and
she strangled out a cry. "I want my lawyer. I'm not going to
say a word. I want my lawyer."

She gulped a lungful of air. "And my husband. Call my
husband — Riley Hannacker — and tell him where I am.

The agents got up and left and she sat alone, waiting.
Some amount of time passed, but she didn't know how
long. The room where she sat was windowless so she
couldn't judge the time. It seemed like hours. Maybe it was
hours. She sat motionless, her thoughts moved like icebergs
through a frozen sea.

And then he was there. Horace Gilbert, the squat
little man who had an office on Chambers Street, a block
off Main. His wife played in the same bunco group as
Sherry Lynn. Beatrice was her name, she'd been at
Sherry Lynn's house playing just two weeks ago. He
smelled like aftershave and breath mints and had a small
dab of white shaving cream beneath his ear. Only then

did it occur to Sherry Lynn that today was Saturday. Somebody had gone out and dragged Horace off the golf course.

Oh, she knew there were better lawyers than this, they'd talked about it. Well, the others had talked and she'd listened. She should have paid more attention! But she did know that Riley had big-time lawyers, expensive big-city lawyers on retainer and they would be representing her.

Representing her.

Horace would have to do until the big guns got here. He needed to get her out of this place and back home … then let the big lawyers fight whatever this was and make it *go away*.

Riley would call — *Riley!*

Did Riley know about what was happening? Had anybody told him? Because when he did find out, heads would roll! He would come roaring in here and … and what? Would they arrest him, too? And Jessie and Willie Ray and …?

"… listening to me?"

Horace was talking.

"Yes, I'm … no, I … What did you say?"

"Don't say anything. Absolutely nothing. I'll handle the questions." He actually patted her hand. "You just be a potted plant."

A potted plant?

When the door opened for the two FBI agents, Sherry Lynn caught a glimpse of a clock on the wall in the hallway. Seven o'clock! How could it possibly be … Drew's party had started at noon!

The agents introduced themselves and shook hands with Horace. Bill Thomas and … Bradigan. She'd missed his first name.

"I want to make sure you understand the charges

against you, Mrs. Hannacker," said Bradigan — *Sidney Poitier!* That's who he looked like, Sidney Poitier.

"She understands the charges and of course will plead not guilty to all of them," Horace said. "She has done nothing wrong and she has nothing to say."

Horace sounded like he knew what he was doing, didn't seem like a befuddled old man at all. She felt a tiny bit better.

The agents looked at each other and Bradigan nodded. Thomas got up and left the room and returned with another agent, a big beefy guy with an Italian name, Zucarini or something, who carried a small box — a tape recorder. He set it down on the table and flipped the play button.

For a moment Sherry Lynn didn't realize what she was hearing. She recognized the voice but couldn't place it — then she did. It was that man — Steve Kaiser.

"*YOU SURE YOU want more to drink? Don't you think you've had enough?*"

"*I can hold my liquor, thank you very much, and that strawberry thing is sooooo good. Just one more.*"

SHERRY LYNN COULDN'T BREATHE.

"Wait a minute. Is that what I think it is … did someone record my client without—" Horace began.

"I don't have to remind you that Kentucky is a one-party consent state," Agent Bradigan said. Then to Sherry Lynn, "That means that it only requires the consent of one person in the conversation to make a recorded conversation admissible in court. The man you were speaking to, Steve Kaiser, has granted his permission."

"I don't remember any — Steve drugged me!"

"Be quiet, Sherry Lynn," Horace snapped. "I told you not to say a word."

"It's right there on the tape that *she* was the one asking for more alcohol," the agent said.

And then he played the rest of the tape. Sherry Lynn was mesmerized by the way Steve directed the conversation to the Cornbread Mafia, marveled at the sound of her own voice on the tape recording, providing intimate information she … she didn't even realize she knew, things she'd merely overheard in passing through a room. Riley had told her about the offshore accounts, but not in the kind of detail she provided to Steve Kaiser. She must have heard him talking on the phone about it or … it didn't matter. It didn't matter how she had come by the information she provided. The only thing that mattered was that she had and that the information was now in the hands of the Federal Bureau of Investigation.

Horace whispered to her that he would fight it, that they couldn't use those tapes as evidence, he'd get them thrown out — not to worry. Maybe he could, but she didn't like the look on his face when he said it. The set of his jaw and the tension around his eyes. He had seemed so certain at first.

She did what he told her. She said nothing. And when the FBI agents finally got tired of the silence they went away. Horace told her then that she would be arraigned on the charges in court in the morning.

"I just want to go home, Horace," she said. "Just get me out of here so I can go home."

Horace looked uncomfortable.

"I'm afraid I can't do that, Sherry Lynn. Bail won't be set until your arraignment hearing in the morning."

"What am I supposed to do until then?"

"They will … take you to a cell."

"Spend the whole night … *in jail?* You can't be serious. I absolutely will *not* stay here."

She did, though.

So did Jessie.

Chapter Seventy-Five

JESSIE SAT LOOKING at a dirty concrete floor, so sick and disgusted and afraid, afraid, *afraid* that she couldn't do anything but just sit there. There were bars — *bars*. Locked bars in front of her, keeping the world out and her in. She was in a cage, and not a gilded one, either.

Though the motion caused stabbing pain beneath the bandages Dr. Callahan had wrapped tenderly around and around her body in the emergency room, she leapt up off the bed, rushed to the metal toilet affixed to the wall and threw up. Again. Tried, anyway. Nothing but stomach bile came up. She'd been vomiting almost nonstop ever since they brought her here, showed her the bunk and the blanket and the toilet … walked out, closed the door behind them. And *locked* it.

She dry-heaved until the pain in her ribs was almost unbearable. The toilet flushed on its own. There was only cold water in the metal sink, and she ran some over her wrists — that's what you did to calm down, ran cold water over your wrists. That's what Mama Ruth had always said.

The image of the old woman bloomed bright in her

mind. Not the woman in the hospital bed, her face slack and placid, on her way to the royal wedding. The real Mama Ruth. The feisty one, who'd invited her to come into her house the first time by saying, "I got coffee. It ain't bad."

She was glad Mama Ruth had died happy, unhooked from the reality that in the other room her only son lay staring with unfocused eyes at the ceiling.

Now, Davie wasn't staring at anything. Davie was dead, gone.

Nowhere in Jessie actually believed that, even after the police officers had confirmed the reality of it. She couldn't believe it, wouldn't believe it until she could see his body for herself.

In the beginning, when he first got home from the military hospital, she had stared and stared at him, her gaze so transfixed that sometimes she imagined he'd stopped breathing. She'd leap up in terror and put her hand in front of his nose to feel the slight, warm breath.

Jessie'd half-expected every time she left him alone, even for a few minutes, that he would be gone when she returned. But he'd lived. Against all odds, he'd lived.

Until yesterday, when Jackson McClusky "finished the job" he'd started nine years ago.

Well, *she* had finished Jackson McClusky.

Jessie and Riley had talked about it once a long time ago, what it was like to kill somebody. She knew he'd been worried about the affect it would have on her when she voted to kill Jackson, black rocks in a box. He'd told her that killing somebody changed you forever and he'd been right. She would never be the same. Killing Jackson was the single purest, most perfect thing Jessie had done since the day she saw Davie for the first time in the hospital, lying there under the white sheet, not a mark on him. It had completed something in her, filled up some emptiness she hadn't known was there. Jessie wanted to brag about it, shout it from the rooftops. "I killed the man who murdered Davie. May Jackson McClusky burn in hell for all eternity."

But she couldn't. Willie Ray had lied with his dying breath to take the blame.

Willie Ray was dead now, too. Another victim of Jackson's evil. Now, it was just the two of them — Jessie and Riley.

And what did the future hold for them?

Chapter Seventy-Six

ELI HADN'T MEANT to awaken Juliette. He'd been up all night and didn't realize it was too early to be calling. She said she'd been awake, that Daniel had been fussy. It wasn't true, but he loved her for saying it.

Leaned back in his chair with his feet on his desk in the Bardstown office, Eli watched the little town wake up around him.

"I want to hear it all," she said, and he found he was reluctant to tell her. He'd certainly censored what he told his wife before, but for different reasons. He'd seen the evil underbelly of humanity more times than he could count and he refused to pollute her consciousness with those images. But this wasn't that. He wasn't ready to tell it because he hadn't yet settled into how he felt about it.

When he described arresting the crooked Commonwealth's Attorney Winona McClusky, he tried to keep the edge of triumph out of his voice but Juliette picked up on it. She didn't miss much.

"She was ready to cut a deal before I even got her into handcuffs, rolled over on her state police detective partner

… and handed me a tape recording, the key that unlocked all the doors."

Eli had listened to the tape recording several times before he questioned Sherry Lynn Hannacker, sprang it on her hoping to shake her up and get her to fill in the blanks in the information, but her lawyer'd been a bulldog. Every time she was ready to crack, he shut her up. Of course, the guy knew he wasn't saving her from anything — she'd already hung herself.

"So Willie Ray Taggart *lied*?" Juliette said. "In a *dying* declaration?"

"He didn't shoot Jackson McClusky — the shape he was in he couldn't have lifted that pistol."

"I thought you said he was a good little Catholic boy — don't they have to tell the truth on their death beds or they'll spend eternity in Purgatory, or something like that? If he didn't kill Jackson, who did?"

"Wasn't Riley Hannacker, I don't think. My guess is Jessica Monaghan. Willie Ray lied about Jackson to protect *her*, said he was the big boss of the Cornbread Mafia to protect *them both*."

"Will you be able to make the case? Is the tape recording enough?"

"Oh, I'll get more than that. Sounds like we're going to make more than a hundred arrests, all the workers in those weed fields all over the country. Someone will make a deal — we'll need it to get Riley Hannacker."

"Why?"

"Because Sherry Lynn Hannacker is on the tape and she can't be forced to testify against her own husband."

～

THE SOUND of Christmas carols was faint, but Eli could hear it. "Joy to the World" floating up from the lobby of the federal building to the office where he sat with Bill Thomas and a group of prosecuting attorneys.

Question: Was there a collective noun for prosecutors? Flock? Herd? Murder? He let it go.

"We can throw the book at Jessica Monaghan and Sherry Lynn Hannacker," said the guy in charge, a man with a Hitler mustache and a really bad combover. "Wire taps on Monaghan's phone and Hannacker's tape are enough to hang them both."

Eli didn't like the smarmy little prosecutor. His name was Reginald Dormont the Third, and Eli pictured him as a fat little boy the other kids called Reggie. Dormont had asked for this case because he was looking to make a name for himself, and he wanted all kind of fireworks. Eli'd tried to convince him that Sherry Lynn Hannacker hadn't been in charge of anything, didn't have sense enough. Bill Thomas had described her as "a brimming cup of piping-hot stupid."

"Doesn't matter whether she really was or not, we can make a case that she was and that's all that matters," the little man had snapped.

"She was a surfer riding the crest of a wave but she was *not* in charge of the ocean," Eli said, but "Reggie" blew him off.

"Even with all the evidence, getting convictions on the Kingpin Statute is *not* going to be a walk in the park, you know. Oh no, no, no! Can you imagine trying to convince a jury that two women, one of them looks like her face belongs on a cereal box and the other is Susie Cheerleader, were running a multi-state marijuana-growing syndicate worth at least fifty million dollars — and that's a conservative estimate."

He glared at Eli. "Can't you get me anything else?"

"Did the best I could."

Eli was tired. Tired of this man, this office, tired of the world of Kentucky farmers where black and white had slowly turned into a uniform sea of gray, from one border of Callison County to the other.

He only needed one. Just *one*. A total of ninety-seven men had been arrested, caught red-handed in marijuana fields or barns in seven states, and Eli only needed *one* of them to testify that Riley Hannacker, Jessica Monaghan and Willie Ray Taggart had worked together to start and build the Cornbread Mafia into a multimillion-dollar cash cow.

Eli had personally questioned every one of them. Not a word.

Taggart had died taking the fall for all of them, and absent testimony to the contrary, wire taps had placed the reins of the operation square in the hands of Jessica Monaghan. The only call that implicated Riley Hannacker was from Jackson McClusky … who'd demanded a ransom of "Jack and the Beanstalk" seeds for Monaghan's life.

Oh, the master bean-counters, comptrollers and CPAs at headquarters, would get Riley Hannacker for *something.* Money laundering, maybe tax evasion. There were plenty of nuts on that tree for the accountant squirrels to find. But without the numbers to those Cayman Island accounts, that money couldn't be used as evidence and the government couldn't seize it. And with a stable full of high-priced legal talent … Riley Hannacker'd walk away with a slap on the wrist compared to the sentences Jessica and Sherry Lynn were facing. They'd be locked up for decades.

It wasn't supposed to work out that way.

Chapter Seventy-Seven

RILEY REACHED DOWN and massaged the swollen knuckles on his right hand as he sat waiting in the interrogation room. The swelling had gone down considerably. He'd slammed his fist into the wall in rage and frustration the day his attorney told him the source of their information about the Cornbread Mafia and the knuckles had swollen up big as plovers' eggs.

Jacob Steiner told him about the wire taps that day, too. How the FBI'd been listening in on conversations he thought were private. They'd heard all the times Willie Ray called in to talk to Jessica, to tell her about the progress of this crop or that, to discuss the hermie he'd found in a stand of weeds that was gonna ruin every plant around it. Plant sex.

The law'd got Jessie and Willie Ray on all those calls, they'd hung themselves by every word they spoke. They didn't have no tapes of Willie Ray and Riley talking about weed, though, because Willie Ray always called Jessie.

Even Riley's recorded conversation with Jackson McClusky had been about magical nursery-rhyme beans.

Bottom line was Riley might go down for other crimes the accountants drummed up — maybe money laundering and tax evasion, which was certainly nothing to sneeze at. But it wouldn't even be as serious as the charges that'd been lodged against the men he'd hired, the ones who'd been caught with tons of marijuana. Steiner believed the courts might be lenient, would take into consideration their clean records — a bunch of farmers — and it being a first offense. There really was no way to tell, though, since every man would be tried separately, and the trials would be held in Kentucky and seven other states.

Then Steiner had explained about the Kingpin Statute, that the FBI had intended to take him, Willie Ray and Jessie down with that charge … except they had to have somebody'd who'd roll over and identify who the bosses were. And nobody would. Almost a hundred men facing sentences from one to ten years in prison and not one of them was willing to negotiate for a lighter sentence.

They'd all been loyal, to a man.

The most detailed, and damning, of all the evidence had come from the least-expected source — Sherry Lynn. Seduced and drugged, she'd reeled out the whole story, chapter and verse, had sent the FBI out to farms all over the country arresting Callison County men. Steiner said he was sure he could kick up enough dust to prevent the information on the tapes from being used against Riley. But Sherry Lynn and Jessie had been nailed.

The door to the interrogation room opened and FBI Agent Bradigan walked into the room.

"I understand you asked to talk to me, Mr. Hannacker — is that right?"

"It is."

"What can I do for you?"

"I want to cut a deal."

It was obvious Bradigan was surprised by the statement, but he hid it well.

Riley had spent a good deal of time with the FBI agent in the past few months — not talking to him … literally, *not talking* to him. The agent spent hour after hour going over information he had about various parts of the Cornbread Mafia operation, asking questions, probing, trying to get under Riley's skin, piss him off, or make him feel guilty. Any edge.

Riley had not said a word. Refused even to confirm his Social Security number.

"I KNOW your friend Willie Ray was lying."

Bradigan is dressed for today's interrogation in a sport coat, no tie, dress pants. Riley's wardrobe is limited to orange jumpsuits. It seems all the Cornbread Mafia are "flight risks," or so the federal prosecutors had been able to convince the judge, and even Jacob Steiner hadn't been able to get them out on bail.

Bradigan had busted him and Jessica wearing a black vest, probably bulletproof, with the letters FBI stenciled in white letters two feet tall.

"He didn't shoot that McClusky guy, just said he did. When I walked in, the man was dying. No way in that condition did he put a bullet in that guy's forehead."

Silence.

"Either you did it or Mrs. Monaghan did it and he lied to cover for you."

Riley says nothing. In the beginning, his lawyer had insisted on being present very time Riley was questioned. But that got old. He'd gotten into some verbal fisticuffs with various law enforcement officers throughout the process, but Riley never said a word, did not utter a single syllable to anybody about anything, so there was no sense in dragging Jacob Steiner in here for every conversation.

And the attorney was getting paid by the hour, after all. Riley figured Steiner gave him special attention because he knew if he didn't get Riley off, there'd be no money for his fee.

"He wasn't running the Cornbread Mafia, either. I figure you were in charge, maybe equal partners with Taggart. I can't figure how a nice woman like Mrs. Monaghan got mixed up with you two. Care to enlighten me?"

Nothing.

Variations on that theme. Over and over and over again.

"WHAT KIND OF DEAL?" But before Riley could answer, he held up his hand. "Don't you want your attorney in here while—"

"When I'm done, I won't need an attorney."

"How so?"

"The deal I want to cut is … I plead guilty. To everything. You get an instant conviction. No wasting taxpayers' money on courtrooms and prosecutors."

That surprised Bradigan, no doubt about that.

"By everything, you mean …?"

"How many things can *everything* mean? All of it. Admit I was the boss, I was in charge. Admit I have numbered accounts all over the Caribbean — and I'll give you the numbers so the government can empty them out."

Steiner had told him that was a big deal — a very big deal. Seizing millions of dollars made headlines and the FBI was always looking for good press.

"I will admit that everything I own, from my Corvette to my underwear was purchased with my 'ill-gotten gains,' and therefore subject to forfeiture. Everything."

"And what is it you want in exchange for … everything?"

"You let Jessie go. You reduce the charges against her

to … *something*, I don't know, you figure it out. Something where she'll be sentenced to time served, or probated. I don't care how you do it, but she walks out of her cell" — *cell!* — "free and clear."

Bradigan paused.

"Your *wife* is also facing the same charges."

Riley hesitated and he could tell Bradigan picked up on it.

He'd been wrestling with his emotional response ever since he'd made this decision. Knew what had to be. But still, it was all Riley could do not to throw Sherry Lynn under the bus. She deserved it. He had absolutely no desire to rescue her.

But she was Drew's mother. If he took Sherry Lynn down with him, the little boy would lose both parents. The change in lifestyle was going to be hard enough — though Drew'd never cared about all the "stuff." Through his attorney, Riley had made certain "arrangements." Drew would be taken care of. And the little boy would get his horse. He would get to raise Coco!

"I was getting to that. Sherry Lynn, too, of course. Both of them. You let them go, and I'll tell you anything you want to know."

Bradigan left, was gone a long time, likely had to run this by the powers that be higher up the food chain. When he returned, he brought with him a tape recorder and one of the other agents — Riley knew them all. This was Agent Peterson, who looked like a Boy Scout. Probably brought him along as the warm-and-cuddly factor, to make Riley feel safe and comfortable, so he'd open up. The law was always clueless.

The agents seated themselves, got the recorder up and running, established for the record that Riley had given up his right to remain silent and the right to have his attorney present. That took a while, and Riley knew they had to get that part right or they were screwed, but he was growing impatient, just wanted to get the whole thing over with.

"Go ahead. Ask me anything."

Bradigan sat looking at him for a moment, then reached over and flipped off the tape recorder. The other agent appeared surprised.

"I want to know about you and Willie Ray Taggart, Davie Monaghan and Jackson McClusky — in Vietnam."

Riley looked deep into the Agent Bradigan's eyes. He could read nothing there. It didn't matter.

"Tell me what happened."

Riley did.

Chapter Seventy-Eight

Riley had certainly had plenty of time to decide what to say, to choose his words carefully. It was showtime now. So very much was riding on Riley being able to pull this off. Guilt was a powerful motivator.

Sherry Lynn looked awful, haggard. Gone was the pretty, bright-eyed cheerleader. The woman sitting in the straight-backed chair on the other side of the table had been through hell. Months locked behind bars had broken her and he suspected the cheerleader would never be back.

They met in the lawyer conference room with no glass partition separating them, though there were handcuffs around Riley's wrists that were attached by a chain to the table. Eli Bradigan had arranged it.

There was a flash of deja vu when she came into the room, babbling and almost incoherent. When she'd come to Fort Knox to see him in the hospital that day a thousand lifetimes ago, her voice had sounded the same, only she'd been hurling accusations then — *why didn't you write, only three letters in seven months* — and now she was pleading for forgiveness.

He blew by the words, didn't listen. Nothing she had to say to him mattered now. All the sniveling apologies, the please-forgive-me's were meaningless. Something from a poem … sound and fury, signifying nothing. He held up his hand.

"Stop it!" He hadn't meant to sound so harsh but that's the way it'd come out and it was honest. Sherry Lynn was totally cowed, stopped talking like he'd flipped off a switch. "We don't have time to do this now. It doesn't matter."

He drew in a breath. Centered himself. Yep, it was definitely showtime. He tried to keep his voice level and even, keep the emotion out of it.

"For the next twenty years" — twenty years, that was an unfathomable length of time! — "I'm going to be locked up in a cage — *because of you*."

"Riley, please, let me—"

"Shut up, Sherry Lynn, and listen, because you're going to recall what I'm about to say hundreds of times, thousands of times in the next two decades. When you go for a walk on a beautiful spring day and smell the wild-flowers in that field that runs along the creek bank — remember there will be no flowers where I am."

An involuntary sob escaped her throat then, but she put her hand over her mouth and didn't make another sound.

"When you hear a chicken hawk in the sky, or see fireflies at night, or stand in the doorway of Drew's room and watch him sleep—" Riley almost lost it then. Saying it all out loud like this was somehow making the abstract concepts real. And reality was too horrifying to contemplate. Telling Drew goodbye had been so gut-wrenching, he had walled off all memory of it. Maybe someday he'd be able to think about it, but if he did now, he would lose some kind of primal scream, wild and Jurassic, that would rip through his being and tear his soul to pieces.

Not to watch Drew grow up … that stopped him, gave him the strength to keep his emotions in check. What he was doing now was for Drew and he had only one chance to get it right. "When you do all those things," he leaned toward her and growled the words, "you remember, you are free — *free* — to live in the world and raise your son and have a life because *I* took the punishment you deserved. You *owe* me!"

She was crying, her head bowed, her hands clasped tight on the table in front of her.

"Look at me, Sherry Lynn!" She looked up and her mascara was making twin black lines down her cheeks. She hated that her makeup smeared when she cried.

"You *owe* me." He said the words softer now. "And you're going to repay that debt — every second of every day for the next twenty years."

She looked confused, but didn't ask.

"You will repay me by how you raise Drew."

Her face went totally blank.

"Your cloying, overprotective hovering is *done*! Over. Do you hear me?"

She nodded, but was still too surprised to really be processing what he was saying.

"Maybe you only did it to piss me off. Whenever I wanted Drew to do something or have something or *be* something, you automatically opposed me, and maybe that was to get back at me for …" He shrugged. "For I don't know what. All these years you've been furious at me and I've never known why."

"It was because—"

"It doesn't matter why. I don't care. Your reasons for being such a terrible mother aren't important anymore."

He could tell that hurt her. Good. "Because you're not going to be one anymore."

"You owe me," he said again and she winced. "Every interaction you have with Drew from this moment forward will be about that debt. From now on, you're going to let him be a normal child. Do you hear me — *normal*."

He grabbed hold of himself, knew he might be shouting and he couldn't chance a guard coming in and hauling him away. He had to be here, say this, right now.

"Every time you open your mouth to say, 'No!' you're going to ask yourself — would Riley say no? If he were here — *where he should be* — raising his son to be a healthy, happy adult, what would he do? Would he let Drew drink from a water hose? Or swim naked in the pond or play baseball or—" He had to stop, couldn't go on. The images of Drew doing those things *without him* was tearing his heart out of his chest.

"You are going to pay for your freedom every day by raising Drew the way I would have done it. Do you understand me?"

She nodded.

"Answer me! Do you really understand what I'm talking about?"

"I'm overprotective, clingy. I tried to wrap him up in cotton because … Drew was all I had."

She was right. Riley had treated Sherry Lynn like a stranger, an inconvenience. He supposed that in some twisted way, he blamed her that he couldn't have the woman he really loved. That wasn't Sherry Lynn's fault.

"I'm sorry, Sherry Lynn … I was never the husband you deserved."

Her face said she was very close to a total emotional meltdown.

"Oh, Riley — all I ever wanted was …" She gulped,

spit out an admission that must have sliced open her soul, "... for you to love me."

It wasn't like that was new information. He had always known Sherry Lynn loved him and expected him to love her back. But it still took his breath away to hear her say it. This was his opening, though, an opportunity to give his son a *life*, the only chance Riley Hannacker would ever have.

Taking in a breath, he put as much conviction into his voice as he had ever summoned in his life.

"If going to prison *for twenty years* to save you doesn't demonstrate my love, what would it take?" He wasn't lying. Going to prison for twenty years *did* demonstrate his love — for Jessie.

Sherry Lynn's face registered the most profound shock he'd ever seen on the face of another human being.

"You mean ... all this time you—?"

"We're not here to talk about yesterday. We're here to talk about tomorrow, and all the other tomorrows out there stacked up in front of Drew. Will you swear to me you'll change, that you'll be the kind of mother ... an incredible little boy like Drew needs?" He reached across the table, took her hand and squeezed. "Swear on ... *our love.*"

Her face glowed with a kind of adoration that was ... sad, pathetic. And Riley was using that, manipulating her feelings. He was ashamed of himself, but not sorry.

"I promise." She squeezed his hand so hard the stone in her wedding band dug into his palm. "I swear I will be a *good mother* to our son ... *your* son."

There was noise from outside the door and he knew his time was short.

"I've asked Jessie to stay close to you, to be a part of Drew's life. She'll help you if you'll *listen* to her."

The door opened, and the guard stepped into the room. Sherry Lynn could barely speak, only whispered. "I'll listen."

Chapter Seventy-Nine

SHE WOULD NOT CRY.

Would not.

An image flashed in Jessica's mind. Jacqueline Kennedy. When her husband was assassinated, she'd held it together with quiet dignity. A story written later said she'd told the other Kennedys, "We'll cry tomorrow."

Jessie would cry tomorrow. And the next day and the next and …

Couldn't go there and she yanked her mind back so forcefully it was almost a physical movement.

Years.

Jessie would have years to cry.

But this, here, right now, was a once-in-a-lifetime opportunity, a gift beyond price. Alone with Riley like this. No … cage.

She shuddered.

No bars.

No handcuffs and leg irons and orange jumpsuit.

The FBI agent had allowed this time, arranged it. Everything was done, over. Riley would be hauled off tomorrow to federal prison where he would remain for the next twenty years.

She had cried a river of tears over it already and there was an ocean more to cry.

But not right now.

Right now, Riley would not see her fall apart. His lasting image of her would not be of her sobbing pathetically, her nose running and her eyes swollen.

This time, right here, she would give him the gift of … normal.

There was a knock at the door and the FBI agent, his name was Bradigan, leaned in.

"You have fifteen minutes."

He opened the door wider, Riley walked in, and the agent closed the door behind him.

Riley was so thin. Standing there in the suit and tie he'd worn as he sat in that huge courtroom where all the sound echoed like you were in a cathedral, the room that was so cold she couldn't stop shivering. Not just physically cold, emotionally cold. Psychically cold.

Riley had lost so much weight. And where he was going, he wouldn't likely be putting any of it back on … *Don't. Just don't.*

He stood there in the doorway looking at her, studying her, as if he were memorizing her, every detail of her face and her body and her being. Memorizing it. Photographing it to pull out and look at later … when it would be all he had.

"I love you, Riley," she heard herself say.

That was not part of her rehearsed speech. And she had a rehearsed speech, about how she would be there for him, no matter what. That time didn't matter, years didn't matter, that she would write to him, visit him, never let go of him …

But now she couldn't remember the speech.

"I love *you*, Jessie."

She knew that he had always loved her, had never stopped loving her, not when she broke up with him in high school, not when she married Davie, not when she was all alone taking care of Davie and he was married to somebody else. Through all that, he had loved her. But he would never admit that now, because to say it would seem to him in some way to dishonor Davie's memory.

Riley had been able to give to her a gift she couldn't give to him. He could save her, rescue her from a life locked behind bars. If she could have given him that gift, she would have. She'd have traded her freedom for his … but they didn't want her. The law had accepted Riley as the sacrificial lamb. Her lawyer said it was "a bird in the hand," a guaranteed conviction — and the millions of dollars seized by the government that went along with it. He said Jessie and Sherry Lynn looked so innocent and "wholesome," prosecuting them would have turned the law into the bad guy. So they'd settled for stringing up Riley.

And then she was in his arms, so tight around her she couldn't breathe and that was alright. He was saying things into her hair that she couldn't comprehend right now, but she'd remember them someday, hear and cherish them someday.

Right now, all that registered on her senses was the feel of him in her arms and the sound of his voice.

They stayed there like that the whole fifteen minutes. It seemed to pass between one heartbeat and the next. They stood clutching each other with all their strength until the FBI agent knocked again on the door, opened it, and said it was time to go.

Riley leaned close and whispered in her ear, "Willie Ray's treehouse. It's there for you."

Then he was gone and still she stood in the room where he'd held her, trying to keep the feel of his touch on her senses, the sensation of him in the nerve endings in her body.

Gradually the feeling faded. Then she sank down into a chair and let herself cry.

Chapter Eighty

JESSIE AND RILEY had never walked together in this field and yet Jessie always thought of it as their *special place*. The field spread out beyond the tobacco barn on the back of Mama Ruth's property, Jessie's now, all the way to the river, and on this bright March morning the meadow was all about springtime, full of buzzing bees and butterflies and the call of birds in the trees.

This was their special place, hers and Riley's, not because they had ever been here together, but because they *would be here together*. Someday.

Jessie and Riley would walk hand-in-hand in the field someday, and she would describe for him again the thousands of images she'd stored up — she'd point out the oak tree full of squirrels she'd written him about and the stand of daffodils. She'd show him where they'd spread the picnic blanket on the soft needles in the shade of the big pine tree on the edge of the woods. She'd take Riley to the exact spot where they'd built a snowman, where they'd made snowballs for fights. They'd have lots of snowball fights, she was sure of it.

As Jessie and Riley walked together, she would describe for him all the times *they* had come together to this field during the years Riley was locked away, she and ...

She'd tell Riley about it this Saturday when she went to visit him. Of course, by then, she wouldn't have to tell him about it. He'd be able to see for himself. She could have told him sooner, but she'd been saving the news, a gift of goodness to him when he needed it. Something to look forward to.

Jessie reached down and touched the growing bulge in her midsection.

If it was a girl, Jessie would name her Ruth.

If it was a boy, she would name him Nathaniel. And call him Nate.

THE END

A Note from the Author

Thank you for reading *Ridin' For A Fall.*

If you enjoyed this book, please consider writing a review on your favorite bookselling site so other readers might enjoy it too. Just a couple of sentences would mean a lot to me.

Thank you!
Ninie Hammon

About the Author

Ninie Hammon (rhymes with shiny, not skinny) grew up in Muleshoe, Texas, got a BA in English and theatre from Texas Tech University and snagged a job as a newspaper reporter. She didn't know a thing about journalism, but her editor said if she could write he could teach her the rest of it and if she couldn't write the rest of it didn't matter. She hung in there for a 25-year career as a journalist. As soon as she figured out that making up the facts was a whole lot more fun than reporting them, she turned to fiction and never looked back.

Ninie now writes suspense--every flavor except pistachio: psychological suspense, inspirational suspense, suspense thrillers, paranormal suspense, suspense mysteries.

In every book she keeps this promise to her Loyal Reader: "I will tell you a story in a distinctive voice you'll always recognize, about people as ordinary as you are--people who have been slammed by something they didn't sign on for, and now they must fight for their lives. Then smack in the middle of their everyday worlds, those people encounter the unexplainable--and it's always the game-changer."

Also By Ninie Hammon

Cornbread Mafia

Fire In The Hole

Blown' Up A Storm

Ridin' For A Fall

Nowhere, USA

The Jabberwock

Mad Dog

Trapped

The Hanging Judge

The Witch of Gideon

Blown Away

Nowhere People

Through The Canvas Series

Black Water

Red Web

Gold Promise

Blue Tears

The Taken Saga

The Taken

The Changed

The Hidden

The Saved

The Unexplainable Collection

Five Days in May

Black Sunshine

The Based on True Stories Collection

Home Grown

Sudan

When Butterflies Cry

The Knowing Series

The Knowing

The Deceiving

The Reckoning

The Fault

Stand-alone Psychological Thrillers

The Memory Closet

The Last Safe Place